FIRE FLOWERS

Ben Byrne

FIRE FLOWERS

Europa
editions

Europa Editions
214 West 29th Street
New York, N.Y. 10001
www.europaeditions.com
info@europaeditions.com

Library of Congress Cataloging in Publication Data is available
ISBN 978-1-60945-248-3

Byrne, Ben
Fire Flowers

Book design by Emanuele Ragnisco
www.mekkanografici.com
Cover photo by John Florea/Time Life Pictures/Getty Images

Prepress by Grafica Punto Print – Rome

Printed in the USA

To my mother and father

Not quite dark yet
And the stars shining
Above the withered fields
—YOSA BUSON

CONTENTS

FIRE FLOWERS

AUTHOR'S NOTE

In early 1945, the United States Army Air Forces began a campaign of low-altitude incendiary bombing against Japan. The raid on Tokyo, on the night of March 9, destroyed sixteen square miles of the city. An estimated one hundred thousand citizens perished in the firestorm.

On August 6, a single uranium bomb was dropped over the city of Hiroshima. Approximately seventy thousand people were killed, with at least as many dying of their injuries and from acute radiation syndrome by the end of the year.

On August 8, the Soviet Union declared war upon the Empire of Japan. Russian forces invaded Japan's colony in Manchuria later on that night.

On August 9, a plutonium bomb was dropped over the city of Nagasaki, killing at least forty thousand people. Associated deaths reached an estimated eighty thousand by the end of 1945.

On August 14, a radio broadcast was made in which the Emperor Showa (Hirohito) announced Japan's capitulation to the Allied powers. It was the first time the Japanese people had heard his voice.

Part One
Surrender
August 1945

1
THE SON OF HEAVEN
(*Satsuko Takara*)

The sun must have just passed its zenith when I looked up. Everyone had already left the workshop except for me and Michiko, who was holding a shell casing, smiling at her warped reflection in the polished brass. I realised that His Imperial Majesty was about to make his unprecedented speech, and so I called to Michiko, and we hurried outside into the bright sunshine of the yard.

The other workers were already kneeling in the dust, facing a rickety table where Mr. Ogura, our foreman, stood fiddling with the dial of a radio which was making piercing whistles and strange whooshing noises. He scowled and waved us angrily to the ground, but just then, a loud blast came from the speaker, and he dropped to his hands and knees with a little whimper, pressing his forehead into the gravel.

The grit stung the scars on my palms as I leaned down, and I stole a glance at the others. Mr. Yamada, the frail student, was staring at the ground, his hair as wild as ever. His fingers were twitching, and I could tell that he desperately wanted to light a cigarette but didn't dare. Behind him was Mr. Kawatake, his lips moving as if he was praying. He looked just like a monk, I thought, the sweat glistening on his shaved head.

The crackling sound stopped, and the signal became clear. A high, reedy voice began to speak, and Michiko sniggered. In fact, I had to stifle a smile myself, because it was true—it sounded like some funny boy speaking, not the voice that anyone would have expected from the Son of Heaven.

I closed my eyes and tried to concentrate on what the Emperor was saying. But it was difficult to understand. His language was formal and ornate, and his words floated in and out of the radio, drowned out every now and then by roaring clouds of static. At one point, I understood him to say that "the trends of the world did not blow in Japan's favour," and I thought that this was certainly true, as I looked around at the crumbling factory walls, the handcarts piled high with refuse in the yard. Then, His Majesty said that he had "accepted the declaration" and my heart gave a leap, as it had sounded so hopeful. But Mr. Ogura gave a hideous groan, like a dying actor at the kabuki. His body sank to the ground, shaking with sobs, and it was then that I understood that Japan had lost the war after all.

Mr. Kawatake really did look like a monk now—he was rocking back and forth on his heels, muttering the name of the Buddha under his breath. Old Mrs. Miyasaki was bent almost double in front of me, and I saw from the little shudder of her hips that she was weeping. I noticed how frayed her uniform belt was, the blue threads unravelling from the hem.

The emperor was speaking now about the soldiers "far away on the field of battle," and I pictured Osamu, sunburned and hot on some island far off in the South Seas. In his final letter, he had written that his unit had been gorging themselves on the bananas and tropical fruits that grew down there, and I'd imagined him lying on a hammock beneath the palm trees, stroking the thousand-stitch belt I'd sewn with ten-sen coins to protect him from the bullets and bring him good luck.

The sun was burning my forehead now, and I wondered if His Majesty would carry on speaking for much longer. He was mumbling now about a weapon the Americans had used, a cruel modern weapon that might "annihilate the entire world," though I, for one, had no idea what he meant. He told us that we would face many hardships, that we must endure the unendurable, and that he hoped we would understand. There was a crackle of static, and then silence.

We carried on kneeling for some time, not saying a word. The old ones quietly wept while the rest of us simply stared into space. Finally, Mr. Yamada stood up, strode over to the radio and turned it off with a loud click. He lit a cigarette and then offered them round to everyone else. For some reason, even I took a cigarette, though I had never smoked before in my entire life.

There was the strain and whir of a cicada somewhere nearby and the scuffle of a rat amongst the rubble. I worried that we should all be getting back to our work fairly soon, but then realised that, in all likelihood, it would no longer be necessary.

2

SHATTERED JEWELS
(*Osamu Maruki*)

Dried victory chestnuts! Lieutenant Koizumi pressed them into my hand that morning, the mad bastard, out of sight of the burly blond American guard, just as if we'd been samurai, preparing our weapons and armour on the eve of battle. I rubbed my thumb over their shells now, hard as the skulls of mice, as we stood in a ragged line within our barbed wire enclosure, facing the field radio our captors had brought out. Half a dozen of us—all that was left of our unit. Heads bowed, necks burning in the livid sun, straining to listen to that wooden oracle, whirling now with our fates.

The emperor's voice was barely audible above the crash of surf, the hiss of insects in the malignant jungle beyond and the screech of the emerald parrots the American captain kept. As His Majesty spoke, a fragment of poetry echoed over and over in my mind.

Je me crois en enfer, donc j'y suis . . .

I believe I am in hell, therefore I am.

The voice slowly dwindled into faint static. The volume of the jungle seemed sharply to increase. Loud, sudden cheering burst from the guardhouse bunkroom; there was the sound of fists thudding planks and the unearthly caterwauling of victory.

An odd gurgle came from behind me. Wetness touched my neck, and I spun around to see Koizumi stagger, a sharp glitter in his fist. His gashed neck squirted crimson blood onto the yellow sand, as with bulging eyes, he clutched the wound, as if to staunch the flow. Horror seeped along my spine as he toppled, like a drunken sacrificial horse, blood leaking through his fingers. A shout came from the guard as he aimed his rifle.

Je me crois en enfer, donc j'y suis.

I believe I am in hell, therefore I am.

3
ASAKUSA BOY
(*Hiroshi Takara*)

The plane twinkled like the morning star in the sky above Fuji-san and I stopped in our tracks and stared. *A B-29?* I shielded my eyes from the sun. *No. Hold on . . .* The plane sailed towards me with a blast of wind, and I clapped my hands over my ears as the engines roared right over my head.

No machine gun turrets at the back of the fuselage. A black "F" mark on the silver tail. *An F-13!* Reconnaissance. I smiled in triumph as it floated off over the charred ruins of the city. They'd never flown low enough to spot properly before.

I carried on trudging northward along the road. *Japan really has lost the war, then,* I thought. *America and Britain have thrashed us.*

It was a shame to think that the planes wouldn't be coming anymore. Night after night, whenever the sirens had started blaring across the city, and the red light had flashed on the telegraph pole outside our bedroom window, I'd leaped from my bed to watch, as wave after wave of silver Hellcats and B-29s thundered past, the bombs drifting down through the night like blossoms. It was as exiting as being at the cinema, I thought, until Satsuko yelled at me to cram on my air defence helmet, and forced me down to the shelter to join our mother.

They were both gone now, though, after the big fire raid back in March. Ever since then, I'd been free to watch the planes whenever I liked. I slept in the ruins, scavenging for tins of food in old houses. The burns on my face had turned squishy with pus now, and my ribs were sticking out from my chest. I was heading to the countryside in the hope of finding something to eat.

The countryside was enemy territory for a fourteen-year-old boy like me. I was an Asakusa kid, fierce and loyal to my noisy neighbourhood and to the Senso Temple, no matter how "tawdry and downmarket" the ward had become, according to my father, since the Pacific War had begun. As for country bumpkins, with their sunburned faces and wooden lunch boxes, well, I'd come to hate their guts during the six months my school had been evacuated from Tokyo to the rural villages two years before.

That night I crouched in a ditch for hours, as a farmer patrolled back and forth across his muddy field. Finally, as night fell, I wriggled out on my belly, and rooted about feverishly in the crop. My hand grasped a withered bunch of leaves, and I urgently tugged at it, my mouth already watering as a spindly shoot slid out from the soil.

A clammy hand fell upon my own.

I leapt up, petrified. Before me in the darkness stood a pale silhouette: a ghost child, I thought, or a gruesome kappa troll! I screamed. The thing screamed back. For a second, we stood there, howling together, until, as my eyes adjusted, I saw it was another boy like me, around twelve years old and sickly thin. A smile crept over his face as he reached out his hand toward me . . .

I jumped forward and smashed my fist into his nose. He fell down with a whimper, and I leaped on top of him, shoving his face into the mud. Then I grabbed the daikon shoot, biting off big chunks as I scrabbled away across the field. I didn't feel especially proud of myself afterward, that was for sure. But I told myself that I hadn't any choice. That he wouldn't have lasted much longer, in any case.

In the days that followed, I hid in the ditches and woods during the day, then slunk out like a fox at night to steal whatever I could from the fields. It wasn't much fun. Farmers patrolled the crop nonstop, beating off vagrants with thick oak staffs. Rats twitched about in the stubble, scuttling over my bare feet, and horseflies bit at my skin with agonizing fury. One evening, as I lay soaking wet in a half-drained paddy field, a hissing sound came from the sprouting stalks nearby. I froze. A moment later, a diamond-shaped head appeared. *A Green General.* It looped toward me in sickly coils as I squeezed my eyes shut in terror. It slithered right over my back and slipped down into the water beside me. I splashed out of the paddy, moaning. I ran into a wood and fell to the ground, crying and sobbing with fear.

The countryside was clearly fraught with terrors I'd never even imagined in my cosy Tokyo bedroom. The supernatural creatures I knew only from kabuki plays I'd watched with my father became suddenly, terrifyingly conceivable as night fell: luminous families of fox spirits roaming abroad to bewitch me; kappa trolls lurking in the streams, intent upon dragging me down to their watery lair . . . All were now eerily palpable in the murmur of the wind across the fields, in every whimper and shriek of the night animals in the forest.

Before long, I began to grow faint, and finally, I began to hallucinate. My mother would run out from the trees at dusk, her arms outstretched, her hair on fire. Scarecrows would wave from the fields, and there would be my burly father, standing in his *happi* coat and chef's apron, grinning and beckoning to me. One night, I was crossing a high wooden bridge over a narrow river when I heard a faint voice calling my name.

Hiroshi! Hiroshi-kun!

I leaned over the rail. There, in the flowing stream, was my sister Satsuko. Crying and pleading with me to come back to her, just as she had on the night of the fire raid, when I had run away and left her to die in the oily water of the Yoshiwara canal.

I collapsed into a shed at the edge of an orchard as the moon shone down through the broken planks. I awoke suddenly in the night to see a broad-shouldered farmer looming over me, cursing as he lifted his staff. As he swung, I darted out between his legs. I sprang through the moonlight and hid amongst the crooked, haunted trees.

The sky was glowing pink and orange the next day as I found myself walking alongside a train track. Before long, a battered locomotive came creaking along the rails. I leaped up onto a coupling and gripped onto the side of the carriage as it trundled on through the countryside.

Before long, the fields gave way to a patchwork plain of ruins. A river grew wide beside us and I realised that I was being dragged inescapably back to Tokyo. The train finally shuddered to a halt at Ueno Station and I slid down and made my way into the cavern of the ticket hall. Throngs of men and women in torn and buttonless shirts lay on rush mats on the floor, their mouths slowly opening and closing like dying fish. Down the steps, in the subway, I curled up on a patch of damp by the wall of a cistern. Dead to the world, I fell asleep, alone amongst the clammy crowd that filled the tunnels and passageways like an army of hungry ghosts.

4
TOKYO BAY
(*Hal Lynch*)

The long white chimneys of the Mark 7 guns still pointed up at the sky. Seamen and airmen thronged the decks of the *Missouri*, spilling over the rails, straining to see the action. I was perched on the ledge behind the rear three-gun turret, holding my Leica camera, legs dangling above the white caps of Third Fleet captains who flocked the deck below. Before them was a triangular space, set with a single table. Upon it lay fountain pens and the documents of surrender.

On the far side of the deck, on a platform behind a rail, the official photographers hunched over Arriflexes and squinted through Speed Graphics, holding up light meters to check exposure one last time. I wasn't one of them—yet—and was instead wedged between an Associated Press correspondent and a petty warrant officer from Alabama, who kept muttering, "Boy, oh boy," like it was some kind of prayer.

A sudden swell of excitement rippled across the ship. Japanese launches were coming alongside the *Missouri*—desperately puny next to our gargantuan hull. Our admirals and generals swiftly stiffened into order below. The solitary table, with its two neatly arranged chairs, looked suddenly as simple and as menacing as a gallows.

I had arrived at Sagami Bay the week before, shortly after my discharge from the 3rd Reconnaissance Squadron. My fellow crewmen had left a booklet on my bunk, entitled *Going Back to Civilian Life,* which I assumed was ironical, alongside a pamphlet, *Sex, Hygiene & VD*, which I opened to read a terrifying warning:

"Japanese women have been taught to hate you. Sex is one of the oldest weapons in human history. The geisha girl knows how to wield it charmingly. She may entice you only to poison you. She may slit your throat. Stay away from the women of Japan, all of them."

Scrawled below was a message from Lazard, our navigator, in clumsy handwriting: *That means you, Hal!!!*

Half the nation was here already, it seemed, in the spirit form of Third Fleet battleships—the *South Dakota*, the *New Mexico*, the *West Virginia*, the *Boston*. They had an awesome look of brute magnitude as they lay anchored together upon the deep indigo water. I spent two days photographing destroyers and carriers as they steamed along the coast. An infinite number of cruisers and transports ferried between them, everyone out on deck, scrubbing and painting and polishing in preparation for our triumphant entry into Tokyo Bay. Beyond the fleet lay the green coastline of Japan, the ghostly shape of Mount Fuji sloping up in the distance, tiny white clouds balled beside it.

It was close enough to swim if you'd been so inclined. Through telescopes and binoculars we watched as old men and women immersed themselves in the water, children splashing in the surf, unhurried and apparently uninterested in the armada that lay before them, the greatest fleet ever assembled. At dusk, we watched the sun set over Japan, the mountain cast into silhouette, the ocean glittering with gold.

I'd seen it so many times, from above. Flying in at dawn at 30,000 feet, my palm automatic on the worn shutter crank of my K-22 camera. Japanese ships out at sea; a white line of surf marking the shore. The black highways and silver railways, the glistening web of canals and rivers; the dense formations of huddled houses, barracks and factories. I knew the whole country, I thought, from above. I'd processed it all inch by inch, shrunk it down to frozen impressions in the silver nitrate crystals of nine-by-nine film. Lugged the cylinders over to General LeMay's Quonset hut for the daily photo briefing at thirteen hundred hours. The big prints on the walls, labeled with arrows and statistics. Circled primary targets. Shaded inflammable zones. Photographs I'd taken of Japan over the past six months. Japanese cities. Before and after.

By the night of the Tokyo raid back in March, the city was as familiar to me as a framed map. We floated up above the Superforts, their fuselages tapering like artists' brushes, guide fires already blazing below. Then, the world became a maelstrom of noise—flurries of bombs screaming down, glimmering pinpricks of light erupting, merging and melding as the inferno took hold. An endless blast of heat, a deep glow as smoke and flames billowed skyward. The next day, when we flew back to photograph the damage, it was all just gutted buildings and burned out ruin. Scarred swathes of cauterized rubble, shimmering with heat waves.

My last photo run: to a city by the coast, our mission, to map out a bombing approach. Down below lay a bustling metropolis, busy streets and market buildings. A harbour full of fishing boats delivering their silvery catch to the dock.

When we returned a week later, Lazard thought we were lost. He simply couldn't identify the place. The valley was ravaged, eerie and desolate. The buildings swept clear, the estuarial rivers glistening down to the sea through char, like tear tracks across a blackened face.

Those nights since my discharge, my mind seemed to be trying to process those thousands of images. As if in my dreams, I could develop them, arrange them into some kind of sequence. I still felt myself flying in my sleep, acutely aware of the vast distance between me and the earth.

I needed to make landfall soon, I thought. I needed to see the world from ground level again.

The launches banged alongside the ship and we all peered down to see who would make up the delegation. An old Japanese man with a cane swung himself forward, followed by his cronies—delegates in absurd silk top hats and frock coats. Then came the generals, squat and drab. They made a grim surly bunch as they stood huddled on the swaying deck, surrounded on all sides by Allied men in blinding white uniform. One question hovered in the air: *where was the Emperor?*

Silence fell over the ship, threaded through with the whir of movie cameras, punctuated by the click of lenses and the puff of flashbulbs.

The door of the bridge cabin swung open.

General Douglas MacArthur. Emerging from the doorway, collar open, shoulders square. He loomed over the Japanese men, hands on hips, staring down, and I was put in mind of my father, the stern headmaster, about to draw the belt from around his waist.

After his sonorous opening remarks, the general gestured to the Japanese to come forward. One by one, in profound silence, they bent over to sign the documents. In a few short moments, the Empire of Japan had surrendered unconditionally to the supreme commander of the Allied Powers.

The general made a fine speech, full of noble sentiment and good intention. Next to me, the Associated Press man doodled an obscene picture in his notebook. I looked out toward Japan as the seagulls cawed above us in the sky. The sun had burned through the cloud. It was a fine day.

All of a sudden, a horde of Superforts and Hellcats and Mustangs filled the air. I lurched, almost tumbling from the turret. They swarmed toward the coast in echelon after echelon, wings glinting in the morning sun. The crew on the upper decks were all hollering now, grinning, slapping each other on the back. Down below, the Allied generals and admirals all shook hands and congratulated each other. I took a deep breath as the planes roared toward Tokyo like a flock of furious birds.

The war was over, I told myself, dumbly. It was all over.

And we were alive.

PART TWO
THE WITHERED FIELDS
September 1945

5
NEW WOMEN OF JAPAN
(*Satsuko Takara*)

Michiko had gone off to the countryside along with half the city to barter with those stingy peasants for food, and I was sitting outside Tokyo Station beneath a sign I had written for Hiroshi, my little brother. The station looked like an old, broken-down temple now, covered with signs and banners addressed to lost friends and relatives, all flapping in the wind like prayer flags. Crowds of people studied them, hoping to read their own names, or sat meekly against the walls, hoping that their loved ones might somehow miraculously turn up.

My own sign I'd hung two days after the huge fire raid back in March. It told my brother I'd gone to stay with Michiko, my friend from the war work dormitory, in her eight-mat tenement house in Shinagawa, and that I promised to wait for him here at Tokyo Station every day at noon. But it had been six months already since then, and still, he hadn't appeared.

The ground had been baking hot beneath my bare feet the morning after the raid, my hands dreadfully burned from the night before. I'd stumbled out of the irrigation ditch by the Yoshiwara Canal and picked my way across the smoking ruins of Asakusa. The whole city had been burned to the ground, it seemed. The wooden teahouses and matchstick tenements had all gone up in smoke and the theatres and picture palaces were just blackened shells. Shriveled bodies lay scattered along the roadways, and sooty figures went by with charred bedding on their backs or pushing bicycles piled with their remaining possessions.

Our old alley had run parallel to Kototoi Avenue, between Umamichi Street and the Sumida River Park. But the whole area had simply been levelled now, with only the odd brick building still standing. After flailing across the cinders for some time, I finally found the square concrete cistern that had once stood in front of Mrs. Oka's shop, our neighbour the pickle seller. It had been cracked wide open by the heat, and a naked man was slumped dead inside. My family's restaurant, with its sliding doors and creaking wooden sign, was gone. The whole alley had been incinerated, leaving nothing but two heaped ridges of ash.

There was no sign of Hiroshi. As I hunted about in the ruins, I pictured him the night before, surrounded by fire on the bank of the canal, shouting that he would come back. My fingers fell upon a scrap of charred blue cloth. It was from my mother's kimono, I thought.

Unfamiliar people, distant relatives, I supposed, were going back and forth with handcarts now. They picked out fragments of bone and piled up any goods that had escaped the flames. I dug about in the char for a while, but found nothing but my mother's battered old copper teakettle. By then the pain in my hands had became agonizing, and I went off to find a relief station, where a doctor gave me Mercurochrome and bandages.

I searched for Hiroshi for hours after that, at Kasakata police station and at Fuji High School, where the injured lay lined up on mats in the playground. But my brother had vanished. As evening fell, I finally returned to the Yoshiwara canal, where he had left me the night before. I started to shake. Troops were fishing out bodies on a big hook suspended from a truck, piling them up in a heap on the bank. I knew I should look for Hiroshi amongst them, but the truth was that I couldn't bring myself to search amongst those slippery mounds of flesh, all pink and boiled.

A train wheezed into the station, windows boarded over with planks. Passengers clambered down from the carriage roofs, and spilled out of the building clutching knapsacks and bundles of whatever it was they'd been able to scrounge from the farmers. Policemen walked up and down, eyeing the crowd for contraband, poking their packages with bamboo night-sticks—as if we didn't have enough to worry about.

Soon enough, Michiko appeared. Her dress was wrinkled, her shoes were covered in mud, and she looked exhausted. Quietly, I asked if she'd had any luck in the countryside.

She wrenched open her bag and gestured inside: three tiny potatoes wrapped up in a handkerchief.

"Three little potatoes," I said. "Michiko, really?"

"It's not my fault!" she said. "Those farmers are worse than thieves!"

She'd bartered away her favourite summer dress, she said, and this was all she'd received in return. It was extortion, pure and simple.

My stomach was gnawing away now, and I wracked my brain to think if there was anything we could use to make gruel. But I knew it was useless. I'd swept between the floorboards two days ago for the last grains of rice bran, and we'd already eaten whatever it was that was down there.

There were a few stalls set up by the station now, but they didn't seem to be selling anything useful except for some kind of rough booze. A couple of old men were already reeling, and one of them shouted something obscene to Michiko. But she just shouted back that she was surprised he could think of anything like that at a time like this, that he should be ashamed of himself, sitting there swilling rotgut while the rest of the city was starving to death.

A little farther on, she suddenly stopped. She put her hand on my arm.

"Satsuko," she said, pointing. "Look."

Nailed to the charred stump of a telegraph pole was a large printed sign. "To the New Women of Japan," it began, rather grandly. Michiko started bobbing up and down and tugging at my sleeve, the way she always did when she was excited.

"Look, Satsuko," she said. "It's jobs for office ladies. We could do that!"

I read the sign with an uneasy feeling. It certainly did mention work for secretaries, but it also referred to "the Contingency of the Occupation," and I felt sure that this must be something to do with the Americans. They'd be here soon, I realised. Large and boisterous, swaggering through the streets and shouting. The idea of working up close to them made me shudder.

But Michiko had a dreamy, faraway look on her face, which I recognized from whenever she would emerge, starstruck, from the cinema.

"New Women of Japan, Satsuko," she said, her voice growing breathy. "Just think. That could be us!"

I groaned and tried to pull her away. But she just stood there, right where she was.

"Michiko," I said. "Please. I'm hot and tired. Please just let's go home."

The starstruck look vanished. "And what are you going to sell for us tomorrow, then, Satsuko? The teakettle?"

A hard lump formed in my throat. This was unkind, and she knew it, as the copper teakettle was now almost the only thing I had to remember my mother by.

"I don't know."

She laid her hand on my arm again, her face softening.

"Satsuko," she said. "We only have three potatoes to eat today. Whatever are we to do?"

She could be surprisingly grown-up sometimes. I knew in my heart that she was right, that we should follow up the information on the sign. But just then, as I thought of the Americans again, another shiver passed through me. Michiko just gripped my arm, though, and the dramatic look came back into her eyes.

"Just think of it, Satsuko," she whispered. "New Women of Japan!"

We dressed up as prettily as we could for our interview, in neat woolen skirts and white blouses I'd pressed beneath our mattress the night before. We never seemed quite able to get all the ash and dirt out of our clothes anymore, but in any case, these outfits were much better than the baggy *monpe* trousers we normally wore, which made us look so hopeless and unattractive. The address was for a building up on the Ginza, which seemed like a hopeful sign, but when we got there, the place didn't seem quite so elegant after all—the roof had partly collapsed, and, inside, cracked paint was peeling from the walls.

An arrow pointed us up a shabby staircase to a lobby, where a large crowd of women were already gathered.

"Do you think we're too late?" I said. I noticed, to my unease, that some of the other women wore bright makeup, and looked like quite vulgar types.

"Michiko!" I whispered. "Are you sure this is the right place?"

"Well," Michiko murmured. "I suppose it can't be easy for anyone to find work right now. Not with things the way they are."

Just then, a door at the end of the corridor burst open. A very young girl rushed out and ran headlong into me. Tears were streaming down her face and I tried to steady her, but she pushed me aside, and clattered away down the staircase.

"Michiko!" I hissed. "Whatever could have made her so upset?"

"Perhaps she wasn't quite right for the job?" Michiko said. "Don't worry, Satsuko, we'll be just fine."

"Michiko," I said, feeling suddenly nervous. "I think perhaps it's best if we try to find some other kind of position elsewhere."

She narrowed her eyes and growled: if I had any idea of where we could go, then I should go right ahead and tell her.

So we carried on waiting for several hours, until finally a secretary came out and gestured toward me. Michiko gave my hand a little squeeze and I followed the corridor to the door.

Behind a heavy desk sat two men as unlike each other as they could possibly be. One was thin and very handsome, his hair slicked back like a movie star. The other was a fat pig of a man, with fleshy jowls and cherry stone eyes that looked me up and down.

"Miss Takara," said the handsome man, brightly, glancing at his list. "An Asakusa girl, no less! Please sit down."

The interview man started pleasantly enough. The handsome man asked me which school I had attended and what my father's profession had been. When I told him that my father had owned an eel restaurant, that I'd been a serving girl, he seemed very pleased, he even said he might remember the place—after all, it had been quite famous if you knew Asakusa at all.

The fat man squinted at me. "No doubt, at school, Miss Takara, you were taught the glorious history of our noble country?"

I wondered whether this might be a trap. Before my class had been sent off for war work with the Student Attack Force, it had been drilled into us that Japan was blessed, that our emperor had descended from the sun goddess Amaterasu and that Japan had a special responsibility to preserve harmony across the Greater East Asia Co-Prosperity Sphere. But I wasn't sure if this was still the case, so I just stayed silent and bowed my head.

The handsome man smiled. "Don't worry, Miss Takara. It isn't a test."

Moving his chair aside, he pointed up at a large painting mounted on the wall. It showed a very beautiful woman from the Edo period, dressed in a pink and white kimono, who knelt at the feet of a fierce-looking Western man with a big white moustache and a red waistcoat. The sea lay a little way beyond them, black-flagged ships sailing back and forth on the waves.

"I wonder," he said, "if you are perhaps familiar with this famous lady?"

As I looked at the painting, her name came into my mind: Okichi. The story was familiar enough. In fact, I distantly remembered an operetta about her, which had been all the rage when I was a little girl. My father had even owned the recording on a gramophone disk.

"Okichi-sama," the pig-man pronounced, to my annoyance, as I'd been about to reply. He explained that Okichi had once lived in Shimoda, on the Izu peninsula, in the previous century, and how, when the foreign barbarians had first landed there and forced Japan to open up to the outside world, she had been presented to the American ambassador as "a consort."

"A peace offering," the handsome man added. "And a clever way to keep an eye on the foreigners!"

I gazed at him uncertainly, wondering where all of this was leading.

The fat man leaned forward. "Do you know what a consort might be, Miss Takara?"

My cheeks coloured. I gave a faint nod.

"Okichi," he went on, his voice swelling now, just like the radio bulletins, announcing a victorious battle, "sacrificed her body for the Japanese nation! Just as our soldiers sacrificed theirs. Now the barbarians will soon land again, Miss Takara." He raised a pudgy finger in the air. "Japan will need a new generation of Okichis. Honourable women who are prepared to sacrifice their own bodies. To act as a breakwater. A seawall which will protect the flower of our womanhood from the savage tide of their rapacious lust."

Silence fell.

"Your sign," I said, swallowing. "It mentioned office ladies—"

"Regrettably Miss Takara, all of our back office positions have now been filled," the handsome man said. "But there are plenty of other positions still available. Fine positions. Noble positions. For patriotic women who are prepared to act as 'consorts' for our foreign guests, once they arrive."

My cheeks were burning as I stood up to leave.

"You would be paid, Miss Takara," said the fat man. "With an allowance for clothing. And for food."

Just then, I felt very faint. My head swam and my legs began to fold. I scrabbled for the desk to stop myself from falling.

The handsome man leapt around the table and caught me, helping me back into the chair.

"Please don't upset yourself, Miss Takara," he said. "But why not at least consider our offer?"

My heart was pounding as they stared at me. I saw myself, sitting in a café with a burly American. What would it be like, I wondered, to be intimate with a foreigner? His body covered in hairy bristles, stinking of sweat and cigarettes . . .

The truth was, I wasn't completely innocent. The night before Osamu had been sent away to the South Seas, he'd visited my house after his leaving party, and we'd gone off to a hotel together for a short time. I wasn't ashamed. After his horrible mother told me he was dead, I was glad that I had given him at least that comfort in his short life.

"Well, Miss Takara?" said the handsome man. I stared at him, thinking of the three potatoes in Michiko's handkerchief. We'd devoured the last one before coming along that morning.

My head began to swim again, and his voice seemed to come from very far away.

"Well, Miss Takara? We're counting on you. Will you help us?"

6
STARS & STRIPES
(Hal Lynch)

I hitched a ride from Yokohama to Tokyo in a jeep with two lieutenants from the 5th Cavalry. Eyes front, they chewed gum rhythmically as they drove. They'd been first into Tokyo, they said, and things were already improving.

Through the rangefinder of my camera, the city seemed utterly obliterated. Fields of rubble sprouted with tall weeds. Ruined factories held from collapse by mangled girders. Abandoned trucks lay on bricks, lichened with orange rust. All the way to Tokyo, along the dirt road, men and women in rags heaved handcarts piled with refuse, swallowing our dust.

The road grew wider as we entered the centre of the city and we veered around deep potholes, edifices rising on each side. Grand once, now licked black, their windows were boarded up, great chunks of masonry torn from their structures. Crowds swarmed the avenue: Japanese women in baggy pants with bundles on their backs; men in battered fedoras and grubby summer shirts. Tall GIs strolled along like stately giants or laughed as Japanese men in split-toe shoes tugged them along in rickshaws. At an intersection of curving streetcar lines, an old man haltered an ox, his cart laden with steaming churns, surrounded by fat flies.

I hopped down beneath the cobweb of overhead electrics and unfolded my map. This, then, was the Ginza—once the grandest avenue in the Orient, its Fifth Avenue, its Champs-Élysées. I drew in a great breath of Tokyo air: smoke and fish guts and sewerage. I wiped the filthy perspiration from my brow.

The *Stars and Stripes* office was housed in a grand old embassy building. Wide concrete steps led up to the doorway, and inside, acres of wooden paneling covered the walls of a high-ceilinged newsroom. Desks were laid out in neat rows, each with a telephone and a gleaming Smith-Corona or Remington. Young men in uniform were typing away and glanced up at me as I entered. They grinned, as if welcoming me to some private members' club.

At the back of the room I spotted a familiar face: Eugene, my old college roommate, the myopic show-off who'd encouraged me to apply to the newspaper in the first place. Skinny as a rake, his curly hair now officially out of control, Eugene leaned back on his chair, an affected green visor shielding his eyes as he spiked stories from a big pile. He whooped when he saw me, leaped up, and proceeded to perform some kind of Indian war dance before bounding over and seizing my arm.

"This—is—it, Hal!" he hollered, hopping back and forth. "The place where we will make our names!"

Oh, boy. He still wore the same round wire spectacles I remembered from Columbia, six years ago, when this "making our names" business had been his obsession. He'd drawn up strategies for us to achieve it in any number of ways—writing for the *Spectator*, acting in amateur theatricals. Finally, under the spell of the French photographer Henri Cartier-Bresson, whose portrait he'd plastered above the desk in our dorm room, he had decided that we would become photographers. For weeks we'd roamed the docks at Red Hook and the tenements of the Lower East Side with our Box Brownies in dogged pursuit of the "decisive moment." Eugene had even gone as far as setting up a darkroom in a storage cupboard beneath the faculty buildings, before he got distracted by a book on how to draw for the funny papers. He'd ditched his camera soon after that. I'd kept hold of mine.

"Hello, Gene. Looks like you're all settled in."

"Sure I am," he said, leading me to a door affixed with a scrawled card. "John Van Buren," it read. "Editor-in-Chief."

"Okay, let's take you to meet Dutch. He's going to give you your press pass. That's your golden ticket, see. Your get-out-of-jail-free card. It's signed by MacArthur himself. It means you can go anywhere you want and talk to anyone you want."

Eugene knocked briefly on the door and we bustled into an office, disturbing a balding NCO who was rubbing his head as he frowned over a typed article. His desk was cluttered with sheets of copy and framed photographs of plump, corn-fed children.

"Hal. This is Dutch Van Buren, Editor-in-Chief of *Pacific Stars and Stripes*. Dutch, this is Harold Lynch. Hal's the best photographer in the Third Army. And he can write too—you just wait until you read what he can write . . ."

"Okay, enough," Van Buren said, holding up his hands. "I've got things to deal with. Lynch, you're very welcome. Sit down. Eugene, why don't you give me a break and get out of here?"

"He's thrilled to be here, Dutch!" sang Eugene in falsetto, skipping out the door. "The crucible of change!"

Van Buren rolled his eyes as he shook my hand. "Oh, my aching back. You know that guy? You've got my sympathies. Well, I guess you're here now anyway. You know much about *Stars and Stripes*?"

"I read the paper on Guam. We all did."

"Sure you did. Well, as you know, the *Stars and Stripes* has been in circulation all the way back to the Civil War. We're here to inform—just as any of the big papers are." His voice took on the tone of a prepared speech. "But in contrast to them, Lynch, we have a very specific audience—the average GI. Doesn't mean we don't go after the big stories. He's interested in the big stories. He understands the political angles. But he also wants to be entertained. He likes to see how the big stories affect the little man."

"Human interest, you might say?"

"Exactly," Dutch said, pointing at me. "You've got it right there."

"Fine. That suits me fine."

"But in addition to that," he said, picking up his pen and waving it at me, "we've got to produce stories that the Japs'll understand. So that they'll see what we're doing here. What we're trying to build. We've got a duty to do that too."

The images of devastation I'd shot on the long ride in from Yokohama that morning were still fresh in my mind. Dutch must have noticed my expression, because he gave a sheepish smile.

"Well, heck, of course, we had to take a wrecking ball to the place first. Only stands to reason. But the next trick is to build something up. A peace-loving, democratic country."

"'The Switzerland of Asia?'" I suggested, quoting MacArthur.

"That's right," he said, pointing at me again. He stood up, gesticulating in the manner of a Roman senator. "Elected representatives. Votes for women. A free press. It's a fine experiment we've got going here, Lynch."

He turned to a filing cabinet against the wall. As he did so, I glanced at the typed article on his desk. A bureaucratic report, something about land reform. Big swathes of blue pencil had been drawn through it, initials and letters circled in the margin. Further down, blocks of text had been struck through with black ink.

"The crucible of change, Lynch," Dutch was saying, as he rummaged about in a file. "It's our privilege to have front-row seats." He turned, smiling, and handed me a small square of paper: "Don't lose it."

My press pass. The scrawled signature of the supreme commander himself graced the back. I was impressed.

Dutch held out his hand. "Welcome to *Stars and Stripes*,

Lynch. I think you're going to fit right in with this bunch of nuts. A man like you could really make a name for himself here."

"Thanks, Dutch," I said, shaking his hand. "I'll see what I can do."

I'd been billeted to the old Continental Hotel, not far from the redbrick ruins of Tokyo Station. When I arrived I was astonished and delighted to find that I'd been given a small room of my own. For the first time in years, I wouldn't be bunking down with a dozen other men, subjected to an unceasing battery of locker-room jaw about pinups and football and the Brass. The carpet was worn down almost to the board and an ancient black ribbon of flypaper hung from the ceiling. But as I unpacked my kit and set up my handful of books on the chipped table by the window, it already felt like home.

The view outside was uninspiring. A streetcar line bisected a gravel road, a row of ruined buildings on the far side. I poured myself a drink, and as the alcohol began to glow in my stomach, I sat on my cot and picked away the epaulettes from my jacket, along with the insignia of the 3rd Recon Squadron. I patiently sewed my woven *Stars and Stripes* press badge in its place. That made it official, I thought.

A clang came from the road and I glanced out. A streetcar was crawling valiantly along the track, so dilapidated that I felt like applauding in sympathy. The windows were cracked, the sides all dented. Expressionless passengers squeezed up against each other on the outer deck, leaning precariously over the guardrails.

It didn't take me long to find a "human interest" piece. While out exploring the neighbourhood down by the banks of the river, I discovered an old man living under a jury-rigged tarpaulin strung between two poles. He was naked but for shorts and an old raincoat, and he held a bamboo fishing rod, the float bobbing out in the river. I took Eugene and a Japanese-American translator named Roy down there one afternoon. We tapped on the tarpaulin, and after a moment the man emerged from his shelter and stared at us. His old face was lined like a boxer's, his beard as coarse as a brush.

He squinted as Roy explained that we'd like him to tell us his tale. After stroking his beard and looking out at the river for a moment, he gestured at his scatter of belongings. We sat down cross-legged on the ground as he filled a bent jerry can with river water and put it on a little hibachi grill to boil for tea.

I'd expected him to be half crazy, but, in fact, he was the model of eloquence. He'd been a bargeman once, he said, waving at the water. Over the years he'd managed to save enough money to buy a boat of his own. After that, he and his two sons made a living ferrying coal and timber from the factories and yards out to the big ships in Tokyo Bay.

I recalled the picture postcards I'd seen of Tokyo before the war: the waterways bristling with lantern-lit skiffs and wherries, ferrymen carrying drunken revelers up and down the canals as fireworks burst in the summer sky. The river was almost silent now, long strands of weed floating around the mooring posts.

After the fire raids had begun, the man said, he and his sons had taken to sleeping on the boat, thinking they'd be safer out on the water. One night, he'd been sleeping out on deck, his sons in the cabin, when the sirens had sounded and the planes started to float in.

I had a sudden premonition of what he was about to describe. Eugene was scribbling away in his notebook, smiling encouragingly.

Mis-tah B—this was what the man called the B-29s, wag-

gling his flat palm toward the horizon in demonstration—
drifted in very low that night. In wave after wave the planes
came, clouds of bombs tumbling from their bellies. From the
river, it soon seemed that the whole city was ablaze, red and
orange flames dancing across the sky. From somewhere, what
he called a "firework" landed on the boat. To his amazement,
it squirted fire all over the deck, fire that stuck to the water and
blazed away in the blackness. He shook his head at the memory. *Napalm*, I thought, picturing the dewy blue flame I'd once
seen spurting from a cylinder that had gone crazy after falling
loose from a bomb bay on Tinian Island.

The deck of his boat, piled high with coal, quickly caught
on fire. The old man leaped into the water, shouting for his
sons to come out. But just then, another white incendiary whistled down and squirted fire all over his body, and he swam desperately to the bank, struggling to escape the flames.

Like an accusing ghost, he opened his coat to show us his
torso—a marbled mass of pink welts and sinewy grey tissue.

From the bank, the man had stared out at the blazing hulk
of his boat, its glowing heart of coal, pleading for his sons to
come out.

He closed his eyes. He shook his head. The barge had
swiftly disintegrated into a mass of ash and cinder. By the next
day it had dissolved away entirely.

The smoke from the brazier fluttered in the wind, the water
in the can still tepid. A sheen of perspiration covered my forehead and a vein was pulsing in my temple. The old man gazed
upstream, as if he hoped to see his boat come floating back
down the river at any moment.

I took off the lens cap of my camera and asked him if I could
take some photographs. With a bow of his head, he agreed.
While I was taking the pictures, Eugene asked how he was now
surviving. The man pointed at the river and made a hurling gesture as if casting a line, then an eating motion with his hands.

"He catches fish?" Eugene said. "Well, how about that."

I could see the story spooling out in his head—"The Lonely Fisherman," perhaps—accompanied by a photograph of the old man proudly holding up his day's catch. But the old man was running his fingers through the air with a repetitive gesture and Roy was frowning. He shook his head: "No, he means rats."

"Rats?" Eugene said. "Don't tell me he eats rats."

The old man ducked his head into his chest, clearly embarrassed.

Roy explained that rats—big bloated ones—often came floating down the river. The old man fished them out and barbecued them on his hibachi.

So there it was. Our first story. We thanked the man and presented him with a packet of cigarettes, which he tucked into his raincoat pocket before touching pressed palms to his forehead.

"Is there anything else he needs?" I asked.

The old man cocked his blunt head for a second. He knelt down, hands on knees. Would it be possible to bring him a flask of soy sauce? I promised that it most certainly would. The old man touched his forehead to the ground.

We clambered up the slippery bank to the main road. When I looked back, the old man had already disappeared back into his shelter.

That afternoon I processed the prints in the darkroom in the basement while Eugene typed the story in the newsroom upstairs. I knew the picture I wanted as soon as it emerged in the developing tray. The old man sat cross-legged like a ragged Buddha, looking out at the lonely river, his carved face and wild fisherman's beard silhouetted against a sky piled with grey cloud. "A certain enigmatical quality," as Eugene later put it.

The piece he wrote was too sensational for my taste. It lingered on the peculiarities of the man's diet and spent little time on his account of the fire raid. Dutch ran it on the third page that week anyway, and I felt a glow of pride to see my byline beneath the photograph. I'd been published for the first time.

Later on that day though, Dutch called us into his office. He looked shaken.

"I've just had a call, gentlemen," Dutch said, "from Brigadier General Diller of the Public Relations office."

I'd heard the name already, generally accompanied by blasphemy. Brigadier General LeGrand Diller—"Killer Diller"—was part of MacArthur's inner circle, his head of Public Relations. A surly, stony bastard by all accounts, he dictated the official line, and took any criticism of the Occupation as a personal slur against his general.

"He demanded to know what I was doing running stories about old men eating rats. What exactly was I implying? That the Japanese population is starving?"

Warily, I pointed out that the population was, in fact, starving.

"Not according to Supreme Command it isn't!" he hollered, slapping a hand on the table. He rubbed his head and accused us of being morbid, of wanting to land him in a whole heap of trouble.

I had a flash of inspiration. I told him we'd planned the story as the first in a series, to show how much life in Japan would improve as the country became accustomed to the Occupation. We'd necessarily started with some poor fellow living in the pits.

Dutch scrutinized me. "Well. You'd better just run anything like this past me in the future," he said.

I told him that we would.

"No stunts!"

I assured him we were not here to play stunts.

As we were leaving, he called out: "I liked your picture in any case, Hal!"

The rest of the staff certainly found it highly amusing. They'd been gathered outside Dutch's office, eavesdropping upon our dressing down. For weeks, we couldn't go anywhere without them holding up their hands like little paws and twitching their noses. One day a spoof story appeared on the notice board, claiming that rat meat was going to be brought onto the ration.

But the publicity didn't do the old bargeman any good. The Tokyo police somehow got wind of the story and they trooped down the next week to clear him out. Half the city was sleeping in holes and ditches at the time, but the authorities apparently considered it a violation of Japanese dignity for the old man to have so publicly shamed himself by talking to us about it. When I went down later that week with a flagon of soy sauce and some sake, he was gone. All that was left of the random clutter of his shelter were some charred sticks and a bent jerry can.

7
THE TICKET-HALL GANG
(*Hiroshi Takara*)

Two *yankii* sailors—enormous black men in flapping white trousers with tiny hats perched on the tops of their heads—were strolling amongst the clapboard stalls and counters of the Ueno Sunshine Market. I was quietly stalking them—*Captain Takara, 1st Ghost Army*. I'd collected half a dozen long cigarette butts already, and one of the sailors was about to fling another one to the ground.

The markets had sprung up like mushrooms almost the day the war had ended, at all the main train stations on the Yamanote Line: Shimbashi, Shinjuku, and here at Ueno. At first, scruffy men and women had just laid out whatever they had to sell on patches of bare earth—cups, pens, any old rubbish. Next came the soldiers, returning home, their houses destroyed and pockets empty. One morning, I'd watched as one of them, thin as a rake, sold off his entire uniform piece by piece. First his greatcoat, then his boots, then his shirt and trousers, until he was standing there shivering in his underwear, and I thought for a moment he was even going to try and sell that, and go off with the money wedged between his buttocks.

Soon enough, though, the yakuza gangs had decided to move in. Now the wasteground beneath the overhead train tracks was just like a real market, with electric lights and speakers chirping music and peddlers selling everything from saucepans to kimonos, blankets to bicycles. There were noodle shops and counter bars, and the place was patrolled day and night by the flashy toughs who worked for Mr. Suzuki, the market boss, who you could see making his rounds every evening in his pale grey silk suit, a felt fedora tilted over his bullet-shaped head.

We called it the American Sweet Shop. GIs came along to swap their B-rations for whisky and fake antiques, and we shined their shoes and scrounged for their chocolate and chewing gum. Kids stole things from their pockets and some of the older girls took them off into the shadows under the railway arches. But I'd promised myself early on I'd never break any laws, no matter how tough things got. My father would have been ashamed of me.

Instead, I became a cigarette boy. The yankiis all smoked like crazy—American cigarettes at that—and if you followed them for long enough, you could collect up a pile of butts and wrinkle out the tobacco into new two-sen smokes. You'd then palm these off onto some poor Japanese, who'd smoke them right down to the last cardboard embers.

The sailor lifted his massive hand and flicked his smouldering cigarette to the ground. I pounced, but suddenly he moved, and I slammed into his leg. It was as thick as a tree trunk, and I sprawled there, stunned for a moment. Then, from nowhere, another cocky boy jumped in and scrabbled for the cigarette himself.

"Get off!" I shouted, grabbing him. "This is my patch!" I twisted the boy's arm, and we grappled and thrashed together on the ground. Above us, the laughing sailors goaded us on, ducking and weaving behind their giant ebony fists.

My hand gripped the boy's throat as I pinned him to the ground. But then, as I slapped his terrified face, I got a shock. It was Koji, the grandson of Mrs. Oka the pickle seller—he'd lived right next door to us in Asakusa.

"Koji?" I said, letting go of his neck. "Is that really you?"

Koji nodded, wiping away snot and tears with dirty little fists.

"Don't you remember me?" I asked.

He grimaced. "What happened to your face?"

The thick welts on my cheeks had gone hard now, like the rubber on bicycle tires.

"I got burned."

His eyes grew wide. "You look creepy!"

I shrugged. "What happened to your granny?"

He thrust out his bottom lip.

"Oh. I'm sorry. Did I hurt you?"

He shook his head sulkily.

"Hungry?"

"Starving to death!"

Over at one of the busy wooden stalls in the market, I counted out a few copper coins from my pocket. We had just enough to share a bowl of cold noodles, and as we stuffed them into our mouths, he told me about some other kids he'd come across since the war had ended. There were quite a few of us Asakusa lot around, it seemed, all in the same boat.

"Nobu's here," he said.

"Really?"

He nodded. Nobu was a ten-year-old boy from the Senso school—his dad had run the fishmonger on the corner of Umamichi Street, where my own father had bought eels for our shop.

"Little Aiko-chan, too." Aiko was Nobu's little sister, I remembered, a funny smudge of a girl who'd attended the elementary school on the corner.

Koji glanced around and lowered his voice.

"Shin's here, too," he murmured. "You know, the boy from Fuji High School?"

I groaned. "Trust him to be here!"

I knew Shin alright. A local bully with a square jaw, he'd been one of the tenement gang up near Sengen Shrine. His father had been a fireman, covered in tattoos, who'd lived on a barge on the Okawa, and my mother said he'd sold Shin's sister Midori, one of the neighbourhood beauties, to the Willow Tree teahouse to become a trainee geisha when she was just eleven years old. Shin had taken after his dad, though—always fighting dirty in the battles we waged in the back streets, throwing chunks of glass on the sly and striding around in a pair of rolled up khaki trousers he swore he'd taken off the body of a crash-landed American pilot.

Over by the Ueno Plaza steps, children were shrieking like monkeys as a pair of GIs revved the engine of their jeep. They clutched at their sleeves, grabbing for the packets of caramels the soldiers tossed out to them. I spotted Shin straight away. He was nearly as tall as me now, and wore no sandals or shirt, just his torn old pair of khakis. As the jeep spun off, he sprinted after it and leaped up onto the bumper. He clung on and rode along the avenue for a second before toppling off and tumbling into the dirt. With an idiotic grin, he picked himself up and hobbled back toward us, elbows streaked with blood.

He grimaced when he saw me. "What does he want? He's even uglier than before."

I gave him a withering look.

Scabs covered his knees and his front teeth were broken. I remembered how, after our schools had been evacuated to the countryside, us Asakusa lot had been given all the heavy jobs in the village, digging octopus holes and cutting fodder for the local garrison's horses. Shin, meanwhile, had wormed his way in with the straw-sandaled village boys by pilfering our barley rations to trade for their silver rice.

Shin sneered. "I bet you want to join my gang now, don't you? Not so high and mighty now, are you? Well, it just so happens that you can't. Not unless I say so."

"Your gang?" I said. "How long have you been in charge?"

He frowned, counting on his fingers. "Ever since—" Everyone went quiet. Ever since March, he meant. The night when Tokyo had burned.

"You must be making pots of money, I suppose?"

He waved a hand at the departing jeep.

"We can always scrounge from the yankiis!"

The children giggled. They were filthy and crusted with dirt. Their shirts were just rags, their hair matted. They would never last another month with Shin in charge, I thought.

"Do you really think they'll always be this generous? What about when winter comes? It's October already. Chewing gum won't be much use then!"

Shin gave another moronic grin and shrugged.

The children looked up at me nervously.

"Listen," I said. "Here's what we can do."

Later that night, Shin and Nobu and I loitered for a few hours outside the Continental Hotel, where the American officers were billeted. We collected a big pile of butts from the ash cans, and back at the station, Koji ground them up in his prize shell casing—a real beauty from a Type 89 discharger. We rolled new smokes from licked twists of newspaper, and the next morning, Aiko took them around the station to sell. When she got back, we had enough money to buy three whole seaweed-wrapped rice balls. We stuffed them into our mouths on the spot—grinning at each other, flecks of rice stuck to our chins.

I never learned exactly what had happened to Koji, Aiko, Nobu and Shin on the night of the raid back in March. It somehow became one of the rules, early on, that we were never allowed to talk about such things. I was still so ashamed of myself that I could hardly bear to even think about that night. The whole city had been on fire as I'd sprinted back toward our house, leaving Satsuko alone in the dark water of the canal. I only made it a dozen yards before the cotton quilt of my air defence cowl caught on fire. I screamed as I tried to pull it off, but it stuck to my cheeks, and there was a smell like roasting pork, which I grasped must be my skin burning. I staggered into a pit shelter by the side of the road, and sat there all night long, the ground vibrating beneath my feet, the air filled with sirens and planes and the stink of smoke as I sobbed in the darkness.

By the time the fires had burned out, my face was already blistering. I stumbled back up the charred street to the Yoshiwara canal, to the iron ladder where I'd left Satsuko the night before. The water below was full of floating corpses, drowned or asphyxiated, bobbing in the water amongst the blackened chunks of sodden timber.

It was good not to be on my own anymore. I missed my family more than I cared to admit, and I didn't know what I would have done without the company of the other children. It felt almost like a big game sometimes, as if we'd all run away from school together. We lit refuse fires in the Plaza and danced around in GI hats made out of folded newspapers. We played destroyer-torpedo in the broken-down houses and built forts in the bomb craters from charred planks and twisted strands of metal. We even marked out a baseball pitch in the wasteground at the back of the station, where we held tournaments with the other gangs, gambling for bullet casings and bomb fragments.

What a liberation from the war! Those days of writing comfort letters to the soldiers until your fingers cramped up, marching around the playground singing patriotic songs. *Children of the Emperor!*

But the children still cried out at night, at the station. I'd wake to see their little faces glistening with tears. So I made it another rule that you couldn't ever let anyone see you cry. If you did, the others had to sit on you, as if you were a sack of rice. I thought that if anyone were to start crying, then someone else would follow, and soon enough, we'd all be crying our eyes out and no one would be able to stop. We might go on crying forever, I thought, until we ended up like empty cicada shells, having cried ourselves away entirely.

I was playing with my metal soldiers at the station one morning when Aiko bustled over. She hovered in front of me for a few minutes, humming away, until, finally, I asked her what was the matter.

She frowned.

"Can people live in holes?" she asked.

"What do you mean?" I said.

Shyly, she told me that she had met a teenage girl the day before, who was living in a hole outside the station.

"You mean the slit bomb shelter?"

There were plenty of single-person earthwork shelters scattered across the city, though none of them had been much use during the fire raids. They'd been more like miniature stoves then. You still had to be wary of exploring them, just in case there was a baked, rotten corpse stuck inside.

"What's she doing in there?" I asked.

"She lives in it!"

"Really?"

Aiko nodded, biting her lip

"Is she nice?"

"She's my friend."

Aiko explained that the girl had been sent to Tokyo from the city of Hiroshima, out on the Seto Inland Sea, in the Chugoko region of Japan. Her mother had packed her off to stay with relatives a few weeks before, but when the girl had disembarked at Tokyo Station, there'd been no one there to meet her. So she'd wandered off on her own until she found herself here at Ueno.

The story sounded common enough. There were lost and

orphaned kids all over the place now, sent to Tokyo from other towns or returning from far-flung parts of the Japanese Empire. They wandered about forlornly, clutching onto the little white urns that contained their parents' remains.

I didn't know much about Hiroshima people, though. Only that the city had been very badly bombed, right before the end of the war. They'd been pretty unlucky, I thought—just a few more days and they'd have made it through.

Aiko's face was crumpled in sympathy and I could tell she'd taken a shine to the girl. It was hardly surprising. It couldn't be much fun for her, hanging about with us grimy boys all the time.

"Can she stay with us, big brother?" Aiko pleaded. "Please?"

I felt a tingle of pride. No one had ever called me big brother before. Maybe it wouldn't be such a bad thing to have another girl in the gang. After all, she could always help Aiko out with the selling work.

"Why don't you bring her over to meet us later on today," I said. "I'll make a decision then."

Aiko's face lit up and she clapped her hands together. "Thank you, big brother!" she said. "Thank you, thank you!"

Tomoko. The name alone was enough to send a delicious shiver down my spine. She wore a blue canvas jacket, a battered water canteen slung over her shoulder. Her hair was cut very short, almost like a boy's, and fell just beneath her eyes, so she blew it nervously out of the way whenever you spoke to her. Her face was quite round but she was terribly thin from her journey from Hiroshima to Tokyo. She was thirteen years old and as shy as a borrowed cat.

That night, she slept on the floor with us in our corner of the ticket hall, Aiko-chan curled up next to her. Just as I was drifting off, something flicked against my ear. I looked up to see Shin leering over me.

"What do you want?" I said.

"I was thinking," he said, scratching the side of his nose.

"That makes a change."

His thick lip trembled. "Listen," he said. "Don't you be so proud. You might have learned all the big words at your fancy school but I'm still Shin from Sengen Alley."

I sat up, a bit ashamed of myself for having been rude. Perhaps he had been a bully in the old days. But all sorts of things had changed since then.

"What's the big idea, then?" I asked.

He jerked his thumb toward Tomoko.

"You know—there's another way a girl like that could make us some money."

I leaped to my feet and stared him down with white eyes. I was furious that I'd ever felt sorry for such a bastard. I held my fist under his chin until he shrank backward.

"What does it matter?" he whined. "We wouldn't be the only ones!"

"Don't you touch a hair on her head," I whispered. "Don't you even dare."

His lips peeled back to show broken teeth. "I get it. Want to save her for yourself, ugly?"

My clenched fist stopped a hair's breadth from his eye socket. He froze for a second, then shrugged and rolled away.

"Suit yourself," he muttered.

Tomoko didn't say much, at first. In fact, I sometimes wondered whether she'd actually forgotten how to speak on her long journey across the Kansai plain. But one afternoon, she came over to us through the ticket hall, holding up a tattered magazine.

"I've found something," she said, in quiet voice.

Tomoko was holding a torn copy of *Women's Club*, a journal that my mother used to read. I wrinkled up my nose, but she opened it anyway to show us an article. I squinted at the title: "Let's Eat Grasshoppers!" it said.

"Grasshoppers?" Koji exclaimed.

It wasn't such a surprise. The newspapers had been full of similar stories that month, making suggestions as to how people could find alternate sources of nutrition.

"Let's hear it, then," I said, nodding in encouragement.

Tomoko blew her hair out of her eyes. Shyly, she began to read.

"Not only is the countryside full of grasshoppers, but despite what some might think, they are in fact quite delicious to eat and are very healthy, being packed full of vitamins . . . "

She trailed off as Koji made a sour face and Shin, not to be outdone, retched loudly. But the idea didn't seem so bad to me. We were all practically starving. Even if we didn't eat the grasshoppers ourselves, we could always try to sell them back here at the market. I'd seen people selling buckets of frogs before, some even sold snakes.

"Perhaps we'll go on a grasshopper hunt tomorrow, then," I said. "First thing."

The children made excited noises, but I quickly dashed their hopes.

"There's no reason for us all to go, of course. Just us older ones. Me—and Tomoko, as it was her idea. Shin, you can stay here and look after the little ones. You're in charge."

The children grumbled away, and I stole a glance at Tomoko. Her cheeks were glowing. She was smiling at me.

It was a cold morning, marvelously clear and bright, as we jumped down from the Tobu Main Line train just past Shiraoka, up in Saitama prefecture. The fields were crunchy with frost and mottled leaves were floating down from the trees, slowly, as if they couldn't bear to land. We'd borrowed some little bamboo cages from an old man at the market to make homes for our grasshoppers. But though we hunted about in the fields for hours on end, as the magazine suggested, it finally became clear that we wouldn't be needing them. There were no grasshoppers to be found.

"I wonder where they all could have gone," Tomoko said with a sniff.

"Perhaps it's not the right season anymore," I said. "Or perhaps they've all been eaten already."

It was still a beautiful day though, and we wandered for a while along a winding path that led through the fields as the dew melted and a warbler called out from the trees. *It must have its nest nearby*, I thought, glancing up the branches, and I wondered if I should try to search for its eggs.

There was a jangling rattle from up ahead. Tomoko was standing by a little shrine set with offerings beside the path, the bell rope swaying. Her eyes were closed, and her head was bowed in prayer.

She looked up and clapped her hands—once, twice.

I began to walk towards her, but as she turned to face me, I hesitated. Her eyes were glistening. I desperately hoped that she wasn't crying. It would have been unthinkable for me to try to hit on her, here.

I cleared my throat. "Tomoko-chan. I hope you're not feeling unwell?"

She shook her head.

"Excuse me," she said. "I was just thinking of my mother. She always said a prayer if ever we passed a shrine out in the countryside."

Two statuettes of fox spirits stood on each side of the shrine, dressed in aprons of red cotton. As I gazed at Tomoko, a strange thought occurred to me.

"Tomoko. Is it really true that your mother sent you away to Tokyo?"

Tomoko looked away as her face screwed up. It all became terribly clear.

"She's dead isn't she?" I said, softly. "You came here on your own."

She gave a tiny nod.

"How did she die?"

Tomoko shook her head. "I don't know, Hiroshi-kun," she said. "She was sick. Something to do with her blood, I think."

"What about your father? Couldn't he help? What did he do?"

"He was a doctor. At the naval hospital."

"He could have helped her then, couldn't he?"

She shook her head helplessly. "Everyone was sick, Hiroshi-kun."

I frowned. "What do you mean?"

She stared at me. "Not straight away. Afterwards."

I stared at her. "After the air raid, do you mean?"

Tears began to leak from her eyes.

"What was it like, Tomoko?" I blurted. "Is it true what they say? That the whole city went up with just one blast?"

She held her arms very tightly against her sides. With a jerk of her head, she began to sob.

I was appalled at myself. *Idiot!* I thought. This was exactly why we didn't talk about such things!

I hurried away down the path, my cheeks throbbing with shame. After some time, I heard Tomoko's footsteps behind me. I finally dared to glance at her. To my relief, her face was calm now, her eyes dry.

"Please forgive me," I said.

"Shall we talk about something else?"

"Like what?"

She considered the question. "Well. What about you, Hiroshi-kun?" she said. "Tell me about Asakusa. Was it really as exciting as all the songs used to say?"

I stared at her. "Haven't you ever heard of the Sanja Matsuri?" I asked, relieved to be on home ground again. "It used to be the best festival of them all!"

Her smile widened. "Is that so?"

"What?" I said. "You country bumpkin. Everyone knows that!"

To my delight, she let out a peal of laughter, and I told her about the rowdy celebrations that took place in our neighbourhood every year in honour of the founders of Senso Temple—the swollen crowds, the bulging-eyed men who carried the three enormous portable shrines up to the temple, swaying and crashing into the narrow buildings of the alley as they passed.

"And did you ever carry a shrine, Hiroshi?" Tomoko asked, her eyes wide.

I hesitated. "Well, yes, of course I did. One of the smaller ones, a little *mikoshi*. But you should have seen it! It was covered with real gold . . . "

I blustered on, hoping to thrill Tomoko with exciting tales of Asakusa. But, the truth was, I didn't remember much about the days before the Pacific War, those wonderful times that my parents had always talked about, of the golden wooden horses in Hanayashiki Park, the jugglers out at Asakusa Pond.

Tomoko was smiling now though, and she happily blew her hair from her eyes. "It all sounds wonderful, Hiroshi-kun."

Her white arms swung by her sides. For a moment, more than anything, I wanted to take her hand and hold it in my own.

"Maybe we could go there one day," I said, carefully. "They're showing American films again at the cinemas now. I could show you Senso Temple if you like."

Tomoko stopped walking and looked at me quizzically. "Hiroshi-kun, would you really?" she asked.

"Well," I stuttered. "Not that there's much left of it, of course." She tilted her head to one side, ever so slightly. She was smiling at me again.

The shadows were stretched out in the copses by the time

we got back to the train tracks. After a while Tomoko murmured that she was hungry. She was very pale, and I realised that, in fact, she was starving, and trying to hide the fact by sheer willpower. I cursed myself for not bringing more food and wondered whether I should try rummaging about in the nearest farmer's field. But just then, a blue-green four-car train came creaking toward us along the track and I hopped up.

"Come on," I said, "Hurry!"

"Hiroshi—" Tomoko was struggling to stand. "Please. I don't think I can. I'm so dizzy."

I grabbed her hand and tugged her along as the train shuttled closer. A coupling came alongside us, and I leaped up, gripping onto the carriage. But Tomoko stumbled, and for a second, I was dragging her along the ground, my arm being wrenched out of its socket. With a great heave, I hoisted her up, and she fell into my arms. Her body was a dead weight. She had fainted.

I struggled to grasp her under the arms, trying to stop her falling from the accelerating train. Somehow I managed to steady her between me and the carriage, holding her around the waist as the train rattled forward. She softly moaned and buried her head against my chest. A caramel scent came from her hair, and her breath fell in hot, delicate waves against my neck.

She made a small sound. As she looked up, the colour slowly came back into her face. I realized my hand was resting on the bump of her chest and I quickly wriggled around so that I was standing behind her.

"Thank you, Hiroshi-kun," she murmured. She turned to face the locomotive, clutching onto the carriage for balance. She looked into the distance as the engine gave a long bellow and the train sped up, its wheels clattering faster and faster along the track. The last light of sunset was bleeding over the trees and bright gold glinted from the windows and the rails.

As we raced back toward Tokyo, the smoke from the locomotive puffed around us, and the wind whipped her hair back
into my face.

It was dark by the time we clambered down from the train
at Ueno Station, and the children were bitterly disappointed
that our bamboo cages were empty. Tomoko took the kids off
to try to scrounge something to eat, and I wandered away on
my own, filled with the urge to lose myself in the uneasy magic
of my sensations.

Not far from the railway arches was a wide bomb crater
with tumbledown houses looming over it. It was flooded with
dark water, and now and then bubbles rose to the surface and
burst with such a revolting smell that I normally steered well
clear of the place. But that evening, as I passed, a glint caught
my eye and I froze. Over on the far bank, there was a tiny pulse
in the air, a bright, thrilling glow, like a green star. I clambered
around the rim of the crater and squatted down to get a closer
look. It was just as I'd thought—though I could hardly believe
it was possible so late in the year. Fireflies—floating up and
down by the muddy bank, like ghostly little lanterns.

With my heart in my mouth, I took a matchbox from my
pocket and shook it empty of tobacco strands. I held it open,
and caught one of the creatures at the top of its ascent. Then I
slid the drawer shut with my thumb, slipped the matchbox
into my pocket, and raced back to the station.

Koji gave a whimper when he saw me coming through the
slumped crowds of the ticket hall. He rushed over and
grabbed my arm.

"Big brother, you've come back!"

"Of course I have."

"Shin said you were gone!"

Beneath the concrete stairwell, Shin was sitting cross-legged

on the floor, a nasty grin on his face. The children looked tear-
ful. When Aiko saw me, she gave a squeal of relief.

"What's been going on here?" I said.

Shin looked up at the ceiling.

"He said you were leaving us!" Aiko said. "That you don't
like us anymore."

"It was just a joke," Shin said. "You damned crybabies!"

I put my hand in my pocket. A tiny flicker came from inside
the matchbox.

"Shut up, will you? I'll deal with this in the morning. Let's
just get some sleep."

The children curled up on their mats. An old woman with
a black shawl rasped away beside us. The station lights were
extinguished, and the hall grew heavy with sleep.

I lay there in the darkness, wide awake, listening to the
snores and night murmurs around me. I held the matchbox in
my palm, picturing the creature trapped there in its miniature
chamber of darkness, its body welling with light.

The children were dead to the world, breathing quietly with
their mouths open. Koji frowned and snorted in his sleep.
Beside him, Tomoko lay very still, her lips slightly parted, the
thin blanket over her shallow ribcage gently rising and falling.
I reached over and tugged her leg. She moaned in her sleep,
then shifted. I pulled her leg again, and this time she jerked
awake and sat bolt upright. When she saw me, she rubbed her
eyes. I beckoned to her. Frowning, she edged forward. I held
out the matchbox in my palm, and then pushed the drawer
open a fraction. As the light pulsed in the box, she gasped, and
a faint green glow lit up in her eyes.

She took the box from my palm and pushed the drawer
open all the way. Suddenly, the creature flew up and out of the
box, and hung suspended in the air between us. We looked at
each other in silent delight. She gestured to the ground beside
her. I carefully clambered over Koji's body. As we lay down,

the firefly spiraled slowly in the darkness and her warm cheek pressed against mine. She fumbled for my hand and picked it up and placed it upon her chest. She held it there beneath her fingers, and then I could feel her delicate heart beat, as we lay there together on the cold, hard floor of the station, gazing up at the magical light as it pulsed softly in and out of existence.

8
THE COMFORT STATION
(*Satsuko Takara*)

The International Palace was housed in an old watch factory, just off the highway out towards Chiba. The name might have sounded very grand, but the walls were crumbling and the partition rooms didn't even have doors of their own, just sheets of cloth hanging from nails. The Americans had found their way there straight away. There was a long line of them waiting outside when we arrived. They all clapped and cheered as our buses pulled up.

A celebration ceremony had been held in the Imperial Plaza that morning. Lines of us modern-day Okichis throwing up our hands and cheering *Banzai!* just as if we'd been schoolgirls off on an outing to the countryside.

The fat pig from my interview—the president of the Recreation and Amusement Association—was already waiting at the entrance, dressed like a cheap stage comic. There was an older lady there too, Mrs. Abe, who was to be our "manager." She led me to a cubicle at the end of the corridor and gave me a crayon and a piece of card and asked me to think of an English name for myself. I couldn't think of any, so, after staring at me for a moment, she wrote "Primrose" in jagged orange letters and tacked the card up on the wall. She told me it was the name of a flower.

"Get yourself ready now, Primrose-san," she instructed. "Our foreign guests will be arriving soon."

The cubicle was tiny, barely big enough for the straw futon that lay on the floor. A grubby window was set high in the wall

and a bare electric bulb hung from the ceiling. I sat on the edge
of the mattress and drew my arms around my legs.

A loud cheer came from along the corridor, the jangling of
uniforms and the heavy thud of boots. My stomach quivered.
The Americans were shouting and laughing as they came in, all
bursting with excitement.

My eyes focused on a patch of bubbly mould on the partition
in front of me. I pictured Osamu, his body thin and muscular in
the bedroom of the Victory Hotel. This wouldn't be like that, I
suddenly realised. It wouldn't be like it at all. My heart started
to pound as footsteps came along the corridor. At that moment,
I promised myself that I wouldn't cry, whatever happened.

Girls were moaning in the other cubicles now, men were
grunting and hollering out. Then the curtain of my room was
tugged away, and the first one was standing in the doorway.

There were little dents in the copper of the teakettle from
where it had been buried in the rubble. I'd been staring at it for
hours, hunched over on the stained tatami in our cramped,
silent house. The dents were dirty with grime which I just
couldn't seem to clean away, no matter how much I tried to polish the metal to a dazzling gleam, as my mother had once done.

I could still smell the reek of tobacco and sweat and hair oil.
They had kept on arriving all day long, in their uniforms and
boots. Most hadn't even bothered to undress. They just pulled
down their pants and turned me around and buttoned them-
sclves up as they left.

After the first one finished, I was stunned. I couldn't quite
believe what had just happened. But then the curtain twitched
open and another one was standing there. Again, and again,
and again. After a while, I just lay dumbly on the mattress and
let them pull my kimono aside.

Only a few had any idea what they were doing. Most of
them were no older than boys. They only lasted a moment,

which was a relief. One was rough. He pulled my hair and twisted me around. I screamed, and he leaped up, clutching his trousers as he ran out of the room.

In the late afternoon, I started to get raw and jittery. The room was filthy and stinking and hot and I felt as if I was suffocating. The curtain opened again, and I let out a sob and rolled up into a tight ball.

But it wasn't an American this time. It was Mrs. Abe, who told me that my shift was over and that I should go home. I fumbled into my clothes, but when I got outside into the hallway, I very nearly did start to cry because most of the rooms didn't even have curtains anymore—the Americans had taken them all away for souvenirs.

A sound came from outside and I jerked up. The door slid open and Michiko's face appeared.

"Satsuko," Michiko said. "Satsuko-chan!" She rushed in and put her arms around me. "Was it really that bad?"

I stifled a sob. She had been working in a different part of the building and I hadn't seen her since she'd squeezed my hand goodbye that morning.

"Did you have to go with an awful many?" she asked, stroking my arm. "Poor Satsuko!"

She unrolled our futon and made up the bed, then gently helped me into my nightclothes and tucked me in beneath the covers.

I heard her yawn as she bustled about by the hearth. She was actually humming to herself as she rummaged about in the cupboard. It was amazing. She didn't seem in the slightest bit concerned.

"Satsuko," Michiko said. "Satsuko! Look what I've got."

I couldn't bear to look.

"Satsuko!"

With a great effort, I twisted round. She was waggling a small square bottle full of dark liquid.

"American whiskey. One of the yankiis gave it to me."

She unscrewed the cap.

"Yankiis," she confided. "That's what all the other girls call them."

She sniffed the bottle, then wrinkled up her face. "Mmm!" she murmured. "Not bad."

She put the bottle to her lips and took a long swallow. Her throat moved once, and she sat there, eyes wide, waving her hand over her mouth.

"Oh," she said. "Oh, oh, oh."

She recovered her breath and poured out the drink into two teacups. She handed one to me, and I sat up and gave it a cautious sniff.

"Who would have thought it?" Michiko said. "An American, giving me whiskey."

I took a tiny sip, and retched. The taste was disgusting and made my eyes water.

"And cigarettes," she said, taking out a packet from her purse and waving it at me. "Have a cigarette!"

She slid one out and lit it carefully, frowning at the glowing end and sucking in the smoke as if she had been doing it her whole life. I took another little sip of the whiskey. It was very pungent, but also sweet. When it reached my belly, I felt a burning, relaxing sensation that was really quite pleasant. My eyes grew heavy and I wondered if I was already drunk. I quickly tipped the rest of the liquid down my throat.

Then I really did feel dizzy. I rolled over on the bed and stared up at Michiko's swaying shape in front of me.

"He was the nicest one, anyway," she said, puffing away on her cigarette. "The one who gave me the whiskey. Even if he was a black one."

I sat bolt upright.

"Michiko!" I shrieked. "You didn't go with a black one?"

"So what?" she demanded. "What do I care?"

She poured more whiskey into our cups and I forced myself to drink it. I closed my eyes and lay back, hoping I would fall asleep straight away. The thought of the next day loomed in my mind. A throbbing pain pulsed in my neck and I felt a tightness in my chest. Finally, Michiko blew out the lamp and slid into bed beside me.

My mind was thick with clouds, but sleep wouldn't come. Shapes were moving about in the darkness in front of me; I could see faces of men flickering and blurring into each other. The floor was moving back and forth, as if I was on a boat, men were heaving up and down on top of me, I was suffocating and there was a filthy, cold wetness inside me . . .

I woke with a shriek and seized hold of Michiko. "Michiko!" I cried. "Michiko, help me!"

She raised herself onto one arm. "Satsuko?" she murmured. "What is it?"

I didn't know what to say. Didn't she understand? She was looking at me in the darkness and I could smell the whiskey on her breath.

"Is there really nothing we can do, Michiko?" I whispered. "Nothing at all?"

Her answer came sharply. "No, Satsuko. There's nothing we can do. So the sooner you get used to it the better. Now go to sleep."

With that, she rolled over and pulled the covers across herself. I drew my arms around my body, shivering. A few moments later, I heard a rasping sound. She was snoring.

Every time I looked up, there was an American standing in the doorway. The building was hot and airless, and my room became a wretched, stinking cave. The murky bathroom where we were told to wash and disinfect ourselves after each visitor was the only refuge, but the smell in there was sickening too, and no matter how much I scrubbed myself I couldn't get rid of the stink of chemicals and men. On the train home at night, I was sure that the other people in the carriage could smell it too, and that they were looking at me in disgust, as if they knew exactly the kind of woman I had become.

At the end of the first week, a rumour went around that one of the girls had killed herself. I remembered her from the bus on the first day—she'd worn a yellow dress with a bow in her hair and had stared at the floor with her hands clasped tight. Mrs. Abe had forgotten to tell her to go home and the Americans had just kept on coming for hours on end. She was only seventeen. Later on that night she threw herself under a train at Omori.

I began to wonder if I might do the same. The rails stretched out at the station at night, glittery and smooth, and I wondered whether it would hurt much, or whether you would faint right away before the wheels went over you . . .

Michiko was already home when I got back that evening. She had a look of glee on her face as she knelt down and took my hands in hers.

"Satsuko," she said. "You'll never guess, but I've fixed it."

"What do you mean?" I stammered.

She clutched my hands. "I've fixed it so that we don't ever have to go back to the Palace!"

I stared at her in disbelief. "Please say it's true, Michiko," I moaned. "Please don't say it's one of your jokes."

"Listen," she said. "I spoke with that fat pig of a boss and he's agreed to transfer us to another comfort station. It's a high-class place, up on the Ginza. Reserved for American officers."

My heart sank. *Another comfort station.*

"Will that really make such a difference, Michiko?" I asked. "Really?"

She stared at me. "Are you mad? Of course it will. We won't have to go with those common types any more. We'll be just like real consorts now, Satsuko."

She squeezed my hand, and I saw the old starstruck look in her eyes.

"Modern-day Okichis!" she whispered.

Jeeps were driving up and down the Ginza, taxis going past with acrid smoke pouring from their charcoal-run engines.

American soldiers and sailors strode along the street in wide groups, and I flinched as one raised his cap to me. His friends all guffawed, and he held out his palms to them in offended complaint.

We hunted about for the address up near the tall, sooty shopfront of the Matsuzakaya department store. The window were shuttered now and the doors barred. I felt a stab of guilt. My mother had brought me here four years ago, on my sixteenth birthday, to buy my first real kimono. It was woven from beautiful green silk, embroidered with golden peonies. I'd had to sell the kimono to buy rice back in June.

Next door to the Matsuzakaya was a low, white building that had clearly once been a communal bomb shelter. A large sign hung outside, English words freshly painted in pink and white.

"There it is, Satsuko!"

Michiko traced the letters in the air with her finger. "Oasis—of—Ginza," she pronounced. "We're here!"

Down a flight of dingy steps, the underground shelter had been transformed into a cheap cabaret. There was a little wooden stage and a small dance floor with chairs and tables set off to one side. Red streamers and paper lanterns adorned the cracked earthen walls, American and British flags tacked up at jaunty angles.

"Very nice," said Michiko, nodding approvingly. A scratchy jazz record was playing on the gramophone, and a very tall and solemn-looking American man was turning slowly around in the middle of the room. A tiny girl appeared, clinging onto him—she could barely clasp her arms around his back.

Mr. Shiga's office was an old storage cupboard piled high with buckets. As we stepped inside, he looked at us haughtily over the rims of his spectacles, and told us how lucky we both were.

"Only the best kind of girls get to work here," he said. "This place has got class." He coughed heavily and spat into his handkerchief. "So you'd better keep all our foreign guests happy. And you're not just here to spread your legs, either."

Aside from the usual services, he explained, we were to encourage the Americans to spend their dollars on drinks and dances and snacks.

"And don't let them palm you off with yen!"

Dabbing at his lips, he quickly went through the financial arrangements, which didn't seem quite fair to me. The Oasis would take practically half of everything we earned, even though we were still expected to pay for our own makeup and clothing and any medical treatment that might be necessary. But it was a sign of how desperate I had become that I just knelt meekly before him and bowed my head. Anything seemed better than the International Palace.

Later that night, we took great care making ourselves up. The dressing room was cramped, the air thick with the smell of perfume and perspiring flesh. Other girls slumped on the floor in their underclothes, fanning each other.

Michiko sprinkled powder on the back of my neck and brushed it until my skin was as smooth and white as china.

"Why, Satsuko," she said, as she stood behind me and pulled my obi tight around my waist. "You look just like a real geisha!"

I laughed at the thought. But as we looked at ourselves in the mirror, I really did look quite pretty, even next to Michiko, who was so stunning.

Years before, I recalled, my mother and I had once dressed up together, just like this, before going out to watch the summer fireworks over the river. We'd painted our faces and glued silk petals to our combs. Then she'd helped me into my beautiful green-gold kimono, hoisting the belt and tying it around me just as Michiko had done.

After things had started to go badly for Japan, that had all changed. There'd been no makeup or jewellery any more. Skirts had been banned, and the busybodies from the National Defence Women's Association went around spying, scolding you in public if you wore the tiniest hint of rouge. *Abolish desire until victory!*

One morning, just after I'd reported for war work, Mr. Ogura ordered all of us girls out into the yard. He told us that we were to unpick every colourful thread from our clothes, one by one. After that, it was nothing but shapeless khaki trousers. *No colour but National Defence Colour!*

"Whatever would Mr. Ogura say if he could see us now, Michiko?" I said.

She applied a last minute dusting of powder to my nose. "I think he'd keel over, Satsuko. Just like he did when the emperor made his speech."

We slid open the door to the cabaret. It was already busy, filled with American officers from the army and navy, with girls perched on their knees, pouring their beer and lighting their cigarettes.

As we walked out into the damp, smoky room, a thought struck me. "Michiko," I asked. "How was it that you persuaded the boss to move us here in any case?"

She gave a low laugh. For a moment, she sounded just like one of the vulgar types we'd been working with until so very recently. It was a nasty laugh, of the kind that asks: isn't the answer obvious?

9
ERO GURO NANSENSU
(*Osamu Maruki*)

J apan appeared like an emerald set in a diadem of glittering blue, and our troop ship at last sailed close to the
winding shore, the peaceful coastline. But the soldiers
sensed something amiss as soon as we clambered down the
gangplank to the damaged harbour: the shops empty, the pop-
ulace unwilling to meet our eyes. At the dock, three old
warhorses, their ribs showing through wan hides, were led
stumbling from the dark hold of the ship, unused to the bright
light of day. A young man in a grubby vest immediately
approached the stableman to haggle for their withered flesh.

We were shunted toward Tokyo in a cramped train full of
poisonous smells and sour faces. The city had clearly taken a
smashing: its ribs were showing too, its carcass was open to the
sky. Tokyo Station swarmed with fellow returnees wrapped in
greatcoats, lying in clumps, or sitting drinking, red-faced and
angry at squalid stalls surrounding the plaza. Civilian eyes
avoided us here too, I noticed, and I longed to shed my winter
uniform, writhing now with lice. But the evening was bitterly
cold, and so I buttoned my woolen overcoat to the collar,
pulled my fighting cap down, and, overcome by an almost
exquisite weariness, began to trudge, disorientated by burned-
out streets and unfamiliar vistas, toward Asakusa, town of rainbow lanterns and sleepless sparrows: my spiritual home.

My letters to my honourable mother from the camp on
New Guinea had gone unanswered for many months. Finally,
I had received a crumpled note from her fellow harridans at

the National Defence Women's Association, which informed me that Madame had died of tuberculosis three weeks before, despite an almost complete excision of her lung. It seemed of little use, then, to return home now. With my mother gone, the main house would revert to the distant Osaka branch of her family, and I held out little hope of much assistance from them. They had long ago let me know how much they disapproved of my "dissolute lifestyle," even after I had received my red call-up papers.

"Across the sea, corpses soaking in water!" the radio had sung that day. "Across the mountains, corpses heaped upon the grass!"

"Congratulations on being called to the front, honourable son," my mother had wept. "Your father would be so proud of you!"

I wandered up the shabby remains of the Ginza. The stores were mostly shuttered and those that were not lay empty and bare. As I passed the pockmarked edifice of the Matsuzakaya, an Occupation bus stenciled with the name of an American city roared up alongside me. It expelled a group of boisterous soldiers, who raced over to what seemed to be a low cabaret further along. Painted girls in cheap kimonos advanced upon them, squealing and clutching at their arms, tugging them through the door of the club like kappa imps dragging wayfarers down into the marsh.

Suddenly, I started. One of them seemed very familiar. The short hair, the white oval face, the jet-black eyes that I once knew so intimately—

Satsuko Takara. The girl who had once appeared to me the embodiment of a beautiful Asakusa Park sparrow. I hobbled over to the other side of the road before she could spot me, a jeep blaring its horn as it swerved in its path.

From the opposite curb, I stood and stared across the road. Satsuko Takara. My brief affair with whom had so scandalized my mother. The girl whose face had hovered before me during all those nights of malarial horror on New Guinea.

Look at her now. In her prancing colours, hovering on the dimly lit street. However had she ever fallen so low? Never had she been a *zubu,* a bad girl, like the crop-haired nymphs who hung stockingless around the Asakusa theatres. She had been a delight, a sweetheart. No more, no less.

I writhed with embarrassment as I recalled my mother's coldness to her on the day of my leaving ceremony. Takara-san had visited our house, only to be turned away weeping at the side door. From upstairs, I had listened as my mother scolded Takara-san for her impudence—intent upon packing my cases, too cowardly to descend.

A sharp feeling of guilt flared inside me as I studied her from the darkness. Lice crawled beneath my cap, and I felt a hopeless sense of destitution. Thank Heaven she hadn't seen me. How would I appear now, anyway, even if I were to approach her? A frail ghost with hollow cheeks, returning so utterly broken by war?

I smiled grimly as I watched, tormenting myself with the vision. At last she claimed her prey: a boyish American with spectacles and a thatch of wiry hair. As she dragged him down the steps, I turned and strode quickly northward. If a girl as proper as Satsuko Takara had fallen to such depths, I thought, then things must truly be bad.

To comfort myself, I took a detour via Kanda, intending to follow the river to Asakusa-bashi and then walk up the Sumida from there. Most of the booksellers were gone, their volumes apparently incinerated in the conflagrations of March. But Ota Books was still standing, and I browsed the shelves for a while in a forlorn attempt to get warm. To my surprise, I found a copy of *Crime and Punishment* on the shelf—the first I'd seen in years. I flipped open the frontispiece and saw the *ex libris* stamp of the Sorbonne University. A pit opened in my stomach. Another one of my dreams the war had put paid to.

Mr. Ota shuffled out, armed with a feather duster. I greeted him hopefully. He stared at me as if I were a stranger. I asked if any of the old haunts or bars were still open—the Café d'Asakusa perhaps, the Dragon, or the Montmartre—but he told me that all but the Montmartre had been destroyed in the air raids. As he hobbled outside to bring in the boxes, I quickly slid the novel into my greatcoat—the pocket flaps at least were conveniently large.

What a relief it was, when I finally turned down a ruined alley and saw a red lantern glowing in front of the Montmartre—Mrs. Shimamura's bottle shop. A lump swelled in my throat. The light was like a glowing beacon, a lonely torch to welcome me home. I pulled aside the curtain at the entrance, and there it was, almost unchanged since the old days. The big map of the Paris arrondissements was still up on the wall, and there, polishing glasses behind the counter, was Mrs. Shimamura herself, still wearing her famous white dress; though, as I came closer, I saw to my dismay that her cheeky rolls of fat had shrunken now to wrinkled folds of skin.

She didn't know me either, at first. As I took my old stool up at the bar, I wondered if I could truly have appeared so altered.

"*Obasan*," I said. "Forgive my presumption. But might you extend a note of credit to a returning soldier—and to a loyal, lifelong patron?"

She stared at me, a dim flicker of amused recognition in her eyes.

"Regrettably, sensei," she replied, "since the war ended, there have been so many hundreds of hungry and thirsty ghosts, crawling about the city seeking credit notes . . . Perhaps sensei would better off talking to his friend Nakamura-san, whom he must surely recognize sitting at the end of the bar?"

I turned. Hunched over the counter sat a skeleton with a drink and a sketchpad. It was him all right! Nakamura and I had been in the same French literature class at Keio; we had even once thought about producing a Sensationalist pamphlet together. But while my stories had withered on the vine, his drawings had won so much acclaim that he had been hired by the noted magazine *Manga* at the outbreak of the Pacific War . . . I remembered his cartoons well. They grew more and more barbarous as the war progressed. Allied soldiers bayoneted to death by loyal children of the emperor; aircraft carriers destroyed by whizzing Zero fighters; not to mention his celebrated masterpiece, "The Annihilation of Britain and America." . . .

Naturally, I was overjoyed to see him sitting there, just as in the old days. As I slid over to him, he gave a sickly smile and quickly turned over his pad to hide whatever it was he was drawing. I asked him what there was to drink nowadays, and he told me that the only thing available was a rotten blend of distilled shochu dregs mixed with aviation fuel to give it a kick. I mulled this over for a few moments, and then remarked, philosophically, that the emperor himself had told us that we must endure the unendurable, after all.

I politely inquired whether Nakamura was still producing illustrations for *Manga*. He gave a ghastly grin, displaying many broken teeth, and, as I hoped, called to Mrs. Shimamura to pour us two glasses of the house spirit, in order to "welcome me home." I thanked him politely and poured the drink into my mouth.

For a moment, I thought my throat was going to explode. I somehow managed to swallow the poisonous stuff, and promptly felt as if my eyes were bleeding. I tugged at Nakamura's sleeve to see what he was drawing. He tried to hide the pad, but I gripped hold of the paper and tugged, until suddenly it tore.

My, my. What an evolution. No foreign barbarians here: instead, a Japanese soldier (who bore a remarkable likeness to Nakamura himself) bowed in thanks to a titanic American with a colossal pair of scissors, who was triumphantly snipping the man free of chains that tied him to a pile of tanks and bombs. I laughed long and hard at this, and told Mrs. Shimamura that we'd better have two more glasses of her awful liquor to celebrate Nakamura-san's new career. I banged my glass against his.

"Well, Nakamura," I said, "'*À l'oeuvre on reconnaît l'artisan.*'" I poured the horrid stuff into my throat, and instantly slid from the chair.

Painful waves beat relentlessly against the quick of my brain. A sensation of helplessness—paralysis. Someone was pounding on the door. I was no longer in a stockade cell on a poisonous island, I realised, nor in the dark bowels of an oceangoing ship. I was somewhere I knew, somewhere as intimately familiar as the womb. Slowly, it dawned on me—with exquisite relief. The room above Mrs. Shimamura's shop. Reserved for customers to sleep off their night's excesses. The banging came again, and my panic rose as the door slid open.

Mrs. Shimamura poked her head into the room. "Time to go, sensei. I've laid out your breakfast."

The thought of the crowds swelling around Tokyo Station filled my heart with fear.

"Obasan, perhaps I could ask you . . . "

"Don't be a pain, sensei—"

"Please, obasan—"

Disgusted with myself, I broke into sobs as I knelt before her. "For just a few days, obasan. Please! I beg you."

Mrs. Shimamura's face crinkled. She hesitated for a moment. I sensed victory.

Kind and noble obasan. She would let me stay—for just a

few days. I was expected to carry out several duties in the bar. I was not expected to sit around the place pickling myself in sake lees.

I stayed on my knees as she strode from the room. I sank back into the soft blankets and closed my eyes. The crowds at the station, the waves of refugees casting about and crashing against each other . . . They were far away now. Here, I was safe, hidden upon my lifeboat, bobbing about on a quiet inland sea. The sky was flowing with the stars of the Milky Way.

The artists who had survived the war were emerging now from the cracks, crawling like valiant cockroaches to the refuge of Mrs. Shimamura's saloon. Every night, around the hour of the dog, the bar filled up with various writers, journalists and assorted poets I had known before the war, as well as the usual students and hangers-on.

My greatest need now was for money. With my mother dead, I was one of the few of the intellectuals with no private income of my own. I discussed the matter with Nakamura and a yawning Mrs. Shimamura one afternoon. What was the role of a writer, I asked, in a world that had fractured so entirely? How could he ever respond to such devastation? And how, I gloomily thought, was he ever to scratch a living? Every crevice had already been swept, it seemed, the dust rolled out into dough. We truly were distilling the dregs.

The following morning in Kanda, I was browsing Mr. Ota's bookshop again, wondering if I dared steal a bound copy of Zola's *L'Assommoir*. Two painters were hoisted up alongside the building next door, working upon its restoration, and, as they slopped whitewash on the brickwork, I overheard the drifting threads of their conversation. To my surprise, they were discussing meals they had once most enjoyed at this time of year. Toasted *mochi* filled with chestnut jam, one enthused.

The crispness of the shell, the wonderfully sweet paste within . . .
The other waxed lyrical about the pressed mackerel sushi he
had eaten as a young man in Osaka—the vinegar tang of the
silver-blue fish! The rice plump and sweet on the tongue! My
mouth began to water, and I recalled a curious pining that I'd
had for persimmons, as we sailed on our long voyage back to
Japan from the South Seas, a craving that had seemed, at times,
almost overwhelmingly intense, the memory of the fragrant
juice, the soft, mottled flesh transporting me back almost
beyond childhood . . .

I strolled over to the men and studied them as they worked.
Their faces did not seem bitter or weathered, despite the cold.
Rather, they were radiant, transported, transcendent even.
They were dreamily happy, I realised, lost in the innocence of
their memories. A thought struck me. I had a sudden inkling
of what I might write.

Nakamura and Mrs. Shimamura agreed straight away that
the plan was a good one. We would sell fantasies.

Mrs. Shimamura summarised things very cogently. She
poured a glass of her clear spirit and pointed at it.

"Look," she said, "if you can't afford sake, you have to settle for this."

I agreed, reaching for the glass, but she snatched it up and
tipped it against her lips, swallowing with a grimace.

"What I mean is, if you can't have the real thing, you have
to settle for its substitute. If you can't find food, you'll have to
settle for articles about it. That's what you'll sell in your magazine. But you're missing a trick, sensei—the most important
fantasy of all."

"Please enlighten us, obasan."

"Sex."

Stiffly, I asked her what she meant.

"Well. It used to be the only thing that was free, didn't it?

But not any more! Think of those trollops in the back alleys. They hoard it up like stingy peasants do rice, and only dole it out to those who can afford it."

I thought wistfully of Takara-san and the gaudy girls on the Ginza, rushing over to grasp the uniformed arms of the American GIs.

"Where's the average man to find comfort nowadays? His wife's most likely dead, and the only girls around are sluts. If he's only got two yen, and a girl costs twenty, whatever is he to do?"

I took Mrs. Shimamura at her word, and jam-packed our new magazine with every possible fantasy—epicurean, erotic, or otherwise—that might appeal to the ordinary Japanese man, so lately oppressed by frustrated desires. I wrote three stories interspersed with Nakamura's drawings and cartoons—the usual erotic, grotesque nonsense we had grown up with.

The first dealt with a soldier who, on returning home, finds that his wife has taken up with his neighbour. Soon enough, he is incapable of arousing himself in any other way than by spying on them from behind a screen.

The second was a more monstrous variation on the theme. A man is forced by circumstance to take work in a brothel, mopping the stained floors and laundering the sheets. He learns that a new girl, a real beauty, is to start work the next day. An uncanny thought occurs to him, and he hides himself under her bed that night. The next day, the presumed beauty comes in with an American soldier. They throw themselves onto the bed and start heaving and cavorting. Aroused, the man's fingers creep into his pants, and, as the bed rattles and shakes, the girl approaches the heights of her ecstasy, and he cannot help but participate in her delirium. "With the roar of a mountain lion," the American completes, and leaves the room.

The man hears the girl dressing. He sidles out from underneath the bed, intent upon presenting her with a diabolical proposition. As he emerges, she shrieks.

He gasps, clutching at his chest. The girl is his own daughter.

The cover was a master stroke, lovingly drawn and coloured by Nakamura. A woman suns herself on a beach, wide hips, jutting breasts, *plus ça change*. But look closer. This is no Japanese bathing beauty. She is a Westerner. An American lady, with just a wisp of hair emerging beneath her navel—for the first time, I was certain, on the cover of a Japanese magazine. The wife of one of the generals, perhaps? Of MacArthur himself? All of this, and more, available to anyone now for just three yen. This, I sensed instinctively, was the true essence of democracy.

The second half of the magazine was more considered and less obscene. Inspired by the house painters, "The Dish I Most Lament" was a feature based upon a series of interviews I conducted at various stations along the Yamanote Line, in which I asked ordinary citizens to describe the meal for which they felt most nostalgic. The reactions were astonishing. Some shook their heads furiously and marched away; one man even punched me on the nose. Others simply froze, then began to reel off a list of dishes as if they were reading from a long menu unfurling in their minds—sea bream cooked in chestnut rice; bubbling stews of chicken and burdock; hot fried tempura and fat slivers of bonito . . . Others smiled, with that dreamy, faraway look I had seen on the faces of the house painters, and talked of cold buckwheat soba from a temple in Kyoto; itawasa fish cakes from a famous shop in Nihonbashi . . . They talked of tofu and oden, horsemeat and clams. But most of all, they talked of miso. Miso, miso, always miso soup, prepared each morning by the hands of once beloved, now departed mothers and wives.

Sometimes I had to stop them talking, as my eyes would be blurry with tears. Their smiles would falter, and the wind would gust past us along the street. The interviewees would look at me bitterly then, as if I had robbed them of something precious. More than anything, I realized, it was our lost past that was the most captivating daydream. In those days of the dried cod, of the rotten sweet potato, it was the most painful fantasy of all.

ERO, as we named the magazine, was an instant hit. Convinced of its appeal, Mrs. Shimamura funded the first printing. By the end of the day, all of the copies we had placed with the booksellers and newsstands had sold out. With the profits, we printed another issue, which itself sold out by the end of the week. It seemed we had struck a peculiar vein.

My financial issues were thus temporarily solved. But I was troubled by the fact that in just five days, my erotic stories had sold a hundred times more than all my literary scribblings had in a decade. Even more disturbingly, while in the past I had agonized over every word and punctuation point, these stories had flowed from my pen like water. I had written them all in one night, in fact, one after the other, sitting up in my room with an inkstone and a bottle of liquor. I wondered if something had fractured in my mind during those malarial months of horror in the jungles of New Guinea.

What irony that I, who fancied myself the Japanese Tolstoy, an Oriental Zola, should find my métier in pornography. That the first thing I should write on my return from the inferno of war should be sensual and erotic!

10
The Touristic GI
(*Hal Lynch*)

My compatriots glanced at me curiously across the dining room of the Continental Hotel as I attempted to lever chunks of rice into my mouth with chopsticks. A small bowl of gelatinous fish swamped in brown paste lay on my table, alongside a slippery white cuboid of tofu and a pot of green tea. The boy had been delighted when I'd asked him for a "Japanese-style" breakfast that morning, but I was now envying the toast and powdered eggs being devoured by the other staff and officers around me.

I had thrown myself into my new Japanese life with vigour, keen to get under the skin of the place. I scoured the markets for books in translation and pored over whatever I could find—folktales, samurai dramas, medieval literature. I undertook a dozen Japanese lessons with an old professor in his chrysanthemum garden in Shibuya, as a sickle of silver moon swelled to a peach in the clear fall sky. I sat cross-legged through six baffling hours of a white-masked Noh play in a dusty, empty hall, as time slowed to a crawl, and the pain in my thighs grew ever more excruciating.

Dutch was still sore at me for landing him in hot water.

"Give this one to Lynch," he would simper at editorial meetings. "He's swell at human interest!"

My assignments so far had included a horticultural show by the Allied Women's Flower Arranging Society and a boxing tournament between the 5th Cavalry and a team of British marines.

In the meantime, I tramped the Tokyo streets, taking photographs of the ruined city and its inhabitants. A bald man in a shanty washing glasses from a bucket. The watchman of the metal mountain up past the Ginza, smoking his pipe amidst the clutter of radiators, bicycles and temple bells.

I was up at Ueno one day, exploring the stalls of the black market. Men chopped slivers of meat with cleavers, unloaded wooden crates of fish from handcarts. Behind the station, a team of tattered children were playing a makeshift game of baseball on a patch of wasteground. A serious looking boy, his face disfigured by burns, was standing against a broken-down section of wall, holding up a charred plank. Another boy in khaki pants flung a ball made of rags, and the scarred kid whacked it, hard. A piece of wood splintered off and he raced around a diamond marked by piles of gravel, the other children hollering in encouragement. I pulled up my Leica and started to fire off shots. The boy tore back just in time to make the home run, sliding along the gravel in a great cloud of dust. The other children cheered and screamed as he rolled home. Then they spotted me. Instantly they abandoned their game, and came galloping toward me in a dusty herd.

I hurled candy bars, of which I now kept a provident supply in my coat pocket, as they swarmed me, shrieking with delight. To give them a treat, I decided to photograph their portraits, and had them scribble their names in my notebook.

"All from Tokyo, right?" I asked, in my new, broken Japanese. "You—Tokyo?"

The scarred boy pushed forward. His hair was thickly matted and he wore dirty blue serge trousers rolled up at the hem.

"We—Tokyo," he said in wavering English, gesturing to himself and the others. Then he pointed. "She—no."

Another little girl was standing a few paces behind him, apparently too shy to come over.

"Oh? Where's she from?"

The boy nodded. "Yes. She—Hiroshima," he said.

I hesitated, intrigued. "Is that so?"

The girl wore a blue canvas jacket and was very frail. An old metal water canteen hung over her shoulder.

I leaned down and beckoned to her, but she barely dared look at me. I offered her a malted milk ball from my pocket, but she quickly shook her head. The other children gathered closely around us.

"You—Hiroshima?" I asked.

She glanced at the scarred boy, then gave a tiny nod of assent.

"You have—mother? Father? Okasan? Otosan?"

She stared awkwardly beyond me, as a faint wind ruffled her short hair.

The scarred boy broke in: "Her mother—sick. Send her—Tokyo."

"Her mother was sick?"

Tears welled in the girl's eyes. All of a sudden, she said something in a strained voice. I turned to the boy.

"What did she say?"

He wiped his forehead with his fist, frowning. "Bomb—fall," he said. He made an explosive noise and threw up his hands. "Every people—sick."

"Sick? You mean dead?"

He frowned, apparently at his linguistic limit. He shook his head. "No die. Sick."

"The bomb? The bomb made her mother sick?"

He nodded triumphantly. "Sick. Dead. So, *desu*."

A memory came into my mind. The surrender issue of *LIFE*, back in September, with MacArthur's face glaring from the cover. A set of photographs of Hiroshima was printed inside, shots of mangled factories, crinkled trees, taken from ground level. There'd been no images of any surviving population.

The other children were scampering about now, hurling stones across the wasteground. The scarred boy was staring intently at my Leica. As a reward for his efforts at translation, I took the leather strap from around my neck and handed him the camera. He examined it with a fierce and concentrated delight, then held it to his face and began to swoop gently around, like a regular Robert Capa.

I smiled as I watched. Finally, I prised it away from him. He gave me a solemn look of thanks, bowing low. A sudden grin broke out on his face and he turned and ran back to his game.

Dutch grudgingly printed the picture a week later. I guessed I was now forgiven. It showed the earnest boy holding his makeshift bat as the ball of rags flew toward him: "The Tokyo Little Leagues," the caption read.

Eugene's interest in Japanese culture was of a different hue to my own. One evening, he asked me to join him and his new friend Bob McHardy, a cartoonist at the paper, at a bar called The Oasis next to the new Postal Exchange by the Ginza Crossing. At the entrance, yum-yum girls coaxed men inside, while laughing GIs lined up at a booth next door, which hair-raising VD posters evinced to be an army prophylactic station.

Downstairs, Eugene sat at a table with McHardy, who had a girl perched on his knee, running her fingers through his curly blonde hair. *Good God*, I thought. She was a knockout. She should have been starring on some cinema screen instead of servicing doughboys down here by the hour.

Another girl, dressed in a kimono, was perched on the chair beside Eugene. She was pretty too, young and neat, with porcelain skin and jet-black eyes.

"Harold, meet Primrose," Eugene winked. "She's a swell sort."

Primrose refilled Eugene's glass every time he took a sip and laughed at practically everything he said. As I drank my lukewarm beer I couldn't help but picture the gangly boy I'd roomed with in college. Just look at him now. Eugene sprawled on the chair with an air of easy and wanton debauch, as Primrose stroked his face and patted his thigh.

McHardy went off to dance with his exotic creature and I told Eugene about an idea I'd been toying with. I wanted to see more of the country, and thought we might try writing some touristic reports, about places the average GI might like to visit on leave.

"It would give us a chance to do some travelling ourselves, Gene. Get out of Tokyo."

"Well, sure," he said. "I guess . . . "

Primrose had taken off Eugene's glasses now and placed them upon her own nose and was generally distracting him. As she reached over to pour more beer into his glass, I noticed that her palms were damaged—they appeared smooth and shiny in the low light, as if they'd been polished.

"Come on, Gene. It'll do you a world of good."

Eugene seemed very uncertain. Primrose put the bottle back down, and for a split-second, I felt her hands touching my face, passing over my back. She caught my eye, and gazed back at me.

A new song came on the gramophone. With a delighted gasp, she hopped up and tugged at Eugene's hand.

"What do you think, Gene?" I said.

"Why don't you talk to Dutch about it?"

"I will." Beer drained, I stood up.

"You're not staying?"

"Uh-uh."

Primrose wiped her forehead in comical fashion. I saw now how pretty she was, and felt dumb to be leaving so soon.

"Suit yourself," Eugene called as Primrose dragged him over to the dance floor. I held up my hand in farewell and strode up the steps to the bustling street outside.

Dutch was enthusiastic about my idea, just as I'd figured he would be.

"It'll be real human interest, Dutch. Aimed square at your average GI."

He beamed. "Attaboy. What'll we call it?"

"How about 'The Touristic GI'?"

"Sure," he said. "Sounds appealing."

Two days later, at six in the morning, a protesting Eugene and I picked our way through the crowd at the station to embark upon our journey to Himeji, a castle complex out near Kobe, having stocked up on tins of spam, sandwiches and bottles of beer from the PX the night before. I'd photographed the sloping turrets of the medieval fortress from our plane back in July, two days before our bombers had poured a few hundred tonnes of incendiaries over the town. Miraculously, the castle had survived.

Japanese crammed into the carriages as women shoved parcels in through the broken windows. With relief, we found the carriage reserved for Allied personnel and clambered into a compartment. It was empty, though hardly luxurious. Most of the windows were cracked and the seats were busted, springs jabbing up through the fabric. But as the locomotive whistled and tugged us out of the station, I felt a cautious thrill to be escaping the fairy-lit toy-town of Little America, and heading out into the wilds of Japan at last.

We jolted through the ruined fringes of the city and out into the countryside. Green paddies stretched along each side of the track, figures in conical hats stooped over as they had, no doubt, for centuries. We ate our sandwiches as the huge, wide slopes of Mount Fuji came into view, ice-cream white now against a cold blue sky. I recalled the conical peak of the mountain from above—we'd used it so many times as a mustering point before the raids that it seemed intimately familiar.

The perspective shifted; my stomach lurched. The world

took on a sudden, febrile intensity as deafening engines thudded in my inner ear.

My head was between my legs. Eugene's hand lay on my
shoulder.

"Hal? Are you alright?"

I took deep breaths until the thudding floated away.
Eugene was staring at me.

"Are you sick?"

"Stuffy in here."

I hoisted down the cracked pane of glass on the other side
of the compartment. Beyond the flat paddies, a stream wound
below a scenic ridge. Eugene opened two bottles of beer and I
took one from him gratefully.

"Here's how," he said.

We clinked bottles and drank. Presently, I took a private
glance behind. The huge mountain was gone, smeared away
into mist.

A little narcotic rivulet trickled pleasantly around my brain
as Eugene told me about the parallel life he had been living over
the past few years, ever since I was drafted straight out of college and had joined 3rd Recon. He'd applied to the newspaper
on a whim, it seemed; up to then, he'd been working at his
father's law office in Manhattan, excused from service due to
his terrible eyes. Japan was his big adventure now. I joshed him
about his "girlfriends" in Tokyo and he coloured, smirking.

"Come on, Hal. Don't tell me you haven't succumbed to
the delights of baby-san?"

The question lacked nuance. Before I'd been sent to Saipan,
there'd been henna-tattooed skin and plump Indian flesh in a
mud shack at Kharagpur; a dose from my favourite girl at the
Phoenix House in Chengtu. Always with a vague sense of bru-
tality, as if I were some kind of marauding barbarian.

"And how is Primrose, Eugene?" I asked, swigging my
beer. "Still blooming, I hope?"

"You should learn to loosen up a little, Harold."

"And how often do you find yourself frequenting such charming establishments, Eugene?"

He adjusted his glasses, a trifle uncomfortably. "Most nights, I guess."

As the train followed the line of the coast, a cold wind blew in through the cracks in the windows. We were starting to shiver when the porter brought in a small, hot brazier of charcoal, which he set on the floor before folding down our bunks. Dusk fell, and we squeezed into our narrow berths and tried to fall asleep under short, thin blankets.

The clattering of the train permeated my dreams, transforming itself into the pounding of aerial bombs. I was alone in a house I somehow knew from my childhood, a place that was at once intimately familiar, yet vastly lonely. The continual whoosh and blast of explosives came from outside and I felt an inexplicable sadness, as a child might feel when he is utterly abandoned. The glass door of a rifle cabinet hung open by the wall. A single lamp burned by the stair. A knock sounded at the door and I knew with instinctive fear who it would be. I hesitated for what seemed like an endless time, before I opened it.

The disfigured Japanese boy was standing there, holding his makeshift baseball bat like some strange oriental cherub. His frail girlfriend stood beside him. Each took one of my hands and together they led me out into a blazing city. Then we were flying high up above a night landscape, villages and towns far below all razed to the ground. We went still higher, miles above the earth, and then we were flying amidst some strange, ethereal hinterland, surrounded by ancient, deserted cathedrals of the night . . .

There was a piercing shriek and I awoke with a shout. The train was shuddering to a halt. The door to our carriage swung open and there was a sudden blast of cold air. People scrambled into our compartment, but the platform guard's voice barked out. He raced to our door, valiantly barring entry, pulling people out and packing them off to the carriages reserved for Japanese. The door finally slammed shut, and I rolled over in my berth with guilty relief.

The rest of the journey was interminable, the train groaning to a halt or stopping at small branch line stations. When we finally clambered out, blurry-eyed, it was into the dim morning light of Himeji, where we were met by Lieutenant Hartley, a shy young officer from the 130th Infantry.

As we walked along the platform, the stationmaster slid out destination plates from their frames on the side of the carriages. Himeji was the junction of three major lines; the train would split here. As he slotted in new plates, two military policemen in white helmets trod past us toward the Allied carriage. They paused by our old compartment and hopped up onto the side, suspending themselves by the open windowpane as they inspected the interior. Apparently satisfied, they jumped down and waved. The stationmaster blew his whistle. As the carriages shunted forward, the new destinations of the onward route came into view, a list of Japanese ideograms next to neatly written English letters:

OKA-YAMA—KURA-SHIKI—FUKU-YAMA—MI-HARA—HIRO-SHIMA.

The artless syllables took me aback—like it was just another town. The frail girl from Ueno Station must have passed through here, I thought. The train pulled away. Just a few stops, now, before its terminus.

Hartley drove us in a jeep through the town—all badly burned, though the castle at the summit of the hill was white as a wedding cake. I wondered out loud as to the significance of the military police at the station.

"Well, sir," Hartley said, struggling with the gearshift as we wound up the hill. "Himeji's the end of the line for Allied personnel right now."

"Is that so?"

A pained look came over his face. "Hiroshima's kind of off limits for the time being, sir."

"Is that so?"

"Yes, sir."

The castle loomed before us. Out front, GIs from the local garrison snapped portraits with their Box Brownies. Inside, the rooms were gloomy and austere.

Eugene was sulking. "I'm sure glad you made me come, Harold. What a splendid view!" From the balustrade at the top of the castle, we could see far into the distance. A burned hamlet huddled beneath us, muddy fields stretching for miles around.

"Okay, Eugene. Give me a break."

Back at the gymnasium where we were billeted, we ate a dull dinner of fried spam. Hartley joined us later and invited us to a bar. I refused, intent on getting my head down. Eugene's interest was piqued. I heard him stumble back several hours later, stinking of cheap scent and whisky.

The next day was cold and Eugene was surly. Halfway home, outside Kyoto, the train halted. After much confused lumbering, it shunted into a siding, where it stayed for over an hour. Finally, the door opened, and a large man whom I recognized clambered aboard. Thickset, big tortoiseshell glasses, a few strands of brown hair scraped over his head, he raised a meaty hand when he saw us. At that moment, the train began to creak backward. He heaved his kit bag up onto the rack, his face brightening as he noticed our green press patches.

"Well, now. The fine men of the *Stars and Stripes.* Always a pleasure." He held out a thick palm.

His accent had a European inflection, I thought. German? Yiddish?

"Mark Ward," he said. "*Chicago Sun-Times.*"

"Hal Lynch," I said, shaking his hand.

I remembered where I'd seen him now. At a press conference in the council chamber of the Diet a few weeks earlier, he'd been haranguing the incumbent prime minister with a vigour the man clearly found unfamiliar and disconcerting.

Eugene shook his hand sullenly. I suspected he was resentful of the men from the "official" papers and the agencies. The *Stars and Stripes*, Japan itself, seemed something of a pet project for him, one he disliked having to share with others. The train started to clang along the rails, and Ward winced as he eased himself onto the seat opposite.

"Lord save us," he said.

"Not quite a first-class Pullman," I ventured.

"Be grateful for small mercies, young man," he replied, jerking his thumb toward the crammed Japanese carriages. He twisted his head until his neck cracked, then let out a groan of satisfaction.

"Interesting assignment?"

"Himeji Castle."

He raised his eyebrows in question.

"Set of touristic sketches. About the historic places of Japan. Kinds of places the ordinary GI might like to visit." A polite nod.

"Castles and such. Famous beauty spots."

Ward squinted as the temple roofs and tall cedars of Kyoto skittered past outside.

"Well. I guess they may as well take a peek at what's left."

I noticed with embarrassment that Eugene was studiously ignoring the man. I speculated on the possible reasons for the train's tardiness and Ward gave a sheepish grin.

"I'm the culprit, I'm afraid," he said. "I was interviewing a major here, local head of procurement, about certain contracts he's just awarded to a local nightclub owner."

A cigar emerged from the side pocket of his kit bag, and he flicked a silver lighter at its tip.

"Well, we just couldn't stop talking and so the interview ran over. The major's secretary was kind enough to telephone the stationmaster, who said he'd hold the train until I got there."

Eugene snorted. "Gee, I hope it was worth it." He hoisted his boots onto Ward's seat and buried his face in a two-month-old edition of *Popular Science*.

"Don't worry about Eugene, Mr. Ward," I said. "He likes to keep abreast of his ignorance."

Eugene yawned deliberately, and went off to lie down in another part of the carriage. As the train rolled slowly eastward, Ward puffed at his cigar in the contented manner of a commercial traveller. He seemed to have visited half of the country already, though he said he'd spent most of the war in China.

"I was based in Chengtu for a spell myself," I ventured.

He examined me, sizing me up. "Well, perhaps we're kindred spirits, then, Lynch."

He took a flask of whisky from his kit bag and handed it over. I swallowed a glug with relish and he nodded for me to take another.

"Well, that's my sheet. How do you find yourself here, Lynch? You must have seen action, I suppose."

"Well, sure," I shrugged. "Where should I start?"

The train gave a loud shudder as the wheels shuttled on the rails. He glanced outside, the dusk gathering now in the paddies.

"We have plenty of time."

As I told him about my war, the sound of snoring drifted from the next compartment. With vague resentment, I realized that Eugene hadn't once asked me about my service in all the time we'd been back together. Ward's manner was avuncular and invited confidences. As the train shunted toward Tokyo, he offered me more whisky from his flask and I recalled to him days and nights hunched over the viewfinders in the belly of *Flashing Jenny*, mapping out the country piece by piece.

"You drew up targets for the Super Fortresses?"

"Eyes of the 21st Bomber Command."

That previous September. Arriving at the Isley Field airstrip on Saipan, fresh and bright in our gleaming new photo-converted Superfort, straight off the line. Bombs out, cameras in. At our first briefing, General Curtis LeMay, then head of strategic air operations, informed us that the best map we had of Japan was from *National Geographic*. Our job was to remedy the situation. All through fall, we flew dozens of missions, debriefing LeMay in his Quonset every day at thirteen hundred, pointing out the spillways of the naval yards; the carriers and cruisers; the munitions factories turning out aircraft engines and locomotives, heavy guns and rolling stock.

At dawn, one by one, the silver dream-boats floated off from the runways. Dipping with the weight in their bomb bays, they ascended, fuselages dazzling bright in the first rays of sun. After dark, the ground crewmen sweated it out on the airstrip, puffing cigarettes, gazing fretfully at their watches and up at the sky, until the low drone of motors sounded far away and finally the powerful landing lights lit up the runway and the first returning planes touched precisely down.

In January, we were relocated from Saipan to Harmon Field at Guam to be closer to LeMay. Operations staff were no longer interested in industrial targets. Instead, we were told to identify the most densely packed residential areas in each Japanese city, and to grade them according to the most inflammable areas.

"The fire raids?" Ward asked.

My scalp prickled. My map of Tokyo hung on the wall of the Quonset two weeks later, the wards marked in varying shades of grey according to their population. By then we had fire jelly and white phosphorus that would stick to skin, paper or wood and burn like hell until everything was gone. To the west of Tokyo, the new suburbs were blank white. To the east, the old wards, Fukagawa and Asakusa, were shaded jet black.

"The Tokyo Raid," I said. "Lord God. You could see the flames from two hundred miles away."

Pillars of smoke rising to 18,000 feet. A sheer of heat, the sky blasting bright outside the windows of the plane. My hand pulling hard on the camera crank, over and over again.

"Next week, Nagoya," I said. "Osaka. Kobe. We were going to burn the whole damn country to the ground."

By July we were running out of places to bomb. My face in the mirror was twitchy, my body listless and unkempt. My CO ordered me to take a week's leave, which I spent swimming around the reef at Tumon Bay, trying to shake my throbbing headaches and chronic dysentery, convinced that a stink of soot and burning flesh had ground into my skin. Floating on my back in the water, staring up at the planes in the sky. The day I returned to duty, I was told to prepare for a photo mission. We were to map out a bombing approach. To identify primary targets around the naval base out in the eastern city of Hiroshima.

Ward was standing over by the window. He hurled out the remains of his cigar, and it flew into the night in a shower of embers.

The next day at thirteen hundred, operations staff were hunched over my prints. LeMay suddenly turned, desperate with impatience, and hollered for a bona fide primary target.

"Sir?"

He stared at me.

"You see a white, T-shaped bridge, sir?"

"Show me."

I walked over and pointed. "See? Right in the centre of the city. Clear as day. Couldn't miss it if you tried."

Ward shoved up the window. He turned to me in the darkness as I wiped the clammy perspiration from my forehead.

"Are you bothered by what you did up there, Lynch?"

Floating over that charred plain one week later, eerie and desolate. The rivers trickling slowly through the char.

"You were just an observer, Hal."

"That's right."

The train came out from behind a hill and curved around a stretch of coast. Black waves in the distance rippled with moonlight.

Ward gave a sudden, jaw-cracking yawn.

"Okay, Lynch. Maybe we should get our heads down."

I rubbed my eyes. "You're probably right."

He looked up at the miniature berths, wincing. "Oh, my aching back . . . "

When we woke, the ruins of Tokyo were visible in the grey light of dawn. Naked children stood outside hovels at the bottom of the embankment, waving up at the train as we passed. At the station, we slung our kit bags over our shoulders and made our way through the departing crowd. Ward held out his hand.

"It was good talking to you, Lynch. Look me up at the press club sometime. There's some folks you might be interested in talking to."

"Okay, Ward. Thanks."

"Well then. I'll see you."

He held up his hand and shouldered his way through the crowd, off to write up his story about procurement scandals and Allied corruption. Eugene and I wandered blearily back to the *Stars and Stripes* office to file our own piece: "The Touristic GI visits Historic Himeji Castle."

11
THE RYOKAN
(*Hiroshi Takara*)

I woke up in the cavern of the ticket hall, my breath puffing in icy clouds. Wisps of vapour floated from the men and women slumped on the floor, as if they were a horde of sleeping dragons. I stood up and picked my way around their mats, dodging the pools of milky vomit that stank like rotten soybeans. At the foot of the concrete staircase, an old man shivered, clutching wretched fingers to shield his eyes from the dawn sunlight. I edged around him warily.

Smallpox. The tunnel people had complained of splitting headaches at first. Then they started to shiver and moan. The rashes came soon after that, bubbly freckles that crusted into sores and spewed white pus all over their faces, as if they'd been stung by a swarm of wasps. The skin of the sickest ones stayed smooth as glass though. Eerie patches of purple welled up and raced across their bodies like patterns on a naval map. They died soon after, mouths gaping, as if something had taken them by surprise.

The children wore rags over their faces and stayed well away from the sick. But Koji had come to me a few days earlier, complaining that he was exhausted and that his mouth stung. When he held up his shirt for me to examine him, I was sure I could see a mark on his chest, like a shadow on a snowy field.

Outside, a frost had covered the city with a sheet of glittering white. It lay crinkled on the wasteground behind the station and on the jagged mounds of scrap metal in the yard. For just a moment, the city was silent, transformed into a secret, sparkling fairyland. I held up my hands, making a frame with my fingers. *Wouldn't it make a good photograph?*, I thought.

The Americans are savages and demons! That's what we'd always been taught. During the war, I'd gazed for hours at the murderous coloured double-spreads in *Boy's Magazine*, picturing myself in the midst of a desperate suicide charge at Guam, firing a submachine gun at those monsters on the beach. *Chun-chun-chun!*

The American in the trench coat hadn't looked like a savage though. He'd looked stylish and rugged as he stooped over to talk to Tomoko, his camera dangling around his neck. When he handed it to me, I rubbed my thumb over the exposure control and twisted the smooth aperture dial, hoping he'd be impressed. I pointed the lens at Tomoko, focusing carefully until her twin images were crisp and clear in the rangefinder. The weight of the brushed metal in my hands was absolutely beautiful.

My father had owned a camera once—a Rolleiflex with a hinged back, which one of his fattest customers had given him at the *bonenkai* party he held to thank his regulars at the end of every year. I took charge of it straight away, constantly tinkering with the intricate dials and mechanisms, copying out the mysterious foreign letters embossed on the front. Finally, after much hinting, my father brought home some photographic film. For two weeks, I waltzed around the neighbourhood with a cutout masthead of the *Yomiuri* newspaper pinned to my jacket, taking "portraits" of the locals: Mrs. Oka from next door, her face as wrinkly as her pickles; two *maiko* girls who giggled behind their fans as they stopped in for snacks on the way to a party.

When my father got his red call-up papers, toward the end of the war, I was sent back to Tokyo from the countryside. My mother was stunned—after all, he'd been borderline at his age.

One Sunday, my father asked me to dig out the old camera. He wanted to go up to Ueno Park to see the cherry blossom before he left to join his unit. There were hardly any families stretched out on the grass that year and no picnic gramophones played amongst the trees as in years gone by. We laid out our blanket and ate a quiet meal together. Before we left, my father asked me to take a photograph. I lined the whole family up beneath the sprays of white blossom, and waved them into position.

My mother wore a pale blue spring kimono, her hand resting lightly on my father's broad shoulder. Satsuko stood beside them, dressed in green and gold. They gazed out serenely, calm and dignified, as all around them, the blossom floated in the air. After a second, I pressed the shutter decisively. When I tried to wind on the film, the lever resisted. The spool was at an end.

I found myself wandering through the heart of what had once been old Shitamachi. The flimsy paper and matchstick workingmen's houses had all evaporated during the raids, but up the hill, past the crimson walls of the Imperial University, was the more elegant quarter where the artists and merchants once had their mansions. Most of the grand old villas were still standing, though they were damaged and silent now behind their heavy wooden gates. Along a shady gravel road, a tree had splintered in one of the gardens, knocking out a section of stucco wall. Grasping the woolly branches, I scrabbled up and hoisted myself into the gap. I sat there for a second, catching my breath as I peered over the other side.

The wide garden was choked with tangled grasses and gnarled ornamental trees. A large, traditional wooden building stood before a gravel yard beyond which gates stood padlocked shut. It seemed solid and imposing enough, though slate tiles were missing from the slanted roof and the windows were boarded up.

I swung myself over, and dropped down from the wall with

a thud. *It must have been some kind of inn, once,* I thought, though it looked very much abandoned now. The fishpond was empty and silted, and by the front door, the welcoming statue of a *tanuki* had toppled over, one of his arms broken off, though he carried on grinning demonically nonetheless.

The lock on the shutters was flimsy, and quickly sprung open when I hammered it with a rock. Past the vestibule, ancient pillars of twisted wood supported the low ceiling of an entrance hall. Dark patches showed where the rain had seeped in. As I stepped over the threshold, the floorboards creaked eerily. I shivered, praying that there were no dead bodies inside.

The air was musty and slivers of light fell from cracks in the window boards. My eyes gradually adjusted to the gloom. Woodblock prints hung around the walls, and as I stepped closer to examine them, I gulped. They all showed ladies, mostly naked or only half-dressed in kimonos, sprawled on futons or cavorting with fierce-looking men. My cheeks throbbed as I stared at the various postures and poses.

Up a wooden staircase was a hallway, with rooms off to one side, marked with nameplates. "Peony," "Cherry Blossom," then, "Ivy," and "Chrysanthemum." I raised my hand to the door of "Peony" and slid it aside.

A dark shape hit my face and I crashed backward. A heavy fluttering filled the air—a huge black moth flew around me crazily, powder thick on its wings, sparkling like coal dust.

Light fell into the corridor as I tugged the rotten boards away from the windows. Down below was a secret garden, a palanquin in one corner, its fabric rotted away. *It must have been a real high-class place,* I thought—*a retreat for the top brass during the war.*

The tatami was frayed in most of the rooms, and in "Chrysanthemum," there was a charred patch where someone had lit a fire. It had seen better days, that was for sure. But as

I explored further, opening cupboards and trunks, I found rolled futons and sheets, soft pillows and blankets. *We could build a huge fort here*, I thought, almost tempted to rush off and tell the other children right away. But then, as I pictured them, huddled up under the dripping staircase at the station, the shivering men and women moaning and vomiting around them, my heart began to beat faster. An amazing idea had just occurred to me.

Night had fallen by the time I got back to the station, and the children were penned into a corner by a group of soldiers, who were snoring away with their hairy overcoats pulled over their faces. The stink of sweat was overwhelming as I clambered over them and shook the children awake.

"Listen! Get ready to leave. We're breaking camp at dawn."

Koji rubbed his eyes. "What? Where are we going?"

"Are we going home?" Aiko murmured, still half dreaming.

"Can't you tell us in the morning?" Shin groaned.

"Listen," I said, urgently. "You need to listen. We're not staying here anymore. I've found somewhere else. A fortress."

"Wonderful," Shin said. "We're going to live in a castle."

Koji frowned. "Will there be other children there?" he asked, hopefully.

I shook my head. "Not yet. It's just us for now. But listen. It's a secret. Don't whisper a word to anyone. Promise!"

The children looked uncertain, still bleary with sleep. Shin rolled his eyes and turned over with a grunt. But Tomoko slid forward and knelt in front of me, pulling her fingers through her hair.

"Don't worry, Hiroshi-kun. Please rest now. I'll make sure the children are ready first thing in the morning."

My heart shivered as she bowed her head. I lay down, and gradually drifted into a twitchy sleep. But in the middle of the night, I woke suddenly. White lights were bobbing across the sleeping bodies around the station, and for a moment, I was filled with panic.

Ghosts! I thought. *Floating above the corpses of the dead!* But the lights were electric torches. Policemen and doctors in white coats were pulling back people's heads and inspecting their faces in the pale beams. Every so often, they tugged someone to their feet and dragged them away into the darkness. A rod of light needled toward us and I urgently shook the children awake. I hustled them to their feet as the figures came toward us, and we hurried outside into the freezing night, as the frost prickled its way across the iron-hard ground.

The house stood silent and ghostly in the morning mist, at the top of the hill. My heart flooded with relief. I'd been convinced by a strange fear that it might all have been a dream, that it would have disappeared overnight like some enchanted foxes' palace. As I led the children over the gap in the wall and on through the garden, they started to rub their eyes and laugh. They could hardly believe it was true.

As I opened the front door, Shin swore softly under his breath.

"It's not really ours, is it, big brother?" Koji asked in wonder. "Not really?" He pulled off his sandals and danced across the tatami of the reception hall.

"It is now!" I shouted.

We raced inside, letting out loud whoops and war cries as we tumbled crazily across the floor and tripped into a hysterical heap.

We got to work cleaning the place up straight away. The children found cloths and buckets and a water pump in the kitchen and as they scrubbed and polished away, I checked the rat traps I had set the day before, then pulled away the last rotten boards from all the windows. As daylight flooded the room, it became clear exactly how run-down the building was—the wooden beams were splintered and the paper screens all torn. But as the children pushed rags up and down the corridors, splashing each other with suds and singing at the top of their voices, they seemed to be in paradise. Clouds of dust smothered Aiko and Tomoko as they beat the futons upstairs, spluttering with laugher, while Koji and Nobu hopped around shouting, sword-fighting with their broomsticks.

Shin, though, came over to me with a sly look on his face.

"What's so funny?"

He sniggered. "I suppose you know what this place used to be, don't you?"

My cheeks throbbed. I'd taken down all the pictures of the ladies the day before, and hidden them all at the bottom of one of the cupboards upstairs.

"An inn, I should have thought," I said. "Some kind of classy place for the higher-ups."

Shin gave a nasty laugh, then made a circle with his thumb and forefinger. He thrust the index finger of his other hand through it repeatedly.

"My father told me all about it," he leered.

By the end of the afternoon, the rooms were airy and the blankets fresh and clean. Beyond the kitchen, Nobu had found a small bathhouse with a big cedar tub, a smaller, private bathroom set off to one side. Part of the roof was missing in this part of the building, and most of the tiles were cracked. Filled with excitement, though, I heaved on the handle of the pump. There was a great gasp of pipes from deep within the building, but nothing emerged from the faucet except for a long, spindly insect.

"Hiroshi-kun!"

Nobu's shout came from the other room. "Come and look!" In a compartment in the wall, he had discovered a large copper boiler and an oil burner covered with dials. After a few experiments and struck matches, we managed to get it to hold a flame.

There was a rumble, and as I turned a wheel, we heard gushing and the clank of pistons, and wisps of steam rose from the boiler.

At the pump, we tried the handle again. With a tremble and a sputtering noise, water began to gush out, lukewarm at first, but growing gradually hotter.

"We did it!" Nobu yelled.

Triumphantly, we marched back to the main hall. The children were lying exhausted on the tatami.

"Well done, everyone!" I announced. "You've all worked very hard. And now, as a reward, we're all going to have a real bath, in our very own *sento*!"

Banzai!

The children screamed with laughter as we raced to the bathhouse. Tomoko and Aiko took the private room, us boys the bigger one. We started to sing Koji's dirty version of the Air Raid Song—*Cover your ears! Close up your bum!*—as we sat on our stools and scrubbed ourselves, the cedar tub gradually filling up.

The filth on our bodies was just incredible. It must have been over a year since any of us had washed, and the tiles were soon covered in grimy suds. But then it was just bliss, as we sank into the big pool of steaming water, groaning like old folk at a hot springs resort. The girls shrieked with delight in the other room—they must have got into their own bath at just the same moment.

As we lay there soaking, I looked up at the sky through the damaged roof. White clouds were passing overhead, and I pretended to myself that we really were at some lovely *onsen* up in the mountains; that after our bath we'd all dress in elegant clothes and be served dinner on floats suspended over the river . . . Tomoko's soft laugh drifted from over the wall, and I closed my eyes, picturing her bobbing in the water. Her hair wet and stuck to her forehead, her skin taut and white; dark, hard peaks on the bumps of her chest . . .

"Look out!" Shin hollered. "He's lifting the tent up!"

To my horror, I'd gone stiff and my tip was peeping out of the water. I crashed my fists into the bath.

"Damn you!" I shouted, desperately hoping that the girls hadn't heard. I leaped out of the tub and covered my privates, wiping myself off with a hand towel.

Shin was still guffawing and even Nobu had a smirk on his face.

"Thinking about someone we know?" Shin crowed, jerking his thumb at the wall. "Why don't you go round and show her how you feel?"

"Shut up!" I hissed.

Shin started choking with laughter. "You'll need something to make up for that ugly face!"

"Shut up!"

My cheeks were burning as I heaved out the wooden plug of the bath. Koji wailed as the water began to slurp away down the drain. I glowered at Shin, praying that the girls hadn't heard his idiotic talk.

"That's enough," I said. "It's not funny anymore."

We decided to play a game later on. Koji thought it would be fun to pretend that we were all working at a real inn, and we all had to make up ways to entertain our guests. He rolled up a cone of newspaper on his head and sat cross-legged on the floor with a broom in his hands, then started to croon, plucking the strings of an imaginary shamisen. Nobu found an old pair of spectacles and sat on the stool in the office, greeting the "visitors" in a wheedling voice, while Shin tied a blue rag around his head and toasted the rice balls we'd brought with us on a little hibachi from the kitchen.

Giggling came from the landing upstairs. Stepping carefully down the staircase came Aiko, leading Tomoko by the hand. They both wore old embroidered kimonos, rolled up at the hem to stop them from tripping. From somewhere, they had found powder and makeup too and had painted their faces white and lips red.

Tomoko stood in front of me. Her hair was still damp and she smelled wonderful and fresh. My stomach knotted.

"Look," Tomoko said. "We're geishas!"

Shin clapped his hands and started to sing a dirty song, but I shot him a ferocious look and he trailed off.

We sat down around the grill, and Aiko and Tomoko served us water from a teapot in little sake cups. I could hardly speak. Tomoko didn't look like a girl to me anymore. She seemed like a fresh, delicate bud about to burst into helpless bloom. When she leaned over to fill my cup, her kimono showed the curve between her breasts and my hand started to shake so much that I spilled water all over the floor.

Koji grabbed the teapot and swigged at it. A moment later, he started reeling, shouting in a slurred voice that he was drunk. As he tumbled over, the children cackled with laughter, and Tomoko put her arm around Aiko, smiling like a proud mother. For a moment, she caught my gaze and held my eye.

I remembered the feeling of her body next to me as we stood on the coupling of the train back to Tokyo, the warmth of her cheek as we lay down together on the station floor. An acute, guilty pleasure crept over me as she came over and sat down beside me, a faint smile on her face. She took my hand and gently pressed it between her own.

It was a soft, wonderful pressure, warm and enclosing. It only lasted a few seconds, but somehow, it seemed to capture the strange magic of those past months entirely.

I jerked my hand away, and leaped up with a short bark of laughter.

"Everybody up!" I shouted. "Time for bed!"

Tomoko's face fell as I hopped around, kicking at the children's legs. "Come on! We're not here on holiday, you know."

The children grumbled as they stood up and trudged sulkily upstairs. We'd already laid out the blankets in the rooms: "Cherry Blossom" for the boys, "Ivy" for her and Aiko.

Tomoko and I stood outside in the corridor for a moment. My heart was still jittering.

"Well. Goodnight," I said.

She bowed shyly.

"Goodnight, Hiroshi-kun."

We went to curl up in our new blankets, and I blew out our lantern. The mattress was deliciously soft after all the months on the cold, hard stone floor of the station, but as I lay there in the darkness, I barely noticed its comfort. From the other side of the wall, Aiko was whispering something, but Tomoko gently hushed her, and soon their lamp was extinguished.

I closed my eyes. Tomoko's image floated vividly in my mind as I drifted off to sleep. Her clumsily painted lips. The soft swell of her kimono. The pale skin of her throat.

12
ENGLISH-SPEAKING PEOPLE
(Satsuko Takara)

The sign I had tacked up for Hiroshi on the wall of Tokyo Station was tattered now, the ink smeared from the rain. I stood shivering in my thin coat, as a group of ex-soldiers huddled around a refuse fire nearby playing flower cards. An old woman squatted beneath a sign of her own, fumbling with her prayer beads. She gave me a sympathetic smile.

"Don't give up hope!" she mouthed.

Not many people came to look for their lost relatives at the station anymore. In fact, we were the only two here today.

I smiled back, faintly. What would her expression be like, I wondered, if instead of my grey dress and mackintosh, I'd been wearing my nighttime clothes, my face plastered white and lips red? What would Hiroshi himself think, even if he did miraculously appear? To discover that his big sister was nothing now but a shameless American butterfly?

It had been weeks since my last trip here, and I felt dreadfully guilty for neglecting my duty to him. They were bringing up children's bodies from the tunnels every morning now, desperately thin and blistered with smallpox. That afternoon, I'd taken his photograph around the main railway stations, holding it up in the faces of the filthy men and women. Crowds of them stretched out on mats across the ticket halls. They squinted for a moment, sucking their rotten gums, and shook their heads. It all felt completely hopeless. I should simply accept the fact that he was gone.

I walked inside to take the Yamanote Line back to Shinagawa. A swarm of filthy brats were clamouring around the passengers disembarking onto one of the long-distance platforms. They slipped their little hands into the travellers' pockets as they took down their suitcases, grubbing about on the floor like insects for the cigarette butts that they dropped.

My heart froze. There, right in the middle, I could see Hiroshi. My heels skidded on the marble floor as I ran toward him.

"Hiroshi!" I screamed. "Hiroshi-kun!"

Barging through the emerging passengers, I thrust my way onto the platform. As I reached him, he was scrabbling around someone's shoes. I seized his arm and pulled him up, rubbing the dirt from this face with my handkerchief.

"Hiroshi!"

The boy shook me off, swearing horribly in a strange dialect. My heart sank in confusion—I couldn't understand my mistake. It wasn't Hiroshi at all.

"I'm sorry—"

The boy squinted at me as I caught my breath.

"Miss?" he spat, turning. "You can wipe this if you want."

He was holding his penis in his filthy hand, a gleeful expression on his face. I gasped and spun on my heel, hurrying away as fast as I could.

When I reached our tenement alley, I paused at the door of our tiny wooden building. There was a radio playing inside—a sentimental children's song that I hadn't heard for years. In fact, the last time I could remember hearing it had been at the old merry-go-round in Hanayashiki Park, with Hiroshi and my mother, one Sunday when I'd gone to visit on my monthly day off from the factory.

Come, come, come and see
Furry friends beneath the tree

In the autumn moonlight
At Shojo-ji Temple!

The song brought back all sorts of memories. I stood there in the alley for a moment, lost in thought. Finally, I slid the door open. Michiko was sitting by the low table with her ear close to the speaker of an ornate radio set. She had a look of intense concentration on her face.

"Michiko!" I hissed, but she waved an urgent hand to the floor beside her and gestured at me to be quiet. The song carried on. But though the tune was familiar, I realized that the words were quite different to those I remembered. In fact, they were in English:

Come, come, everybody
"How do you do?" and "How are you?"
Won't you have some candy?
One, and two, and three four five . . .

Michiko was trying to mouth along to the words.

Let's all sing a happy song
Tra-la, la la la!

She looked up at me in excitement.

"I'm learning English!" she whispered. A man's voice began to speak from the radio and she turned back with what she clearly thought was a studious expression, which mainly involved frowning and nodding at everything the man said.

Another one of Michiko's crazes! I thought, as I sat down beside her. But, as I listened, the programme really did seem quite fun. The presenter's name was "Uncle," and it was the same man who had translated the Emperor's speech into common language back in the summer. Now, it seemed, he was going to teach the Japanese people how to speak English.

Uncle was very kind. He explained that the lessons wouldn't be like school. In fact, they would be more like us playing a game together through the radio. This sounded very pleasant, and so we sat there, fascinated, and after a while, even I tried to repeat some of the English words back. I found myself smiling and nodding as the theme song came on at the end. It was funny, I thought—the new words were already standing in for the old ones in my memory.

"Satsuko!" Michiko exclaimed, after the programme had ended. "We can listen to this and become proper English speakers. Just imagine."

We already knew some English, of course, from our dealings with the Americans, but I didn't think that any of it would have been especially suitable for polite company.

"'How are you? How do you do?'" Michiko said, imitating Uncle's manly voice. Suddenly, in a fit of laughter, she leaped up, took my hands in hers, and spun me around the room.

"'How are you? How do you do?'" she sang.

Finally she let go of my hands and sighed. "Just think, Satsuko," she mused, as she poured water into the teakettle. "Now we really will be 'New Women of Japan.'"

I suddenly remembered what I had wanted to ask her. "The radio, Michiko. Where did you get it from? Surely you didn't buy it yourself?"

"Ah! The radio," she said. "It is handsome, isn't it?"

"Yes," I said. "It certainly is. I wonder where it could have possibly come from?"

"It was a present," she replied. "Isn't it splendid?"

"Another present, Michiko? Anyone would think you had a rich old man off somewhere!"

But she just smiled mysteriously, as if she hadn't heard, and then poured out the tea, still humming away to herself: "How are you? How do you do?"

The afternoon was gloomy as I walked through the ruins of Asakusa. I had promised myself that I would visit the site of our old home and light some incense for my parents; and for Hiroshi, now that it seemed likely that he was gone.

Empty brick shells were all that were left of the trinket stalls along the Nakamise Arcade and a cat scuttled along the low, broken walls to escape the first streaks of rain. At the end of the arcade, the Senso Temple had more or less vanished. All that was left now was a big gravel precinct set with the charred stumps of the ginkgo trees, and craters full of muddy water, crinkling in the drizzle. Sadly, I turned and walked toward Umamichi Street.

How dismal it all was now! I thought. Even when I'd been a girl, there'd been *kaminari-okoshi* sweets and bear paw charms. Fortune-tellers and jazz dancers and troupes of actors. Overhanging stalls painted with bright scenes from the kabuki which sold wood prints and postcards and windup toys. Pots billowing with fragrant steam and mouthwatering smells from the *yakitori* sellers as they brushed their smoking skewers with delicious sauces, the serving girls running between the tables as the oil lanterns bathed the street with a soft, rosy glow.

The war had sucked all of the colour away. All that was left now were hovels of rotten planks and sagging tarpaulin, the streets all churned to muck.

I finally found the square cistern in the middle of our alley. But I couldn't make out the site of our home anymore. Eventually, I found a burned patch a little way on, which I thought must be about right. I wedged my sticks of incense into the black mud. It took me a whole box of matches to get them lit. Water dripped down my neck as I stood up to say a prayer.

The sky seemed to turn several shades darker. All of a sudden, rain hurtled against my umbrella, and I had the intense feeling that I wasn't welcome there. It was if my mother and father were standing behind me, ashamed and angry, hissing at me to go away. The impression grew so vivid that I became quite frightened. I hitched up my skirt and hurried away down the alley, stopping only to glance back at the incense sticks, still just about smoldering in the rain.

The tram was packed on the way back to Shinagawa, the windows misted with grimy condensation. An ex-soldier was squashed up against me, a short man of about forty. The brim of his army cap poked into my nose and I could tell by the dirt on his neck and the sour smell that he hadn't washed for quite some time. I closed my eyes, hoping that Michiko would be home by the time I got back.

A cold hand grasped me between the legs and I froze. The man in the cap was staring at my shoulder, his lips writhing beneath his dirty moustache. His hand clasped me firmly, squeezing, and I shut my eyes, burning with shame. Tears welled up in my throat as his fingers gripped harder.

I suddenly opened my eyes again. *What right did he have to do this?* I thought. *Did he think he could touch me without paying? Who did he think he was?*

I jerked my shoulder violently into his face.

"Pervert!" I shrieked. "You filthy pervert! Think you can just grab anyone you want?"

The passengers jostled around us, happy for the diversion on such a rotten day.

"Who do you think you are?" I said. "Are you such a hero? You couldn't even win the war. You should be ashamed of yourself!"

The man stared at the floor. His face was twitching and, at that moment, I didn't know whether I felt hatred or pity for him. The tram shuddered to a halt, and I elbowed my way out and jumped down into the wet street. As the tram clanked off, the passengers stared back at me through little rubbed windows in the condensation.

I had left my umbrella on the tram in all the confusion, with the result that I was quite soaked by the time I got home. When I went inside, the house was cold and empty. Michiko was nowhere to be seen.

I let out a sob. I took the bottle of whisky from the cupboard and poured myself a cup. The fiery liquor soothed my heart, and I sat on the floor, stock-still, listening to the rain as it thrashed against the roof.

Michiko was probably off at some expensive restaurant or inn with her rich new lover, I thought, whoever he was. I started to feel quite sorry for myself and poured myself another large cup of whisky. Then, though I tried to resist, my thoughts drifted to Osamu. I remembered the time he'd taken me to a comic show at the Café D'Asakusa, how the students had howled with laughter and he'd held my arm encouragingly as I tried to smile at the jokes. I pictured the look of disbelief on his face the day he had received his call-up papers. He'd trembled and stammered—his mother could have applied for exemption for him, he said, he was an only son! I thought of his body, thin and muscular, in the back room of the Victory Hotel, after he'd come to my house on the night of his leaving ceremony. I wished now that I had let him do what he had wanted to much earlier. I'd been with so many others since then, after all! If I had given in sooner, then I'd have those times to remember now as well, not just that solitary night, when he'd shuddered with joy once before falling asleep next to me. The next day, we were waving them all off at the station, the soldiers wearing their thousand-stitch belts wrapped tight around their bellies. His horrid mother had stared at me as the women from the Defence Association cheered and the train pulled away. *Congratulations on being called to the Front!*

I wondered if memories were like precious porcelain that should only be brought out on special occasions, whether they were like fruits that lost their lustre if they spent too long in the sun. If that was the case, I told myself, I would have to be careful how often I thought of Osamu now. Or of my parents, or Hiroshi, for that matter. I didn't want my memories of them to shrivel away like withered flowers. They were the only thing I had left of them now, after all. Except the charred scrap of my mother's kimono. And the teakettle, of course . . .

The door slid open and Michiko came crashing in. She tumbled amongst the pots and pans, making a terrible racket. Then she started to sing so loudly that I was terrified she would wake the neighbours.

"Michiko," I hissed, "be quiet!"

She stumbled toward me.

"Satsuko," she wailed. "Satsuko, help me. I'm so drunk!"

She slumped down onto the floor and clasped me around the neck, giggling.

"He's in love with me!" she shouted. "He wants me to be his only one!"

I clamped my hand over her mouth. I was sure I didn't want to hear her secrets, least of all in the middle of the night. Viciously, she bit my finger and burst into laughter. Then she slid over, waving her head from side to side.

Suddenly, she sat bolt upright and made an odd sound. She rushed over to the door and heaved it open. The she fell onto her hands and knees, and was retchingly sick into the alley outside.

The next morning, when I awoke, Michiko was already up. She was wearing a pale green dress as she hovered over the stove. A delicious smell was rising from a pot.

When she saw me, she knelt down in front of our futon, pouting unhappily.

"Please forgive me, Satsuko, for my juvenile behaviour last night. It must have been very distressing for you."

I admitted that she had seemed rather drunk, but said that she should think no more about it. She smiled, and bowed again.

"Thank you, Satsuko," she said. "Now. Please come and eat your breakfast."

She took the lid from the pot on the stove with a flourish, and I cried out. A silver fish, a herring, I thought, was bubbling away in a sauce of miso and sake. The aroma was just wonderful. I glanced toward the door to check it was closed—the neighbours would have been madly jealous if they could have smelled the food.

"Wherever did it come from, Michiko?"

She raised her eyebrows and put her hands in the air, performing a little swaying dance. Then she drew an envelope from inside her blouse and handed it to me.

"Look."

I gasped. The envelope was full of money, an astonishing amount, more than we could have possibly earned even if we'd worked at the Oasis for months.

"Whatever are you going to do with it?" I asked. "Save it up?"

She gave a short laugh. "No, Satsuko. First we are going to have our breakfast. Then I'm going to get some sleep. And then, you and I are going shopping."

The Matsuzakaya department store might have been burned out, but the Mitsukoshi had reopened and I felt a glamorous thrill as we stepped through its wide doors. The shop had always been famous for its opulence and luxury, and even its wrapping paper had seemed beyond the reach of a family like mine. But there wasn't much opulence or luxury left now, I thought, as we wandered amongst the empty shelves and rails. An icy draft was blowing through the place and rubble crunched underfoot, beneath the torn carpet. The staff stood shivering in their uniforms—they didn't look quite so haughty anymore.

They scuttled after Michiko as if she were a noblewoman visiting from her country estates, as she picked out a dress here and a shawl there, telling the attendant to wrap them and have them delivered to our house. But when she gave them our address at the counter, they looked at us suspiciously. After all, Shinagawa wasn't the kind of place that anyone would have associated with nobility. From then on, I had the distinct feeling they were giving us looks and muttering behind our backs. It was as if they knew there was only one way girls like us could afford to shop at the Mitsukoshi.

"Please can we go now, Michiko?" I whispered uncomfortably. Michiko glanced at the assembled staff. A mischievous gleam came into her eyes.

"Yes, Satsuko," she said in a loud voice. "Perhaps you're right. Let's leave all this rubbish behind and go down to the Shimbashi blue-sky market instead. After all, there's so little to buy here!"

And she flounced through the door as they bowed down low, their faces frozen. As soon as we got outside, she burst into laughter.

"Those stuck-up prigs!" she cried. "No one looks down on me anymore, Satsuko!"

In fact, there wasn't a great deal to buy at the Shimbashi blue-sky market that day either. Michiko finally had to be content with some sheer silk stockings and a floral scarf that the old woman claimed was from Paris. But then, just as we were leaving, we passed another stall, piled high with old, elegant kimonos.

I froze. Right on the top was something I recognized intimately. A beautiful green kimono, embroidered with golden peonies—the very kimono that my mother had bought me on my sixteenth birthday, and which I'd been forced to sell months before to buy rice.

I leaned over to touch the hem with my fingertips, remembering at once how fine the stitching was, how delicate the embroidery. All sorts of memories and feelings passed through me then. Michiko must have noticed my expression, because the next thing I knew she was airily asking the stallholder how much it cost.

"Don't be silly, Michiko!" I said, but she shushed me and asked the stallholder again. As I suspected, the price was many, many times more than I had been paid. But without even bargaining, Michiko simply snapped out four hundred-yen notes from her purse and handed them over.

"Michiko," I begged. "Please! Don't be ridiculous!"

But the woman was already wrapping the kimono in colourful crêpe paper and tying it with a ribbon. Michiko wordlessly took it from her and handed it to me.

Then I started to cry, for the first time in many months. As I stood there, shaking with sobs, I pictured my mother, helping me dress in the kimono for the first time, with such a look of pride in her eyes. I remembered how Osamu had noticed me wearing it at the Spring Festival, how he had strolled over to compliment me, blinking with embarrassment. Then I saw the face of his horrible mother, the day I'd gone to her villa, trembling with nerves, to ask if there'd been any news of him from the South Seas. Her mouth had puckered, as if she'd sucked a sour apricot.

"Dead," she hissed. "Shot in the stomach. Now get away from here, you slut."

I was sobbing so much now that the woman who owned the stall sidled round and took my arm, patting it affectionately until I had recovered.

Later on that evening, after dinner, Michiko brushed my hair and made me try on the kimono again. It was as beautiful as I remembered, though quite loose around my shoulders now. I hadn't noticed quite how thin I'd become. Michiko insisted on painting my face and then held up a mirror so that I could see my reflection. Then she took out a small vial and began to scrape a bright red paste onto my fingernails. To my horror, they began to turn crimson.

"What on earth are you doing, Michiko?" I said.

"Don't be so old-fashioned, Satsuko!" she said. "It's just nail rouge. One of the Americans gave it to me. It's very modern."

Suspiciously, I let her paint them all. Afterward, as I admired the colour, she poured us both some whisky and we giggled together for some time before going to bed.

Michiko left me just a few weeks after that. In my heart, I'd always known she would. Every night now, she joined the band up on the stage, a red plastic rose in her hair. She smiled into the piano player's eyes, and sang into the silver microphone in her birdlike voice, occasionally pausing to throw out expressions she'd learned from Uncle English to the audience. A white-haired American officer reserved the seats directly beneath the stage every evening, his legs spread wide, gazing up at her as if spellbound, clapping and bellowing with laughter.

One morning, she returned home and told me that the man—some general, or admiral—wanted to set her up in an apartment of her own in Akasaka, where he could visit her whenever he chose.

"Michiko," I murmured. "Perhaps I could come and visit you sometimes? I could even come and stay at first, just to help you get settled in—"

"No, Satsuko," she said quickly, shaking her head. "You can't, he's very jealous, you see. He'll expect me to be there for him at all hours."

A hard lump grew in my throat. "Well then," I said. "It doesn't matter."

Michiko clung onto my arm, and rubbed her lovely face

against my shoulder like a cat. "What do you think you will do now, Satsuko?" she asked in a small voice.

"Well," I said with a forced smile. "I imagine I will just carry on working at the Oasis. With all the other, less beautiful, girls."

Michiko's face crumpled and she burst into tears. She hugged me, burying her face in my hair.

"But you *are* beautiful, Satsuko," she cried. "You are!"

But whether I was or not, at the end of that week, a swish black sedan rolled up at the end of the street, and a driver with white gloves came in to help Michiko move her things. He loaded up her trunks of dresses and gowns, her boxes of creams and vials, and, as she strapped on her new high-heeled shoes, she took one last look at our leaky room. We bowed to each other and she tottered outside to the car. With a wave, she clambered into the backseat. The chauffeur closed the door and, with a whining engine, he reversed back down the alley.

13
No.1 Shimbun Alley
(*Hal Lynch*)

A grizzled mongrel nosed about in the dark fluid welling from a broken standpipe on a street of ruined buildings near Yurakucho Station. On the front of the dilapidated hotel was a hand-painted sign: *Tokyo Foreign Correspondents' Club.* A staff car ground to a halt in the dirt road outside and I followed two Allied colonels up the worn steps, through a set of glass doors to a lobby, where correspondents stood in telephone booths, dictating stories on the overseas lines. After a creaking ascent in the iron elevator, the old operator wrenched open the guardrail to reveal a hallway redolent with the smoke of pipes and cigarettes and cigars. Two Japanese busboys bowed, and swung open a further set of doors. A polyglot clamour emerged from within.

The ballroom was crowded. A gleaming baby grand stood in the centre, a diplomat with a white bouffant and dinner dress sat upon its stool, holding uproarious court to an obsequious coterie. A clump of reporters harangued a U.S. Army major, who spread out his hands in apparent defence as their pencils jabbed the air around him. A pair of British naval captains stood with white caps under their arms, woollen socks pulled high, as they were cheerfully molested by two old ladies in grey chiffon and horn-rimmed glasses. To the side of the room, crumpled correspondents interviewed nervous-looking Japanese; Chinese generals slumped on leather sofas and Allied officers sat drinking with women too pretty to be their wives. Between the encampments floated Japanese boys in red and gold uniform, carrying trays laden with square bottles of whisky, delivering glasses, squirting soda siphons, slipping their tips into their side pockets and tapping them for good luck.

"Glad you could make it," growled Mark Ward, as he materialized by my side. He gave a lopsided grin when he noticed my expression.

"Where are we, Ward? Casablanca?"

An exquisite Japanese girl came down the steps, black hair piled high to show a snow white neck, a string of silvery pearls tracing the prow of her ruffled silk dress. I'd seen her before, I thought, in surprise—the pinup from the Oasis club, who'd sat on McHardy's lap that night. She was clearly moving up in the world. A grizzled, white-haired Third Fleet admiral barged forward to greet her, and she let out an almost genuine cry of delight as she took hold of his outstretched hands.

Ward led me into the crowd, signalling to a boy for drinks. "This is the nerve centre, Lynch—the reliquary!"

The boy handed me a glass of raw Japanese whisky and I took a large gulp.

"Who runs the show here?"

"We do."

"How's that?"

"Wherever newsmen gather in the world, Lynch, needs must that they have a bar. Without such a place, stories go untold, confidences unshared. Last September, MacArthur decided that Japan didn't need any special correspondents, with their irritating habit of independent thought and inquiry. He stopped giving them billets. So we took over this place instead."

A grunt came from behind us and a heavy hand fell on Ward's shoulder. Two bulky, shaven-headed men glared at us. One pushed Ward contemptuously on the arm, as the other jerked a warty thumb toward his mouth and emitted a phrase in some Slavic language. Ward grinned.

"Lynch, meet Gorbatov," he said. "Boris One. The other fellow's Agapov. Boris Two. Don't ever get them confused or they'll break your arm."

"Good evening, comrades."

Boris One jerked his bare head at Ward. "We drink soon," he ordered, and the pair headed off toward the bar. Ward smiled as he watched them go.

"Friends of yours?"

"If you ever want insight into the dark recesses of the Soviet mind, Lynch, they're the men you should talk to. Oh, look who it is . . ."

As we worked our way toward the back of the ballroom, Ward recounted his mental encyclopaedia of all those present. At the piano, the diplomat prodded the ivories to delighted applause, and the first notes of a Chopin sonata floated through the ballroom.

"Anyhow," Ward said. "We're all in the library. Something that ought to interest you."

"Oh?"

We proceeded down a corridor to an underlit, smoke-filled room. A couple of cracked leather armchairs had been set up and dozens of foreign and Japanese newspapers were draped over wooden rails. A crowd of men, waistcoats lined with pencils, shoes scuffed, were gathered around a wide table. A man with a thick brown quiff sat behind it, gesturing at a series of photographs laid out under a green-shaded lamp.

"A friend from Chicago," Ward murmured. "George Weller. Just got back from an unauthorized trip."

As we slid into the huddle, a couple of men nodded at Ward in greeting.

"The Mitsubishi shelters were useless, of course," Weller was saying. "They were at the epicentre of the blast. The factory makes a strange sight now, I must say—like a metal rib cage, only all the bones are bent outward."

I stiffened. I knew with instant conviction what he was talking about. We'd flown over the big Mitsubishi works at Nagasaki a month before the city was A-bombed. The firm manufactured torpedoes and ammunition for the Japanese navy and I'd been surprised to see the place still standing. A graceful city by the seaside, just like Hiroshima, sprinkled with the spires of Christian churches.

"Most of those that died did so straight away, or within a few hours of the blast," Weller continued. "But then something else happened. Something strange."

Weller held up a photograph of a ruddy-faced Japanese girl, smiling into the camera with a knapsack on her back. It triggered a memory somewhere in my brain.

"This young girl escaped the blast itself with no more than a burn on her leg. She left the city that day to stay with relatives. She came back two weeks later. Days after she returned, she looked like this."

Another photograph. The girl was sitting up in a hospital bed now. She had the look of a scarecrow—bald patches on her head, prickles covering her skin as if she had been dragged through a thornbush.

The memory came to me. The trembling girl and her scarred boyfriend at the back of Ueno Station.

"This is her two weeks later."

The girl once more. Withered almost to a skeleton now. Completely bald, her body covered in thick welts.

Weller paused, gauging the reaction of the men.

"But here's the thing, gentlemen. This girl didn't start to get sick until she came back to Nagasaki. And that was three weeks *after* the blast."

I struggled to recall the boy's garbled tale as Weller handed around the photographs. The men scrutinized them, muttering soft prayers and obscenities before handing them on. I studied the print of the ruddy-faced girl. She looked out with empty eyes from a frayed hospital mat, dark blood clotted beneath her nose.

The bomb? The bomb made her sick? The boy's fervent nod.

Perspiration prickled on my forehead as Ward took the photograph from my hand.

"What is this, George?" he asked.

Weller shook his head, lit a cigarette.

"The doctors won't make a diagnosis. Because they don't know how to diagnose it. It's sinister."

"Does it have a name?"

"No. For now, it's just Disease X."

"What's the official take?" Ward asked.

"Headquarters don't buy it. Or they don't want to buy it. They say it's a scam. That the Japs are looking for sympathy. Easier terms."

Weller unfurled a newspaper. To my dismay, I saw it was a copy of *Stars and Stripes*—the same copy, in fact, that had our piece on Himeji Castle printed toward the back, just before the sporting green.

"This is from one Colonel Warren, of the University of Rochester medical school."

"That august institution," Ward murmured, to snorts of amusement.

"He states, quote: 'There absolutely is not, and never was'—note that," said Weller, his finger raised, "'any dangerous amount of radiation in that area.'"

He paused. He had the men's entire attention now.

"'The radioactivity of a luminous dial wristwatch is one thousand times greater than that found at Nagasaki.'"

He set the newspaper down on the table. "Do any of you gentlemen wear a luminous dial wristwatch?"

A few raised forearms. "Ever find your intestines choked with blood? Blood spots in your bone marrow?"

Furrows spread across the assembled brows. My mouth was dry as I raised my hand.

"Mr. Weller?"

He glanced up. I swallowed as the faces of the other men swivelled towards me.

"Disease X. Has it been reported in Hiroshima also?"

Weller shrugged.

"God alone knows. Both cities are now out of bounds. Under penalty of court-martial."

I pictured the MPs loping along the platform, scrutinizing the Allied carriage for passengers.

Ward stepped forward. "When's this going out, George?"

Weller stubbed out his cigarette with sudden bitterness. He slumped back in his chair.

"It's not."

Incredulous noises came from the assembled men.

"How so?"

"I was fool enough to file it in Tokyo. Headquarters have killed it. Every last word. Diller told me I was lucky to still be in the country. I doubt I will be much longer."

Noises of anger and disenchantment came from all sides of the room. Ward slid behind Weller's chair and raised big, calming hands.

"Okay, boys, here's what we do. We form a delegation, we go to Diller. We impress upon him that this is unacceptable censorship . . . "

I barely heard him. The photograph of the girl was propped up against the lamp, her eyes boring into my own. *Sick. Dead. So—desu.*

The newspaper had fallen open at our story and the photograph I'd taken outside Himeji Castle: Eugene holding up a samurai sword, baring buckteeth with a ferocious expression.

I pushed urgently out of the library. The noise and chatter of the ballroom washed over me again, along with the frenzied crescendo of the Chopin sonata. I signalled urgently to a boy for a drink and when it came, I threw it back, feeling the alcohol liquefy the pressure in my temple. Men began to stream out of the library as the meeting wrapped up. They lit cigars and made a beeline for the bar. Ward approached me, thick eyebrows raised.

"Everything okay, Lynch?"

"Little claustrophobic in there."

He nodded. "Pretty strong salts, huh?"

"Yes. Pretty strong."

"Another drink?"

"Some other time."

"Okay, Lynch. Make sure you come again."

A thick cloud of blue smoke curled over the ballroom as I strode through the animated crowd and took the elevator back down to the lobby. Outside, the night was cold, and I stumbled through refuse and mud. Just before the junction, I glanced up at a building. The front was still there, but the back was missing, like the façade of scenery in a cheap Western. You could see right through the walls, and where the roof should have been there were stars.

I bought a pint of whisky from a hood at the Ginza crossing, and swigged it as I strode home. Back at the Continental, I lay down on my bed and swilled some more. Then I switched off the light, still fully clothed, and drank in the darkness until the face of the skeletal young girl had dissolved from my mind.

Down in the dusty basement of the press club, I scoured archive boxes of newspapers for any article concerning the A-bombings of Hiroshima and Nagasaki. There was precious little to read. Access to both areas was interdicted now, and there were no official reports on the state of things in either city. The London *Express* had carried a report by a correspondent named Burchett who had raced down to Hiroshima in advance of our lines—"The Atomic Plague!" screamed the ghoulish headline—but the article itself had been suppressed and the copy in the archive was scored with black ink that stained my fingers. There was the set of photographs in *LIFE*, the surrender issue, which showed the familiar ruined plain of Hiroshima. It made a brief, tantalizing reference to reports from local doctors of bleeding gums amongst the surviving population. But the article abruptly cut to a consideration of the future of war and the place of the atom bomb within it, and no more reference was made to its victims.

The only other piece was in the *New York Times*, by a man named Laurence. He'd flown as official observer upon the *Bockscar* to Nagasaki. His writing was lyrical, almost poetic, as he described the swollen tub being loaded into the bomb bay on Tinian.

"A thing of beauty to behold, this gadget," he wrote, as if extolling the virtues of a new refrigerator or vacuum cleaner. The pilot had taken the bomb up to 17,000 feet, and from there, in the air-conditioned cabin of a reconfigured Superfort, Laurence had pondered the fates of those on the ground below.

"Does one feel any pity or compassion for the poor devils about to die? No. Not when one thinks of Pearl Harbor and of the death march on Bataan."

I'd heard the line so many times now, it seemed worn smooth by repetition.

His tone became rapturous, almost sexual, as he described the blast and the mushroom cloud exploding into the sky:

"The smoke billows upward, seething and boiling in a white fury of creamy foam, sizzling upward, descending earthward . . . "

Floating over that desolate plain. The city swept away. *Poor devils.*

The last paragraph of the article struck me as odd. As if in preemptive defence, Laurence emphasized that there was no "mysterious sickness" caused by radiation in either of the two A-bombed cities. Any such reports were "Jap propaganda," wily attempts to wring concessions from the Allied powers, a cynical ploy to win sympathy from the American people, with their big hearts and deep pockets.

I lay the paper down, and closed my eyes.

Hibiya Park was located auspiciously. To the north lay the Imperial Palace, aloof and remote behind its moat and thick stone walls. At its eastern corner stood the granite fortress of the Dai-ichi Insurance Building, now General Headquarters of the Supreme Command of Allied Powers—SCAP—as contained in the body of General MacArthur, Japan's most recent and now omnipotent emperor. The country's feudal past and democratic future faced off, so to speak, across its patchy fields, and, suitably enough, the park had become Tokyo's premier site for demonstration, a rallying point for the new political parties that had burgeoned in the wake of the war's end.

A small crowd was gathered when I arrived. Up on the bandstand, a stout man in a green jersey was striding about like a boxer, bawling through a whistling microphone. Jeeps lined the flowerbeds, bored military policemen observing the events. The crowd seemed very much of a type—early middle age, circular spectacles, drawn faces. Despite the bitter cold, they were rapt, cheering loudly as the speaker's hoarse voice rolled across the park. Red flags and banners were unfurled and then came the first, eerie, ululating note of a chant. It was haunting and somehow melancholic and it made the hairs on the back of my neck stand on end. The men began to sing in chorus, their voices welling up above the mud of the park, floating high into the crystalline fall air.

A familiar bulky figure clapped gloved hands and cheered

along. I strode over and touched the arm of Mark Ward's woollen overcoat.

He turned to me, eyes bright behind thick spectacles. "Intoxicating, isn't it?"

A phalanx of men and women started to jog back and forth, waving their banners with balletic fluidity. They danced forward, halted on a dime, then went back the other way. I had a sudden impression of migrating geese, of brittle red maple leaves drifting down along the Hudson. I stood there for a moment, letting the feeling wash over me.

Ward seemed cheerfully nonplussed by the whole affair. He scribbled briefly into his leather notebook, then slammed it shut.

"Well, I guess that's enough for one day. How about we get ourselves a drink?"

"That would be grand."

The night's first hookers stood shivering against the trees at the edge of the park, scuttling out in pursuit of the GIs who sauntered along in pairs. All were very young—their breasts hardly made a bump in their sweaters—and they wore motley woollen skirts and dowdy jackets. Not many were pretty, but there was a certain sharp eroticism in the air that sprang from their brazen approach. After brief negotiation, they pulled their man off into the melding shadows, and, as the sun went down, the edges of the park came furtively alive with the faint, mingled caterwaul of swift, preprandial copulation.

A girl in a grubby yellow dress skipped over and slid her arm through Ward's, as if we were all out for a pleasant Sunday afternoon promenade.

"Okay, Joe—very cheap!" she promised, swinging his arm from side to side.

"No, sweetheart," Ward said. "I'm not your john. Get on home."

She frowned. "Very cheap—"

He raised a thick finger in warning, and she dropped his

arm, glaring at him. She peeled off along the path with a muttered curse, and Ward watched her go.

"And so the country is truly conquered," he said, gloomily.

"At least we pay for it. Unlike our Russian buddies."

He glanced at me sharply. "What good capitalists we are."

The windows of the Dai-ichi building were still lit, the
teams of bright young men burning the midnight oil as they
drew up their plans for Japan's future. Down in the plush bar
of the Imperial Hotel, the strictly temporal reigned. An old
Japanese band played soft Ellington covers, while colonels in
well-cut uniforms lounged in armchairs, enjoying the first
drinks of the weekend. The waiter brought us whisky and I
sipped at mine gratefully.

"So, Lynch," Ward said, settling back. "How goes life at the
Stars and Stripes?"

I shrugged.

"That well, huh?"

"Should I be diplomatic, Ward?"

"No need."

"How should I put it? It's not quite what I visualized when
I decided to become a reporter."

"What did you visualize?"

I considered the question. The eyes of the correspondents
at the press club had been shrewd as George Weller told his
uncanny story. As he'd slumped in his chair afterward, he'd
seemed both noble and pathetic.

"Something more than 'The Touristic GI.'"

Ward nodded as he slid a large cigar from his breast pocket.
He puffed away, squinting at me through the smoke.

"Something eating you, Hal?"

As on the train, I felt encouraged to confide in him. I told
him of my hunt through the archives; of the MPs searching the
train at Himeji Station; of the trembling girl at Ueno who'd
fled from the ruins of Hiroshima.

He stared at me for a long moment, then studied the glowing embers of his cigar.

"I'm afraid I'm not a psychologist, Hal."

I hesitated. "I never implied that you were, Mark."

He pointed his cigar at me. "But you must understand that what you witnessed from up there was the greatest feat of destruction in all human history."

"What's your point, Ward?"

He jabbed the air with the cigar for emphasis.

"The fall of Troy. The sack of Rome. The Mongol Horde. Nothing compared to what happened here. The destruction we achieved in the space of, what, six months? It's no wonder you're a little . . . stunned."

I was grateful for his tact. "Shell-shocked" was no longer the current expression in any case.

"What's your take on Disease X, Ward?"

He raised his heavy eyebrows. "You heard Weller. He's a strong reporter."

"You think they're still dying?"

Ward shrugged. "Who knows? You can see why SCAP would want to keep it quiet. It's embarrassing, to say the least. Sinister at worst. Especially if it turns out we knew it would happen all along."

"There was an article in the *New York Times*. A man named Laurence—"

"William Laurence?"

"That's him."

Ward shook his big head. "Man's a stooge."

"He is?"

"Sure." Ward screwed the remains of his cigar into the ashtray. "He's on the army payroll. He's their cheerleader for the bomb."

"Are you serious?"

"Yes I am." He nodded, then swallowed the remains of his

drink with a grimace. "Are you interested in chasing this, Lynch?"

In my mind's eye, I saw the sparkling inland sea, temple roofs, fishing boats unloading their catch at the silver harbour.

"Maybe so."

"Might help you sleep at night."

I laughed. "I doubt it."

The place had filled up now. Tables of military men brayed and drank, and I gestured to a passing waiter for the cheque.

"Did you ever meet Wilf Burchett?" Ward asked, as we stood for our overcoats. "The reporter who went down to Hiroshima after we landed?"

I remembered the blocked-out article in the London *Express*. "He's still here?"

"Not for long. MacArthur's throwing him out. But I'll introduce you if you like."

A blast of cold air met us as we approached the revolving door. It spun about, expelling a group of staff muffled against the cold. A tall Japanese man in a camel coat glanced at us through round spectacles, then touched the arm of a hawklike general. He wore an immaculately cut uniform, his hair parted in dark waves, a monocle screwed into his eye socket. The Japanese muttered something into his ear, and the general glared at Ward for a moment. Ward stared back, rocking on his heels. The general thrust out his overcoat to a boy and marched into the bar, his subalterns skittering behind him.

Ward's nostrils were flared.

"Buddy of yours?" I asked as he shoved his way through the door. The cold air outside stung my cheeks.

"Major General Charles Willoughby," he said, as he gestured to the doorman for a cab. "G2. Chief of Intelligence. Shady character."

The doorman blew a whistle, and a taxi veered toward us in the road.

"Born Karl Weidenbach in Heidelberg, Germany. 'My own dear fascist,' as MacArthur calls him."

The doorman opened the cab and I buttoned up my collar in preparation for the brisk walk back to my hotel. I thought agreeably of my cosy room at the Continental, the old woman who would bring up a little brazier of charcoal whilst I poured myself another drink.

"How do you know him?" I called.

"Willoughby?" he called back as he clambered inside. He threw his cigar butt onto the road and stamped on it. "He's an old pal."

The door slammed shut. The taxi drove off along the road, smoke pouring out into the bitter night.

I met Burchett two days later in the guest room on the second floor of the press club, the air ripe with the aroma of men in close confinement, unmade beds draped with newspapers and damp underwear. Burchett was packing his kit bag with stacks of notebooks and clippings. He wasn't British, I realised, but a blunt, amiable Australian with a cynical and amusing manner.

"Lucky you caught me. They're slinging me out next week. The bastards."

He was impressively cheerful. The men at SCAP had removed his press accreditation a month before, a fact which he ascribed to the article he had written, with a typewriter on his knees, in the ruins of Hiroshima, just a few days after we had landed. When I told him I was curious, he raised his eyebrows.

"Oh, you are? Well, you're in the minority. I bet they're still dropping like flies. If there's any of them left, that is. We'd not hear a dicky bird about it in any case."

"How did you get down there?"

"How? I got the bloody train like anyone else. Caused quite

a stir, I don't mind telling you. Bunch of army samurai chappies didn't quite take to me . . . "

He described landing with the first parties of marines on a beach near Yokosuka. As soon as he entered the surreal wreckage of Tokyo, he rushed to the station and boarded the first train toward Hiroshima, looking for a scoop. The carriage had been packed with Japanese officers, bitter and glowering—it had been the day of the surrender signing aboard the *Missouri*—and he'd been the only white man on the train but for an old German priest.

"Drank some of that sake stuff with them though. Seemed to calm things down a bit. Just goes to show, doesn't it?"

"What about Disease X, Burchett? This—radiation disease?"

His face became suddenly serious. "Atomic Plague. That's what I called it. At first the locals thought it must have been caused by a kind of poisonous gas from the bomb."

He'd stumbled across a makeshift hospital on the outskirts of Hiroshima, scores of people lying on rush mats, deteriorating almost before his eyes.

"Came in complaining of sore throats. Days later, their gums were bleeding. Then their noses, then their eyes."

After that their hair began to fall out. The doctors, desperate, injected them with vitamins, but the flesh rotted away around the puncture points.

"Gangrene," Burchett said, his nose wrinkling with the memory. "You can smell it a mile off."

Some died soon after. Others held out for a while longer, complaining of an overwhelming inertia, a strange, heartbreaking malaise. Then they died too.

Burchett let out a long sigh. "And that, sir, is more or less the size of it."

"Who else knows about this?"

He snorted. "Brass are doing a bloody good job to make sure no one does."

"And do you have photographs?"

"Ha!" he barked. "Did have!"

My stomach tightened. "There's no photographs?"

"Therein lies a tale," he said. "After I got back to Tokyo, I was ordered to visit a military hospital. No doubt to check I wasn't glowing. Two days later, my camera disappears from my kit bag. Along with my notes, my typewriter, and five rolls of film. 'Sorry Mr. Burchett, must have been that shady chap on the other side of the ward.' All very mysterious."

My head began to swim. "There's not a single image of what you've been describing to me?"

He shook his head.

It seemed astonishing, terrifying—that an entire city and its inhabitants could disappear without a trace.

"Unless you chaps took any snaps for posterity. Or the Japs did. Even so, I doubt we'll be seeing any of those at the flicks any time soon."

Wild thoughts swirled around my head.

"Anyway. Need to pack up now, old chap. Getting shipped back to the mother country in the morning. Oh, for London in the winter."

He gave a theatrical shudder and I wished him luck.

"Good luck yourself, mate," he said, looking me straight in the eye. "Believe me, you're going to bloody well need it."

My dreams that night were relentless and harrowing. Standing on a desolate plain, the wind howling around me. An inferno swept from the horizon, fireballs pelting down from the sky. A ruined schoolhouse, a stench of rotting meat. The assembly hall piled with skeletal bodies. The little girl from Ueno, her mouth agape, her body covered in welts.

Endless corridors, men in pursuit. A door to an office. Behind the desk, a chair. My father. A shotgun barrel in his mouth, still open in a ghastly smile. His brains thickly smeared on the wall behind.

*

Two days later, I woke early. In the pale light of dawn, I sliced off the *Stars and Stripes* blazon from my jacket and sewed back on my lieutenant's epaulettes. My knapsack was bulging from a visit to the PX the night before, packed with chocolate, tins of Spam, a bottle of Crow, and two cartons of Old Golds, along with ten fresh rolls of 35mm Kodak film.

I travelled in the Japanese section of the train, despite the insufferable crush. People blankly made way for me and my uniform, and I squeezed myself into a cramped seat by the cracked window. Babies hoisted on women's backs swung perilously close to my head. The carriage was filled with the tang of unwashed bodies and wet wool. The windows were mostly gone and cold blustered through the carriage.

The inspector looked at me in mortification after examining the ticket I'd had a Japanese boy buy for me at the station. Brow furrowed, he rubbed his hat back and forth over his bald head. I held my fingers to my lips in question, and his eyes lit up. I handed him the first of my packets of cigarettes, a five-dollar bill folded inside. After a moment of shameful deliberation, he gave a sickly grin, slid both into his pocket, and politely clipped my ticket.

The train stopped often throughout the night, halting in lonely tunnels, shunting into sidings for what seemed like an eternity. Snow whirled outside and there were clangs and shouts as men tried to restart the engines. The passengers pressed their faces to the windows to watch, their breath freezing against the broken glass. There was the lonely sound of metal being hammered in the darkness as handcarts of coal were hauled up to the locomotive.

Later, we passed through Kyoto, where most of the passengers disembarked. A few hours later, I recognized the white alabaster of Himeji Castle up on its hill, pale in the light of a bright full moon. I fell into a troubled sleep against the comforting bulk of a large, warm woman who sat beside me, my pack drawn close against my knees.

I was awoken by the woman jabbing me in the ribs, repeating Japanese words in a loud, obstinate voice. I tried to crawl back into the drowsy shelter of my dreams, but she poked me again, hard, and I sat up, rubbing my eyes.

The carriage was almost empty now, and, outside, the first light of dawn lent a rose-grey tint to the horizon. We were passing down onto an immense, bleak plain, rugged mountains looming in the distance. The wheels screamed on the rails as we slowed on our approach to a shattered station. The train shuddered to a halt. The platforms were gone, and there was a sharp drop from the train to the compacted dirt below. A solitary wooden sign was nailed to the wall of a battered brick building and I struggled to identify the ideograms as the woman, still jabbing her finger into my side, began to intone the syllables, over and over, in a strange, mellifluous voice:

"*Hiroshima, desu, Yankii. Yankii—Hiroshima desu.*"

14
UNAGI
(*Hiroshi Takara*)

From where Koji and I sat on the stone bank of the canal, Fuji-san was just visible beyond the ruins of the city, its peak sprinkled with snow. We had set off that morning with our bamboo fishing rods, crossed the Kototoi Bridge and made our way up to the lock with its little castle keep. Our lines were hooked with chicken gizzards, dangling now in the black depths of the water, the slick surface glistening with rainbow whirls of oil. We were fishing for eels.

My father's shop had sold eel, of course. The rich, sweet aroma had infused my childhood. The shop had been popular with the patrons of the theatres and cabarets that lined the streets of Asakusa, a regular haunt of the stagehands, theatre managers and actors who came in at odd times of the day for snacks and a glass of sake between shows. My father was a true fan of the kabuki himself—the rough-and-tumble style popular in Tokyo back then, and prints of the Danjuros, the famous dynasty of actors, were plastered all over the walls. He liked nothing better than to banter with the customers about famous performances of the past, cracking jokes in that gruff, smart way that Tokyo people liked, steaming and grilling the strips of eel all the while. He brushed them with a thick secret sauce from his famous pot—an earthenware thing he'd inherited from his own father, bound with wire, sticky and smeared from generations of service. As he stood there, surrounded by smoke and fire, he looked almost like a character from a kabuki play himself. One of the wilier, earthier types.

Ours was an old-fashioned shop in that the live eels were kept in a big glass tank at the front by the street. My mother skinned them on a block: she pinned them through the head and tore away the slimy skin with a swift movement, pulling out the backbone and slicing the fillet into strips in an instant. Sometimes I pressed my face up against the glass and watched the animals flap their fins and slip around each other, glistening like they'd been freshly coated with lacquer. My father once told me that every eel in the world was born in the same place, out in the middle of a distant ocean. I dreamed about the place sometimes, the sea crashing as the glassy elvers drifted away, to be tugged apart from each other by the ocean currents.

The first day my father took me to the Kabuki Theatre was the day after the Pacific War had broken out. Our headmaster had gathered us in the assembly hall of my school, and we'd nudged each other, trying not to laugh, because Sensei had tears streaming down his cheeks.

"Children," he said, his voice wavering. "Japan has entered the great war against America and Britain at last!"

Banzai!

We were thrilled, of course—we could hardly believe that Japan had actually gone and done it. Our country was going to annihilate the enemy. That afternoon, our teacher unrolled a huge map of the Pacific Ocean and we pinned it up on the classroom wall. We spent the lesson searching for Honolulu, and stuck on a little rising sun flag when we finally found it.

The next morning, my mother was washing my father with warm water from the cedar tub. She passed the cloth over his muscly back, then toweled him down and helped him dress in his yukata. She arranged my clothes and brushed my hair as the radio burbled away with another excited report of the glorious attack. I noticed that she and Satsuko were still dressed in their normal work coats and aprons.

"Why aren't you getting ready, mum?" I asked.

"Your mother and sister aren't coming," my father said, with a wink. "It's just us men today."

Us men! I was beside myself with excitement as we made our way into the theatre, blazing with lanterns and filled with smells. His big hand gripped mine as the patrons called out to him, sprawling in their boxes with *bentos* and bottles of sake laid out in preparation for a good long afternoon's entertainment ahead. When my father told them I was his son, they studied me with approval, remarking on my dark eyes and declaring that I had the ferocious glower of a Danjuro myself, which made my father's face crinkle with pleasure.

We took our place in the centre of the hall and he set out some rice crackers to nibble on. The national anthem played at a deafening volume, then there was a loud bang and the lights went out. I seized my father by the arm and he laughed uproariously as a cloud of smoke billowed on the stage. I smiled at him in bashful excitement and we settled back to watch the play.

There were flashing lights, sudden explosions, the wail of horns and voices and clouds of colourful smoke. As the actors came onto the stage, men cried out *Banzai!* and the audience all roared with approval. At the climax, the clappers rang out and the audience exploded, pounding the sides of their boxes as the actors pulled their faces into ferocious, cross-eyed tableaux. Afterward, everyone spilled out into the light of the bustling evening to eat and drink amongst the stalls and shops, and I rubbed my eyes as if emerging from a dream.

Later, somehow, it all went wrong. A few years after that, rice was being rationed and the fishmonger had gone out of business, and, finally, my father was forced to close the restaurant. The women from the neighbourhood association came round the next day, and asked him to donate his grills to the military as they were made from such good iron. *Let's send just one more plane to the front!*

Then the real tragedy occurred. The fire raids began, and the theatres were shut down and my father's last pleasure in life was taken away. His call-up papers arrived soon after that. On the evening of his purification ceremony, we ate a solemn meal of sea bream and red rice. Afterward, my father put a lid on his ancient pot of sauce and sealed it with wax. He wrapped it up in oilcloth and placed it in a cedar box, which he stood in the alcove underneath the family altar. As we stood before it, he put his hands on my shoulders, rubbing them over and over.

"Take care of that until I get back, Hiroshi-kun, do you hear me?" he said.

I nodded. He pointed at the box.

"That's our only family treasure."

My father heaved his kit bag onto the train at Ueno Station the next day. He was going to report at the Yokosuka air-naval base. He squatted down on the platform and embraced me tightly as the platform guard blew his whistle.

"Remember what I told you," he whispered.

I nodded.

"I promise, Father," I said.

"I'm counting on you, Hiroshi-kun!"

There was a shriek from the locomotive as the wheels began to turn. The train pulled away from the platform. He leaned out of the carriage window for a moment, and waved his fighting cap.

And then he was gone.

Koji shrieked as something writhed violently on the end of his fishing line. I leaped up and quickly wound the string around my arm as it veered from side to side. The taut line angled up, and I prayed that it wouldn't snap as I staggered backward, heaving as hard as I could. There was a sudden splash, and then, there it was! A dark, shining eel, coiling and writhing on the bank. Koji hollered in triumph as we dangled the spiraling creature into our bucket, spluttering with delighted revulsion as slimy water flicked in our faces. We dropped it into the pail, where it whumped away with a dull clanging noise. We covered it up with a plank of wood, and together we hoisted it up. We triumphantly carried it down the canal toward the river as the water sloshed back and forth.

The light was just fading as we met the other children at Ueno Station. They crowded around us excitedly when they saw that we had actually caught something. When I slid the plank away, they gasped. The eel was curled up like an evil black snake in the bottom of the pail. Aiko leaned over, very warily. Suddenly, the thing wriggled and flicked water into the air, and she screamed and fell onto her backside. The children cackled with laughter as Tomoko helped her up. Aiko began to wail as Tomoko brushed her down.

"Cheer up, Aiko-chan! You won't be bellyaching when Hiroshi's cooked the eel for our dinner."

Tomoko glanced at me, amused.

The lights of the market glowed, and spattering flecks of black on the brickwork of the railway embankment marked the start of rain. GIs went to and fro in their rain capes amongst the stalls to haggle for stockings and trinkets for the night ahead. Shin was showing off now, dipping the tip of his finger into the water to goad the eel while Koji and Nobu watched warily over his shoulder.

Aiko's high voice piped up. She pointed over toward the far railway arches. Two GIs were walking along in the shadows. We had four last cigarettes left—should she go and ask if they would buy them?

"I'll go!" Tomoko said, brightly.

Aiko handed her the remaining cigarettes and Tomoko sprinted off. I sat down on the gritty bank. The children were daring each other to touch the eel, jerking back whenever it moved. A train rumbled up on the tracks as I closed my eyes, smiling to myself.

Some instinct made me look up. Through the drizzle, one of the distant soldiers was looming over Tomoko, pulling her toward him. I leaped up. Tomoko ducked away, but then, with a quick movement, the soldier grabbed her. There was a scuffle, and then, somehow, her monpe were around her knees. The man pulled her toward the iron struts of the railway bridge and she cried out as he pushed her up against the column.

The world melted as I tore toward them, a sharp stone in my hand, my mind filled with a piercing roar. Tomoko stood pinioned to the wall, the soldier pressing one hand beneath her chin as the other pulled at his open trousers. He suddenly turned and saw me. Tomoko dropped just as I leaped into the air and swept the stone down hard toward his forehead. His brawny arm shot up and struck me in the jaw and I crashed down into a heap of charred, wet timber. I looked around desperately for a weapon. My fingers fell upon a piece of rusted pipe and I started to swing it as the man hovered in front of me. His shirt was billowing from his fly, and he was breathing heavily.

A sudden wave of fear came over me as the man came closer. I swung wildly with the pipe, but to my horror, he caught it with one fist and ripped it from my hand. He grabbed me by the scruff, and I screamed and flailed at him as he slapped me with his hand, swearing. His companion grabbed his shoulder, but the man bellowed and he shrank away. I was hoisted slowly upward. The veins in his neck bulged and I could smell his beery breath. Sweat and blood and rain were dripping from his brow—I'd caught him, I thought, with a glancing satisfaction. I kicked out wildly. He slammed his left fist into my eye—there was an explosion of pain and I collapsed onto the ground. A boot stood by my head, smeared with mud, the laces looped and tangled around the ankle. I was deaf except for a far-off ringing in my ears.

I felt the tremble of iron rivets. Another train was passing along the track high above and sparks flew down from the rails. Passengers hung from the side, peering down the embankment. There were shouts. The other soldier clasped his friend by the neck, pulling him away. The GI resisted for a second. He stared down at me, then swung his boot again, straight into my belly. It lifted me from the ground, and I collapsed in agony, struggling to inhale. The train screeched off along the rails as the soldiers disappeared beneath the tracks, their shadows jerking up along the brick wall behind them.

My head was ringing. I couldn't get up. Tomoko stood a few yards away. She struggled to pull up her monpe as I crawled toward her.

"Tomoko? Tomoko-chan?"

Dread spread from my stomach to my fingertips. She clutched her arms around her body and began to shiver. I reached out to touch her but she jerked violently away with a whimper.

"Tomoko?" I said. "Tomoko-chan!"

The rain poured down around us, saturating our thin rags, as she shook against the iron column.

I clambered to my feet and forced myself to walk back toward the children. It was dark now, and the lights of the market were bright smears in the rain. The children stared at me as I approached. The zinc bucket was still there, perched unevenly on the ground. With a sudden fury, I kicked it as hard as I could with my bare foot.

It reverberated with a dull clang and the water slopped onto the ground.

There was a movement and the black shape of the eel slithered forward. It shivered up the slope and waved over the broken slabs and gravel until it reached the edge of the bomb crater, flooded with icy, dark water. It paused for a second at the edge, then slid in. The silhouette hovered at the surface, as if stunned. Then it slipped away, writhing, and disappeared down into the blackness.

15
PHILOPON
(*Osamu Maruki*)

hilopon. Drug of the hour. Glint in the eye, pulse in the vein. Saviour of the downtrodden. Sacrament of the lost. Bright white light to the woe-struck, the lice-ridden, the starry-eyed artists: the stupefied, raving philosopher-poets of the burned-out ruins.

Mrs. Shimamura's bar swirled for hours each evening now, the intellectuals variously mournful and long-faced or else frantic and electrified, circling sections of the newspapers spread out on the bar, their eyes shining with morphine and methyl.

We came together as drunks or tramps do—to hold each other up in swaying arms. The bar was a sanctuary to which we retreated to comfort ourselves with raw, amniotic liquor, to keep our minds numb and distracted with absurd toasts and peculiar drinking games. What conversation there was now was of rashes, blisters, coughs, ticks, rations, hunger, thirst, and cold. Mostly though, we just drank, night after night, holding our glasses aloft and crashing them together—*shoo shoo shoo!*—before tipping the fluid down our throats. Glass after glass, until the light compressed into pinpricks and we slumped facedown on the bar. The bright stars of Japan's literary firmament. We were nothing now but slurred aphorisms and pulmonary complaints.

Everything was so bleak and petrified in Tokyo that winter that it was no surprise that many of us began to supplement our meagre diet of rotgut and sweet potato with the small, crystalline Philopon pills we'd fed upon during the last days of the war: those little tablets of courage that had steeled our nerves against the battery of Australian and American guns, that had kept us feverish and alert through those long nights of grisly carnage. A glut of the drug flooded the city sometime in December: thousands upon thousands of green ink bottles appearing in pyramids at the black markets, passing from hand to chafed hand in the cramped, leaky bars. Before long it seemed as if the whole city was munching the pills like sardines, washing them down with tears and tiger's piss in an attempt to blunt the teeth that gnawed at our bellies; to propel our battered bodies through the freezing streets, the cluttered train compartments.

Prior to this, I had developed another, more sinister addiction. Those evenings when I had reached my alcoholic peak, as it were, my mind illuminated by stars, I would board a tram to the Ginza, alighting near the American PX and the Oasis cabaret. There I would take a place on the curb on the side of the avenue, beside the peddlers with their straw mats of figurines and fountain pens, and watch as the Americans crammed down the staircase of the brothel. Once in a while, I would be rewarded with a glimpse of Satsuko Takara, as she performed her shamming routine outside, pulling at sleeves and enticing officers to enter. Sometimes, I would spot her as she left, hours later, buttoning up her raincoat as she strode away into the dawn like a departing angel.

I tormented myself with the thought of her, down in that secret cellar, American hands sliding over her back and along her pale thighs. I recalled the brief hours we had spent on a straw-filled mattress in the Victory Hotel, the night before I was sent to war. A victory of sorts. My last. The Americans had polluted her now, just as they had polluted me. One night, I stood with a grubby girl at the back of a ruined building, my eyes brimming with tears as I handled her, urgently trying to imagine her Satsuko—

It was no use. They had taken my very manhood.

Philopon came not a moment too soon. A glimmer of life came back into my eyes, my spirits leavened. Lazarus clambered from his tomb. I still drank, of course, until I collapsed, but the periods of consciousness between now grew more animated and urgent, my actions more sprightly and vital.

Night after night, I sat on my mattress, attended by a flask of shochu and a vial of Philopon, and wrote, until the tiny room was littered with balled-up clumps of paper, the air clotted with ink fumes. I wrote stories inspired by the strange articles that filled that day's newspapers: the grandmother murdered by her grandson on his return from Manchukuo; the blind children found living in the sand dunes of Izu. My stories were macabre, catastrophic, stygian. They were also unreadable, I realized. Yet I thought, perhaps, they might represent a kind of literary self-immolation, a spiritual disembowelment that might somehow purify me, and set me free from the past.

One evening, I came upon a writer I was somewhat familiar with, tottering on his stool at the bar. He was breathing heavily, giving occasional tubercular rasps into his silk handkerchief. His conversation became increasingly feverish as the evening drew on, his pen scribbling faster as he yelled out choice epithets to us all. At last, he leaped up, seized the arms of his nearest companion and dragged him off into the night. After he had left, I found his notebook on the bar amidst the confusion of newspapers. As I flicked through it at random, I found a page of dislocated words, which together seemed to form a kind of occult, chemical sutra:

Morphine. Atromol. Narcopon.

Pantapon. Papinal. Panopin.
Atropin. Rivanol. Philopon.

Philopon. Could we have survived the winter without it?
Philopon was the true hero of our age, our Eucharist. In the
paralysis that followed surrender, it was the rod that kept our
spines stiff, the glue that kept flesh adhered to our bones.

The special attack pilots, in those last, surreal days of war,
had tied emblazoned bands around their foreheads, and,
together with their brother officers, had sung the national
anthem and offered *banzai* to the emperor. They toasted each
other with ceremonial sake, just as samurai had once sprinkled
it upon their swords on the eve of battle. Then, however, they
had ingested Philopon, before climbing into their flying
machines and roaring off into the suicide of the setting sun.
What modern men they had been.

Philopon was the crystalline symbol of our new age. Who
needed an emperor when we had MacArthur? Who needed
sake when we had Philopon? From the emerald paddy we had
been transported to the laboratory, from the bloody field of
battle to the dissection tank. We had traded fireflies and
lanterns for the flood lamp and the phosphorus shell, kabuki
for cabaret, rice for amphetamine. Who needed tatami in the
age of concrete? What use was steel in the age of plutonium?
Goodbye, Nippon, goodbye! Farewell Amaterasu—hello
America! And welcome, Japan, welcome: to the bright, white
chemical age!

16
AFTERMATH OF THE ATOM
(*Hal Lynch*)

I vaulted down from the train as a dozen other people, mainly women, trudged over to the station building. They eyed me with frank hostility as I approached. I was aware of how conspicuous I was in my uniform. The train gave a piercing whistle and lumbered away. I lingered, watching it disappear along the tracks. An acute, heavy silence descended.

The roof at one end of the narrow ticket hall had caved in. Riveted iron beams hung down from the brickwork and rubble was heaped high on the floor. The other end was bare but for a solid desk, at which sat a guard, his moustache bristly beneath his peaked cap. He gasped audibly when he saw me, springing to his feet and bobbing there for a second, as if unable to decide whether to salute me or not. I extracted my crumpled train ticket from my pocket. He shrank away as I tried to press it into his hand.

In broken Japanese, I asked him the way "to the city." He tugged at his moustache for a second, then beckoned for me to follow him through a pair of splintered wooden doors. He pointed. A desolate plain stretched for several miles until a heavy ridge of rugged mountains. About halfway across, hazy outlines marked an isolated outcrop of buildings. Nothing else was standing but charred spindles of telegraph poles marking vanished avenues.

"Hiroshima desu," the guard said, staring at me with watery eyes.

I heard a cry. A policeman, his nightstick dangling against

his leg, hurried over from a corrugated hut, a rusted bicycle leaning against its side. I twisted my shoulder to make sure he could see my epaulettes of rank, and he halted and glowered for a moment, before finally twisting his hand against his forehead.

I pointed toward the buildings in the distance.

"Hiroshima?" I asked, quite aware of how ridiculous the question sounded.

He seemed torn between his misgivings and instinctive submission to my authority. Eventually, in painfully slow English, he asked: "Why you go Hiroshima?"

I took out a folded piece of paper upon which Burchett had scribbled an address.

"Hospital?" I asked.

He studied the paper, then conferred with the train guard. Finally, he raised his hand and wriggled his fingers in the general direction of the ruined buildings.

"Thank you, gentlemen." I gave them a curt nod and slung my bag over my shoulder.

As I started to walk down the track, footsteps followed and I felt a tap on my shoulder. The policeman held his fingers to his lips with a cringing motion. I split another pack of Old Golds from the carton in my bag and tossed it to him. He bowed, then strode as imperiously as he could back to his shack.

I surveyed the blank plateau before me: a hardened, empty desert. The sky was swirling with heavy cloud that obscured the ridge of mountains in the distance, and flakes of snow were drifting down. I took a deep breath and started to walk, my footsteps crunching upon the earth.

Tokyo didn't come close, I thought, *even at its worst*. There, at least, the remnants were identifiable—the broken frames of buildings, hewn chunks of masonry and cauterized brick. Here, any human vestige, any recognizable form had been ground into abstraction. The landscape was moulded from pulverized fragments as fine as sand, and thick, gravelly dust formed strange, surreal hummocks and formations, solidified now by the rain. It was a wasteland.

Every so often, a bicycle creaked toward me. The riders wore cloth masks over their mouths and turned their handlebars to steer around me in a wide arc as they passed.

I began to detect a vague tang in the air—a bitter, acrid smell I couldn't place. I followed the shadowy outline of what must have once been a streetcar track, the overhead lines swept clear away. Fifty yards away, in a solitary heap, lay the twisted metal frame of a destroyed trolley.

Up ahead was a high step to a stone bridge. A stream of pungent water trickled at the bottom of the channel. Corpses of fish and mangled bicycles cluttered the riverbed. I took out my camera, and started to take shots.

For a long stretch after the bridge, though, there was nothing to document. No broken-down houses, no graves, no signs of settlement whatsoever. Just a vast expanse of thick, reddish-brown dust, punctuated by clumps of bushy yellow grass and spiky, poisonous-looking shrubs. The light was hazy and grey, the sun a pale, far-off disk, and I had the feeling of walking on the surface of a distant planet. Time seemed somehow disjointed, as if I was floating through a dream landscape. There was no sound of birdsong or human activity; no trees or vegetable gardens. The place was poisoned, stricken, dolorous.

By the banks of another, much wider river, a shattered dome loomed, resembling the frame of an observatory. I recalled the umbrella roof of the central market building from my aerial photographs, and realized I was coming close to the hypocentre. Clumps of plaster still dangled from the curving struts of the dome, and plants were growing in the ruins—tendrils of dying morning glory that spiraled amidst the broken tiles; tangles of thorny herbs and small yellow broom-like flowers that clutched at the blackened brick. There were signs of life on the other side of the river now as well. A man led horses, pulling a cart laden with furniture while others went by on bicycles.

I picked my way out of the dome and walked over to the bank. Fifty feet to my left, I saw it. The big, white bridge that I'd proposed as a primary target. The cement structure was askew, as if it had been shoved from its supports. The stone itself seemed ancient. As I crossed the bridge, I was put in mind of mythical tales of rivers to the underworld. Fields of lost souls on the other side.

Shanties stood alongside the avenue, lines of laundry strung between them. Down by the river, women were scrubbing clothes in wooden tubs and children splashed about in bathing caps.

I was so absorbed that I didn't notice the rumble of the army convoy until it was almost upon me. I turned and froze. Figures stood in the backs of trucks, silhouetted by the cloud of dust raised by the heavy wheels. I wondered whether I should run, but some instinct told me to stay and so I stood rigid, my hand held up in stiff, formal salute. British markings were painted on the sides of the vehicles. My panic turned to relief as the cheerful troops in the back called out, thumbs held up in salute as they rolled past. The friendly sound of a horn blared out as they disappeared into a haze of red dust, my heartbeat slowly subsiding.

I strode along the avenue toward a tall building that looked as if it had once been a five- or six-storey office block. On entry, the impression turned out to be illusory. Only the outer shell was still standing. The interior walls had collapsed, and the ground floor was gutted and charred, leaving nothing but rubble and emptiness.

Further along, another tall building seemed solid and undamaged. People were coming and going through its main doors. They glanced up as I approached, stopped in their tracks and stared.

Inside was a large, high-ceilinged hall, clerks at desks flipping through ledgers and stamping forms, counting out coins and notes for people lined up before them. At the end of the room, a huge clock hung on the blackened wall. I glanced at my own watch. The hands of the clock had been frozen in time.

I raised my Leica, and the image of the clock sharpened as I focused the lens. A hand pulled at my arm. For a second, I thought that I was being robbed, and I raised my fists as I spun around. Two policemen stood cowering, while another stepped gingerly forward and attempted to grasp me again.

"Come—please," he said, clutching at me with bony fingers.

"Hands off," I said, shoving him away. He stood there for a second, apparently contemplating another attempt, before clearly deciding discretion to be the better part of valour. He walked toward a wide stone staircase that led away from the lobby.

"Come—please," he repeated. He waved his fingers at me as if beckoning to a cat. Up the puddle-stained stairs, on the third floor, was a set of doors that bore the insignia of the police force. Inside, men sat at splintered desks laid with maps, scrolls, and jars of cloudy tea. They wore overcoats as they worked— the room was cold enough to see the vapour of their breath. They glanced up at me curiously as I was led through the room. The officer knocked softly at a door. At the sound of a bark from within, he opened it, saluted, and hustled me inside.

A man with a silver beard sat behind a desk, glaring at me with sharp eyes under a beetling brow. The room was bare except for a beige raincoat slung over a screen in the corner and a portrait of the emperor that hung askew on the cracked wall.

The man fired off a torrent of angry Japanese.

"I can't understand you, Chief," I said. "No matter how loud you shout it."

He stomped around the table to face me. He was tough and grizzled, and about a foot and a half shorter than me. He jabbed a sharp finger into my chest.

"Hold on now, Chief," I said loudly, grasping my epaulettes and thrusting them into his face. "Let's not forget who's who."

A timid knock came at the door, and a disheveled man with a toothbrush moustache came inside.

"Excuse me," he said in English, with a hesitant bow, "I am translator."

The chief growled and retreated to his desk. He snapped at the man, who nodded meekly every now and then, penciling words in a small notebook. The translator turned to me and cleared his throat.

"He asks, 'Why are you in Hiroshima?'"

"That's a good question."

He gave me a look of anxiety. I took pity on him.

"I'm here to visit the hospitals."

"You are doctor?"

I shook my head. "No, I'm a reporter. *Shimbun kisha desu.*"

As the man started to warily translate, the Chief uttered a guttural volley of Japanese that crescendoed with a slam of his hand on the table. The translator cringed.

"He says—no reporter in Hiroshima. Forbidden."

I wondered whether I should try to bluff it out with my press pass. I thought I might do better with cigarettes and a few tins of Spam. The chief tapped his fingers against the table, apparently unable to decide what to do with me. He picked up the telephone, and barked into the receiver. There was a crackling voice on the other end. The chief grunted as he listened.

Over by the window, I looked outside. Flat ruins stretched for miles all around. Millions of tiny snowflakes were falling through the air. They stuck to the glass for a moment, before melting away into tiny droplets of water.

The chief replaced the receiver. He stood up and put on his coat and hat. He flung a few words at the translator and wrenched open the door.

I looked askance at the man.

"Where are we going?"

The translator dipped his head. "He says—to visit hospital."

"We are?"

"Yes. We go now."

"Why should he take me to the hospital?" I asked, hurrying after him. A look of painful embarrassment passed over his face.

"Excuse me."

"Yes?"

"He says—to show America what it has done."

The chief himself drove the battered sedan, the car toiling over the pits and crevasses in the road. The translator sat next to me in the back. As I asked him about the state of the city now, he responded with terse, nervous answers. Yes, people were returning, though most still clustered on the outskirts, too scared of sickness to venture further in. No, there was no electricity yet. They still relied on the army generators. No, they rarely saw any Westerners. Teams had come a few weeks after the surrender, dressed in protective clothing and carrying peculiar pieces of equipment. They had drilled in certain areas and taken away samples of rocks and brick, but had not returned since.

I rolled down the window and started photographing. Men in rubber boots and helmets shovelled debris, sawed planks, dug foundations. In an open patch of ground a long, low building was painted in crude camouflage, scrap metal piled outside—warped radiators and railings. Men in blue overalls dragged over still more, sorting and arranging it by type.

We bumped along a dirt track lined with rows of identical, newly built wooden huts. Black squares of vegetable gardens lay between them, the earth dotted with tiny sprouts of green.

Past a long yellow brick wall, we emerged into the muddy yard of what had once been the Red Cross hospital. The car slid to a halt and we clambered out. The chief snapped at the translator, gesturing toward the building.

A doctor, a bespectacled man in his mid-fifties, his beard cut in a tapering European style, emerged from a side door, stepping delicately around the muddy puddles as he approached. I thanked the police chief for his help, and he laughed mirthlessly.

Frankly, the translator said, he should have had me arrested at the station when he had been alerted to my arrival. He had orders to call the Allied commander of the area if any unfamiliar personnel arrived in the city.

"And yet he chose to ignore his orders," I said.

The chief scowled at me.

"He says—it is better for you to see for yourself."

"I agree."

The chief's eyes narrowed and his face became full of contempt. He gestured once more at the hospital. With that, he climbed into the car and slammed the door shut. It trundled away, the worn wheels splashing through the flooded potholes.

Dr. Hiyashida had studied medicine at the University of Heidelberg and spoke good English. He had come to Hiroshima from Osaka to make a special study of radiation disease. Shamelessly, he told me that he hoped his thesis would glean him a position on the medical council.

"You weren't here yourself on the day of the blast?"

"No," he said, frowning. "And now there are no more than a few A-Bomb cases still in the hospital. It is most unfortunate."

The inside of the hospital was a shambles. The window frames were warped, the glass gone. An icy wind blew in from the hills, visible in the near distance.

"How are conditions now?"

"Improving," he said, apparently without irony. "We have more medicine now, vitamins and plasma. But we still need more operating tables, X-ray machines."

Patients wrapped in bandages were lying on mats on the floor, sleeping or quietly reading miniature books.

"You see?" he said in a frustrated whisper. "Few of them have any interesting symptoms any longer. They just say they feel empty and listless. They complain of tiredness and melancholy. I find that difficult to ascribe to radiation. After all, who ever heard of a bomb causing melancholy?"

In another ward, he kept his more "interesting" cases—the more grotesquely injured victims of the bomb whom I assumed he hoped would form the notable chapters of his thesis. I felt acutely awkward as he strode from one patient to another, ordering them to display their symptoms as if they were performers in a circus freak show.

One young man raised his shirt to expose his midriff. It was covered with the same thick, rubbery colloidal scars that the victims in Weller's photographs had shown. Another man's skin was burned with the striped pattern of the yukata he had been wearing at the time of the flash. The doctor urged me to take photographs—"For your newspaper!"—as he poked and prodded his patients, snapping at any of them who appeared too listless or embarrassed to respond. I grew irritated: he put me in mind of a particularly difficult superior officer I had known during my service, and I felt an incipient wave of hatred for the man.

Up ahead, an old woman, her white hair pulled into a bun, was sitting on the edge of her bed. I asked the translator to politely inquire whether I might talk to her. Dr. Hiyashida rushed over and took her arm, shaking it, which made me so angry that I almost struck him. I ordered him to leave us, and he slunk back to the doorway, glancing at us every now and again with a sulky look.

She had been beautiful once, that was clear. Her eyes were almost pure black, and her nose was still a soft, elegant curve. But her face seemed to have slid an inch or so around her skull, like a loose mask, and her skin was etched with a deep web of ancient lines and whirls.

She spoke in a low voice, almost without intonation. She had been a dance instructor, she said, though she'd had very few students left by the end of the war. She had arrived at her studio in the centre of the city at around eight o'clock on the morning of the blast. She had been walking along the corridor on the first floor, where she had paused for a moment to open a window to let in some air, glancing as she did so up at the mountains, thick with green against the blue summer sky.

There was a flash. An explosion of glass pitched her backward. She tumbled in the air with the last thought that a bomb had landed directly upon her. When she awoke, she was pinned facedown in the darkness, her mouth full of plaster. The floor above her had collapsed and she lay there for several days until men finally dug her out of the ruins. Outside, the city was flattened. Drops of oily black rain were falling from the sky.

Barefoot and dressed in rags, she made her way along the river to the park where hundreds of women and children lay dying. Some were vomiting up their innards; the flesh of others was peeling off. She saw two women from her neighbourhood association squatting by a fire, and hurried over. When they saw her, they turned away, aghast. The next morning, she went to a pool in the river to look at her reflection, and realised why.

She closed her eyes, gesturing toward her face. Her brows

seemed to have been pushed in by the thumbs of a sculptor, her lips almost entirely smudged into her face. With an almost imperceptible noise, the old woman hunched over. Her medical chart lay on the edge of her bed. My scalp prickled as I deciphered it. She was only twenty-five years of age.

On the other side of the room, two men were lying side by side in bed. One sat up and smiled vaguely as the translator and I came over. His scalp was bare and blotchy, his arms as thin as twigs. As with the girl in the photographs that Weller had showed us, his withered chest was speckled with red liver spots. The other man was asleep and his breath came in rasps.

The old man spoke so softly that I could barely hear. He smiled and made tiny gesticulations to illustrate his story. Sir would never believe it, he whispered, but they'd both worked on the railroad as labourers until just six months before. They'd been brawny and tough back then, with full heads of hair—wives, mistresses! They'd both been working on the tracks that morning, when the man had noticed the far-off glint of "Mr. B" in the sky, but they'd assumed it was just the weather plane and ignored it. There'd been an air raid warning earlier that morning, and it had passed without incident.

"Hiroshima was lucky, we used to say. The Americans didn't want to touch it."

He'd never been on a plane himself, he said, but as he'd looked at the silver glint in the sky, he'd wondered what Japan must look like from above.

"How beautiful it must be to fly, sir," he murmured, "to see the whole country stretched out beneath you."

He'd watched the plane as it passed. He'd put his hand above his face to shield his eyes from the dazzling sun. That was the moment.

There was a flash. There was no sound. He felt something strong and terribly intense and there was a pulsing of colour as he was hurled forward. He lay splayed on the ground with fragments of stone like teeth in his mouth. He thought he was dead.

Great crashes came from all around and he saw train carriages tumbling across the ground like toys, as an immense cloud rose up and blotted out the sun. Then, all around, debris and dust began to rain violently down from the sky.

He fell silent, staring into space.

"How do you feel now?"

He drew in a breath, then let out a long sigh. He rubbed his hands together dreamily, as if he were washing them. Last year, he said, he'd used his hands every day. Flinging a pick, hammering rivets, laying track. His body had been all muscle. He held up his shaking hands for me to see, then laughed. He didn't even think he could lift a glass of beer now. He felt so light that he thought he might float off into the wind like a feather. I took his photograph and thanked him. He gave a trembling smile and bowed, pressing his hands against his forehead as if in prayer.

As we left the ward, Dr. Hiyashida shook his head and crossed his hands behind his back. "Awkward cases, these A-Bomb people."

Darkness was seeping from the hills and I needed to catch the train back to Tokyo. It was the only passage for two days and the idea of being stuck here in this strange city at night filled me with a baffling fear. Dr. Hiyashida insisted that one of the hospital ambulances drive me to the station and this at least I gratefully accepted. I told myself I should be wary of encountering army personnel, although, in all honesty, it was the thought of traipsing back across that mournful wasteland in the dark that filled me with dread. What I desired more than anything was to be back in my room in Tokyo, a brazier smouldering away on the floor, a large glass of whisky in my hand.

Dr. Hiyashida waved me off at the hospital gate, the translator having now departed. He promised to send me a copy of his thesis when it was published. He urged me to be sure to mention his name "in my newspaper."

"Oh, I'll make sure I do," I called back.

The driver of the ambulance was a handsome young man of around twenty. To my surprise, he spoke English too—his parents had been Christians, and he'd been taught German and English by the monks at the church school, though the English lessons had come to an end some years before. He'd lost both parents in the blast, but he himself had survived largely unharmed, a feat which he ascribed—admirably, under the circumstances, I thought—to "God's grace." All he'd suffered were some small burns that wouldn't seem to heal. Out of thanks to God, he had now dedicated his life to helping the sick and the injured.

As we drove along the dark, wide dirt road, he recounted some of the grim stories and grotesque myths that had sprung up in the wake of the blast. The bomb had been the size of a matchbox, people said. The bomb had been tested on a mountain range in America, which it had destroyed entirely. Some other stories had a ghastly ring of truth. A group of soldiers had wandered lost in the park that night, holding each other's hands in a macabre line, their eye sockets empty, their eyeballs having melted down their cheeks. A whirlwind tore through the city a few hours after the blast, uprooting trees and sucking dead bodies up into the sky.

I pictured the old man as he lay on his hospital bed, the dreamy look in his eyes. He'd been imagining what it would be like to fly, thinking how beautiful the world must seem from up there.

Poor devil.

I asked the driver if he'd suffered any effects of radiation disease himself.

He said he didn't know. He'd lost some hair, but it had grown back. Far worse were the headaches he got at night, the inertia that sometimes pinned him down for days.

He frowned, then carried on in a low, confidential tone.

"The worst of it is that the women's menses have stopped. There are fears over whether they will ever begin again. My wife and I were only married last year, and we so want to have a child one day."

It was pitch black by the time we reached the station and I said goodbye to the boy with a fervent handshake. The snow was coming down in steady drifts now, and in the ticket hall, the shivering inspector made me understand through sign language that the train would be delayed.

I wandered around the back of the station to the railway sidings. A long chain of carriages lay tipped on its side, the wood scorched. There was a low hill nearby, and partway up, exactly one half of a *torii* arch marked the entrance to what had once been a temple. Nothing remained now but the broken stones of the votive pool, still bubbling with water from some mysterious spring, and the stumps of what must have once been enormous cedars. Beyond them was a mound of rubble, and atop it, two perching Buddhas, about to fall. The face of one was sheared away. The other gazed at the ground, his hands resting in his lap, a silent, secretive smile on his face.

As I walked back down the hill, soft snowflakes brushed my face and settled between the tracks and along the rails. From the lonely platform, I watched the snow fall until finally, with a distant glow, a train approached the station. When it pulled in, I clambered up into an empty compartment and took a hard wooden seat by the window. With numb fingers I slid the whisky bottle from my knapsack and took a long swig as the train jerked into motion. I craned my head out of the window as the train gathered speed. The station passed into the distance as snow whirled silently in the black sky. For a second, there was a faint glimmer of light somewhere far out on the plain. Then came a scream of wind as we plunged into a tunnel, and it was gone.

17
THE BLOOD CHERRY GANG
(*Satsuko Takara*)

The Ginza was bright and crowded with American GIs in fur hats and thick woollen gloves. A boisterous bunch were stamping along the frosty avenue in front of me as I walked toward the tram stop, flinging little icicles at each other and bellowing with laughter. I tried to dodge around them, but as I did so, a girl suddenly barged right into me. Short and plump, she wore a violet dress and reeked of liquor—she was clearly a streetwalker. She glared at me, slurring a curse. Then she spat full in my face.

I stood there, speechless, as she started screaming, her face twisted with rage. Who did I think I was, she demanded, with my airs and graces? Was I somehow superior to her?

"You're just a whore like me!"

It was awful. A crowd had gathered to watch the show: Americans pointing and sniggering, the eyes of the Japanese men blazing in spiteful satisfaction. I stepped away down the avenue, wiping my face with my handkerchief as the dreadful girl hurled insults behind me.

There seemed to be legions of streetwalkers out in Tokyo that night. Lurking in the doorways, darting out like crabs from their holes to grab any passing man. They really were a wretched mob, I thought, their makeup smeared, bare legs puckered from the cold.

I drew my coat around me. Was it true what that floozy had said? That I saw myself, somehow, in a class above them? Girls such as I drank Scotch whisky in cabarets, after all, while they swigged shochu dregs in dead-end alleys . . . Naval captains reserved my company in orderly private rooms, while they were pummelled by hideous old Japanese men in storefronts and frozen bomb craters.

Michiko had despised them all. Harlots and tarts, she called them, filthy *pan-pan*. While she, of course, was a courtesan, a modern-day Okichi.

It just went to show, I thought, as my tram pulled up. People always needed someone else to look down upon, no matter how far they had fallen themselves. After all, even the dogs that roam the streets and eat trash have hierarchies of their own.

The next morning, when I woke up, I felt very odd. A great weight was pressing upon my rib cage and it was so cold that I could see my breath. When I finally dressed, I grew dizzy, and had to lie back down again. I felt like a butterfly pinned to card.

Drifting in and out of sleep, I began to have the uncanny sensation that someone else was there in the room with me. The feeling grew stronger and stronger, until I became convinced that my mother was sitting over on the tatami by the table. I closed my eyes tightly and hid my face in the blanket, but the feeling grew so intense that I suddenly spun around and looked.

And there she was. Sitting on the floor, staring at me with lashless eyes. Her blue kimono was scorched, her hair all burned away. A terrible smell of char filled the room and I screamed out loud and fainted.

When I came to, she was gone. But I could still picture her, grimly staring at me, smouldering in accusation, and I knew that the reason she had returned from the other world was to punish me for having betrayed our family's honour by becoming a prostitute.

Over the following days, I wondered whether I should go up to the temple to say a prayer, or light some more incense in our street, but I doubted if either would help. Perhaps I should set out once more in search of Hiroshi, in the hope that by finding some trace of him, I might somehow quiet her restless soul . . . but I knew it was useless. There were no graves I could visit, no fragments of bone that I could inter.

I grew frightened that other ghosts might come to haunt me now as well. Some nights, when I left the Oasis, I thought I saw a pale figure standing on the other side of the avenue, gazing at me with solemn eyes. My heart would patter and I would hurry away through the crowded streets, terrified that Osamu's spirit was following me. But whenever I turned to look, the figure was gone.

Mr. Shiga must have noticed that I was on edge, because one night he summoned me to his office.

"Takara-san," he said, "if you can't get a grip on yourself, then you're fired. Your gloomy face is causing our customers discomfort."

I gave a shrill laugh and bowed low, asking him to forgive me. I explained that I just felt very tired.

He opened the drawer of his writing desk and took out a small green bottle.

"Take one of these each evening, Takara-san, before you come to work." He shook a small white pill onto his palm. "Our noble troops were given these at the end of the war to revive their stamina. You may find they help."

Later that night, I swallowed one of the tablets shortly before sitting at a table of American sailors. Soon enough, my mind became quite calm, and I started to feel pretty and sparkling. Their conversation was very amusing, and I began to laugh and chatter away in broken English, an unusual confidence and excitement quivering all through my body. It was quite extraordinary. The Americans smiled at me and joked with their friends at the other tables, and they all asked me to dance one after the other, so that in a few hours I earned more for tea dances than I normally did lying on my back for the whole night.

Girls were sprawled, drinking, in the dressing room when I finished my shift. They grinned when I showed them the bottle of magical pills.

"We've all been taking them for weeks now," they laughed. "They really are amazing!"

The pills had the added benefit, they said, of stopping you from getting hungry, so you wouldn't get too fat, either. We all laughed at that one: none of us were more than skin and bones in any case.

From then on, I swallowed a chalky pill as soon as I arrived at the Oasis each evening. It fizzed inside me as I dressed and painted my face. The Americans gave me swigs of whisky, and the club turned into a glowing merry-go-round as they twirled me across the dance floor. Finally, I took a yen taxi home, still wide awake, but then I just drank more whisky, and the room would spin deliciously around me as I sank down into a deep, dreamless sleep. And then, even if my mother, or my brother, or Osamu did come and visit me from beyond the grave, I was always too dead to the world to notice.

I was far out on the Pacific Ocean, on a battleship ploughing through the waves. My father was tucking me into a bunk, but the blanket wouldn't quite stretch. He climbed in beside me, and I was ashamed, but then he turned around, and he was Osamu. There was a loud explosion, a clanging alarm. Sailors were running through the galleys—we had been struck by a torpedo, the boat was sinking, and I was deep beneath the ocean, the sea pouring into my lungs—

"Satchan!"

Water dripped down my cheeks. Michiko was leaning over me, holding an empty glass.

"Satchan, really!" she said. "I thought you'd never wake up. You should be ashamed of yourself."

Michiko unpacked tins from a bag and laid them out on the table, a silver bracelet sparkling around her wrist. A thick, luxurious looking white fur coat hung by the door. *She's put on weight*, I thought. She had a lovely, sleek look and there was a rose-pink flush in her cheeks.

Michiko sat down and drew up her knees with a sigh. I groggily climbed out of bed to make some tea as she launched into a tirade about her admiral.

"Such demands, Satsuko!" she wailed. "I sometimes think I was better off at the Oasis."

I smiled thinly as I glanced at the fur coat.

"He won't keep away, you know. He treats me like I'm a prisoner!"

"It must be very unpleasant for you, Michiko," I agreed, swirling the kettle.

She gave a sad nod. "But he loves me, you see, Satsuko. He's going to tell his wife in America that he's leaving her."

I stifled a laugh.

"And marry you, Michiko?" I asked. "Is that honestly likely?"

"He's very wealthy," she said airily, ignoring the question.

She took a small, jewelled mirror from a leather purse and applied an invisible dusting of powder to her face.

"And you'll never guess, Satsuko," she said.

"What's that, Michiko?"

She cleared her throat and stood up. With one hand against her breast, she sang the notes of an ascending scale in a pure, clear voice.

"Very melodic, Michiko," I said, impressed. "You're much better than before."

"Do you think so?" she said, proudly. "Guess what else. I'm learning how to act as well."

She had apparently persuaded her admiral to pay for lessons with some old stagehands from the Minato Theatre, and had even cajoled him into buying her a piano. In fact, she said, it was to be delivered later on that very day.

As the kettle boiled, I felt queasy. I thought urgently of my vial of pills in the dresser.

"It's kind of you to visit, Michiko," I said as I poured out the water, "what with all your new distractions."

My stomach suddenly heaved.

"But I've missed you, Satsuko!" she said.

"Do you know," I said, inhaling sharply, "I was at the cinema just last week. An American film. There was an actress who somewhat resembled you—could it be possibly be Ingrid something?"

"Ingrid Bergman?" she cried, clapping her hands. "How clever you are, Satsuko! I think so too. There's a definite resemblance."

I turned away, swallowing bile. *Could I politely ask her to leave?* To my relief, Michiko waved away her tea in any case.

"Satsuko," she said, "please forgive me. I must go now. My piano is to be delivered at any moment."

"Please come again, Michiko. You're always very welcome."

"As soon as I can. Oh, and before I forget . . . "

She took a box wrapped in red crêpe de chine from her bag and placed it on the table.

"Michiko-san," I stammered. "Honestly, I've no need for gifts. I'm doing perfectly well . . . "

"Please accept it, Satsuko," she begged, kneeling in front of me. "You really must."

A horn blared outside. Before I could respond, Michiko had scuttled to the door and pulled on her fur coat. She whipped out her mirror and applied a last, rapid puff of powder to her face. Then, with a wave of her gloved hand, she was gone.

The powder hovered in the air, pungent and flowery. Suddenly, I gasped, reaching for the pail. I heaved up the milky contents of my stomach, my eyes blurry with tears as I clung onto its cold metal rim.

When I had finally recovered, I slid over to the table and held up the package Michiko had left. Several silk bows and ribbons criss-crossed the box and I fumbled with them for some time, until I gave up and ripped open the red tissue paper.

Oh, Michiko, I thought.

A fur stole lay in the box, taken from a white fox or some other expensive animal. It was so beautiful that tears sprang into my eyes. The fur was the softest thing I had ever felt in my life, delicate and supple and luxurious. I held it against my cheek for a long time. Then I lay back down on the futon and drifted away, lost in its fleecy softness for the rest of the afternoon.

A Joe with a pockmarked face was fast asleep on top of me, snorting violently in my ear. He had been celebrating his birthday that night and his cronies had strong-armed him into swallowing one bottle of beer after another. With an effort, I heaved him onto the floor and rang for Mr. Shiga. The man's companions finally came to fetch him, deciding first to dress him back to front in his uniform, which was just the kind of childish joke the Americans seemed to continually enjoy playing upon on another.

So I wasn't in an especially good mood as I waited in the cold drizzle for a tram that never came. Eventually I decided that it would be just as well to walk to Shimbashi Station and take the overground train back from there. I drew my fur stole close around my neck and walked off into a slanting wind.

It was deep winter now and I wondered how they survived, the pan-pan girls. Rows of them were sheltering in the low tunnels beneath the railway line, each with a leg bent up, cigarette smoke curling around them in wisps. I quickened my step, dodging the icy pools of water as I went.

A crunch of footsteps came from the shadows. I glanced over my shoulder. A knot of girls were walking fifteen paces behind me, silent in the darkness. I focused intently on the lights of the station, a hundred yards ahead, as my heart began to beat faster. The footsteps were coming closer. I suddenly hitched up my skirt in panic, about to run, but already they were behind me—

A fist struck my face and I sprawled to the ground.

Voices chorused above me, brutal and shrill. A tooth was loose on my tongue, my mouth full of blood. Thin, strong hands grabbed my arms and heaved me to my feet. I was trembling helplessly. Three women stood in front of me, and I saw the fat girl in the purple dress who had spat at me the week before. She stank of tobacco and sour sweat as she stepped forward and slapped me as hard as she could. Then she hawked and spat at me once again, her chewing gum catching in my hair.

"Where have you been tonight, you bitch?" she demanded. I gulped. "Still think you're better than us?"

Her fingers dug into my wrist, and she twisted it until I cried out in pain.

"You American whore!" she screamed. "I should stab you in the heart right here and now!"

I gasped as she shoved me and I stumbled backward. She seized my bag from the floor and began to rifle through it. Another woman stepped in front of me. Tall, dressed in a crimson frock, her eyebrows were painted high up on her forehead, giving her a puzzled expression. She grasped a clump of my hair and twisted it until tears sprang into my eyes. Her voice came in a low rasp.

"What are you doing here, anyway? You know this is our patch."

I gasped in pain, unable to speak. In the darkness, her other hand moved. A cold, sharp point suddenly pressed against my lip and nose.

"We own this ward," she said, staring at me with startled eyes. "You'll pay your share like everyone else."

The point jabbed into my flesh and I screamed. She pulled it away, and I fell sobbing to the ground. The other girl was pulling things from my bag now, like a fox devouring a chicken. The fat one wore my stole around her own neck, and was stroking it as if it was a kitten.

The woman in the crimson frock squatted down. Her knife was long and thin—the kind used to slice up fish.

"I've seen you," she said, in an empty voice. "I've seen how you look at us."

Frantically, I shook my head.

"You really think you're any better that us?"

The knife touched my neck, and my entire skin crawled. A humiliating seepage flooded my thighs and she smiled as drops leaked against the ground. "See? You're no different after all."

The world swam before my eyes and I fainted dead away.

When I came to, the women were disappearing beneath the iron struts of a railway underpass, animal shrieks echoing behind them. I staggered to my feet. My blouse was torn and my stockings shredded. My mouth was swollen and numb, and as I touched my lips, my fingers wetted with dark blood.

Something lay on the ground in front of me. I reached down to pick it up. It was a large card—like a visiting card. Ornate, emblazoned with a red satin peony, it was inscribed with hand-painted words: *Ketsueki Sakura Gumi.*

The Blood Cherry Gang.

So it seemed we really were to have equal rights in Japan. Women would be able to vote and men no longer allowed to divorce us whenever they chose, and now we even had our own lady gangsters to terrorize us, just as the men had had the yakuza all this time.

The Blood Cherry girls were already notorious, it seemed. The rumour went that they had all made a blood pact, that their leader, Junko—the woman in the crimson frock—had once been the famous geisha "Willow Tree," the mistress of Akamatsu, the ace fighter pilot. They were witches in human form; they were *kitsune,* fox spirits, who could bewitch men and even shift shape. All superstitious nonsense, of course, but enough to send a shiver down my spine when I recalled my nightmarish meeting with them.

I took a taxi home from the Oasis every night now, despite the expense, too frightened to walk anywhere alone. The gang was made up of the very worst kind of pan-pan and worked the area between Yurakucho and the Kachidoki Bridge, which they now claimed as their own territory. Dressed in lurid clothes, their faces garishly painted, they demanded the right to organize all the girls in the surrounding streets, which, of course, meant harassing them and stealing from them whatever they could. And it was my bad luck that these girls, for some unfortunate reason, had decided that I needed to be punished.

I was squatting in the filthy lavatory shed outside the Oasis when I felt a sharp pain, as if hot needles were passing through me. I didn't need to guess what it was. The other girls had worried about it often enough.

The doctor confirmed my suspicions as he made his rounds the following week. I was distraught. Mr. Shiga would be informed and I wouldn't be able to work for weeks. Money would have to be found for medicine—which wasn't cheap, only available on the black market—and during that whole time I wouldn't earn a single sen.

When Mr. Shiga summoned me to his office, I got down on my hands and knees and begged him to advance me a loan. To my horror, he dismissed me on the spot.

"You've been an embarrassment for months now, Takara-san," he said. "Just look at yourself. You're spent."

Stunned, I packed up my makeup and my collection of trinkets and walked out of the old bomb shelter for the last time. When I got home, I filled the pail from the standpipe in the street. Inside, I undressed and slowly sponged myself down. I studied myself for a long time in the mirror. Mr. Shiga was quite right. Hollow sockets stared back at me, and my hair was lank and brittle. A red sore glowed at the side of my mouth and my belly was swollen, my ribs showing beneath my breasts, shrunken now like old gourds. I looked like a ghost.

Wearily, I wrapped up my beautiful green kimono, and took it back down to the Shimbashi market.

"Back already, dear?" the old lady clucked. She smoothed out the fabric and counted a few notes and coins into my palm. Confused, I asked if she had made some kind of mistake: it was less than half what Michiko had paid just a few weeks before.

"Take it or leave it, dear," she said, her nose wrinkling. "There's plenty more like you about."

I felt at a complete loss. Then, from over by the railway arches, there was a flash of colour. This was the heart of Blood Cherry territory. I quickly stepped behind the old woman's table, laden with kimonos, as unfamiliar girls headed toward the market.

Somehow, in the light of day, they seemed different. Glowing with life, they scoured the stalls, biting apples and flinging the cores over their shoulders. They barged their way through the dreary crowd in their bright Western dresses the colour of bruises, picking out whatever they fancied and flicking banknotes under the noses of the peddlers. As I stood there, hiding, I felt a sudden stab of realization. They really were different from me.

They were honest. All this time, I'd let Michiko and the managers fill my head with sheer nonsense—we weren't common prostitutes, no, we were Butterflies, Foreign Consorts, modern-day Okichis! But we were all just whores, plain and simple. At least these girls admitted it.

In one fell swoop, they'd cast away the twisted ideals, the slogans and the lies we'd been fed for so many years, the deceit which had brought our country to the brink of ruin. So much for honour. These girls were the lowest of the low, and they just didn't care.

These were the New Women of Japan, I thought angrily, not us. No happy endings for them. No imperial palaces, no tragic affairs like Kyoto geishas. They would smoke and spit and sell themselves for the last penny, until one day they would collapse in the gutter: dead and honest, and free.

The next day, I washed, dressed in my brightest clothes and painted my eyes in vivid colours. I took the Yamanote Line to Shimbashi and walked in the direction of Tokyo Bay, past the old, abandoned market, toward the dull steel arches of the Kachidoki Bridge. The sky was pale and blustery, and there was a reek of fish. I examined the card that the Blood Cherries had left.

The house was a big, broken-down mansion that must have belonged to some merchant at one point. A girl dressed in a short green skirt opened the door. She wore a sprig of clover in her hair and her eyelids were shaded with silvery-green powder, like the wings of some exotic butterfly.

I bowed meekly as she showed me through to a gutted hall. The place looked like an enormous, smashed-up doll's house. Landings jutted out from the walls, splintered stairs and ladders led up through holes in the collapsed ceiling. Dozens of girls lounged about in their underclothes on the bare flag-stones with cigarettes in their mouths, playing flower cards and swigging from a large bottle they passed between them. Piles of clothes were scattered all around and a large mirror stained with verdigris was ratcheted to the split wooden panelling of one wall.

Underneath the staircase, a gaudy little shrine had been set up, decorated with star-shaped scraps of silver paper and burning candles. Torn-out pictures of angels had been pasted in a circle on the crumbling plaster, and in the centre, a carved statue of Jesus Christ was splayed upon a wooden cross. He was naked but for a loincloth, his head turned away, as if he couldn't bear to look at the world.

The plump girl was kneeling before it, hands clasped, mumbling to herself. Junko stepped forward from a large, dark hole in the wall, steadying herself as she came toward me. Her face was smooth and white, framed by tight black curls, and she wore an enormous pair of round sunglasses. Little prickles, like bedbug bites, lined the white skin of her inner arms.

"Did you know that Maria-sama was a virgin when she gave birth to Jesus Christ?" she rasped. She waved at the fat girl. "Yotchan over there believes that if she prays hard enough, Jesus Christ will make her a virgin again!"

She laughed, her neck wrinkled and sagging beneath thick powder.

"How old-fashioned!" she spat. "Relying on a man for everything."

She smiled tightly and took off her sunglasses. Her eyes shrank as she looked at me.

"You've come to work for me now, is that it?"

I nodded.

"They always do."

She held up bony fingers in front of my face, counting them

off. "Eight yen a time. That's the standard rate. Four goes to us. Two more for food and drink. You work out the rest."

Two yen. It really wasn't much. A packet of cigarettes alone cost twenty. But I bowed my head, feeling a painful itch between my thighs and a sharp desire for one of my little pills.

Junko came very close and pressed her fingernail against the skin of my cheek.

"Holiday season for the yankiis," she mused. "Plenty of work for a pretty girl like you."

The other girls had abandoned their games now and crowded in front of the big mirror, painting their faces and trying on different pieces of clothing.

"Well, then," Junko said, "time to get ready."

Nervously, I prepared myself behind the scrum of girls. After half an hour, Junko clapped her hands, and the girls gathered in a wide circle, turning to face each other. One of them pulled me in, stretching out her tongue. All the other girls were doing the same, placing little tablets into each other's mouth as they stared into each other's eyes. The girl beside me gave me my tablet, and I felt my heart pounding as it dissolved. The big bottle of shochu went around the circle and I took a deep swig, washing the pill down my throat.

The girls held each other's hands. We stepped forward and swooped them into the air. *Banzai!*

Excited and nervous, the girls streamed toward the door. As I passed, Junko gripped my wrist.

"You see?" she hissed. "You were one of us, all along."

The night was freezing and there were patches of black ice on the ground. The girls were dressed in all the colours of the rainbow, their hair styled in rumpled permanents, their lips swollen like dark petals. Restless from the pills they had taken, they screeched out vulgar comments to nervous passersby.

Junko walked beside me with Yotchan following. The faint

smell of the sea drifted toward us from the nearby bay, and as we passed the pale green roofs of Hongwan Temple, girls peeled away down side streets. Junko prodded me in the back to indicate that I should carry on. My throat was very dry and my heart was beating fitfully as I thought about the night ahead.

The streets grew busier as we crossed the Ginza and turned north toward Yurakucho, following the brickwork of the overground train track. Deliverymen rode by on bicycles, their baskets piled high, and Americans strode muffled up against the cold, grinning and clapping hands with each other.

"Over there," Junko commanded. We were at the back of Yurakucho Station. She pointed to a low-slung tunnel beneath the train tracks and I went in and leaned against the cold, glazed tiles. Junko stood beneath a nearby streetlamp in a freezing cloud of mist.

Soon enough, an elderly Japanese man approached, peering into the tunnels like a nervous crab. His breathing was heavy as he inspected me through his glasses.

"How much?" he asked.

"Eight yen, sir," I said. "Worth every penny."

He grunted and wrenched my arm so violently that I cried out.

"Not so rough!"

"Hurry up," he said, already unbuttoning his trousers.

Junko was standing against the streetlamp as he pushed me deeper into the low tunnel. Her arms were folded, and her face was filled with triumph.

Headlights blazed white. Sirens blared and there was a roar of engines as military trucks careened wildly toward us. The old man thrust away my hand and hobbled off as fast as he could. Jeeps screeched to a halt on each side of railway track, men leaping down from the cabs, searchlights flashing in bright beams. Women ran out of the tunnels like rats from their holes, screaming as American and Japanese police caught hold of them. They hauled them by the waist and swung them into the open-backed trucks as if they were sacks of rice.

I was blinded for a second as a truck veered toward me, its wheels sliding across the icy gravel. Two Japanese policemen leaped out, advancing upon me with torches. I gasped as one of them grabbed my wrists and jerked so hard that my arms nearly came out of their sockets. The other gripped the collar of my dress, and I heard the fabric tear as he dragged me toward the back of a truck like an animal.

"What are you doing?" I shrieked. "Get off me!"

"We're clearing up tonight," the policeman snapped. "You whores are giving Japan a bad name."

Us? I thought, speechless with rage, despite myself. *Us, giving Japan a bad name?*

"How dare you," I cried. "We're the only honest ones left!" I kicked at his leg, but he shoved me heavily into the back of the truck and I tumbled onto the cold, rumbling metal floor.

As I pulled myself up, I could smell cheap perfume. Girls were perched on the narrow benches that lined each side of the truck bed. All of them were pan-pan and they had covered their faces with their hair in shame.

"Where are they taking us?"

Nobody answered. Through the canvas flaps, I could see lights and decorations and Americans crowding the Ginza. We came to a juddering halt by the Continental Hotel, as a line of staff cars dropped off men and women in dinner dress. As the truck jerked forward, a sleek American sedan pulled up, and a bellboy rushed over, saluting as he opened the back door. A man in white dress uniform climbed out, holding out a hand to his companion. A petite Japanese woman emerged, taking a second to smooth the black velvet of her cocktail dress as she handed the bellboy a white fox coat.

"Michiko!" I screamed, leaping up. "Michiko!"

For a second, I thought she had heard me. She cocked her head to one side. Then, as the officer took her hand, she stood on tiptoe and kissed his cheek. His hand slid down her back and he guided her up the red-carpeted stairs toward the lobby.

The truck pulled away, the figures shrinking as we accelerated up the avenue.

We crossed the Kanda River and turned onto the Edo Road. We would pass through Asakusa next, I thought, picturing the Sumida Park to one side of the road, the charred remains of my neighbourhood on the other. As we passed the Kototoi Bridge, an ominous feeling came over me. I had an sudden inkling of where we were being taken.

The Yoshiwara canal was dark, the water low. As we crossed the bridge, I had a vivid memory of Hiroshi, standing on the high bank as I floundered down there, fire pelting from the sky.

I groaned and pulled my hair over my face. Thank heaven he couldn't see me now, I thought. Thank heaven he was dead.

The truck crunched to a halt. The canvas flaps were pulled aside to show a huge, solitary building with flat grey walls lit by floodlights. Women shouted and screamed as policemen hauled them from the trucks, and I climbed down, shivering in the freezing night. American soldiers and Japanese doctors herded women toward a gatehouse, and from high above came an eerie shrieking. I gazed up at the towering building, shielding my eyes. Women were leaning out the windows on each level, waving and howling. We swarmed toward the building as truck after truck rolled up to deliver yet more girls, and the women called down in a dreadful chorus, their hair falling wild about their shoulders, tattered white gowns swaying in the wind. It was as if they were a horde of screaming souls, welcoming us to hell.

18
PUBLIC RELATIONS
(*Hal Lynch*)

The corridors of the Continental were quiet and the peace of the Sabbath reigned throughout the building. A smell of roasting chicken drifted from the basement dining room and from the recreation hall came the echoing tap of an eternal game of ping-pong. I locked my door and heaved my knapsack onto the bed and retrieved my rolls of film. Jittery and exhausted, I needed to sleep, but felt a deep and anxious need to develop my photographs straight away.

I figured I could use the darkroom in the basement of the newspaper office without being disturbed, so I took a taxi without changing my clothes. As I'd hoped, the newsroom was empty, the building silent.

I felt a tightening in my stomach as I drew the first spool of glistening negatives from the reel. On the train, I'd been gripped by an irrational fear that something would have gone wrong with the exposure, that radioactivity in the city would have somehow damaged the film, that all I would be left would be blank prints and uncertain memories. But now the tiny scenes threaded out in miniature under the red glow of the safety lamp, mute testament to all that had occurred.

Once the negatives were dry, I lined up the paper beneath the enlarger head and fed the strip through. I exposed the paper to the light, ticking off the seconds until they were done. One by one, I shook the sheets in the developing fluid. Slowly, the mysterious images welled back into existence.

As the pictures hung there, dripping on the drying line, a

deep sensation of loneliness washed over me. The mangled pile of bicycles in the riverbed. The curving ribs of the ruined dome. The silent Buddha, smiling enigmatically as snowflakes settled upon his head. I recalled a strange story the ambulance driver told me, of how people's shadows had been seared into the stone of the bridge at the moment of the flash, and as I looked into the ancient eyes of the dance instructor, the frail, smiling face of the withered railwayman, I had a sudden comprehension of the deep, lingering malaise the victims had complained of, the terrible void that had developed within them, as if a cancer had consumed some vital part of their souls.

While the prints dried, I went upstairs to the empty newsroom. At my desk, I fed a sheet of carbon paper into the drum of a Smith-Remington. I stared at the blank page for what seemed like an eternity. Then, almost without thinking, I began to press my fingers on the keys and a confusion of words and letters slowly clicked out onto the page.

"*The Aftermath of the Atom,*" I titled the piece. I described the day simply and clearly, from the moment I arrived at the station to the second my train back to Tokyo passed into the tunnel. Darkness had fallen outside the big plate windows by the time I was done. The pool cast by my lamp was the only light burning in the building. I rolled out the final sheet and read the last paragraph out loud.

"*While most of the victims of 'radiation disease' are now dead, it seems clear now that this terrifying new weapon has a capacity to destroy even beyond that which its creators foretold. It has the capacity to plant the seeds of a lethal sickness into men's bodies, to scatter poison into their very souls. Whatever the justification for the atom bombing of Japan, any government that believes in justice surely has a duty to help those that it has unwittingly—or wittingly—exposed to this sickness, this creeping death that still lurks in men's bloodstreams so many months after the smoke has cleared.*"

The heavy newsroom door creaked open and I lurched up in my chair. A tuneless whistle came from the corner of the room and the big overhead lights glimmered on. Eugene. He assumed the comical expression of a boy caught with his hand in the cookie jar.

"Hal!" he exclaimed, striding toward me. "Don't tell me you're working? On a Sunday night?"

I smiled, hastily covering up the pages on my desk.

"How about you, Eugene? Feeling guilty about something?"

The corners of his mouth turned down.

"Let's just say I forgot something." He opened the drawer of his desk and palmed a package of prophylactics into his overcoat pocket. He parked himself on my desk with a grin.

"Where have you been anyway, Hal? We never see you anymore."

I felt a pang of sympathy for my old roommate. He'd never seen any action, just like all the other fresh recruits now garrisoned in Japan. The country was like a playground for him.

Grime and dirt were ground under my fingernails and developing fluid stained my skin. As I looked up at his cheerful, freckled face, the crooked wire-rimmed glasses beneath the wild thatch of hair, I felt a curious collision of instincts. After a moment of hesitation, I gathered the sheaf of papers on the desk and handed it to him.

"Proof this for me, Eugene."

He licked his thumb and forefinger as he flipped through the pages. Surprise, astonishment, confusion progressed across his face as he read. I slumped in my chair, aware of the sour reek of my unwashed body. When he finally finished, he gave a low whistle.

"Boy oh boy, Hal. Do you think Dutch'll go for it?"

I laughed, despairing. "You know I wasn't planning to file it to the *Stars and Stripes*, Eugene."

He adjusted his glasses. "Right. So—where are you going to file it?"

I shook my head. "I've no idea. One of the nationals, maybe."

His face crinkled with apparent distaste. "So you're a Fancy Dan now, Hal?"

I shrugged.

"I don't get it Hal. Why are you so bothered about the Japs all of a sudden? They started it, right?"

I didn't know what to say. I just led him down to the basement and gestured at the prints. He examined each in turn, pausing every now and then to take a closer look. He became silent for a long time, brow furrowed.

"They're quite something, Hal."

"Thanks Gene."

"SCAP was upset enough about the rat guy."

I laughed, picturing Dutch in his office, accusing me of being morbid.

"They sure were, Gene."

He glanced at me in doubt.

"You're sure you want to do this, Hal? You know it means trouble. Why not let sleeping dogs lie?"

"I can't."

"You can't?"

I shook my head.

"Discuss it over a drink?"

I shook my head again. I suddenly yawned, my eyelids like lead.

He sighed. "Well. Okay, Hal. Suit yourself."

He patted me on the shoulder. "You get some rest, Hal, do you hear me? You'll be here tomorrow, right?"

I nodded.

"Okay. See you around."

There was a vague sound of whistling as he climbed the

stairs, and the heavy office door closed with a thud. I was hopelessly fatigued. The lights and the scent of chemicals made my head swim as I unpegged the prints from the line. Upstairs, I peeled the carbon from the line and slid the photos and the story into my drawer.

The next day at noon, freshly showered and shaved, I walked back into the newsroom. Faces glanced up at me, then swiftly dropped away. The room fell silent but for the echo of typewriter keys.

"Someone die?" I asked, with a pang of trepidation. "Who was it? The Emperor?"

Upon my desk lay a scribbled memorandum in Dutch's handwriting: "ASAP."

As casually as I could, I sat down and opened my drawer.

It was empty. Over in Dutch's office, figures were silhouetted against the glass. The muffled sound of argument was rising from within.

Keeping an eye on the door, I walked to the stairs, and then ran down. In the darkroom, I switched on the lights. The developing tins were neatly stacked in the corner. Even the drops of fluid on the floor beneath the drying line had been mopped clean. I got back upstairs just in time to see Eugene arriving at his desk. When he saw me, his smile froze. Over his face passed the look of a whipped dog.

The door to the office swung open and two military policemen stepped out. Behind them followed an extremely anxious-looking Dutch.

"Ah, our roving reporter!" he called when he spotted me.

The MPs loped over as Dutch stood rubbing his head. One of them squared up to me.

"Mr. Lynch?" he asked. Puffy-faced, his skin was as soft as a boy's. I realized, absurdly, that I recognized him: the petty officer who'd sat next to me on the gun turret of the *Missouri*, the day of the surrender signing. He showed no sign of recollection.

"We've been asked to fetch you, sir."

The friendly southern drawl was incongruously loud in the newsroom. Everyone was still staring at their typewriters in studious concentration.

"May I ask by whom, officer?"

"Just come along with us, would you, Mr. Lynch?" he said, placing an encouraging hand on my arm. "There's some folks who'd like to talk with you."

The Public Relations office was located in a sinister-looking building that had once been home to Radio Tokyo: the voice of the Japanese Empire. From here, bulletins of lightning victories had rung across the Pacific, the shortwave siren song of Tokyo Rose. The concrete box was painted jet black—camouflage against night attack.

Flanked by the MPs, I walked up the stairs as a man I somewhat knew emerged from the doorway. George LeGrand was a photographer from *LIFE* magazine who'd approached me a few weeks earlier, to ask my advice on aerial photography.

"Hello, Lynch," he said pleasantly, nodding toward the MPs. "Everything in order?"

"Hello, LeGrand," I said. "It seems the brigadier general wants to speak to me about something."

"Baker?" he asked, raising his eyebrows. "Good luck."

Brigadier General Frayne Baker was MacArthur's new head of Public Relations—a stony, white-haired North Dakotan, as mean and surly as his predecessor.

"In any case, you'll find him in good cheer."

"Is that so?"

"I've come from him just this moment. We've all been on an exciting duck hunt."

"Oh?"

"That's right. The Imperial Palace invited him to the Imperial Wild Duck Preserve to try his hand. They give you these big nets, you see . . . "

The southern boy cleared his throat.

"I'd best be on my way, LeGrand."

"Okay, Lynch. See you around." He glanced at the MPs, then winked at me. In a stage whisper, he said: "Don't worry too much about Baker. He's had a damn good lunch."

The office door was open and I walked in. Baker was sitting behind his desk, cap askew, eyes closed, hands clasped across his chest. A trio of ducks lay on one side of the desk, necks tied together with twine, beaks hanging disconsolately open. There was a musty smell, and I was reminded of my father in his den, a bottle on the table, sleeping off his lunchtime load.

My missing piece was on the table, heavily scored with blue pencil, thick initials circled in the margins. Two photographs lay beside it. I recognized the picture of the schoolteacher. Next to it was the photo of the Buddha statues. The print had been torn precisely in half.

Baker's eyes flickered open. He spent a second staring at me, attempting to focus on my face.

"What the hell are you doing in here?" he snapped.

"I was told to come, sir. Obliged."

He gave a sullen growl and rubbed the stubble on his chin. "Who's your editor?"

"Dutch. That is, John Van Buren, sir."

"*Stars and Stripes*?"

"That's correct."

He placed his big, liver-spotted hands down on the table. "You do him a great disservice. As you do your paper."

"With the greatest respect, sir—"

"Respect?" His eyes flashed. "What does a *Stars and Stripes* man know about respect? Do you respect military interdict?

What in the hell is a *Stars and Stripes* reporter doing in a restricted area in any case?"

"With the greatest respect, sir, the *Stars and Stripes* has a tradition—"

"Damn the *Stars and Stripes*, sir!" The fist slammed down upon the table with such violence that the beaks of the ducks rattled faintly together. "Damn you. Don't you know I could have you court-martialled right here and now? Do you understand that?"

My mouth was dry. "The public has a clear interest in knowing what is happening in Hiroshima—"

"The public has all the information they need about Hiroshima, son!" A vein bulged in his forehead, and I tried not to flinch, picturing my father at the height of a fit. "Don't you worry about that. This—" He gestured at the table. "This—horseshit? You think you know better than our best medical men?

"I want to report what I saw, sir—"

"What you saw? What you were shown, don't you mean? And who showed it to you? The Japs!"

He stood up, perspiration shining on his forehead. As he leaned forward, I could smell the boozy cave of his mouth.

"Did it ever strike you as convenient, what you saw? Gave you a guided tour, didn't they? Your own private freak show. Ever consider why they were so keen to show you around?"

A pang of doubt struck me. In my mind's eye, I saw the police chief scowling at me: *Now—show America what it has done.* Dr. Hiyashida's familiar wave, his gleeful pride as he showed me his most pathetic victims. *Take more pictures! For your newspaper!*

I swallowed. Baker's eyes twitched. "Played you for a fool, you idiot. Don't you see? You're a sap. A first-class fucking sap."

He picked up my article and slapped it with one hand. He snorted, as if faintly amused. "Radiation disease."

He threw the pages in the air, and they fluttered incoherently to the floor. "Horse. Shit. Tell me, son. Were you ever in a battle against the Japs?"

"I was a lieutenant in Third Recon—"

"Well, I was a general at fucking Bataan, Lieutenant!" he hollered, smashing his fist upon the table again. "You ever hear of something called the Death March? That mean anything to you? You ever hear of a place called Pearl Harbor?"

His eyes were blazing, consumed with fury. He pointed to the door.

"Get the hell out of here." His ruddy face had ripened to a deep maroon, his tongue lolling from his mouth like an overheated dog's. "Get out!"

I rotated swiftly and marched out the door, as tiny, ruffling feathers floated up from the corpses of the ducks.

Dutch stroked the ginger-blond hair that he grew long below his pate, looking at me with watery eyes.

"There's no chance, Hal, I'm sorry. No chance at all."

His face was grave, like a doctor informing me of a terminal illness. "And there's trouble. It's gone all the way up. They've been asking me some pretty tough questions about you."

"Such as?"

"Such as whether you are, quote, some kind of subversive. Whether you are a communist."

"Am I, Dutch? In your opinion?"

He gave a long sigh. "Times are changing, Hal. I think there's going to be another war coming soon."

"So. What did you plead?"

"I told them about your fine work in reconnaissance. I told them about your commendations. I told them that you may have been . . . disturbed by what you saw from up there. That you may be feeling the need to make some kind of recompense."

"I'm a bleeding heart, Dutch, is that it? Or are we pleading insanity?"

"Hal. I'm putting my neck out for you here."

"What's the verdict, Dutch?"

He shook his head. "You're suspended, Hal, for the time being. Pending their decision on what to do with you."

"What about my other pieces?" I said, sullenly. "'The Touristic GI?'"

"I'm sorry, Hal," he said, with more emphasis.

"And you've agreed to all this, Dutch? What kind of newsman are you? Whatever happened to the crucible of change?"

He laughed. "What do you want me to do, Hal? They're threatening to have you court-martialled for travelling to a prohibited area. How can I publish journalistic pieces from a military prison?"

He looked down at the desk, guiltily. "And I've been asked to take back your press pass, Hal. I'm sorry."

An unexpected lump rose in my throat as I slid the square of crumpled paper out of my wallet, the scrawl of MacArthur's signature smudged now as I placed the pass upon the desk.

"What's going to happen to me, Dutch?"

He leaned forward. Sotto voce he said: "Strictly between you, me and the gatepost, Hal, I think you've been lucky. Believe it or not. I gather there's been some kind of falling-out upstairs about what to do with you. There's a certain amount of . . . tension between Intelligence and the New Dealers."

"So they're not slinging me out?"

"Not yet."

"I can't write, but I can stay?"

He shrugged. "For now at least."

Limbo, I thought. *The realm of lost souls.*

"Okay, Dutch," I said. "I'm going to go get my head down."

A pained look came over his face. "That's another thing I

need to tell you, Hal. You're going to need to find another place to live. They're taking away your billeting rights."

I let out a short laugh.

"That's right. They're a petty, vindictive bunch when they want to be. And you won't be able to draw rations either. You've got two weeks."

"No more powdered eggs, Dutch?"

"'Fraid not."

"No more gratis Luckys?"

"No, sir."

"Alright. Thanks, Dutch."

"Wait, Hal," he said as I stood to leave.

"Don't tell me. I'm not invited to the Christmas party."

His face was serious. His throat moved. He opened up his drawer and took out a slim envelope and slid it toward me.

I glanced at him in question. His brow rippled.

"You know, it's very bad form for a photographer to leave negatives in the enlarger head, Lynch."

I stared at him. I could hardly recall leaving the darkroom the night before, I'd been so tired. He nodded at the envelope. I half opened the brim.

Inside was a cut spool of maybe twenty photographs, shots I'd taken at the hospital. My heart leapt, and I grasped Dutch by the shoulders, kissing his bald head.

"Alright, alright," he spluttered.

"I won't forget this, Dutch. I mean it."

He wiped his head with his handkerchief. "Merry Christmas, Hal. Enjoy your tinned turkey while you still can."

I suddenly pictured Dutch in his paper Christmas hat, playing Santa amongst his horde of redheaded children. I couldn't help but smile.

"And your eggnog!" he called out plaintively, as I left the room.

19
CHILDREN OF THE EMPEROR
(*Hiroshi Takara*)

Tomoko and I were lying on the floor of Ueno Station, gazing up at constellations of fireflies. The Yoshiwara canal was strewn with fire as we sat on the concrete embankment and I kissed her and stroked her black hair. Then we were beneath the iron rivets of the railway track, a train screaming overhead as I fumbled with the fly of my khaki uniform, twisting her hair as I pulled her toward me—

I woke with a shout. The room was dark and Koji was whimpering in his sleep beside me. My heart pounded as the dream floated away, leaving me utterly appalled and ashamed.

Tomoko had hardly said a word since the night of her attack. Once again, she had retreated into that silent, distant world where she'd hidden after leaving her home, as lonely and haunted as her old slit-bomb shelter. No one had spoken as we trudged home that night. The children were all aware that something awful had happened. When we reached the inn, Tomoko went straight through to the bathhouse and slid shut the door behind her. I realized that the water would be icy cold and so sent Aiko in to ask her if I should light the boiler. When she came back a moment later, she shook her head.

"Go upstairs and lay out the blankets, then."

She nodded and darted up the staircase, not daring to look at me.

There was a clanking of pipes, and I gazed at the paper screen of the bathroom door. On the other side, Tomoko would be sitting on the cedar stool, her monpe crumpled in the corner and growing dark and soaking wet. Naked, her skin white, splashing the cold water over her breasts—

To my horror, I was becoming stiff.

There must be a kind of demon living inside me, I thought, as I tramped along the Ginza. That was the only answer. I'd taken to walking for hours across the city every day now, watching the Americans with their arms around Japanese girls, indulging in wild and violent fantasies of revenge.

The Matsuzakaya department store had been turned into a shop for the Americans. Behind the steamed-up windows, Westerners crowded the aisles, picking out tins and boxes. Next door was a club, set in an old bomb shelter. Japanese girls stood hopefully outside, trying to coax the GIs in.

I'll find a pistol, I thought. *A Nambu Type 14. I'll track that bastard down to some brothel, wait outside until he comes out drunk into the street. And then—fire. Bam! Right in his face. Bam! Bam! Bam!*

Long after nightfall, I found myself walking past Hibiya Park, at the corner of the Imperial Plaza. Two huge pine trees stood erect and glittering in front of the American headquarters, and on the higher floors, yellow lights were burning. I wondered about the men who worked up there. Every one of them would have slept with at least one woman, I thought. A Western one and probably a Japanese one as well. Even the ugliest one amongst them would know all about the great, masculine secret that still lay beyond me.

The moon was full in the sky. You could see the rabbit in the moon tonight, I thought. Silvery light was rippling in the water of the palace moat, and down below, something bobbed in the darkness. I squinted, wondering if it was a dead rat. Another lump floated over, and, slowly, more and more came into view, bumping against the stone wall of the bank.

A thin American in wire-rimmed spectacles came over and stood beside me, his mouth open in a yawn. He threw something down into the water, fumbled for a moment, then began to piss into the moat. The splash slackened and he shivered like a dog before belching and buttoning himself up. I looked down again, slowly realising what the shapes were. Legions of used prophylactics were floating in the palace moat.

From the Imperial Plaza came faint sighs, grunts and cries of surprise. Against the wall of the gate, twisted shapes humped against each other in the moonlight, white buttocks of men encircled by coils of legs as women moaned out softly, then sharply.

It was hopeless. A moment later, unable to stop myself, I ran over to the trees and thrust my hand into my underwear. I rubbed myself swiftly and furiously until, after a few seconds, I felt a dark warmth flood inside my belly, overpowering me, and I shuddered, gasping, hot and cold all at once, feeling as if my stomach had melted out all over my thighs. I stood there breathless in the shadows, gripping onto a branch and quivering with shame.

It was a freezing cold night, and we were rummaging about in the garbage cans by a row of warped tenement houses. The eaves were low and stank of fish guts and night soil and the sickly sweet smell of rot swamped me as I stood arm-deep in refuse. The other children were hunting a short distance away. Tomoko was hunched over, her tunic sleeves rolled up. She was desperately thin now, and her skinny arms showed as she delved in a heap of peelings.

My fingers touched something and my heart suddenly leaped. A smooth sphere, soft and squashy. I clutched hold and tugged it out, flooded with excitement.

It was exactly what I'd hoped. A whole bean jam bun, untouched except for a tiny solar system of silver blue mould.

My mouth began to water as I held it to my face, inhaling the sweet smell of mochi.

Tomoko had once told me that they were her favourite thing to eat. She was still standing nearby, ghostly in the moonlight. The dough was sticky in my fingers as I urged myself to go over and give it to her, to make her a present of it. Here was the chance, I told myself, to break down the impossible wall that had come between us, a magical token that might somehow shatter the awful spell that had been laid upon her.

Aiko was standing beside me, her eyes wide.

"Look what you've got!" she trilled. The other children started to wander over.

"A whole bean jam bun! Will you give it to Tomoko?"

Tomoko glanced up as she heard her name spoken.

I suddenly noticed Shin standing in the darkness, a nasty grin on his face. My stomach knotted and my cheeks began to throb with embarrassment. I gave a short laugh.

"Give it to Tomoko? Why should I? I found it, didn't I?"

"But you always save bean jam for Tomoko," Aiko insisted.

Tomoko was still gazing at me in the moonlight.

Without knowing why, I stuffed the bun into my mouth. I tore at it with big wolfish bites, chewing with my mouth open like a peasant. Aiko stared at me, aghast, as I swallowed it piece by piece. It was dry and mealy, not nearly as nice as it had smelled. But I carried on regardless, stuffing it all into the wads of my cheeks.

The dough was so dry that it finally made me gag. I choked, and spat out the last mouthful. Aiko stared at the remains, as if she was about to cry. Tomoko stood, hunched over, gazing at the ground, her arms by her sides. My eyes filled with tears of shame.

Koji's voice came from the alleyway at the back of the houses. "Come quickly!" he hollered. "Come and look what I've found!"

I hesitated for a second. I wiped my sleeve across my eyes and rushed after him into the darkness.

It was the yard of what must have once been a teahouse. Crates of rubbish and empty bottles lay all around and a powerful stench floated from an old latrine shed.

"Look!" Koji crowed. He pointed at the ground. In between the crates lay obvious and ripe morsels. Apple cores, fish carcasses, mouldering pumpkins. The children scrambled forward, and I was just about to do the same, when I caught a movement from the corner of my eye.

"Stop," I said. "Don't touch anything."

My eyes adjusted to the darkness. The sleek corpse of a rat was twitching in the corner. Another appeared by the latrine, then another—dead and unmoving, wiry tails coiled, mouths open, tiny teeth bared in pain. I gingerly poked one with my foot and tipped it over.

The puffy flesh was writhing with maggots. My stomach heaved.

"Get back," I said. "Don't touch anything."

Koji's face fell, and his frail chest began to heave up and down.

"Leave it. Leave all of it. It's been poisoned."

The children stood there, mouths open, as if unable to believe we'd be leaving all of this feast behind.

"Let's go. Move!"

They still hesitated.

"Now!"

One by one, they slid back under the fence to the alley. As we gathered in the darkness, I suddenly felt horribly tired.

"Let's just go home," I said. "Let's all just get some sleep."

The children began to whine in frustration, still ravenous.

"Be quiet!" I yelled. "I can't stand it any more!"

I rushed ahead, tears in my eyes, not wanting the others to

see. Icicles hung from the eaves of the tenements as we stumbled through the back alleys like a clan of starving goblins. We were just passing through the wasteground at the back of Ueno Station when I heard a commotion behind me. Filled with helpless anger, I spun around, my fists raised.

My heart stopped.

Tomoko lay on the ground as the other children stood above her, trying to pull her up. She shivered uncontrollably, as if she was having a fit. Aiko started to scream as I rushed over and knelt down in the earth. Tomoko's hand was gripping onto something tightly and I tried to prise open her stiff fingers as she started to choke.

I thrust my fingers into her mouth and tried to wrench out whatever it was she had eaten. But she writhed violently from side to side, vomit seeping from her mouth. She suddenly retched and half-eaten fragments of fruit emerged. There, in the moonlight, were the black teardrops of apple pips on her glistening chin.

She gave an awful bark and her back arched and her limbs thrust out. She stared straight up at me and gripped onto my hand, her eyes filled with blurry tears. Her head shook, and she started to gasp. She froze, and then her whole body rose up, as if a terrible pain were passing along her spine. She shuddered and sank back down again, her eyes still staring at me as a fine, white froth leaked from her lips.

Her fingers slowly released their grip on my own. She slumped to the ground. A strange gargling emerged from deep within her body, and I fell backward.

Her features seemed to soften. She was gazing up at an uncertain point high above, as if toward some distant star, far away in the sky.

20
SILENT NIGHT
(*Hal Lynch*)

The festive season was upon us, and in celebration, SCAP hoisted two Christmas trees outside headquarters with a ten-foot banner across the façade: "Merry Christmas!"

After I got my marching orders, part of me considered leaving Japan. I'd go back to New York, I thought, get on the GI Bill and return to Columbia. Join one of the big agencies or magazines or dailies and make a living snapping mobsters and sports stars. Or I'd move to some honest-to-God small town, a Knoxville or a Jacksonville, take a job at the local paper and cover the high school football games, the petty brawls and larcenies that came to the county court each week. I'd arrive at the office bright and cheery in my gleaming new Cadillac every morning, settle down with a Southern girl and raise a litter of my own.

Then I thought of Christmas dinner with my mother and my aunts in the depths of a New England winter—the empty plate laid for my father, his sullen portrait glaring down from the wall. The snow falling silently outside, as if it were passing over the very edge of the earth.

So I decided to stay in Tokyo, to get drunk, and to see what the new year would bring. The men that still haunted the Continental were subdued now, almost meditative, resigned to another Christmas away from home. Most of the boys who'd seen action were already back home, their feet up in front of their well-deserved hearths in Lexington and Harrisburg and Worcester and all the other countless villes and burghs that make up the vertebrae of our nation. Those left behind walked the halls in their socks, wrote letters, played rummy and whist, busying themselves with innumerable small tasks to while away the time.

On Christmas Eve, SCAP organized a party. There was to be a dinner and a movie show, followed by a performance by "native musicians." I pictured the overheated hall, the red-faced officers in their paper party hats attacking their tinned turkey and eggnog. Douglas MacArthur standing up to make some flowery speech as the officers slumped over their trifles. It was all too god-awful to contemplate, and so, early in the evening, I wrapped up warm and headed out into the streets, alone.

It was bitterly cold that night, and everyone had their hats pulled down over their foreheads, mufflers pulled up to their eyeballs. I hitched a ride to Shinjuku on an infantry truck, but the driver got lost and took an unaccountable detour and we passed through the abandoned districts, the shantytowns of the old city. The water that flooded the bomb craters had turned to ice, old pieces of metal and timber frozen within, sticking out like the limbs of witches. Between the craters, clumps of people huddled around miniature braziers, burning paper, kindling, pieces of old furniture—anything that could hold a flame. Their hands cast flickering shadows over orange faces as they stared into the fires. They didn't look up as we passed.

The Infantry finally let me off outside the brightly lit, newly covered market by Shinjuku Station, where fresh, excited young GIs were swapping their cigarette ration for beer and whisky. I did the same and took a couple of nips right there to warm myself up. Then I wandered the streets with no particular goal in mind. Tacked to a newly cut telegraph pole, I discovered a handbill advertising a concert: Handel's *Messiah*. This intrigued me, so I asked a man for directions, and headed for the theatre. As I strode up the street, a couple of kids ran past me, frosted white from head to toe, as if they'd been rolled in sugar. I wondered whether this might be some strange Japanese seasonal custom, but then the rumble of a truck came from around the corner with GIs hanging from both sides, pumping out a great, whirling mass of white powder like a blizzard of fine snow—DDT. Folks were hurrying along after the truck to get disinfected as the powder drifted down and settled in restless shoals on the frozen ground.

I finally found the old theatre. Elderly couples in Western dress were walking inside as I paid my entrance fee to a beaming young woman. The roof of the amphitheatre was mostly gone—the building was open to the sky. From a slat seat above the stalls I could see a silver needlework of stars. Down below, the orchestra and choir tuned up on metal chairs, their breath emerging in glistening clouds. A couple of GIs were scattered solitary in the aisles, hunched up, clutching themselves for warmth. Everyone was shivering, so I had the bright idea of passing the whisky around. I tapped the shoulder of the man beneath me, who glanced at his wife, and then took the bottle with a murmur of surprise and gratitude. After he took a sip, I gestured for him to pass it on. It went steadily around members of the audience, who directed glances of appreciation in my direction, before it finally returned to me with the barest sip remaining.

Down below, the conductor tapped his stand and counted two silent notes in the air with his baton. Then the voices began to fill the frozen night and there was an exhalation from the audience. We all sank back into our seats, watching and listening as the exquisite voices of the choir billowed up into the sky in clouds of tiny diamonds.

I pictured the notes floating up, rising high above the ruined city, above the men and women who lay shivering in their shacks and hovels far below, huddled together around their flickering fires, silently staring into the flames and wondering what the future would bring. The voices flowed out across the night, and I thought about the folks back home in America, the Christmas trees lit up and the children scampering about in the snow as their mothers stood in the doorways, calling them in for dinner. I saw men and women all across the world, reunited after all these long years of war, mothers hugging sons, girls embracing sweethearts, fathers with tears in their eyes as they welcomed their children home, home from the war, back home to where they belonged, at last, for the war was over—*and they were alive.*

I saw stricken refugees trudging across the plains of Europe, frozen and weary as they settled down by their campfires, snowflakes whirling around them as they held each other's hands and haltingly began to sing. I saw solemn glasses being raised to lost fathers and brothers and sons—to the ones who had not returned—and I heard prayers of requiem and the sob of quiet mourning float up into the sky, mingling with the precious, holy notes of the chorus. I heard the great, melancholy music float out across the world, over the shattered cities and the bombed-out ruins, the fields of carnage and the tangled remains of the living and the dead, the terrible music that floated through the darkness that shrouded our silent, injured world that Christmas night, as, far below, its men and women all sat huddled together in front of their fires, staring into the flames and wondering what the future would bring.

When the concert ended, I applauded the orchestra for a long time, my hands numb within my gloves. I climbed down the steps to congratulate the conductor, then presented another bottle of whisky to the members of the orchestra, who smiled and bobbed their heads in thanks. I bowed back, and we all laughed and took sips, trembling with cold. The rest of the audience quietly departed.

There were few people on the streets as I headed for the station, and those who were out looked grim and unhappy. I offered another bottle to people at random, but most veered away, and I realized that I was drunk. Only one fellow took it—he unscrewed the cap, took a big swig, then grinned and gave me a thumbs-up: *Merii Kurisamasu!*

I finally reached the station. The chemical truck had just passed and dashes of white powder were drifting about in the air. Time for bed, I thought.

Then, from nowhere, a group of elegant old ladies in colourful kimonos were tugging at my sleeve, their eyes twinkling, their faces as wrinkled as walnuts. They must have been freezing near to death, but their hair was styled to perfection, their kimono belts exquisitely tied, and they were bowing and smiling for all they were worth.

"Please, please," they asked me in English, "can we *sing* with you?"

I didn't quite understand. Then one of them explained—they were Christians, she said, and this was the first Christmas they had been allowed to celebrate for several years. This made me pretty emotional and so I said yes, of course they could, in fact, we would all sing together, and so we took each other's arms. And then, this bold young man and these delightful, wrinkled women whose country I'd helped raze to the ground, well, we all stood there together outside of a ruined train station as flakes of DDT floated down from the sky like snow, and then, God help me, we began to sing "Silent Night."

PART THREE
APRÈS GUERRE
January 1946

21
YEAR OF THE DOG
(*Osamu Maruki*)

Mrs. Shimamura sang along to the radio as she washed the glasses: the inane and mournful chorus of "The Apple Song" was playing for the tenth time that day. She picked up the glasses one by one from the basin, twisting them this way and that so that drops of water flicked away from the rims, then swaddled them in the dishcloth and rubbed them vigorously, as if drying a child in a towel.

Her dimples had returned, I thought, as I watched her from my seat at the bar. I had my head in the pages of a story by the master, Jiro Tanizaki, my old idol, from his erotic, grotesque period. Once again, I revelled in his description of a lurid children's game, a leg bruising blue beneath sharp slaps. Ever since the end of the war, I had felt a jolt of excitement whenever I read the story, taken an odd pleasure in the thought of a sudden, stinging palm striking my own numb flesh.

A cold draft gusted in from the doorway and I gulped back my drink and shuddered, feeling a kind of sordid torpidity settle upon me. I studied the cover of the book. Tanizaki would still be writing, I thought, he would still be slogging away. Wasn't it at times of just such extremity and extenuation that art truly flourished? Japan eviscerated, a foreign army parading the streets—what would Tolstoy have made of it? Maupassant?

And yet here I sat, my lice-ridden overcoat draped over my shoulders, scribbling fantasies for the lost and the lonely. Hunched over my foul rotgut, tormented by constipation, a cough racking my lungs, my toes dissolving into the mouldy morass of my boots. Keening around a decent woman like Mrs. Shimamura like a camp dog, whining for scraps and sympathy. A wave of disgust washed over me, and my hand instinctively reached to my pocket for the tablets I kept there for just such moments of despondency. I popped one into my mouth, and bit down on it.

I felt a sharp crack and a shooting pain screwed all the way up the front of my face. I urgently probed my mouth with my tongue. There was a gap next to my front incisor, the rotten gum spongy like dank vegetation. I tasted rotten, metallic blood and spat the split remains of my tooth and the dissolving Philopon pill into my cupped hand: a swirl of blood and saliva, the amphetamine fizzing into tiny bubbles, the decayed tooth a black pearl.

Whatever next? I thought. Would my eyeballs dim with rheum, the last of my hair fall out? The dull ache in my liver seemed to pulse and flare. I felt utterly destroyed.

"It's all gone," I muttered. "Everything's gone."

Mrs. Shimamura came over. To my utter surprise, she put her tender, matronly arms around my neck. Disgusted with myself, I began to sob into her bosom.

"There, there," she said. "Stop being such a baby."

She turned to the bar, and poured me a glass from her private supply. Then she folded her arms and became stern.

"Now, sensei. Don't go getting yourself so upset about everything. You don't have it so bad. You're no worse off than a million others. So pull yourself together."

She turned back to her sink of dishes and started crooning again. I shrugged meekly, and went off for a lie-down upstairs.

There were many things that I pined for in those days following the war. Things that I fleetingly craved with an urgency I had never known before in my life. Persimmons were one of these; as for some reason, later on, were tangerines. I had always been partial to persimmons, of course, but tangerines I had never had any particular feelings about, until, on my return to Japan, quite suddenly, their dimpled, waxy skin, their tart sweetness, and, more than anything, their bright orange colour began to exert a powerful hold on my imagination. I could spot them from a hundred yards off at the black market, amongst the covered stalls and booths, the cups cast from melted fuselages and the muddled heaps of cast-off army garments: the tangerine vendor, his vivid fruit wrapped in newspaper at the back of a handcart. Cruelly, their price shot up almost as soon as they became more widely available; they all came via the American Postal Exchange, descending to us from the gods, as it were. And so they were to remain, perpetually hoisted just beyond my reach.

What I longed for more than anything, however, was a really decent, proper pair of shoes. Since my repatriation from the green hell of New Guinea, I had worn my hobnailed army boots day and night, as did most of the other returnees from the battlefield. After countless miles of trudging, swelling and shrinking, the cowhide had welded to my feet, so much so that it was now an effort to remove them. They entirely repulsed me. They were a badge of shame, a decrepit symbol of servitude to a suicidal ideal. They were uncomfortable as well: the metal heel rims had long since worn away, the seams split, and icy water leaked in around my toes whenever I stepped into one of the freezing puddles that lurked all across the city that winter. I cursed them every time my heel poked through the worn sole, every time the sodden laces squeezed the fragile bones of my foot. I had heard that certain black market shops sold looted officers' boots—high, elegant cavalry affairs cut from soft leather or European kid. But the thought of their buttery smoothness made me nauseous: they reeked of everything I despised. Perhaps, I thought, I could revert to wearing split-toe *tabi* and wooden clogs, as some of the other writers had done. But for all their homely charm, they too seemed fundamentally feudal to me, and, after all, they were hard and uncomfortable, and so very cold in winter.

No. What I truly aspired to was a good, sturdy pair of Western shoes. Enviously, I had observed an American civilian on the tram a few weeks previously wearing precisely the style I desired. A smart pair of burnished Oxford brogues, reddish brown, aglow with heathery tints. A thick lock of coffee-coloured hair fell over the man's angular brow; a neat, moulded camera case was slung over his shoulder. He sat holding his book, chin perched on hand, elbow on knee. One leg dangled casually over the other, a neat argyle sock clasping the ankle beneath. Then there was the beautiful shoe, rocking faintly back and forth to the rhythm of the tram. I was racked by a sudden, violent desire. When he alighted near Yurakucho Station, I pressed my face to the window, picturing myself casually clipping along the street, just as he did now. *Well*, I said to myself. *There at least goes a serious man.*

Perhaps as a man with real shoes, I might feel like a human being once more, after years of being nothing but a soldier and subject. The stopped clock of my life might start ticking once again—as a man of purpose, striding boldly into the future. Rather than just another faceless nonentity in a city of pinched, weary men, our service caps pulled over our eyes, our shoulders sparring with the wind as we trudged the disconsolate streets.

I hoarded every penny like a miser, denying myself tobacco, even shochu. I avoided the temptations of Kanda, and busied myself instead with my third edition of *ERO*. To my delight and good fortune, it met with considerable success. Struck by the popularity of the feature in our last issue, "The Dish I Most Lament," I decided this time to expand it to encompass the entire panoply of frustrated desires hidden in our citizens' souls that winter. Once more I circumnavigated the Yamanote Line, stopping passersby and asking them to describe their heart's most secret desire. They were hesitant at first, unsure of how to respond. Then, the words began to spill out like a flowing river of dreams:

"My wife."

"My son."

"A good, long Noh play."

"Pickled plums."

"The knowledge that all of us Japanese were on the same side."

"A real coat."

"A working watch."

For me, though, it was always the shoes. I had taken to leaving my boots in the street at night now, plugged with newspaper to contain their rotten smell of fermenting soybeans. The cowhide was crinkled and frosty by morning, and I had to rotate the boots over the brazier to thaw them out. But even from there, they haunted my sleep. I would dream they were calling to me, that they might somehow slip back into the building, hop up the stairs and lace themselves earnestly back onto my feet while I slept.

I was in Shinjuku one afternoon when I saw a man wearing a sandwich board. When I read it, I thought that heaven must be smiling upon me at last. A shoe shop was opening that very day, not half a mile distant. I rushed over to the place, and urgently scanned the display.

There, in pride of place, was my heart's desire. A stout pair of russet Oxford brogues, stitched on each side with bronze thread. Barely worn, looking to be more or less my size. I darted in, demanding to try them on. The shopkeeper eyed me suspiciously while I wrestled them onto my feet. They were a perfect fit, snug and tight. I asked the man to tell me how much they cost.

The price was absurd. But I barely gave it a thought, and told him I would return directly. I hurried home to fetch all of my hoarded savings. Walking back to the shop, I became suddenly nervous, wracked by the thought that someone else would have purchased them in my absence. But when I arrived, they were still there. I thrust the money into the man's hands and tore my old army boots from my feet. I took the Oxfords in my hands, inhaling the cedary fragrance of the dappled leather, turning them to admire their subtle, coppery tints. I slipped them onto my feet, and firmly laced them up.

"Should I wrap these old boots in newspaper, sir?" asked the shopkeeper.

I glanced at them with loathing.

"Please dispose of them as you see fit, sir," I said. "I have no wish to see them again."

I turned on my heel and left the shop, feeling as if I were walking on air.

I made my way along the street, pausing every now and again to glance down. The leather pinched a little; I told myself it would take a while for my feet to become used to real shoes again. On the tram, I experimentally tried to cross one leg over the other, as I had seen the Westerner do, but it was an uncomfortable, constricting position and would take practice to perfect. Several of the passengers, I was sure, gave me sidelong glances. I casually extended my legs, rotating my feet from side to side in order to impress upon them the dazzle and flash of the shoes' superb leather.

So absorbed was I that I entirely missed my stop. I was now some distance from home. My feet were becoming quite painful, though this was only to be expected at first—this was simply how it was with proper shoes. An alley led off from the main avenue, and I was surprised, halfway along, to see the glowing lantern of a public bathhouse. This was an unexpected treat. Most of the *sentos* had been badly damaged during the bombings and those that remained had little fuel available to heat the pipes. For a people who so valued cleanliness, this was a considerable discomfort. I myself had not had a chance to bathe for several months. The thought of taking off my shoes and immersing myself in a hot pool of water filled me with exquisite pleasure.

It was a run-down tenement area and two children were tormenting a cat outside the building. As I approached, the cat went mewling away and the children slunk off—glancing, I noticed with helpless pleasure, at my bronze beauties as I ducked underneath the curtain.

The place must have been old-fashioned even before the war. Against the wall of the entrance hall was a row of wooden compartments with slotted hatches in which to store one's valuables, and a scrawny woman dozed away in a booth, her neck a mass of chicken skin. I unlaced my Oxfords, with some relief now, admittedly, and placed them in a compartment. I rapped a ten-sen piece on the counter and the woman yawned and waved me over to the male changing room.

The place was deserted but for the trickling sound of water, a faint mould growing over an engraved relief of furiously bay-onetting soldiers along the wall. As I peeled off my clothes, I was appalled by the odour of my body. I piled my coat, shirt and underclothes into a basket. Covering my nether regions with a hand towel, I slid open the door to the bathroom.

The air was dank and there was a chemical smell. But steam rose appealingly from the main pool and I shivered in antici-pation at the thought of climbing in. I took a wooden bucket, filled it from the tap, and then, on my low stool, began to soap and rinse myself with the deliciously hot water. The hue of the bubbles that ran off down the drain was disturbingly grey. My body was speckled with a patchwork of sores and bites from legions of ticks and fleas and the rampages of bedbugs. It was horrifying. I made a solemn vow to myself that I would track down one of the American trucks that were criss-crossing the city blasting out insecticide, and subject myself to a frosting.

Eventually, I seemed more or less clean enough, and I slipped into the big, steaming pool. I moaned with pleasure—it was utterly divine. I placed my hand towel on my head, and submerged my body in the hot water. After a minute, I opened my eyes.

What a startling sight. Somehow, I hadn't noticed how pale and shrunken my body had become. My skin was as white as tofu and my rib cage seemed to have sunk entirely into my chest. What a transformation had occurred since I had been called to the front. What an old man the war had made of me.

I sighed and sank back into the water. I mustn't feel sorry for myself, though, I thought, picturing Mrs. Shimamura's kindly face with affection. After all, didn't it seem now as if things might finally be on the up? The magazine went from strength to strength; it kept at least some flesh adhered to my bones. Perhaps I could fatten myself up a little. Cut back on my daily doses of shochu and Philopon, regain some of my prior sturdiness . . .

My thoughts drifted to Satsuko Takara, and I felt an acute sense of shame. The last time I had gone to the Ginza in the hope of glimpsing her outside her cabaret, she had not appeared, though I waited, shivering, until dawn. Perhaps she was dead now, I thought. Perhaps those visions of her on the street had been heaven-sent driftwood, to which I should have tightly clung.

I thought of the night when I had taken her to the anarchic revue at the Moulin Rouge, when she had laughed along as heartily as the students, even though she was just a shopgirl by trade.

A shopgirl. What did that matter, in any case? The war hadn't cared much for class, had it? The careful social grada-tion my mother had ruthlessly applied to every facet of her universe, from the pattern of a kimono belt to the arrangement of a teacup. What a mockery death had made of it all. Of rank, of ancestry. As if our blood type had mattered as the crimson poured from our veins; as if the bone fragments of a lowly private could be distinguished from a general's as they sluiced into the sinking mud of that tropical hell.

And if Satsuko Takara was a fallen woman, wasn't it I who was to blame? The man who had taken her virginity, as if it were a prize, the day before going to war?

I would find her again, I thought. I would seek her out, wherever she was in the city. There was little hope that we might rekindle our lost, unlikely love, such as it had been. The war had slaughtered my romantic capacities in any case. Yet, I might apologize to her for my failings. Make some small recompense.

I emerged from the bath feeling entirely cleansed. I dressed in my clothes, overwhelmed by their tarry stench of cigarette smoke and sour sweat. I vowed that I would make a bonfire, burn them all up in a great blaze. I'd buy myself a new set entirely, before going on my search for Takara-san.

I stood in front of the mirror; combed my hair; gave my teeth a quick scrub with my finger. I might even visit a teahouse on the way home, I thought. I felt more refreshed than I had in years.

As I emerged from the changing room, a sudden panic struck me. The scrawny old woman in the vestibule was asleep, her head tilted backward, a line of drool dangling from her mouth. The door to the compartment where I had left my shoes was open. I rushed over. The latch was up. The compartment was empty.

I seized the woman and shook her violently. She stared at me in dull incomprehension.

"Where are my shoes?" I demanded. "Why have you moved them?"

"I haven't moved them anywhere, sir," she complained, "Why should I?" She'd been right there, she said, keeping an eye on things all this time.

I had a sudden vision of the two boys outside. With choking trepidation, I darted out. The street was empty. Back inside, the woman was looking vexed, sucking at her lips and shaking her head.

"Oh sir!" she moaned. "Those two dirty children! They were playing right outside! They must have noticed sir's handsome shoes, and taken it into their heads . . . "

Oh, it was wicked, sir! Those dirty, wretched, evil little shrimps. Scampering about right by the entrance, she had told them to clear off, but she must have just dozed away for just a second. Oh sir! Whatever must the honourable gentleman think? Such nasty urchins. What a wicked place Japan had become, that two innocent little children could do such a shameful thing!

Methodically, I opened every other compartment as she prattled away, praying that I had somehow been mistaken, that I would open a wooden hatch to see amber contours glinting calmly back at me.

It was to no avail. They were all empty. I felt a hard lump in my throat, an intense sensation of loss, as if someone close to me had died. Wretchedly, I went back outside and looked up and down the street. It was no use. The area was deserted. The shoes were gone.

I shuffled from the bathhouse with bales of newspaper wrapped around my bare feet. They grew sodden and bitty as I negotiated the puddles, and soon threatened to disintegrate altogether. People passed by with smiles on their faces.

I stubbornly filed a complaint at the police box. The officer on duty rolled his eyes as he wrote out a form. He suggested that I go down to the nearby black market and search for them there—that was where most of the stolen goods in the area ended up, he said.

If he knew that, I asked myself sullenly, as I prowled up and down the aisles at the market, then why didn't he do something about it? Icy water had risen up the legs of my breeches now, and my feet were almost naked. It was dark by the time I found a stall selling shoes on the very edge of the market. It was just as the officer had suspected. My Oxfords were sitting there, in pride of place upon the trestle table.

I pointed at them. "Those are mine."

The stunted stallholder squinted up at me.

"Four hundred," he said. He glanced down at my naked feet. "Perfect for a gentleman like you."

"Four hundred? What are you talking about? I paid three for them just this afternoon."

He shrugged. "Take it or leave it."

"But they're mine!" I shouted. "They were stolen from me this afternoon."

The man came a little closer. "So I'm a thief, am I? Is that what you're saying?"

"Yes, yes, you are," I said. "They were stolen from me this afternoon by two urchins, no doubt paid by you—"

A heavy hand fell on my shoulder and twisted me around. Beneath a felt fedora, glittering little black eyes stared at me—the sharp yakuza boss who ran the place.

"What's the problem here?"

I stuttered, acutely aware of the pincerlike grip around my arm, the bulging muscles beneath the man's pale silk jacket.

"Those are my shoes," I managed to say. "This man has stolen them from me."

"Oh yeah?" the man slurred, picking them up and looking at them with a bored expression. "Well, they look like a pretty common style to me. There must be thousands like them in Tokyo. Don't you think you've made a mistake?"

"I should hardly think so. I had them on my feet not two hours ago."

He rubbed his forehead with a pained expression. "Look, mister, I think you've made a mistake. There's no need to be making wild accusations in public."

"But it's true," I said frantically. "Two children stole them from me this afternoon!"

"Look, mister," he said, squaring up. "You've made a mistake, now calm down."

"But they're mine!"

There was a piercing pain in the socket of my right eye, as his knuckle crunched against bone. I collapsed onto the ground, my vision black on one side, my head ringing.

"You've made a mistake, mister," said the tough, looming above me. "So forget about it now. Either buy something or push off."

He strolled away, wringing out his fist.

I slowly picked myself up. My glasses were dangling from my ears, smashed and useless. I could still see the dim, reflective red glow of my shoes upon the table, the man standing over them protectively.

"Alright then, damn you," I said. "I'll buy them back. But look. I can only afford a hundred."

I took out all the money I had left from my pocket, and laid it in a pile on the table. The man straightened up, as if I had offended him.

"One hundred!" he said, haughtily. "Outrageous. Don't you know these are Oxford brogues—they're made in London! I couldn't take anything less than three."

I almost started to sob as I looked helplessly down at my numb feet. The last of the newspaper clung to them in soggy strips, and my toes were raw and shrivelled, as if they'd been steamed.

The man grew more sympathetic.

"Look," he said. "A pair of these wouldn't suit you anyway. They're far too fancy. But I'll tell you what I can do. I can sell you a good pair of boots for fifty yen."

Good heavens, no, I thought, *not boots again, not after all this time.*

He reached beneath the table to pull out a hulking pair of army boots and laid them heavily down upon the table.

I recognized the smell straight away—the rancid odour of rotten soybeans. I picked one up, fingering the chafed cowhide, poking my finger through the familiar holes. Wearily, I pushed fifty yen in coins across the table to the man, who pocketed it neatly. I bent down and tugged the boots back onto my feet.

"Look!" the man said cheerily. "A perfect fit. You're lucky after all."

Wordlessly, I strode away from the market as the darkness and rain fell about me. As I trudged back home along the mucky street in my old, detested army boots, I had the curious feeling that they had somehow magically engineered the whole affair, that they possessed some supernatural power. That now, reunited with me again, they were finally content, and were smiling in secret triumph.

22
THE YOSHIWARA
(*Satsuko Takara*)

My ward was on the top floor of the crumbling grey venereal hospital, up five worn flights of stone stairs. Once the most notorious building in the busiest pleasure district of all Japan, chunks of plaster were missing from the walls and you could see the brickwork and horsehair beneath. The high-ceilinged hall was lined on each side by thin straw palliasses, the patient's belongings laid out beside them: wiry blankets, envelopes of tea, tangled strips of dried cod.

Every morning, we were given a bowl of rice gruel and set to work cleaning the never-ending wards and corridors. The tarry smell of the carbolic soap reminded me of the International Palace, and the chemicals turned my hands bright red and as scaly as snakeskin.

One afternoon, as I trudged back from work, my back aching from scrubbing and polishing the floor of the dining hall, I found a plump lady laying out her things by the mattress next to mine. When I knelt down and introduced myself, she smiled, dimples appearing in her cheeks. Ishino was her name, she said, in a husky voice, she ran a restaurant down in Nihonbashi. There was something familiar about her face, I thought. It was as if I'd seen her on a forgotten theatre poster, many years before.

"Help yourself!" she said, holding out an earthenware jar. "Pickled plums. Nothing like them to keep the doctors away."

I almost gasped as I tasted the sour juice for the first time in years. Mrs. Ishino spread a mat between our mattresses and laid out some rice crackers and dried seaweed, urging me to help myself. As I nibbled away, she glanced toward the door, and pulled a small flask from beneath her kimono jacket.

"Have a nip of this as well, dear," she said, handing it to me quickly. "Nothing like it for the cold."

It was strong and she nodded at me to take another sip. As the liquid reached my belly, it made me dizzy, and I started to smile.

Mrs. Ishino told me her story as we ate, kneeling on the ground like a comic raconteur on the stage. The day before, she said, the police had paid a visit to her bar in the middle of the night. I might not have heard, but they were enforcing new regulations now. In any case, they had carted her off to the hospital, along with the two girls who worked for her, Masuko and Hanuko. It was all very awkward. The doctors had performed their usual tests, and Masuko and Hanuko had been given the all-clear and sent home. But Mrs. Ishino herself had been unexpectedly diagnosed with something very unpleasant, and was obliged to stay on.

"And I know exactly who's responsible, Takara-san!" she said, waving her finger at me in a menacing fashion. "And he'll be for it when I get out of here, you just mark my words!"

I clapped my hand over my mouth, trying desperately not to laugh. But Mrs. Ishino just took a long swallow from her bottle, and burst into loud peals of laughter herself.

The patients wore padded kimonos of faded grey-green as they slouched on the floor. Some got on with piecework they'd been given to pay for their treatment, stitching trousers and dresses from strips of old uniform, or painting dolls as souvenirs for the hospital shop. It was shivering cold on the ward, yet they insisted on opening the tall, cracked windows in the late afternoon, when they would clamber up onto the sills to look out over the road below. It was like the cinema for them, as they hung there, screeching like vultures at anyone who passed. They saved their loudest chorus for any American soldiers, who waved up even as the girls made vulgar gestures.

Those first nights, after my diagnosis, I lay there, parched and desperate for one of my pills. I thrashed and shivered with feverish nightmares, my blanket soaking wet. But finally, after several weeks, I began to feel calm once again. My terrible dreams began to fade. One morning, when I awoke, I felt fresh, as if snow had fallen while I had slept. I realised that the suffocating spirits that had haunted me for so long had finally left my side.

There was a glint in Mrs. Ishino's eye as she sat down on her mattress that morning. A frayed towel hung over her shoulder and her hair was wet from the bathhouse.

"Good news, Satsuko-san," she said, as she tugged a comb through her hair. "I'm finally escaping at the end of this week. I've been given the all-clear."

Her news took me aback. I realised I'd become quite used to her comforting, matronly presence at my bedside each day as I woke.

"Well. I'm certainly very pleased for you, Mrs. Ishino."

She gave a sly smile. "And that's not all," she said.

"Oh?"

"I've heard a message on the wind that you'll be getting out of here too, Satsuko-san!"

I glanced at her in alarm. Despite the stink of the bedpans, the vulgarity of the patients and the backbreaking work, the gloomy ward had become something of a refuge, a place where I could hide away from the world and all its horrors.

Mrs. Ishino twisted her hair into a knot and knelt down beside me. "Satsuko-san, I wonder if I could ask you something."

"Anything you like, Mrs. Ishino!"

"I hoped that you perhaps you might consider coming to work for me. When you get out of here, I mean. The shop could always do with another pretty girl. Someone who's worked in the trade before, you know."

For a moment, my heart leapt, as I pictured myself in the old days, working at my father's restaurant—going back and forth amongst the tables with a big bottle of sake on my back, my skirts hitched up, serving dishes and joining in all the banter . . .

Mrs. Ishino was studying me. It dawned on me that this wasn't the trade she meant. She'd mentioned that her bar was popular with "a certain kind of American."

The picture faded as she took my hands in hers. "Why not come and join us, Satsuko-san? It's not such a bad place. You're sure to get on with the other girls. You could do much worse, you know."

I knew that she was right. The comfort stations had all been shut down, in any case. There'd been too many Americans going back home to their wives with unfortunate conditions. The only other place to go now would be the streets.

The thought of the broken-down mansion in Tsukiji, the drugged girls in their livid dresses, made me shudder. I took a deep breath, pulled together my kimono and knelt down on the floor in formal thanks. After all, it didn't seem that I could stay here any longer.

Mrs. Ishino herself came to collect me in a taxi on the day of my discharge. She made comforting noises as the doctors stamped my forms and wrote my name in the ledger.

As I walked out into the bright spring sunshine, I blinked.

"Look," I said, pointing.

Opposite the hospital, the first plum blossom had budded white against a row of scorched trees.

23
THE HOLIDAY CAMP
(*Hiroshi Takara*)

Plum blossom sprouted prickly white all over the trees in the Yushima Tenjin shrine. Bundles of wooden prayer plaques covered the racks outside so I guessed that the snobby students at the Imperial University must be having their examinations. A crowd of GIs were gathered in the garden beyond the arch and I wandered toward them to find out what they were looking at.

Beneath a blossoming plum tree, a Japanese girl stood dressed as a geisha. She wore a purple and crimson kimono and held a tasselled parasol over her shoulder, a gold fan hiding her face. The soldiers were all pointing cameras at the girl, squinting through the viewfinders, and the air was full of the exciting sound of the shutters clicking and film whirring. The girl shook the fan delicately, then snapped it shut.

Satsuko.

The girl looked so much like my sister that my heart actually stopped. I saw her treading water in the fiery canal; I almost felt the flames scorching my cheeks. One of the GIs called out and she shifted. Her eyes fell upon me, and my heart filled with terror.

There was no sign of recognition in her white-powdered face. I struggled to recognize the wide, deep black eyes of my sister as she turned her head, raising the fan again in another pose. Her nose was not quite right I realised—and she was much shorter that my sister, stocky even. An awkward sense of guilt and relief flooded my heart. Satsuko was dead, after all.

Down by the woman's feet was a cardboard sign scribbled with clumsy English: *Genuine Japan Geisha Girl. Photograph— 1 Yen.* There was a little tin can next to the sign, already filled with banknotes. She started spinning her parasol, pouting and pushing out her chest in a way that no real geisha would ever have done. Her face was as wooden as a doll's as the soldiers pulled her into position by her kimono sleeve, pushing their cameras right up in her face.

I thought of the tall American in the trench coat, who'd taken photographs of us that day by our baseball pitch. I remembered how I'd held the solid bulk of his camera in my hands, and how, for a moment, I'd caught Tomoko in the rangefinder, the twin images of her shy face blurred and sharp. There must be a photograph of her, somewhere, I thought. Perhaps I could track down the American somehow, ask him for a copy . . . Then, at least I would have something to remember her by.

A soldier was squatting in front of me. All of a sudden, I shoved him as hard as I could, and he fell over onto the gravel. I leaped on him, grasped hold of the camera and pulled, the man gasping and clutching at his throat as the leather strap garrotted him.

The strap snapped, and I tumbled backward, managing somehow to keep hold of the camera. I sprinted away through the garden, angry voices hollering behind me. A second later, heavy, crunching footsteps came hot on my heels.

Nearly stumbling in front of a bus, I sprinted across the avenue. As I ran alongside the university walls, horns blared— the soldiers were trying to hold up the traffic and negotiate their way to the other side. I spun around the corner and slipped through the famous Red Gate. Students and professors were coming out of the buildings and shouted at me as I dodged around them. I ran out past the quadrangle and through the back gate at the other side, then slid down against the wall, completely out of breath. As I pulled the camera out from beneath my shirt and examined the elegant dials and embossed serial numbers, my heart started to pound even harder. It was a Leica, just like the one that trench coat had used. I slid it into my canvas satchel, a fantastic idea forming in my mind.

Shin's hoarse voice was bellowing from inside as I paused outside the entrance to the inn, my hand on the wooden screen door. I slid it open a crack, and peered into the darkness. The children were all kneeling on the tatami of the reception hall, clearly engrossed in some kind of game. Nobu, Koji and Aiko had their heads bowed low and were whimpering as Shin strutted up and down before them, a blanket around his shoulders.

"Take me, sir," Koji said. "Please!"

Aiko jerked up her head. "No, sir! Take me!"

"What's in it for me?" Shin asked, in a strangled voice, as if he was an aristocrat. "You." He pointed at Nobu.

"I'll do anything you like, sir," Nobu pleaded.

Shin waved his muddy straw sandal in Nobu's face. "Kiss my feet then." Puckering his lips, Nobu gave his foot an unhappy peck.

Shin spun around and squatted over Nobu's head, gripping his shoulders as he spread his bandy legs. "Eat my shit!"

Nobu brayed like a donkey and pulled away. "No, sir!" he shouted. "Please don't make me!"

I heaved aside the rattling door and rushed into the hall.

"What's going on?"

Shin's face froze. Slowly, he began to give his wide, idiotic grin, showing the broken teeth behind his thick, curling lips.

"Well now, big brother's home at last," he said. "Got any treats for us today?"

"Shut up."

"Bean jam buns? Or is it apples again?"

I felt as if he had punched me in the stomach. Tomoko's body had lain for hours in the wasteground, as we struggled to dig down into a frozen bomb crater to inter her. Pale and blanched in the moonlight, her body had been withered away almost to a skeleton, black apple pips glistening on her chin.

"We were just playing a game," Koji stammered. The other children stared at me nervously. Shin slapped his hand over Koji's mouth. "Shut up! It's none of his business!" he shouted.

"What's none of my business?"

"It's none of your business!" Shin's face was red and he was furious.

Koji struggled to pull Shin's hand away. "Why don't you just tell him?" he whined. "Just tell him!"

"Tell me what?"

Aiko was bobbing up and down as she piped up: "About the holiday camps! The holiday camps!"

An eerie feeling passed through me as I heard the phrase.

"What's this?"

Aiko was nodding earnestly. "The holiday camps, Hiroshi-kun. We're going away to be adopted."

The hair prickled up on the back of my neck. I sat down cross-legged on the floor.

"You had better tell me what this is all about. Please."

Slowly, they all sat down on the floor in front of me.

"Well," Aiko began, "I don't really know—"

"It was the Americans, wasn't it?" Nobu said. "It was their idea—"

"One at a time."

Koji frowned, tracing a vague shape with his finger in the dust on the floor.

The Americans, he began, had apparently decided to set up holiday camps in the countryside, for all the Japanese children who had lost their families during the war.

"Just like us!" Aiko said, excitedly.

Some of the camps were in noble houses by the seaside, Koji continued, some of them up in the mountains, in old monasteries, but all of them had warm beds and three meals a day, hot rice and soup with them all. You could choose whether you wanted to help out on the farm, digging the fields or feeding the animals, or you could go back to school and have lessons with the teachers. There were all sorts of toys and games, model airplanes for rainy days, activities and trips to the countryside or the beach, swimming galas, running races, butterfly collecting—

Koji was panting as he trailed off. The other children were gazing at him like they were hypnotized.

It all sounded so marvellous that, for a second, I let myself imagine that it was true. I pictured us all, miles and miles away from Tokyo, racing along a shimmery beach, splashing and diving amongst the blue waves. For a moment, I imagined Tomoko, standing by a rock pool. Wearing a white swimming cap, the skin brown and sunburned around her shoulders.

"Tell him about the family visits," Aiko whispered, nudging Koji in the ribs.

Koji nodded. "They're the best of all."

Every Sunday, he said, mothers and fathers who had lost their children in the war drove up to the camps to inspect the children. They asked the headmaster about their behaviour, then chose the ones they liked best to take home to bring up as their own.

"We're going to be adopted," Aiko whispered. Her eyes were shining.

A horrible, empty feeling welled up inside me. I clasped my hands around my knees.

"Who told you all this?"

"All the gangs are talking about it," Nobu said. "Everybody knows."

As I looked at their bright faces, I felt utterly helpless. I gazed around the room, at the dark, damp patches in the ceiling, threatening to collapse at any moment; at the rotten tatami on the floor and the broken window shutters.

"I'm sorry," I said. "I'm very sorry. But someone has been filling your head with fairy tales."

Silence fell. It was as if I had smashed a mirror with a hammer. Koji smiled doubtfully, as if he thought I was joking. Shin's face was still red, and he looked at me with pure hatred.

"I'm so sorry," I said, my voice wavering. "I wish it was true as much as you do. Really I do. But it's just not."

I waved a hopeless hand around the decaying house. "I'm so sorry. But this is all we've got."

Shin leaped to his feet, staring at me with white eyes. He smashed his fist into his palm as he loomed over me.

"You're always so clever, aren't you, you bastard?" he snarled. "You're always right about everything, aren't you? Well, this time you're fucking wrong!"

To my complete astonishment, there were tears in his eyes. His thick lips were trembling.

It was appalling, the worst thing of all—that such a bully as Shin could be caught up in such a tangled dream—

Shin rotated his shoulders and I slid backward.

A horrible feeling of shame dawned on me and my cheeks began to throb. Could it truly be that he missed his violent, drunken brute of a father, as much as I missed my own? Wasn't a boy like him from Sengen Alley too stupid, too vulgar to feel pain and hurt like I did, a clever, sensitive boy from Senso High School—

Shin edged closer, his face twisted in animal rage. The children stared at me tearfully from behind him.

All those times when they'd cried out at night, and I'd forced them to be quiet. Every time they'd started to snivel, and I'd made the others sit on top of them, as if they were sacks of potatoes! Forcing them to work the streets day and night, to pick up spit-stained cigarette butts, to root about in filth and night soil when all the time they'd all just wanted nothing but their mums and dads—and I was supposed to be their big brother! What kind of big brother would act like I had? Forcing them to work as if they were nothing but animals, locking them up at night in this collapsing ruin, which was really nothing more than a filthy old whorehouse, and where we would all probably die together—

"We're sick of you, you bastard," Shin hissed.

They would have been better off without me, I thought.

Shin curled his fingers into a fist, and I backed away, suddenly scared.

Tomoko would still be alive—

Shin's fist slammed into my face. I sprawled backward, my ears ringing, stunned by its force.

He loomed over me and the other children gathered behind his legs, as if for protection.

"We're going away, big brother," he said, waving a thick finger. "There's nothing you can do to stop us. We're tired of being your slaves."

My slaves! Tears began to spill down my cheeks. I spoke through wrenching sobs.

"Go on then. Do whatever you want. See if I care."

I grabbed my satchel with the camera inside and raced outside through the long grass of the garden. I sank to my knees, and pounded the earth with my fists, howling and whimpering with bitter tears.

Up in Ueno Plaza, the signs for lost relations were peeling in soggy strips from the bronze statue of Saigo Takamori. Last year they'd been everywhere, covering every inch of space. I'd sometimes stopped and gazed at them, imagining what it would be like if, by some miracle, I read my own name there. One night in winter, a bunch of kids had gone around tearing them down from the walls and telegraph poles. They'd made a big bonfire up here in the Plaza, dancing around the flames and whooping as the names and addresses and hopeless messages all went up in smoke.

The shoeshine kids were playing a game of baseball down below. Maybe I could join them—I'd somehow grown taller over winter and could probably hold my own against them now. I could get a wooden shoeshine box, wait outside the hotels and government buildings at dawn with my brushes and tins of blacking. Polish the shoes of the Americans stiff shoes until I could see my ugly face in the leather.

I glanced up. For some reason, the shoeshine boys had abandoned their game—they were slinging their boxes over their shoulders and racing off down the steep banks of the Plaza. There was a flash of blue and for a split second, I saw the policemen coming up behind me, just before they pounced. A bamboo stave struck my spine and I sprawled forward in agony. A boot pressed against my head, pressing my face into the ground, and my arms were jerked up behind my back, tears springing into my eyes.

My head was lifted up by the hair. An inspector with round glasses and a straggly loach moustache started bawling at me, spraying my face with saliva.

"You filthy shit!" he hollered, banging me on the head with his fist. "What kind of impression do you think you feral dogs are giving us?"

A feral dog—that's what he called me. Down in the Plaza, policemen were swarming up the steps, holding out their hands, attempting to corral the remaining kids as they tried to escape.

With a twist, I managed to slip out of the inspector's grip. But then his hobnailed boot swung up and caught me right in the balls. I collapsed, unable even to make a sound.

"You little shit," he snarled, kicking my behind, knocking

me all the way to the steps. Down on the road, there was a truck with a wide canvas awning, its engine rumbling. Policemen were standing at the back, hoisting children in, counting them off on their fingers as if they were a herd of animals. My camera satchel was around my neck, and I clutched it against my chest, desperate to protect it, as I half fell, half rolled down the steps, my head cracking against the stone. I landed at the bottom, stunned senseless. The inspector grabbed me between the legs and hoisted me into the truck. The tailgate slammed up behind me.

There were about a dozen other kids in the truck, and as the truck lurched forward, they started panicking and crying as we were thrown about the floor. Liquid was trickling from the trousers of the smaller ones—most of them had already wet themselves. A few of the older ones were familiar—shoeshine boys from the market, mostly—but there was an another boy too that I'd never seen before, who sat on the flat metal truck bed with his head between his legs. His thin arms were covered in purple and yellow bruises and a gash across his forehead was crusted with dried blood.

"Let us out!" I shouted, hammering the tailgate with my fist.

"Where are they taking us?" one boy asked.

"Prison, maybe," whimpered another.

"No," one of the older boys said. "They're taking us out to the Arakawa River," he said. "They're going to shoot us one by one and shove us in, that's what I heard. They don't want kids like us around anymore."

"You're all wrong."

The boy on the floor had lifted his head. His face was like a skeleton and his eyes bloodshot. We all stared at him. Fresh blood glistened as he scratched the wound on his head.

"They're taking us to an orphanage."

The word sent a chill down my spine.

"How would you know?"

"Because I only just got out of one." He spat on the floor.

Something started to nag at my mind. In a terrified voice, one of the little kids asked him what it had been like.

"Worse than hell. They feed you less than on the streets and keep you cooped up in shitty cells and half the time they take your clothes away and leave you naked so you can't even run away."

My skin crawled. *The holiday camps.*

I took a running leap at the tailgate of the truck and just managed to get my fingertips over the lip. I scrabbled my feet against the metal, and hoisted myself up. We were driving down a dirt road between suburban houses. The truck was moving fast as I swung my leg over the side. Terrified, my head started to swim as the ground raced away below me. Suddenly, I leaped.

The sky and ground were spinning, then my bones were cracking as I rolled over and over in the dirt. My satchel strap was strangling me, the metal of the camera smashing against my rib cage. A horn blared violently, and I twisted into the tall grass at the side of the road, a split second before the massive wheels of another truck crunched past my head. One after the other went past in convoy, dark green and anonymous, their cabs covered in dust.

When the last one had disappeared up the road, I crawled out and stood up. An agonizing bolt went through my ankle and I collapsed back down again. For a few minutes, I lay there, my heart fluttering, trying to steady my breath. I took hold of my ankle, squeezing the flesh and bone. It was broken, I thought, or at least completely sprained.

The holiday camps. How had it all got so horribly tangled up? We must have really been desperate—if we'd believed that, we would have believed anything at all.

I struggled to stand up, wincing with pain as I started to

hobble back down the road. An hour or so later, I crossed a bridge and came across the overground train track. My ankle was white and swollen now, twice its normal size. My forehead was clammy and I felt sick and I had to lean against a wall to rest. The children's faces flashed into my mind. I needed to hurry.

The sky was darkening to grey and drops of rain started to speckle the road. Almost crying with pain, I pushed myself up straight. Grasping my satchel, feeling the shape of the camera inside, I started to hobble, agonizingly slowly, up the hill toward the inn.

The wooden gates to the courtyard were wide open and the broken locks dangled in the scrubby weeds. Heavy juddering came from inside, and there were shouts and unfamiliar voices. I hid behind the gatepost. A long Fuso bus was parked in the yard, big white headlights glowing in the rain. A driver in cap and spectacles sat behind the wheel, staring out through the windshield. Toward the back of the bus stood a policeman, facing the front door of the inn.

Nobu and Koji came out first, carrying little bundles tied with string, and I struggled not to cry out as they hopped up the steps into the vehicle. Aiko came next, smiling at the policeman: she was carrying a little metal suitcase I'd found for her one day in the rubble, with the scratched face of a cat painted upon it. Shin emerged, finally, in his torn khaki trousers, instinctively dropping his head to the policeman. The man said something, and he grinned. Shin glanced back at the inn for a second, before turning and hurrying up the steps of the bus. The officer slammed the door, and banged his palm on the side. The faces of the children appeared, struggling to open the windows and poke out their heads. The engine throbbed loudly. As the officer clambered into the front, the heavy wheels of the bus lurched forward.

"Bye-bye!" Aiko yelled, leaning out of the window and waving toward the inn, and the others all joined in chorus. "Bye-bye!"

I pressed my back against the stone gatepost. The nose of the bus edged through, and the driver glanced up the road before heaving the wheel around. The heavy wheels crunched into the gravel, and the bus drove past.

"Bye-bye! Bye-bye!"

Aiko and Koji were leaning all the way out of the windows, still waving desperately at the inn.

"No!" I shouted, as I tried to stumble after them.

Aiko suddenly spotted me and her mouth fell open.

"Hiroshi!" she screamed. "It's Hiroshi! Hiroshi-kun!"

Nobu's face appeared and he started to wave urgently.

"Come on, Hiro! Come on! We're going to the holiday camp!"

I hobbled along for a few paces, but then, in searing pain, my ankle gave way beneath me.

"No!" I shouted. I staggered to my feet again, and somehow made it another few steps as a sob clutched at my throat. "Please! Come back!"

My ankle was burning as I stumbled forward. The children's faces were screwed up with excitement and they started banging on the side of the bus with their fists.

"Run, Hiro! You can do it!"

I was crying so hard I could hardly speak. "It's an orphanage!" I shouted in a strangled voice. "An orphanage!"

I tripped, the gravel tearing my knees open. My satchel flew to the ground and the camera spilled out. As the bus reached the brow of the hill, I grasped for it, and held the camera up, waving it desperately in the air.

"What about your portraits?" I shouted, tears streaming down my face. "I wanted to take your portraits!"

The bus reached the brow of the hill, the children still waving at me from the windows. I collapsed into the mud, clutching the camera to my chest. The rain poured down as the bus rolled away. As it drove into the distance, I could still hear their faint voices, calling out my name.

24
PRIMROSE
(*Hal Lynch*)

My new home was the guest room on the second floor of the press club. I had a lumpy mattress and a coarse woollen blanket that reached either my neck or my toes, depending on my preference, and a part share in an electric lamp along with three other men. I'd hunted around for Mark Ward, anxious to talk to him, to show him my negatives and ask his advice. But he was travelling in the north now, up in the Snow Country, working on some piece about unions and sharecroppers, and wouldn't be back for weeks.

One afternoon I found myself walking along the riverbank, near the Nihonbashi Bridge, not far away from where I'd first encountered my bargeman all those months ago. I paused for a while as I looked out at the grey river. Dusk was falling, and I became seized with a powerful urge to drink a whisky—perhaps several whiskies—in the warmth and comfort of some homely saloon. I ventured into a warren of low shops and run-down tenement houses. Halfway down an alley, a red lantern was glowing like a votive candle. I hurried toward it, already feeling the drink warm and radiant inside my belly.

I ducked under the blue half-curtain. A hefty woman was polishing glasses behind the bar and called out to me in welcome, waving to a line of stools set up at the empty counter. The place was neat and snug—exactly what I'd had in mind—and I took my seat with a pleasurable sense of anticipation. The woman was taller than any of the others I'd seen in Japan, and deep dimples appeared in her cheeks as I requested

248 · BEN BYRNE

whisky. She poured me a glass of Suntory, which I sipped with intense satisfaction.

"American?" she asked.

I tipped my glass toward her in a rueful gesture of acknowledgement.

She placed her elbows on the counter, supporting her chin with her hands. She gazed at me with a frankness that I found somewhat disconcerting.

"GI-san?" she asked, and I braced myself for the inevitable offer of a girl. But then she frowned, shaking her head.

"No, you not GI type, I think."

I was amused. "Oh no? What type am I then?"

She squinted. "You artist type, I think."

I grinned. "Is that so?"

She nodded, apparently sure of herself. "Yes. I think."

I liked the woman already. She was burly and maternal all at once, with a dash of sultry sexuality lurking somewhere beneath it all.

"I wish I was," I said. "But I'm just a reporter. *Shimbun kisha desu.*"

"Oh." She raised her eyebrows. "*Repootaa.* Very good Japanese."

She topped up my drink and poured one for herself.

"*Chis-u.*" She held her glass in the air. I clinked it against my own. She knocked hers back. I did the same and an agreeable warmth hit my guts. Why hadn't I visited pleasant places like this more often?

"Where you stay now?" she demanded.

I laughed again. "Well, that's a funny thing . . . "

Leaning over the counter, as if I were a regular soak in a downtown speakeasy, I found myself explaining that I'd recently been obliged to leave my quarters. She looked me up and down for a second, then her eyes brightened and she hurried around the bar and took my arm.

"Come—look!" she said, pulling at me.

I was pleasantly tight by now, and I let her lead me away through a back door to a flight of narrow steps. At the top of the stairs, a door opened to a small room with a stained ceiling. There was a futon in the corner and a battered-looking desk pushed up beneath the window. Big raindrops were trickling down the cracked panes.

"You stay here," she said, excitedly. "Very cheap!"

Stay there? I thought. Maybe it wasn't such a bad idea. Privacy. Exclusive rights to my own reading lamp. A good place to lie low, plot out my next steps. I could rewrite my Hiroshima piece, take photographs, read books, drink whisky. What a change from the Continental, with its officers doing jumping jacks in the halls, scratching at their white bristles in the mouldering bathrooms.

I turned to face the lady and negotiate terms.

A mischievous gleam appeared in her eye: "One more whisky?"

The next day I heaved a knapsack and suitcase up the steep wooden staircase to my new home. I lined up my tattered collection of Japanese books along the window ledge and lay a typewriter case I'd requisitioned from the *Stars and Stripes* on the desk. The room was quiet, secluded. At one corner of the room, I prized up the floorboard with my jackknife. I placed my Hiroshima negatives beneath it, the envelope hidden inside a cigar box and wrapped up in a cotton sweater for good measure.

I lay back on the futon and lit a cigarette. The room was filled with a pale grey light, and I listened to the rain patter against the roof and the windows. The place reminded me of an old forestry hut in the woods near our home, where I'd hidden out for a week when I was a teenager, just after my father had died. My uncle had finally tracked me down. He'd put his arm around my shoulder: "Come on home, Hal. He's gone now. Your mother needs you . . . "

Glancing, butterfly dreams. When I awoke, I was disoriented. Night had fallen, and the crackling voice of Josephine Baker drifted up from the bar below. As I came downstairs, I saw my new landlady, Mrs. Ishino, arranging bottles of liquor on the shelves. A portrait of a Japanese man in a flying jacket hung above them on the wall. Officers sat at tables; a couple of girls in plain dresses laughing away with them, hands over their mouths. They weren't exactly beautiful, I thought, but seemed warm and friendly and were somehow the more appealing for that. As I took a stool at the bar, Mrs. Ishino smiled indulgently and poured me a drink.

"On house," she announced, proudly. From a tiny kitchen behind her, wisps of steam were emerging. She called out in sharp command. An answering voice sang out with a long, high-pitched, "*Hai!*"

She turned to me maternally. "You like room?"

"Yes. I sure do."

"You welcome."

A girl came out from the kitchen with a plate of small dumplings, which she set in front of me with an incline of her head.

"Lynch-san," Mrs. Ishino said. "This is Satsuko-chan. My new favourite girl."

The girl looked at me. She had the darkest eyes I'd ever seen—almost entirely black from the pupil to the iris. Her face formed a smooth oval, the lips slightly parted to show small, regular teeth. Her pale skin was flushed from the heat of the kitchen and there was a faint perspiration on her brow. She wore a blue cloth tied around her forehead, which gave her a vaguely boyish, piratical air.

"Well. Here's to her," I said, raising my glass.

Hands tight against the sides of her apron, she bowed. Mrs.

Ishino gave another sharp command. With another obedient "*Hai!*" the girl scurried back to the kitchen.

"Satsuko-chan . . . " Mrs. Ishino began, but just then, a couple of officers wearing rain capes emerged through the curtain with Japanese dates on their arms. They held up hands in greeting, as if they knew the place well. Mrs. Ishino led them over to a table and I sat alone at the bar for a while, sipping my drink and feeling almost absurdly content.

The girl bustled in and out from the kitchen several more times that night, bringing small plates of chipped potatoes and fried egg sandwiches for the men. Before long, I realized I was drunk. The place filled up, and, at one point, I helped Mrs. Ishino move the tables aside to make a space for dancing. There was none of the wild jitterbugging of the Ginza clubs here—the men were stately and senior, and moved their partners gracefully back and forth like ballroom dancers, hands on backs, swaying expertly to the music. Others played cards while the girls poured their beer, and a soft haze enveloped the place as Saturday evening toppled gently into the arms of Saturday night.

Later on, the girl came out to me. She'd removed her headgear and had her face made up now, a simple brush of powder and a crimson curve of lipstick. She wore a green flower-print dress, a red plastic peony in her hair. Eyes downcast, she placed a light hand upon mine.

"You sit with me?" she asked.

Her hand was cool, the impression of skin smooth upon my wrist.

"Let's see now," I said, turning over her palm. She resisted, and I dropped her hand, afraid that I'd offended her. But then, with a curious look in her eyes, she relented, and held out her hand in front of me.

There were no lines on her palm at all, just a smooth, shiny surface, like polished marble. I had a sudden recollection of

Eugene, in the Oasis that night, the girl pouring out his beer. *Hal, meet Primrose. She's a swell sort!*

I studied her. It was the same girl, I was sure. I felt a strange collision of emotions as I looked into her coal-black eyes. Curiosity. Admiration. What kind of life had she lived? What bleak encounters had she witnessed since the last time we met . . . I felt a frank, swelling attraction as I glanced at the curve of her chest, the pale skin taut across her breastbone.

My throat grew suddenly thick, and from nowhere, a loud roar thundered into my ears.

Her smooth palm was touching my cheek, holding my head steady. She looked into my eyes with an expression of concern.

"You tired, I think?"

The thundering faded. The music from the gramophone and the sound of conversation gradually reasserted themselves.

"Yes," I stammered. "Yes, I am tired."

She patted the side of my face.

"You go sleep," she said, before walking to a table in the corner of the bar. As I sat there, clinging onto my drink, she threw me occasional darting glances. Finally, I stood up, determined to approach her again, but just then, another Western man—a civilian—entered the bar and walked over to her table. They talked for a short while, and she stood up and took his hand. She led him away through a low door at the back of the room and I caught a glimpse of her bare arm as she pulled the door shut. Into my mind's eye came the unwelcome image of his scratchy white legs, the red peony askew amidst stray strands of the girl's black hair. I threw back my drink and said goodnight to no one in particular. Then I clomped up the stairs to my new abode. I took a long drink of water from the jug, and passed out on my new bed.

In the lobby of the press club, correspondents hammered out copy with typewriters on their knees. The long-distance booths were jammed, urgent stories being dictated into the glossy black telephones. The *Asahi Shimbun* that day was dominated by stories of unrest sweeping steadily across the country in the wake of the crop failures. The first reports of starvation had already emerged; there'd been rice riots in the north and strikes at the coal mines and here at one of the Tokyo newspapers. A leading communist had been welcomed home from China that week like a movie star. Philip Cochrane from the *Baltimore Sun* told me that mobs had greeted the man at the station, the whole place a sea of red flags.

Mark Ward had an inch of beard on his face and a glitter in his eye when we sat down for drinks in the bar later on that evening with Sally Harper of *TIME*.

"Welcome home, Ward. How was the Snow Country?"

As we drank our raw Japanese whisky, he regaled us with stories of evenings spent in sharecroppers' huts, peasants gathered around fires with padded blankets on their knees, telling tales of despair as the oxen moved about in the mulch, the snow thick on the ground outside.

"This country's a tinderbox, my friends. Believe me. A powder keg, just waiting to explode."

"You're a true believer, Ward," I said.

"Right." His eyes narrowed. "Did you know G2 pulled me in yesterday?"

"Are you serious?" Sally said, her eyes wide with concern. G2 was Intelligence, the most muscular and secretive of the Occupation divisions, presided over by General Charles A. Willoughby—MacArthur's chief of intelligence, and, I recalled, Ward's nemesis.

"What did they want?"

"They wanted to ask me why I was writing a piece on Japanese union organizers. Whether or not I sympathized with them."

"What did you say?"

"I told them that people were starving to death because our land reform directive was taking so long to draft, and that you could bet your bottom dollar that I sympathized with them."

As I looked at him, I was put in mind of a painting I'd once seen in the Metropolitan Museum in New York. Chagall: an old bearded man in a thick overcoat, a sack slung over his back, floating across a dream landscape of snow and yellow baroque architecture.

"What did they say to that?" Sally asked.

His voice fell in surly imitation. "They said: 'Listen, Ward. Things have changed since we arrived. We're at war with the Russkies now. Whose side are you on?'"

He shook his big head, his voice sour. "You know they slung out two of your friends last week? Brown and Christopher?"

I vaguely remembered a demure, grey-haired Californian and an effeminate New Yorker, both of whom had been working at the *Stars and Stripes* when I'd arrived.

"You're kidding? For what?"

Ward waved his meaty hands in the air. "'Communistic leanings!'"

I laughed. They'd been poring over baseball statistics when I'd first met them, apparently more concerned with sport than politics.

"They're Reds?"

"Sure! They've been sprinkling the whole paper with subversion."

"What's happening to them?"

"They've been sent to Okinawa. To keep them out of trouble."

"That's real tough for them.

He glanced at me sharply.

"You don't understand, Lynch."

The wattle of skin beneath his jowls swayed as he shook his head sullenly.

"Are you in some kind of situation, Mark?" I asked.

He stared at me, mildly incredulous. "Don't you get it, Lynch? I'm next on their goddamned list!"

Sally left us, and Ward and I went out to get a snack at a low noodle place. It was bustling with GIs and their dates and we drank lukewarm beer and slurped at our noodles in the Japanese fashion. Ward began to pluck at his plate of fried dumplings with his chopsticks.

"And how about you, Lynch?" he asked, absently. "The *Stars and Stripes* send you anywhere interesting?"

"They fired me," I said.

The chopsticks paused in midair.

"What happened?"

"I took a train trip. To Hiroshima."

The chopsticks clattered onto the table and an incredulous expression suffused Ward's face.

"You actually did it?"

"Yes. Yes, I did."

The edges of his wide lips curled up.

"How did it look?"

"More or less the same as the last time I saw it. By the way, Disease X is real."

The jowls shook and the inevitable cigar appeared. I told him of the long walk across the red fields, the pulverized city centre, the victims I'd met at the hospital. He clutched my hand, steam beading on his brow from the billowing stockpots.

"Did you take photographs, Hal? Please tell me you took photographs."

I nodded.

"Where are they?"

"Safe. Most of them. The first prints got confiscated."

"How? By whom? Got a name?"

"SCAP. Public relations." I realized that I hardly knew. "They raked me over the coals when I got back, anyhow."

His eyes narrowed behind a cloud of fragrant smoke.

"Who's the pigeon?"

"Does it matter?"

Eugene's face the next day had been grey and artless, though that could just as well have been his daily hangover. It could have been anybody in the newsroom, I thought. I'd been so tired that night I couldn't even remember if I'd shut my drawer.

Ward's face was animated now, the glow of the restaurant lanterns reflecting in the wide lenses of his spectacles.

"How are you going to play it, Lynch? I can help you. We could file the story here, overseas line. But what about the pictures? They'll never make it out. And the pictures are the story."

"I know that, Ward."

He frowned, puffing at the cigar, releasing several big clouds of smoke. Finally he spoke again. "There's only one way I can see it, Hal. You've got to get back to the States. Take the negatives with you. Or have someone else go for you. Then pound on some doors until they're published."

I pictured a ship, somewhere mid-Pacific, sapphire waves crashing against the hull. An editor's office in New York, overlooking the Hudson. Snowflakes touching the glass, shivering away to nothing.

"They won't let me back in, Ward."

"Probably not."

He considered the glowing end of his cigar. "Anything special keeping you in Japan, Hal?"

I pictured my drafty room in Nihonbashi. My mess of blankets, the typewriter on the battered desk. Mrs. Ishino leaning over the bar and pouring me another glass. The serving girl, Primrose—Satsuko—sat at a side table, with her scarred hands and a red plastic peony in her hair.

"I guess not."

He suddenly grinned, shaking his head.

"My goodness, Hal. You really are a dark horse. You know that? A real dark horse."

He rested his big paw on my shoulder and looked me straight in the eye.

"Just remember me when you get your Pulitzer, okay?"

I took a long walk home along the river, past dark fields of ruin. When I ducked past the curtain, the place was busy.

Satsuko-san wandered over as soon as I sat down, as if she just happened to be passing. She opened up a beer and poured it into two glasses.

"*Cheers*," she pronounced, smiling at me.

"Cheers," I replied.

We exchanged pleasant banalities for a while, the familiar patter about food in Japan and in America, and she gave polite gasps of surprise and admiration as I regaled her with a list of the exotic dishes I had tried in her country. There was a lull in the conversation. Her lips moved, silently, as if she were phrasing a question in her mind. She looked back up at me with a very serious expression. Slowly, she asked: "Do you have pet?"

I laughed.

"Well, yes, I do. Or rather, I did once . . . " I found myself telling her about Finn, the adored glossy red Irish setter I'd had as a boy.

"When I was young, I used to sleep with my head on his fur. Like it was a pillow. You know—pillow?"

She looked startled. "You go sleep?" she asked, mimicking slumber.

"No, no. Not yet."

Finn had gone lame as I'd gotten older. One winter morning, just after my twelfth birthday, I was awakened by a distant noise. My breath billowed in the air as I came downstairs. The glass door of my father's gun cabinet hung open, one of the rifles missing. I creaked open the door and touched the smooth metal barrel of its twin. At that moment, my father came tramping back in, holding shotgun and shovel. There was sweat on his brow, and a frail scent of sulphur.

"You have any pets, Satsuko-san? A dog?"

She smiled.

"Cat," she pronounced with a look of satisfaction. "We feed—" She slithered her hand through the air.

"Eels?" I asked, in a moment of inspiration.

"*So.*" She made a snapping movement with her mouth. "Eel head."

A great wave of warmth and sympathy coursed through me. I felt curiously privileged to have this fragmentary glimpse into her past, into her life before all of this began.

I started to laugh and she looked at me in surprise. Then, slowly, to my delight, she began to laugh too. Not the giggle of a whore, eager to please, but the genuine laugh of a live woman, with a childhood and a past, who considers her reflection in the mirror, and nods with wistful acceptance.

Finally I stood up, fully intending to head upstairs.

"You sleep now?" she asked.

"I'm going to try."

She placed her cool hand on my wrist. Her eyes were candid.

"You want take me?"

I hesitated, the delicate pressure of her fingers upon my skin.

"Maybe another time."

The corners of her lips turned down sulkily. She crossed her arms.

"Well," I said. "Goodnight."

I lay fully clothed on my bed, cursing myself as I pictured the inevitable events unfolding below. Men arriving, the gramophone playing, couples swaying back and forth. Satsuko leading another man to the back room. What exactly was I trying to prove? I pictured her smooth, slim body as she pulled her dress over her head, the glimmer of light in her jet black eyes. I almost got right up and headed back downstairs to ask her to come up after all. But before I knew it, I had fallen dead asleep.

25

MRS ISHINO'S SPECIAL EATING & DRINKING SHOP
(*Satsuko Takara*)

The water was just coming to a boil as I dropped the scrubbed potatoes into the pan. From the crates piled up in the narrow kitchen, I took cans of spiced meat for sandwiches and tins of dried egg to mix bowls of gluey omelette for the night ahead—those simple snacks that the Americans seemed to find so delicious. They kissed their fingers and applauded as I set down bowls of chipped potatoes and greasy fried egg sandwiches. A far cry from eel liver soup and *unagi-don*!

As I poured the water into the sink, Mrs. Ishino sidled into the kitchen through a big cloud of steam.

"Well?" she asked, pinching my arm. "What did you think?"

I frowned, concentrating on the potatoes as they tumbled into the draining basket.

"What did I think of what, Mrs. Ishino?"

"What did you think of the Westerner, of course!"

The American who slept in the attic room upstairs had taken me to the cinema that afternoon. I shrugged.

"I'm sure I don't know, Mrs. Ishino," I replied. "Does he really seem that different from the rest of them?"

Mrs. Ishino frowned as she considered the question. "Don't you think, Satsuko-chan? More the 'sensitive type,' I would say."

"Really, Mrs. Ishino?" I said, pouring oil into the pan. "Do you really think any of them are sensitive?"

Mrs. Ishino let out an exasperated noise.

"Why not find out, Satsuko?" she said, stamping out of the kitchen. "It might not be such a bad idea to have a foreigner looking after you these days!"

I spluttered with laughter as she marched out. As I slid the potatoes into the spattering oil, I pictured the American sitting beside me in the cinema, gazing up in bemusement at the screen.

Men in short sleeves had been bustling around the cinemas on the Rokku as we stepped down from the tram in Asakusa that afternoon. Several of the theatres had reopened along the wide avenue now, their brickwork stained by black smoke. Banners for new shops fluttered on bamboo poles in the brisk spring breeze, and cinema posters were mounted on billboards, mostly showing Western men in cowboy hats and blonde women with large bosoms.

Just past the old Paradise Picture House, a big painted sign on the side of the wall advertised a new Japanese film. When I saw it, my jaw fell. I grasped hold of the arm of the American. Up there, larger than life, was Michiko.

The resemblance was unmistakable. But the American misunderstood my expression. He walked over to the booth and bought two tickets for the film. Still stunned, I tried to explain that it would be in Japanese, that he wouldn't understand a thing. But he just shrugged and smiled, took my hand and led me inside.

There was only one row of seats left at the front of the damaged theatre and as we took our places, the audience standing behind us seemed restless and agitated. The light flickered onto the screen and my stomach tightened. The thought of seeing Michiko again—and in such a manner! My eyes widened as the names of the actors blazed up on the screen. There it was: *Michiko Nozaki.*

The film began. Almost straightaway, she appeared. Wearing a white, pleated skirt, casually twirling a summer parasol—

I almost clapped my hands in delight. As I settled back in my seat to watch the film, I couldn't stop smiling. The American squeezed my arm and offered me a hard candy from a paper bag.

I could hardly remember the plot afterwards. It was a simple love story, all faintly ridiculous. Michiko was the true star of the film. Her beauty simply flooded from the screen. The audience jostled behind us whenever she appeared, sighing and murmuring with delight when she flashed that eager, encouraging smile I knew so well.

Her leading man was very handsome, with sharp cheekbones and piercing eyes. I glanced up at the American, who was quite unaware of my emotions as he munched away on his snacks. He looked rather handsome himself, I thought, and I squeezed the tiniest bit closer to him.

Toward the end of the film, there was a shock. At the height of the drama, the man grabbed hold of Michiko, accusing her of covering up a crime. She tore herself away with tears in her eyes, but he rushed over and took her in his arms. She turned, half-resisting. And then, quite openly, he leaned forward and kissed her.

A gasp came from the audience. He had kissed her! Full on the lips, in public—just like that. Of course, we had never seen anything like it on the screen before, and the audience shouted in astonishment. My American laughed, quite bewildered by it all.

As the crowd poured out of the cinema into the spring sunshine, he took my arm and we walked together through the streets of Asakusa. Men were going by with sandwich boards advertising new shops, and some of the stalls on Nakamise Arcade had reopened, selling flimsy mirrors and trinkets to the passing soldiers.

Cherry blossom hung from the scorched trees that leaned over Asakusa Pond, more like a flooded bomb crater now. We sat on a bench and gazed at the flowers for a while, and I pointed out the scorched patch that had once been Hanayashiki Park with its golden horses, the mound of rubble on the other side that had once been my old high school.

"Where did you live, Satsuko?" he asked, quite suddenly.

I frowned, and waved my hand vaguely in the direction of Umamichi Street, on the far side of the temple precinct.

He fell silent for a long time, deep in thought. Perhaps he really was different from the other Westerners. Darker, somehow, more brooding. I knew so little about him. Where had he fought during the war? Had he been a pilot, up there in one of the planes?

It was a question that none of us girls ever asked. I might have seen him one night, as he flew low across Tokyo. His handsome face beyond the quilted nose of the cockpit, the glass glinting with the light of the fires raging below.

A muscle tightened in his jaw. I should hate him, I thought, for what he had done. But as we sat there in silence together, he took my scarred hand and held it between his palms. For a moment, as the breeze blew blossom onto the surface of the dark water, it felt as if the sky was exhaling, as if the earth itself were silently offering up flowers for the souls of the dead.

The potatoes hissed and sizzled in the pan as Masuko came into the bar and switched on the radio. My ears pricked up straightaway.

"Who Am I?" was a programme which had come on the air that month. It featured displaced persons from all over the Japanese Empire who had lost their memories during the war, and now, on their return home, were trying to discover exactly who they were and where they had come from. The presenter interviewed them in the hope that someone out there might recognize their voice or recall some clue about them.

"Can you remember anything about your childhood, sir?"

he was asking, as Masuko turned up the volume. "The village festivals, perhaps, or where you went to school?"

A man's voice crackled in reply. "I can't remember much of anything, sir, just that we lived in the countryside. Our teacher was Matsukawa-sensei. He was so strict! I remember he beat me once when I lost one of the buttons of my school uniform . . ."

Masuko laughed out loud as I took the pan from the heat and walked through to the bar in my apron. She was a short girl, as chirpy as a sparrow, with a lovely hint of the south in her voice. We'd quickly fallen into an enjoyable routine together, visiting the market for vegetables in the morning, cleaning the bar in the afternoon, and gossiping about Mrs. Ishino and what we referred to as her "mysterious past."

Masuko certainly found the show very entertaining, though for all the wrong reasons. A sly smile played on her wide lips as we listened to the next segment.

"And now for some success stories," announced the presenter. "Last week the loyal wife of Mr. Kawachi heard her husband's voice on our programme, and boarded a train straightaway from Kobe to come to our studio and collect him. They are now reunited in joy in their marital home."

"What rubbish!" cawed Masuko. "I bet Mrs. Kawachi's just some old hag who can't find herself a husband. She heard his voice on the radio and thought that a man without a memory would do her nicely!"

I gave a thin smile. But the truth was that I listened intently to every minute of the show, my stomach quivering as the men began to speak. What would it be like, I wondered, if Osamu's voice suddenly emerged from the crackling radio? If he had been lost somewhere in the South Seas, falsely reported dead by his colleagues? Would I have telephoned the radio studio if I heard him? Even now?

My memory of him was fading, I realised. The picture of us

together in my mind was frozen in time, ageing, like an old photograph.

Young boys spoke too sometimes, telling tales of lost mothers and fathers. Tears had welled in my eyes one afternoon as an Osaka boy described losing his family in the fire raids, just nights after I had lost my own. I'd been flooded with hopeless guilt. What would I do if Hiroshi's voice suddenly, miraculously came out from the speaker?

"I lost my sister, Satsuko Takara, on the night of the Great Tokyo Fire Raid, but can remember nothing more. My only wish is to see her again . . . "

Perhaps I had given up the search too soon? Mrs. Ishino told me I'd performed my filial duty, that I must simply get on with my own life now. But so many of us were still lost, it seemed, so many still struggling to find their way back home.

I sighed as Masuko switched off the radio. She began polishing ashtrays and laying them out on the tables and I went back to the kitchen to salt the fried potatoes. After a while, I heard footsteps coming from upstairs. I put my head back around the door. The American was sitting at the bar, reading his book. He glanced at me in surprise and I smiled at him shyly. His face lit up as his deep blue eyes gazed directly into mine. He slid a match into the pages to mark his place and placed the book down upon the counter.

26
LA BOHÈME
(*Osamu Maruki*)

I spent much of spring in a state of dissolution, my vow to seek out Satsuko Takara blurring steadily away to transparency in countless glasses of *kasutori* shochu. I had relapsed into torpor, paralysis, as if the natural cords between motivation and action had been entirely severed.

Then I was seized with a bout of the stunning, virulent malaria that had tortured me in New Guinea, and while the cherry blossoms blushed along the canals, I spun in and out of high fever, harrowed by visions of green chasms and purple corpses.

Thus it was not until the end of April that I had the energy, or the application, to take up my pen once more. I dedicated my convalescence to writing a novella, which, I was convinced, would capture the elusive spirit of our times. It followed the transmission, in excruciating stages, of a mysterious virus from an American soldier to a young Japanese artist. I felt it by far my most compelling work to date, and I confidently submitted it to several of the leading literary reviews of the day, entitled simply, "The Germ."

It proved too avant-garde to be published. "Obtuse," the responses noted. "Incoherent." But this was just further proof, I realized, of something I was rapidly coming to understand.

Men were starving to death in the Tokyo streets, our nation knelt grovelling before an army of occupation. This was no time for deep examinations of the human condition. What was needed now was diversion and distraction: American pinups and bare-knuckle wrestlers; baseball games and "The Apple Song" piped through countless speakers. It was an age for fairy tales, for the rabbit in the moon.

I received the last of my rejection notes in the morning, and was slumped drunk by midday, the manuscript of "The Germ" crinkling to cinders in the stove. When I awoke later that evening, I felt maudlin and out of sorts, and I reached in my drawer for a faithful tablet of *courage*. As it dissolved beneath my tongue, a cheery chemical abandon erupted into my bloodstream. The room seemed suddenly claustrophobic, and I slipped downstairs to immerse myself in the comforting waters of the *demimonde*.

The bar was busy. A haze of acrid smoke lapped the walls, the revelries already in full swing. Two editors from a leading review of the day were sitting in an advanced state of disrepair at the counter, dribbling over their glasses.

In the centre of the room was a clique I didn't recognize. They were celebrating, and I hovered nearby on the off chance they might offer me something to drink. At the centre of the party was a man with a goatee beard, wearing dark, round glasses and a wine red beret. The young people at his table refilled his glass each time he took a sip, laughing uproariously at every word he said.

"Who's that?" I asked Nakamura, who had appeared by my side. He was grinning drunkenly, and seemed very pleased with himself.

"You're behind the times, sensei," he said. "That's Kano, the famous film director."

"Oh," I murmured. "Well, the cinema . . . "

I had heard of the man, of course—his "kiss" film had been the talk of Tokyo for weeks. One could hardly enter a room without overhearing allusions to his genius, his "distillation of the modern spirit."

"Why don't you come and meet him?" Nakamura suggested.

"You're acquainted with him, I suppose?"

"Oh yes," he said, grinning. "He wants me to work on his next film. Just some sketches for scenery, you understand . . . "

That wily old raccoon. Taking advantage of my illness to cozy up to film directors . . . Several of Nakamura's new cartoons had been published in the *Asahi Shimbun* that month. He had even started to ramble about founding a new magazine, devoted entirely to manga.

"Well," I said, "perhaps I'll drop over later. Though I haven't much time for cinema people."

"Come on, Maruki," he said, gripping my arm. "Don't be such a snob."

"Nakamura, not now, please . . . "

"Come on," he said bluntly, and I smelled the booze on his breath. "It's his birthday. And he's buying."

With a sigh, I let Nakamura draw me over to the table, sharply aware of the Philopon now off on its gleeful spirals around my bloodstream. Most of the men at the table were young, with slick hair and gaudy shirts, shrieking with laughter. None looked up as we approached, and I found myself considering them resentfully, when, to my embarrassment, Nakamura suddenly shoved me forward and I banged into the table.

"Maruki-sensei!" he announced, sniggering. "The famous, talented writer!"

The group looked up at me askance. I tried to back away, cursing Nakamura for his boorishness, but Kano held up his hand. He took off his dark glasses and turned to me with a twinkle in his eye.

"We were just discussing our traditional Japanese culture, Maruki-san. Whether it still has any place at all in a modern nation. What is your view?"

I wondered if it was a trap, noticing the shining eyes, the arch smiles. Someone pushed a glass of shochu toward me and

I drained it. As I looked at their smug faces, I felt a sudden wave of recklessness—inspired, no doubt by the combination of shochu and amphetamine now pulsing through me. I'd throw their superiority right back in their faces.

"I think our 'magnificent culture' has all turned to piss, sensei," I said, turning on my heel, deciding that I would march straight out to another, less condescending watering hole.

To my surprise, a peal of high laughter came from Kano. Quickly, the rest of his disciples followed suit.

I turned. Kano was smiling at me.

"Thank you, Maruki-san," he said. "You see, we've just returned from the theatre."

I felt a tinge of doubt. "Well, the kabuki, of course—" He cut me off. "Actually, I was thoroughly bored by it all."

A smile played on his lips. The heads of the others swivelled toward him, like acolytes waiting for a sutra to drop from the mouth of the Buddha.

"Is that so?"

He smiled. "Don't misunderstand me, Maruki-san. I have always been a great fan of the theatre, ever since I was a boy. But so much else has been lost that it seemed somehow meaningless to me. Hence my boredom."

"I see," I muttered, not quite following.

"It was as if one was attending a birthday party, surrounded by all sorts of delightful guests, and treated to all manner of delicacies, only to be told that the host had just died."

The acolytes chuckled, though none had any clue what he was talking about, clearly. Kano took a cigarette from a packet in his side pocket—French, I noticed, they must have cost a fortune—lit it, then blew out the smoke in a tangled ring.

"And then. Just think. I visited the urinal."

There were snorts of laughter. Kano was smiling dreamily. "I thought to myself—how many thousands must have pissed here on this same spot in the past? How many generations have passed water here over the decades, the centuries, even? How many gallons of sake and shochu have drained away; how many fathers and sons have stood here, aiming, shivering with the same primordial satisfaction? That most universal, absent-minded moment of pleasure, when even the most sophisticated man approaches the divine simplicity of the Buddha . . . The smell was overwhelming, and yet I stood there, inhaling the fumes, thinking to myself—how wonderful! How delightful! And then—do you know what I thought? I thought, *This is it. This is the true smell of culture.* This is where the soul of a nation truly resides."

The disciples shook their heads at such erudition. Mrs. Shimamura approached the table carrying two large bottles of sake. Kano looked at me directly. "Culture's a pretty sorry thing if it lives in a few temples and monuments, isn't it?"

I nodded.

"But it's always still there, you see? In the habits, the manners, the customs of the people. They can't be destroyed, Maruki-san. The way people talk. They way they laugh. And, yes—the way they piss. And so thank you, sensei, you are indeed correct. Our magnificent culture has indeed all been turned to piss. And that, if I may say so, is where it's always been. When everything else has been stripped away—that is where any culture finds its true essence."

Loud and enthusiastic applause burst from all sides of the table, there was a hammering of feet upon the wooden floor. I hardly knew where to look. Kano raised his glass, and proposed a toast: "To a true scholar of the modern age!" Another large glass appeared in front of me. With an unsteady grin, I raised it to the assembled company and tipped it down my throat.

Room was made for me at the table. Mrs. Shimamura set down bottles and snacks, glancing at me in amusement. Soon enough, I felt relaxed and cheerful. Every so often, someone would bang the table and stand up and declare that they were "off to analyze our true culture" and everyone would laugh as the man went outside to urinate in the alley.

I found myself sitting next to Kano. He pushed his cigarettes toward me in an encouraging manner. The tobacco was delicious, and he talked to me in a conspiratorial way, as if we were both men of the world.

"And how are you surviving these morbid times, Maruki?" he asked politely.

"Well," I said, hesitantly, "I print a small journal. Nothing of any great consequence, you understand."

Mrs. Shimamura was leaning over the table, wiping away a spillage.

"Oh?" Kano inquired.

"It's been a great success, sensei!" Mrs. Shimamura piped up. "Better than half the other rubbish out there at the moment."

My face flushed. Hastily, I insisted: "Just popular entertainment of course, sensei. Nothing of any artistic merit."

He frowned. "What's it called?" he asked.

"It's called *ERO,* sensei," interjected Mrs. Shimamura, her eyes twinkling with amusement. "It's really very popular. I was just thinking, in fact, that sensei might like to take a look at it himself. I think we have a few spare issues behind the bar."

I jumped up from my seat. "Thank you, Mrs. Shimamura! That won't be necessary! Now, if you'll excuse us . . . "

But Kano was looking at her. "There's no need, obasan," he said. "I've read every copy."

I was stunned. *Kano,* I thought, *reading my rag?*

"Not so much for the erotic pieces, you understand," he went on. "More for the 'man-in-the-street' interviews. I think they are an act of genius."

I was speechless.

"Yes, they're quite remarkable. I look to them for inspiration. You truly have the 'human touch,' Maruki-sensei. You are a true pioneer."

A lump formed in my throat. "I had always hoped . . . "

"There is a childlike simplicity to your work."

"You don't say?"

"Oh yes," he murmured. "And now, as never before, we must return to a state of simplicity."

I was dizzy as Kano himself poured me another large drink. I felt absurdly pleased with myself. I had started out the evening as a pornographer and a literary flop, and now looked set to end it the pioneer of a new *naïf* school. The room began to glitter around me and I felt a great warmth toward everyone there.

"I'd like you to write something for me," Kano was saying, his figure blurring in and out of my vision. "Something about the men and the women of the Tokyo streets. You're the expert, after all."

Mrs. Shimamura drew up a stool.

"How much?" she demanded.

"Mrs. Shimamura, please," I protested, "Sensei, you must ignore her."

But Kano was smiling, and he casually named a sum that made my jaw drop. Mrs. Shimamura jotted figures on a piece of paper, crossing out numbers and totting them up as she murmured to herself.

"That's five months' rent—overdue now, if you please—shochu, food, breakages . . . Well, sensei, I think that should do nicely to start with."

She stood up and put out her hand, Western-style. Kano shook it with a smile as the rest of his disciples gathered their things.

"He'll start on it first thing tomorrow, sensei, don't worry," promised Mrs. Shimamura. "I'll make sure he does."

"Please do," smiled Kano. "And thank you, Maruki-sensei. I look forward to reading your work."

As I stood up, I felt the floor sway beneath me.

He bowed formally. "Maruki-sensei. Please write it from the heart."

The heart, I thought—the heart, of course. I started to slip toward the floor, and felt Mrs. Shimamura's hand underneath my armpit, more to soften my landing than to raise me up again. As I rested my cheek against the hard wood, I was vaguely aware of Kano and his party hovering just above me. His words came to me as if through water.

"Just look. We're all at the bottom now. Isn't it glorious!" Metallic laughs echoed from all sides.

"After all—it's only after one collapses that one can learn to stand on one's own two feet."

The next day, I took myself to Asakusa to watch Kano's famous "kiss film," in order to gain some understanding of his style. The damaged theatre was packed to the rafters, though most of the seats had been removed, and I squirmed through an excited crowd to stand behind the sole remaining row of chairs at the front of the auditorium. Before me was the glossy head of a Japanese woman, and that of a tall Western man sitting next to her. As the projector rolled, the woman turned to whisper something into the foreigner's ear. For a moment, the reflection of the screen lit up her face.

A bolt of shock.

It was Satsuko Takara. Her hair cut to a bob, smiling up at the man, those obsidian eyes with long lashes that threw into relief the glittering pupils. As she turned back to the screen, her hand fell lightly upon the man's well-clothed leg. A man, I realized, with growing astonishment, whom I also recognized: last seen on the Yurakucho tram, reading a newspaper and wearing a glossy pair of chestnut Oxford brogues . . .

I felt a ridiculous sense of wounded pride, a dismal, masochistic satisfaction. To be so justly punished for my hopeless vacillation, my impotent conceit.

Takara-san gazed at the screen as if in wonder. After a while, the American put his big arm around her, and she rested her beautiful head upon his shoulder.

With a rueful smile, I pushed my way back through the crowd. The spring sunshine was bright as I walked slowly back to the Montmartre. My heart was spinning with hopeless desires. When I got home, I marched straight upstairs. I locked the door and took out my notepad and pen.

I wrote the script entirely from the heart, as Kano had asked me to do. I poured every atom of my being into its pages, scribbling away until long in the night.

I infused the story with "childlike simplicity." I captured the spirit of the times. From the crystalline vials of Philopon pills to the dimpled tangerines at the market, I employed every image I had seen on my long voyages around the Yamanote Line that winter, every encounter I had witnessed on my solitary peregrinations through the freezing streets. The American, with his moulded camera case and shoes. The urchins outside the bathhouse. Satsuko Takara, standing poised outside her brothel, the night I returned home, broken from war.

The script became a love story, as is so often the case. But it was one far removed from the frustration and obscenity that made up the dreary leitmotifs of *ERO*. Much of the action would take place overground. The city itself would play a starring role. As I wandered the streets of Tokyo that week, fresh-cut cedar flashed yellow from the newly-built houses, green shoots sprouting from the charred black soil. Could there be hope here still, I wondered, despite all the death and ruin?

I cannot pretend that the script was not sentimental, even melodramatic at times. But Kano was overwhelmed when I showed it to him. It made him weep to read, he said. We were then required to submit the script to the American censors for their scrutiny. It emerged back a few weeks later, thick with blue pencil—shaved of some of its limbs, but with its heart mostly intact.

The day after, we set out jubilantly from the white warehouses of the Toho Studios with a young and excited crew to film the first scenes in the streets of the city. And it was there, in those burned-out ruins, that I saw our star in the flesh for the first time, as she practised her lines outside a broken-down house. The actress I knew straightaway would come to define our age, who would capture the hearts of an entire generation of cinemagoers. For our leading lady was none other than the glorious, the exquisite, the unmistakable Michiko Nozaki.

The flats beside the river park were strewn with rubble, and all that was standing were charred telegraph poles and tin shelters from which emanated wisps of smoke and the scent of charcoal. Faint outlines showed where houses had once stood, though there was nothing inside now but strands of rusted iron, broken tiles, shards of crockery. Satsuko led the way through the labyrinth of soot.

I'd asked her if she would take me to see her old neighbourhood. She had seemed terrified for a moment, as if a ghost had appeared before her. But then she looked up at me, searchingly, and finally she nodded, apparently resolved.

We walked in silence through the char, negotiating mounds of earth and ditches filled with brambles and weeds.

There was a quality to Satsuko that I couldn't quite define. Behind the frank warmth she exuded as she sat beside me at the bar was an aura of profound tragedy, and endurance. She was an enigma to me, I accepted, but not one fatally inscrutable, as so many of my countrymen tediously asserted the Japanese to be. Despite the short length of our common frontier, the depth of our hinterlands, I felt a curious bond with the dark-eyed girl, as she sat in her woollen skirt and white blouse and poured beer and dealt out playing cards on the counter. We had established a wonderful shelter of the subtle and banal, a sanctuary of the trivial and the everyday, within which we both seemed tacitly content to hide. I flattered myself that we were more than just another man and woman cast together by the great currents of the world. That the flashing sensation I felt when I was with her was correct: that I understood her, and—even more puzzling—that she understood me. But the nights of fire that lurked on the borders of my dreams lay between us still, and I knew that I needed to see the site of her home—the place of her ruin—if I were to hope to fathom her mystery; if I wished to salvage something of myself.

We reached a canal, and walked halfway across a green, iron-riveted bridge. She leaned over the side. Down below was a concrete bed, flowing with shallow water. She pointed upstream.

"Factory," she said. "Chemical."

I nodded, imagining the explosion. She rested her elbows on the metal, slim-waisted and willowy as she gazed out. Along the banks of the channel were lumberyards. Wet, black ash soiled their cobblestones, and frail stacks of wood stood like piles of burnt matchsticks, waiting to be blown away. Further up, a set of lock gates were warped and splintered. She pointed, making a swimming motion with her arms.

"Swim? You used to swim there?"

She nodded. "Children. I. My brother."

I pictured boys and girls diving into the water, ducking and playing hide-and-seek as they swam around the timber barges. From the other side of the canal came the faint sound of high-pitched chanting. We passed a schoolyard and finally came out onto a wider avenue. A little further down, by the entrance to a furrowed alleyway, she stopped. She clasped her arms over her chest, and I saw that she was scared and was trying to summon up courage. I attempted to take her hand, but she pulled it away and shook her head. She took a deep breath and strode forward.

We walked down a row of incinerated buildings until we reached a square concrete cistern. She stopped and frowned.

"This. I think—"

She crossed an invisible threshold onto a patch of ground, littered with ash and broken glass. I hesitated at the boundary. Weeds had sprung up, as high as my thigh. She closed her eyes, holding out her arms, and then gently spun about, like a little girl in a daydream. As she stood there, the field of rubble stretching to the river beyond, I imagined her that night, the air quivering as the planes roared over in a great metallic typhoon.

She turned to face me. She sprinkled her fingers in the air to mimic falling bombs.

"My house," she said. "Burn down."

I nodded. On my map, the whole of the Asakusa ward had been shaded the darkest of blacks. *Inflammable Area—Grade 1.* She was standing, arms extended, palms down, as if measuring the space around her. She pointed into the air. "My mother—"

I frowned. "Your mother's room?"

"So."

She turned and pointed again. "There, my brother—"

"Your brother's room?"

"So." She frowned and touched a finger to her nose. "My room also."

"What happened to your mother, Satsuko?"

She held her hands up, waving her fingers around her head. "Fire."

I swallowed. "And your brother?"

She looked down at the ground and slowly shook her head. It was then that I stepped over the threshold. I walked to her and took her hands in mine. When she looked up, her eyes were wet with tears.

"Satsuko—"

What could I say? Please forgive me, Satsuko? I'm sorry, Satsuko, for burning down your house? For killing your mother and your brother? I rubbed my thumbs against her smooth palms, as if, like some saint of old, I could miraculously heal the scars.

"Satsuko—"

She looked up at me, gasping, as I held her shaking body in my arms. I pulled her forward and clasped her frail torso. As our cheeks pressed against each other, I imagined the two of us together like this, that night, silhouetted on the blackened plain, the chemical works burning like a livid green candle behind us as rivulets of fire streamed across the sky.

Finally, we drew apart. The wind gusted around us, ruffling the feathery fronds of the weeds. I gripped her hand in my own, and, together, we picked our way out of the rubble and walked back toward the avenue.

Our shadows cast long in the afternoon sunshine as we strolled among the bustling crowds on our way to the train station. Satsuko drew closer to me. Western men and Japanese girls passed us occasionally, the men glancing at me with expressions of awkward complicity. I put my arm around Satsuko's waist. I imagined the two of us walking together along Fifth Avenue, Christmas shopping in the December snow. At the Metropolitan Opera, drinking cocktails before a concert. The pompous looks of disdain from the fur-coated women; the envious eyes of the patrician men in their dinner suits. I was still smiling as we reached the scaffolded gate of the Senso Temple. A jeep skidded up beside us. A press card was wedged behind the windshield.

Eugene took off his aviator sunglasses as he clambered out the door. Japan had filled him out—there was a mottled fleshiness to his face now, a hint of gut beneath his khaki shirt.

"Hal," he exclaimed, holding out his hand. "I didn't know you were still here!"

"Hello, Gene. Where else would I be?"

He hesitated. "I figured you'd gone back to New York."

"How so?"

He paused, then glanced at Satsuko, raising his eyebrows in lewd question. I pictured her for a moment in her cheap kimono, tugging him onto the dance floor of the Oasis, and felt a stab of panic that he might recognize her. *Primrose.* Her face betrayed nothing.

"Gene, this is Satsuko."

He grinned and saluted.

"Hello, Satsuko."

Satsuko nodded demurely, and drew closer to me.

"Working on something, Gene?" I asked, pointing at the Speed Graphic around his neck.

He rolled his eyes. "The monks here," he said, jerking his thumb toward the temple. "Apparently they keep prize chickens."

"Huh. Sounds like Dutch. Human interest?"

"Can't all be hotshots like you, I guess, Hal."

I studied his face. Acne had erupted across his cheeks and thin hairs were growing on his upper lip, as if he'd just now entered adolescence. Satsuko excused herself, and walked over to browse a stall. Eugene watched her appraisingly, then gave a low whistle. He turned back to me with a triumphant leer.

"So you finally succumbed to yellow fever, Hal. After all your inoculations. Maybe you're human after all."

I forced a smile. "It's not quite like that, Gene."

"Oh no?" He squinted back at her. "What is she? An imperial princess?"

"She's just an ordinary girl."

He laughed. "She's got her claws into you, Hal. All of them try sooner or later, trust me. They all want to see New York. She ask you to marry her yet?"

"No."

"So what's the deal, then, Hal? Angel with a broken wing?"

"Does it matter?"

He shrugged. "I guess. I'm glad you've found yourself a piece at last. Do you good."

My fist tightened involuntarily.

"She's not a piece of anything, Eugene."

My house, she'd said, staring at me with tears in her eyes. *Fire.*

His eyes widened. "Is this what they call penance, Hal? Atonement for your sins? Or is it just good old Catholic guilt?"

I felt a flare of rage and moved forward.

He jumped back, fear in his eyes. Then, suddenly, his face became wreathed in a smile. Satsuko had wandered back over. She put her arm in mine and I felt her fingers squeeze my own.

"Well, it was good to see you again, Hal," Eugene said. "You two look swell together. Mind if I take a snap?"

My rage slowly ebbed as he held up the camera. Satsuko combed back an invisible wisp of hair and looked up at him. I waited for the flicker of the shutter behind the lens.

"Smile!"

When we got back home that night, we went straight upstairs. I shut the door and when I turned around, Satsuko was naked. It was cold in the room, and she stepped lightly over to me, putting her arms around my neck. I rested my chin on her head for a moment, rubbing the ridges of her spine beneath my fingertips. She looked up at me, and I kissed her gently, feeling the soft warmth of her lips on mine, her small tongue darting timidly into my mouth. I quickly undressed, and she led me over to the futon and I blew out the light and pulled the covers over us.

Moonlight was falling into the room as we lay there, very close, holding each other tenderly. Haltingly, she moved around until she was lying on top of me and pressed against my rib cage. I felt her hand move, and then her chin tilted upward and she gave a small gasp. Her pale belly was trembling in the darkness, black tresses of hair falling down over dark-tipped breasts. She placed both of her hands on my chest and, with a deep sigh, pushed down. Slowly, she arched her back, and I could see the indentations of her ribs rippling like shadows beneath her breasts. Her eyes closed and her cheeks flushed and finally, with a moan, she twisted her hips and gasped. Her breath came out slowly, in shivers. She gazed at me, and whispered my name; in the moonlit darkness, I could see her black eyes glistening with blurry stars, the smeared reflections of far-away fires.

28
An Only One
(*Satsuko Takara*)

America.

I couldn't remember ever having seen a map of the United States before. But Mrs. Ishino had an old atlas of the world on her shelf, and I sat with it now at the back of the bar, spelling out the unfamiliar names of the cities and rivers and prefectures, trying to commit them to memory.

New York, where Hal-san had studied, was famous, of course, and so was Chicago, with its skyscrapers and gangsters and jazz cabarets. But what about Nebraska? Utah? Albuquerque? Half of the names were unpronounceable, even if I had been able to speak English fluently. I closed the atlas in frustration. The thought of America was becoming an obsession. I was worried that I would bore Hal silly by asking him about it. I picked up the wrinkled magazine that someone had left on the bar earlier that week. There was a long feature with a set of colour photographs of California inside. While New York and Chicago might have been exciting places to visit, I'd decided that California was the place for me.

San Francisco seemed almost Japan-like, I thought, as I studied the photographs in the magazine for the hundredth time. Brightly painted wooden houses stood up on the hills and fishing boats were docked at the bustling wharves. There were forests and mountains in the distance, and Mrs. Ishino had once told me that other Japanese people lived there too, so I might still be able to buy miso and *katsuobushi* whenever I had a craving for Japanese food, or felt homesick for Tokyo.

Not that there seemed much chance of that. The magazines were so glossy and the colours so startlingly rich that I wondered if the sun might somehow be brighter in America than it was in Japan. The pages were packed with pictures of healthy-looking men playing baseball and tennis and golf, lounging by swimming pools and smoking cigarettes, whilst neat, smiling housewives in bright calico dresses stood next to refrigerators laden with meat, churned yellow butter, and glass bottles of orange juice. There were advertisements for everything and anything, from syrup to stockings, spectacles to hats. Silk gloves, leather shoes, bedsheets, perfume, whisky and wedding rings. Everyone was happy, and judging from the way America looked in the magazines, that was hardly surprising.

I sighed and placed the magazine down. I walked over to the open doorway. The sky was grey and the street outside was full of churned mud. Children ran half-naked past the shanty houses, and a toothless man walked slowly past with hollow eyes, his clothes loose upon his body.

The idea that I might go to America started as a joke. One evening, as we sat at the counter, Hal-san was telling me about his old college in New York, which sounded similar to the castle-like buildings of the Imperial University. Just at that moment, he caught my eye.

"Would you like to live in America someday, Satsuko?" he said.

My heart rose to my throat. For a moment, I thought he had actually asked me to go away with him, just as casually as he might ask me to the cinema. I started to stammer. Then my cheeks flushed as it dawned on me, that, of course, he had just been asking the question in a general kind of way.

I tried to laugh. America certainly sounded wonderful, I said, but I couldn't speak English very well, and of course, I'd miss all of my friends. He put his hand on my wrist and stroked it gently and I wondered if he wasn't a little bit drunk.

"We could find you a teacher," he murmured.

I laughed again, more cynically this time. Teaching you English was something they all promised to do.

"Cat, sat, mat," I muttered. "How are you? How do you do?"

It was a stupid thing for him to have asked, and I was annoyed at him for suggesting it.

But then I saw that he was looking at me quite seriously. For a moment, I let myself imagine what it might be like, living far away in a foreign country. A house beside a shady park that stretched all the way to the ocean. I could grow daikon and burdock in the garden. The days would come and go. Hal would go off to work at his newspaper every morning, and I would visit the beach, listening to the seagulls, as our children played around me in the sunshine.

Posters were appearing all over Tokyo with Michiko's beautiful face upon them. Everyone was looking forward to her new film. The cinema magazines reported that the action was to take place in the burned-out streets of the city itself, and I found myself watching out for the film crew whenever I visited the market.

For weeks, I had been convincing myself that I should write to Michiko and tell her where I was living. But as I pictured her, lounging in her glamorous apartment, surrounded by clothes and magazines, I wondered if she would even open a letter from me. She might fling it from her in terror when she saw my name, repelled by the thought of any contact with this spider from her past.

But finally, one afternoon, I sat down to write in any case, intending to keep the note brief and to the point. I gave her my address, and told her that I was working in a restaurant again, that I had several warmhearted companions and that life was full of possibilities.

"I was so thrilled to see you on the screen last month,

Michiko," I wrote, "when my American and I visited the cinema together."

I stared at the words I had just written. My American? My heart started to patter, as I picked up the pen once more.

"Yes, Michiko, it's true. I too have found an 'only one,' as you yourself did last year. I very much hope that you will have the chance to visit us. Please do not be too embarrassed to come. I admit that I was upset when you moved away, but I know now that it was all for the best. After all, you were simply choosing to live, Michiko, in the only way you knew how. Just as we must all try to live."

I started to feel quite emotional. The images from the magazine were still fresh in my mind. It was at this point that I may have got carried away.

"I hope, in any case, you will be able to come to visit before too long, though I know how busy you must be with your cinema activities. Because very soon, Michiko, my American will be taking me away from Japan. We will be going to live in San Francisco, and I may not return for a long time. So you see, Michiko, it is not only film stars like you that can have exciting romantic adventures!"

My heart was in my mouth as I sealed the note and copied out the address of Michiko's studio from the back of a film magazine. I couldn't quite believe what I had written. But as I handed the letter to the postmaster, I felt as if the flimsy note was a votive plaque that I was hanging at a shrine, a hopeless prayer that I dreamed might somehow come true.

When Hal came back to Mrs. Ishino's that evening, he seemed worried and drew his fingers through his thick hair. My stomach tightened as I went to make him a sandwich. I poured him a drink. After a while, he seemed to relax.

Later on, casually, I took down Mrs. Ishino's atlas, and opened it up to the map of America. His eyes lit up and he laughed. Taking my hand beneath his own, he drew my finger to the eastern side of the country.

"New York," he said, pointing at himself. "The Empire State."

I smiled and shook my head. I drew his hand back to the other side of the map again.

"No empire. San Francisco," I said.

He started to laugh again, that warm, glorious laugh that poured from his chest.

"You want to live in San Francisco, Satsuko?" he said.

I smiled. "Yes. You take me."

"You want me to take you to San Francisco?" he said, sweeping his fingers through his hair. "Sure! Why not? Let's go to San Francisco. We'll take the next boat!"

I couldn't quite tell if he was joking or not. He shook his head with a faraway smile. He gazed at me for a second, then looked away, rubbing my hand over and over again.

We went up to his room soon after. His body was strong and taut and I felt a great, piercing sense of relief sweep through me. In the middle of the night, I woke up and gazed at his smooth, white skin, his chest moving softly up and down. I wondered whether I should slip downstairs to my room, but the nest of blankets was so cozy, and there was such a gentle warmth emanating from his body, that I just lay beside him, clasping my hands around his broad chest, and fell away into a deep sleep.

When I woke in the morning he was already getting ready to leave. I lay there dozing for a while, taking pleasure in the sound of him washing and getting dressed. Just before he left, he leaned down over the futon and kissed me on the forehead. For a moment I could smell the musky scent of his cologne on his smooth cheeks. Then the door closed and I lay there in a shaft of spring sunlight, breathing in the scent of the sheets, watching the motes of dust dance in the air. I thought that I should probably get up and go on with my work quite soon, but then I told myself I should stay for a little while longer, that I deserved to be happy, just for this short time. And so I lay there, smiling secretly to myself, stretched out on the bed like a satisfied cat.

29
THE YAKUZA
(*Hiroshi Takara*)

From the top of the old railway bridge, I scanned the market through the sight of my sniper rifle: *Captain Takara—deep behind enemy lines.*

Slowly, I swept from side to side, as the huge American flag flicked on its pole, casting a shadow over the GIs who were ambling amongst the stalls below. *Easy targets*, I thought. *One bullet each. Aim for the heart—*

There was a flash of colour as the three girls flounced toward the market. I fumbled with the aperture of my Leica and urgently twisted the rangefinder. Through the lens, I focused on the stocky one in the middle, the one they called Yotchan.

I could almost make out the shadow that curved between her breasts. *Fire!*

I pressed the shutter and the flutter lens closed. *Bull's eye!*

A hand cuffed me on the back of the head and I spun around. Mr. Suzuki was laughing at me, hands on his hips. The shoulder holster of his pistol showed beneath his grey silk jacket.

"Getting some cute pictures, are you, little shit?" he said. "No wonder you spend so much time up here."

My cheeks began to throb.

"Put your dick away. It's lunchtime."

Mr. Suzuki wasn't a man to argue with. The market boss had almost killed me two weeks before, when I'd gone to the station to drum up portrait business. I'd spotted him at the mouth of the market, looking up and down the road as if he was waiting for someone. The grey felt fedora was pulled low over his forehead, and a white silk handkerchief ruffled from his breast pocket.

I ran over and held up my Leica in question.

"Sir—"

I didn't get a chance to finish.

"You want me to break that thing in your fucking face?" he snarled.

I backed off right away—I got the message all right. He glared at me, a faint squint in his eye. A memory came to me then, of an afternoon long ago, years before the Pacific War had even broken out.

Back in the days when our shop had been open, my mother sometimes asked me to deliver box lunches to especially important customers in the neighbourhood. One afternoon in July, a huge order had arrived just after midday. It was the busiest time of the year—the real dog days when the line snaked all the way down the alley, with everyone desperate to eat their fill of unagi-don to revive their flagging spirits.

My father glanced at the name card. He gave a low whistle and wiped the sweat from his brow. Politely, he told the customers out front that there would be a short delay in serving them, and tightened the cloth around his head. He piled up charcoal on the grill, and started frantically brushing the sizzling strips of eel with sauce from his pot as fast he could, calling to my mother to pile them onto rice in our best lacquered boxes.

As she loaded the parcels into the carriage of my delivery bicycle, she grasped my arm and wiped my face with her sleeve. "Go as quick as you can," she said. "And keep a civil tongue in your head!"

When I reached the address on the card, in a row of tenements up by Sengen Shrine, I thought I was lost. There was nothing there but an abandoned house with broken shutters, stray cats stretched out asleep on the roof. Then, from inside, I heard faint voices—shouting out numbers, intriguing rattles and slams. Nervously, I tapped on the door. A moment later, a half-naked man slid it open, waving a silk fan against his upper body as he squinted down at me. The rippling torso was completely inked over with colourful tattoos.

Now, Mr. Suzuki stepped toward me.

"Do I know you?" he said, his voice slurring like a proper yakuza.

I bowed my head. There was no way he could remember me, I thought, not a chance.

"What the fuck happened to your face?"

"I got burned, sir," I said.

"You don't say."

He peered at the camera around my neck. "You know how to use that thing?"

I nodded.

"So come over here."

On the other side of the station, a huge sign was hoisted up alongside the overground train track. Made of high-powered electric lightbulbs, it spelled out the name of the market, so that people could see it for miles around. Mr. Suzuki stood underneath it, and tipped his hat over his eye, almost daintily.

"Be sure you get the sign in the picture," he said, jerking his thumb into the air.

As I twisted the lens, his blunt face came into focus. A ribbed, crescent-shaped scar dimpled one of his cheeks.

"And make it a good one, kid," he called. "I might not be here so long."

I stifled a grin. This was exactly the kind of thing that gangsters were supposed to say! I held up my hand in a professional manner, and pressed the shutter firmly. He strode back over and roughly pulled the camera from around my neck, grunting as he turned it about in his clumsy hands.

"You really know how to use this?"

"It's not so hard, sir."

He stared at me for a moment. Then he draped the camera back around my neck. "Hungry?"

My eyes lit up as he jerked his head toward a stall just inside the market. Clouds of fragrant steam were billowing from the pots and my mouth started to water. The spry old chef welcomed us in like royalty: he hurried out to wipe down our stools and poured a frothing bottle of beer into a glass he set on the counter in front of Mr. Suzuki.

"Make yourselves at home, young sirs," he said as he bustled around his pots and pans. "You're very welcome!"

"What filthy soup are you using today, granddad?" Mr. Suzuki drawled.

"Dog and crow, sir." The man giggled and stirred the big metal vat on his makeshift stove with a long ladle. Mr. Suzuki grunted.

"Two of those, then, granddad. Extra chives, extra jewels, hard-boiled egg."

"Coming right up!"

As I shovelled the almost unbearably delicious noodles into my mouth, I wondered what Mr. Suzuki could possibly want with me. A lot of the other street kids were going into the gangs now, but I didn't want to be any part of the yakuza, even if I had stolen the camera. My father would have been ashamed of me. Even so, it was pretty exciting to be sitting next to a real live gangster. People going past glanced at me with interest, and I cocked my head casually, as if eating with Mr. Suzuki was something I did every day of the week.

"Where do I remember you from, kid?" he said, taking a sip of his beer. It was amazing. I guessed a man like him needed a good memory.

"My father used to own a restaurant, sir. Not so far from your old office."

He grinned, as if remembering far-off, sunlit days. "Takara Eels?"

My heart almost burst with pride—my dad's shop!

"Fucking great," he said. "Shame it closed down. All dead now, I guess?"

A pit opened in my stomach. I bowed my head. "Yes, sir. I'm sorry."

"Even that cute girl? Was she your sister?"

I glowered at him. Mr. Suzuki raised his eyebrows and held up his hands in apology.

"Alright, little shit—don't go upsetting yourself. Where'd you get that contraption from in any case?"

He pointed at the camera, and I drew it closer to my chest, fingering the knot in the leather strap.

"Steal it?" he smirked.

I stared at the table in silence.

"Suit yourself."

He drew a big pile of noodles onto his chopsticks and gazed at the steam that came off.

"No family left at all?" he asked, stuffing the noodles into his mouth.

I shook my head.

"That makes two of us."

He slurped down the last of the soup, then lit a cigarette. "Want to take some pictures for me?" he asked, as he squinted through the smoke.

"Photographs, sir?"

"I could use someone with sharp eyes."

Despite what I had told myself, there was something about his face that made me nod straightaway.

"Good boy," he said. "Work hard for me and I'll see you're treated right."

There were little wrinkles on his forehead. As I stared at his blunt features, I realized that he was older than he looked. He snapped his fingers in front of my face.

"See?" he said with a grin. I found myself grinning back at him. "Now you've got a friend in the world."

I left the inn soon after the children had gone away. It felt too lonely after that, the paper screens torn, the tatami littered with dead moths and butterflies. The grass was waist-high in the garden when I went, the cracked statue of the tanuki still lying grinning on the threshold.

Now that the weather was warmer, I slept in Ueno Park, beneath a tarpaulin stretched from a tree not far from the shogun's graveyard. The lotus plants in the pond were leafy now, and green and black ducks dabbled in the water. I hung around the clapboard bars in Yurakucho where the Americans drank at night, holding up the camera hopefully as they lurched out. They posed drunkenly, arm in arm with their friends, or with giggling Japanese girls hoisted up on their shoulders. They scribbled their names and their billet in my exercise book, and I wrote down the number showing on my exposure counter. An old chemist developed the film for me at the back of his tiny studio in Kanda, and I delivered the prints to the Americans a week later to collect my fee. I stood in the marble lobbies as they flipped through the shots, guffawing, and tried to smile as they patted me on the head and I waited for my money.

Mr. Suzuki gave me a ninety-millimetre screw-mount lens for my camera and a big pair of field binoculars that must have belonged to some officer during the war. From the top of the old railway bridge, you could see people approaching from any direction. Mr. Suzuki told me to take pictures of anyone I didn't recognize, and showed me a series of flags to shoot down a wire stretched over the market if there was ever any sign of trouble—white for American military police, red for Koreans or Formosans. Sometimes, too, he had me take stealthy photographs of the American soldiers who came to the market in military trucks to deliver crates of cigarettes and rations, and who took sheaves of cash from Mr. Suzuki, holding up their thumbs and slapping the sides of the cabs before roaring away.

The rest of the time, I was free to roam about taking photographs of whatever I chose. The market became my personal cinema as I gazed through the rangefinder of my camera, the cool, heavy frame a comforting weight against my face: the traders laying out piles of old boots, bony women stalking the aisles with babies on their backs, the ex-students who ran the liquor stall and drank glass after glass of booze at the end of the day until they collapsed on the ground.

Then, there were the pan-pan girls, who strutted through the market as if they owned the place, shrieking like vixens and yammering insults. They grabbed any man that they fancied by the arm, or the crotch, and dragged him away beneath the railway arches.

The girl in the purple dress gave me a sharp erotic thrill whenever I saw her. Yotchan must have been about eighteen and wore heavy lilac makeup, her hair cut in a straight line so that it fell just above her eyes. There was something about her thick legs and giant breasts that made my stomach melt, and sent me scrambling up the ladder to the top of the railway tracks to helplessly relieve myself. As I watched her through my camera, day after day, a plan began to take shape in my mind. Mr. Suzuki had told me that I was getting paid at the end of the week, fifty yen. Yotchan, I'd heard, cost ten. Finally, I decided. It was about time.

Mr. Suzuki must have noticed that I was distracted, because, toward the end of the week, he called me over to the office, a wooden hut on the edge of the market. A pile of crisp black-

and-white photographs lay on the desk in front of him, and he frowned as he flicked through them. At the end of the stack was the blurry shot of Yotchan. He grinned.

"Cute," he said. "Not my type, though."

He leaned forward. "You want to see some real pictures of girls?"

My heart began to thud as he took an envelope from his desk drawer and slid it over to me. I quickly stuffed it under my shirt as he gave me a wink.

"Don't worry, kid. I was just the same at your age. Though I'm guessing you're a man already, right?"

I swallowed, glancing at the picture of Yotchan. He grunted.

"No? Well. I'm disappointed in you. It's about time, then, isn't it?"

My pulse started to race.

"You've worked hard all month," he said. "You could do with a break. I'll tell you what, next weekend, we'll go to a place I know in Shinjuku. They'll show you the hills and the valleys."

I started to tremble. *This was it!* I bowed my head, my fingers clutching the envelope beneath my shirt. Just as I was leaving, he called out behind me.

"They're all good girls," he said. "Not like real geishas. More like *Daruma* dolls."

I stared at him, lost. He started to wheeze with laughter.

"You can roll them over as much as you like!"

I kept my head down as I shuffled through the market, painfully aware of the envelope hidden beneath my shirt. I didn't even notice the girls until I had walked straight into them. Something soft bumped against my head and I was suddenly surrounded by a choking cloud of perfume.

"Hey, look where you're going, you little prick!"

Clouds of coloured nylon and cotton swirled around me. The girls' faces were plastered with makeup and they grinned at me like jackals. Yotchan jerked her hand up in a brutal sexual motion.

"Gone blind, have you?"

My cheeks throbbed. It was as if she could see right through me.

A nasty grin came over her face. "Well. I don't suppose you get much with that melted face of yours. How old are you anyway?"

"Fifteen," I muttered.

Her eyes narrowed as she edged closer. "Well. You're practically a man already, then, aren't you?"

My face was nearly touching the pale skin between her throat and her breasts, my nose swamped with the sour animal smell of her sweat.

"Want to take me on, kid? You've got money, don't you?"

Despite my panic, I felt an almost excruciating excitement. *Please*, I thought, *don't let me lose control, not right here and now.* Yotchan was staring at me slyly, her bright red lips moving round and round as she chewed her gum.

Suddenly, her hand shot out and she gripped my privates. She squeezed and I gasped as her eyes grew wide.

"Well!" she said. "You are a man after all."

She pulled my head toward her and crushed it against the pillow of her bosom. I heard the other girls shrieking with laughter, and I struggled to free myself, spluttering. The stallholders had all gathered round now and were cackling away, enjoying every moment.

Yotchan snorted. "Well. He knows where to find me."

I stumbled backward, bent over double. Yotchan fluttered her hand in the air. "Come back tonight. Make sure you bring enough money."

I slunk away, my cheeks throbbing.

Yotchan suddenly exploded with a splutter of laughter. "Hey! You've forgotten something."

I froze, rooted to the spot, suddenly aware of the lack of weight within my shirt.

I hardly dared to glance back as I ran toward the railway embankment. Yotchan was bent over, shrieking, waving the photographs in the air for all the world to see. The stallholders were all roaring with laughter, tears of amusement streaming down their faces.

30
SENTIMENTAL JOURNEY
(Hal Lynch)

Ward was subdued as he sat at the kitchen table in his fine new house in Shinjuku, freshly decorated in preparation for the arrival of his wife, Judy, from Chicago. A new set of wicker furniture graced the room and the sliding doors were wide open to disperse the lingering smell of fresh paint and pickled radish. I felt a pang of jealousy as he showed me the neat garden outside—the wisteria in bud over the doorway, a cherry tree ablaze with white blossom and filling the air with scent that mingled with a thread of incense from the nearby temple. His beard was thick now, streaked with silver, and he wore a long silk robe, as if he had just stepped out of some antique Japanese painting.

"So where are we, Ward?"

"I've talked to more people this week, Hal. Harry Welles from *LIFE*. Auberon Fox from *TIME*. They're intrigued. They want to see your pictures as soon as you arrive home."

The whir of a cicada came from the trees. I went over and stood in the doorway. From up above the slanted tiles of the temple roof floated the thudding sound of a drum.

"Are you ready?" he said.

The drum beat faster and faster, until, with a bang, it suddenly halted.

"Almost. When's Judy arriving?"

"Friday."

"Everything fixed up?"

Ward grunted. "Almost."

He stood up to fetch a bottle of Guckenheimer from the sideboard and poured us two glasses. Birdsong trilled from the garden; there was the faint, far-off drone of Buddhist prayers being recited.

"It's a beautiful home, Ward. I'm sure you'll be happy here."

He nodded steadily and sipped at his drink.

"You're going to miss Japan, Lynch. Isn't that so?"

I thought of the imprint of Satsuko on my bed that morning, silently echoing the contours of her body. Stray strands of black hair upon the pillow. The cedarwood cigar box hidden, waiting, under the floorboard in the corner of my room. I needed to talk to her, and soon.

"You won't look back from this, Lynch," Ward said. "Believe me. It'll be the making of you."

I nodded.

He draped a sandalled foot over his big thigh and blinked heavily. He rubbed his eyes and gave a lopsided grin. "You know that I'm proud of you, don't you, Hal?"

I nodded. "Thank you, Mark."

He poured more whisky into his glass and sighed again, then turned to look at the last cherry blossom in the garden. My throat tightened. In the pale sunlight, sitting in his chair, for a moment, he looked just like my father.

The first warmth of summer was hovering outside my window as I gazed over the crooked planks of the tenements below. A horse-drawn cart paused in the alley, and a ragged child stroked the animal's flank. I rolled out the carbon from the drum of my typewriter. I was in shirtsleeves, rewriting what I hoped would be the final draft of my Hiroshima piece.

There was a quiet knock at the door and Satsuko came in. She was carrying a glass of beer and some rice crackers. I sat her down upon my knee as I read over what I'd written. I ran my fingers through her hair. I kissed her. The sweeping horns of "Sentimental Journey" were drifting up through the floorboards, and streetcars clanged in the road as the dusky sunlight streamed over us.

The USS *New Mexico* was leaving the following week for San Francisco. I'd booked my passage that morning; the ticket was safe in my jacket pocket. At the Military Affairs office, I'd made inquiries about the legal procedure of Japanese emigration and entry to the United States. The captain had rolled his eyes and told me I was the third person to ask that day. The Alien Exclusion Act was still in place for Orientals, he said, but everyone thought it most likely would soon be rescinded, judging from the number of potential war brides strolling around on the arms of American soldiers. Satsuko could join me later, I figured, after the restrictions were lifted. Five months, six at the most. After my photographs had been published. After my whole world had changed.

We undressed and lay down on my futon and I inhaled the scent of her pale skin, feeling the warmth of her body against mine. She was naked except for a narrow wristwatch that I'd bought for her two days before.

She reached over for her purse. From it, she took a small velvet jewellery box, which she shyly presented to me. Inside was a small silver crucifix on a chain. She took it out and draped it around my neck, then fastened the clasp. She pulled me over so that we both faced the cracked mirror leaning against the wall. She pointed at the reflection of our entwined bodies.

"Look," she said. "Adam—and Eva."

31
THE BRIGHT LIGHT FROM THE WEST
(*Satsuko Takara*)

Not long after breakfast, I felt suddenly very sick. I dashed to the latrine outside, where I retched up the miso soup and pickles I had just eaten. Dizzily, I looked down at the filth, swamped by the smell of rot and sewage. As I shuffled back inside, Mrs. Ishino emerged from her parlour room at the back of the bar, wearing a plain kimono. She saw straightaway that something was the matter. She ushered me onto a stool at the counter and asked me what was wrong.

When I explained what had happened, she fell silent. She looked at me closely.

"How long, Satsuko?" she asked. "Since your last cycle?"

I puzzled it through, doubtfully. All of our cycles had been highly erratic for some time, just like everything else, so it was very hard to keep track. But I suspected that it had been several months now, at least.

Mrs. Ishino picked up my hand and squeezed it.

"Please don't worry, Satsuko," she said. "I'm convinced that Lynch-san is a good man."

I stared at her for a moment as I grasped what she was saying. Then I burst into tears.

Sheets of typewritten paper were piled up on Hal's desk next to his typewriter, socks and shirts draped over the back of his chair. The futon was still on the floor, the blanket crumpled up where we had left it that morning. There was a faint film of dust on the windowsill, and I drew my finger through it absently. A battered pigskin suitcase stood in the corner of the room. A curious feeling came over me. I knelt down beside it and pushed the hasps. The locks flicked open.

A couple of vests were balled up inside, and there was a smell of mildew. Beside the vests were newspapers, and as I spelled out the title, I recognized the name of the paper that Hal had worked for. I leafed through the copy on the top. Photographs of men and soldiers, as usual. Carefully, I began to study the names typed beneath the pictures, with a tingle of expectation. Wouldn't it be lovely if I found Hal's name written there? Toward the end of the stack, I flipped over a front page. My finger paused. There it was! "Harold Lynch."

I studied the large, blurred photograph above it. A group of street children were playing a game of baseball on a patch of wasteground.

I screamed.

A boy with a disfigured face held a charred plank as another boy flung a ball of rags toward him. It was Hiroshi. Unmistakably, I thought, as I brought the page close to my face and stared at the blurred dots of the image. Despite the tangled hair, the disfigured face, it was him.

I started to feel very faint. It was my brother. He had that earnest look of concentration on his face, just like when he and my father had thrown baseballs in Ueno Park, the same excited tension in his eyes as when he'd gazed at the cinema screen of the Paradise Picture House, when we'd gone to watch a film together on a Sunday.

I realized that I was softly moaning. All this time. Hiroshi.

I stood up and placed the newspaper upon the desk. I held my palm over my belly. There was the faintest swelling beneath the cotton. Hopeless images flashed through my mind. The boiled bodies being hoisted on a hook from the Yoshiwara canal. My hand-drawn sign at Tokyo Station, smeared from the rain. The horrible urchin on the railway platform, exposing himself to me. I closed my eyes. What if Hiroshi had seen me, I thought, standing outside the Oasis, my face plastered white as I clutched at the arm of another passing GI? *Come in, yankii! Very cheap!*

Into my mind's eye came the pictures of America from the magazine. The smiling families in their motorcars, the advertisements for soap, for lacework wedding dresses. The photographs of San Francisco, the white city rising between green hills, thousands of miles away, far away beyond the ocean.

Before I knew it, I was clawing at the thin, rough newspaper, tearing the photograph from the page. Urgently, I ripped it into shreds. I heaved open the window, and flung the fragments of paper into the air outside. They fluttered for a moment, like falling blossoms, then drifted randomly down, scattering into the muddy puddles in the alley below.

Election posters were pasted up all across the city, painted with doves and slogans. That week, the ration fell, and the Imperial Plaza grew crowded every day with gaunt men and women waving placards and chanting. A rumour went around that the grain ship from America had sunk, that there was only enough food left for a few days. Prices shot up at the black market, and gunfights broke out in the streets. Men dangled out of the windows of the office buildings, using magnifying glasses to light their cigarettes with the weak rays of the spring sunshine.

At the table at the back of the bar, Mrs. Ishino was drinking a glass of clear liquor. She was in a sentimental mood. Masuko had found the disc of a Puccini opera that morning while we'd been out shopping, and the soprano was warbling away now from the gramophone.

"Madame Butterfly!" Mrs. Ishino said, pointing at me and laughing. "Do you know we used to dance to that, Satsuko, here in Tokyo?"

Her arms swayed in the air.

"So many rules, Satsuko! They shut us down because Lieutenant Pinkerton was an American."

I pictured the huge portrait of Okichi, the maidservant presented to the Americans in the Edo period, framed on the wall of the sooty building on the Ginza at my interview all those months ago.

"What happened to your husband, Mrs. Ishino?"

She glanced at me abruptly. I had always been too shy to ask about her mysterious past. I thought she would tell me now.

She shuffled over to the phonograph, and lifted the needle-arm from the disc. The music stopped. She took a stool around to the other side of the bar, climbed up, and reached for the picture on the wall above the bottles on the top shelf—the framed photograph of a handsome man in a flying jacket. Masuko and I had long ago decided that the man must have once been Mrs. Ishino's lover. She clambered back down and placed the photograph on the table between us.

"Lieutenant Ishino," she said, touching her fingertip to his face. She swallowed her drink and wiped her mouth. "We were childhood sweethearts, though he was a year younger than me. Can you imagine?"

I bowed my head.

"He chose to die."

I looked up sharply. She nodded, staring at me.

"Yes, Satsuko. He did. He was stationed over at the Tsuchiura airfield. My dance school had been closed down by then. Planes used to pass over the city every day and I'd always jump and wave, imagining that it was him up there, looking down at me."

She stared at the empty glass.

"What happened to him?" I whispered.

"He came back home one night, last April, without any warning. It was raining, I remember. I'd been asleep when I heard knocking at the door. There had been an air raid earlier, and it was still pitch-black. I could only just see him on the doorstep."

"He'd come to visit?"

"He said he'd been given overnight leave. He'd been selected as group leader for a special mission. He didn't know when it would happen, only that it would be soon."

She swallowed, and I saw tears in her eyes. She looked at me.

"I knew there was only one reason men were given overnight leave back then, Satsuko. He knew he was going to die. He had come back to say goodbye."

I felt a hard lump in my throat.

"We held onto each other all through the blackout that night. I begged him to try to get out of it somehow—what was the point of dying? I asked. But he refused. It was his duty, he said. He asked me to forgive him. He left at around five in the morning, without telling me where he was going. 'Look for me in the spring,' he said. Those were the last words he spoke to me."

I felt myself starting to cry. Mrs. Ishino opened up the frame and removed the glass. She slid another photograph from behind the first. It showed the same man, in his flying jacket, standing beside a Zero fighter. Around his forehead he wore a headband, emblazoned with the rising sun.

"Eiji flew the lead airplane. He took off just after six a.m. He's smiling. Look."

She pointed at his face and stared at the photograph for a long time.

"Why, Satsuko?" she said. "Why is he smiling?"

She wiped her eyes and went to the bar and poured out another glass of liquor.

"Did you know one of his friends tracked me down last winter, Satsuko?" she called. "Eiji had written me a letter. Do you know what it said? He implored me to forgive him. He asked me to live purely and honourably after his death." She laughed bitterly, gesturing around at the wooden tables and chairs. "Honourably! What chance did I have, after what he had done? After he went off to fly his plane into some American ship? After he left me here alone?"

She let out a sudden sob, and I rushed over and put my arm around her as she shook with tears.

"For what, Satsuko? Why did my husband choose to die?"

I drew her close as she spoke.

"I'll never forgive him for that, Satsuko, never. No one should ever choose to die."

She turned to me and held my hands tightly in hers, tears trickling down her cheeks.

"You see, Satsuko?" she said. "We can choose to live, now. Don't you see, Satsuko? You must choose to live!"

My fingers were clumsy as I helped Hal button his shirt. Protests were slated all across the city that day, and he was going along to take photographs. In a quiet voice, I asked him to meet me at Asakusa Pond later on that evening.

He stroked my hair and held my scarred palms to his lips. He kissed them, then kissed me goodbye and walked out the door.

I listened to his footsteps going down the stairs and I walked over to the window. As he emerged from the door down below, I held my hand over my belly and he strode away up the alley.

I spent most of the day preparing. Mrs. Ishino and I walked to the bathhouse, where she soaped me and scrubbed my back. Afterward, she rubbed a special almond-smelling salve onto my hands. Back at the bar, she took me into her cluttered parlour room. A spring mattress lay on a Western-style brass bedstead, with horsehair bursting from its seams. A row of ivory-coloured ballerina shoes were draped on a rail along the wall. She sat me in front of the mirror and spent several hours combing and arranging my hair, painting my neck and face before she carefully helped me on with my clothes. We decided upon the green and gold kimono my mother had given me, which I had finally bought back from the pawnbroker after several months of saving.

Mrs. Ishino stood behind me and pulled tight my embroidered brocade sash. As I looked in the mirror at my reflection, I saw that she really had done an expert job. My neck was pale, my cheeks were pink, and my hair was beautifully styled and pinned up with a mother-of-pearl comb.

She would come with me as far as the Asakusa tram stop. Evening was darkening outside and I became suddenly nervous and started to tremble. Mrs. Ishino made me drink a glass of whisky and told me that everything was going to be all right. She stroked my wrist as I drank the fiery liquid down. Then she looked up at the clock on the wall. It was six o'clock. She pinched my cheek and said that it was time to go.

32
Tokyo Giants
(*Hiroshi Takara*)

Ueno Station was swarming with people arriving on packed trains from the towns and villages outside the city, all decked out in their best spring suits and kimonos, wearing sashes and aprons and holding up painted banners and placards: *Mothers for the Rice Ration! Railway Men for Reform!*

I watched them warily. The demonstrations had better not interfere with our big night out. Beneath my shirt was an envelope of cash as thick as my finger that Mr. Suzuki had given me that morning. He'd told me to scrub up at the bathhouse, to get my hair cut, and to buy a collared shirt and a tie.

"Get yourself nice and relaxed, kid," he said. "Then you won't be so nervous later on."

As I boarded a tram for the Ginza, I looked down at my new watch. Five hours to go. At eight o'clock, I was going to meet Mr. Suzuki at his office at the market. From there, he was going to drive us both over to Shinjuku himself, in his luxury black Daimler with the brown leather seats.

As I sat in the barber's chair, and the old man fussed around me with his comb and scissors, I wondered why Mr. Suzuki liked me so much. Maybe it was because I was from Asakusa. Maybe he'd just liked my dad's eels. Every night, after the market closed for business, I sat with him in his office as he went over the accounts in his oilskin ledger and totted up the day's profits. When he'd finished, he had me check the numbers while he took a square bottle of whisky from the iron safe in the corner of the hut and poured himself a glass, full to the top. With a sigh, he'd loosen his collar, put his feet up on the desk, and shove the cigarette box toward me.

"You and me, little shit," he'd say. "We're like two badgers from the same hole."

My real job, I sometimes thought, was to listen. As he worked his way through the bottle of whisky, he told me violent stories from the market: about vendors who hadn't paid their dues, about the vicious Formosan gang who'd blasted him in the shoulder. The American officers who double-crossed him and were worse than crooks, the bastards who'd taken all the reconstruction contracts by paying out bribes, the lying politicians in the Diet, General Douglas Fucking MacArthur, and all the other pigs and snakes who were making Mr. Suzuki's life a misery, keeping him from his only true pleasures in life, which, it was clear, were gambling and women.

Asakusa was like his great lost love. "You should have seen it, little shit!" he roared one night, as the bottle got close to the end. "Nowhere else ever came close."

He told me about the Casino Folies, the Russian dancers who kicked their legs right up into the air; how, when he'd been a kid, there had been two Bengal tigers kept in a cage at Hanayashiki Park. But it was the games of flower cards he'd run up in the old abandoned house by Sengen Shrine that seemed to be the pure land of paradise for him. His eyes sparkled and his hands fluttered when he talked about them, as if he was still rattling ghostly dice cups.

"Shirt off, blue and green flashing, sweat dripping down my back. Howling out the bets as the old ladies doled out the cash from their kimonos, the grocers slapping down their wages on the table. That was the real Japan, little shit, not the crap all those military bastards shoved down your throat in school."

I told him how our heads had been shaved right after the attack on Pearl Harbor, how every Friday they'd given us a lunchbox full of rice with a pickled plum in the middle to look like the flag of the rising sun.

Mr. Suzuki would slump forward, cross-eyed on the desk, the bottle now empty. "Look at us now, little shit," he'd slur, as he stubbed out his last cigarette. "We're like carp on the fucking cutting board."

As he started snoring, I'd drag him over to the futon in the corner and pull a woollen military blanket over him. He'd be rolling about, muttering and grunting, as I left, the crows flapping around the market in the first light of dawn.

Rain hammered against the window as my train curved around the overground tracks toward Ueno Station. Up in the distance, I could see the bright spotlights of the market sign blazing away in the dripping night. My hair was trimmed and brushed neatly now, and I wore a grey worsted wool suit and a white cotton shirt I'd bought at a tailor shop off the Ginza. The old man had stared at me over his spectacles as I walked through the door, but sure enough, the pile of notes I slapped down next to his sewing machine was enough to get him on his feet in a second, pulling out his measuring tape and getting on with his cutting and stitching as quickly as he could.

I stared at my reflection in the window glass. I bared my teeth. *Monster*, Shin had called me. I turned my head this way and that. I looked almost respectable now, I thought. Almost handsome. It was amazing what a collar and a tie and money in your pocket could do.

The train curved around the embankment, the wheels screeching on the rails. Down below was the wasteground where Tomoko had been attacked the day Koji and I had caught the eel. I remembered her body pressed against mine, as I'd held her up on the carriage coupling, and the train rattling through the countryside all those months ago. It all seemed like a dream to me now.

On the other side of the track was nothing but blackness. It stretched across Asakusa all the way to the Sumida River. Buried below it, somewhere, were my mother and my sister, charred into ash, dissolving now in the rain that fell across Tokyo, washing away into the river that flowed out to the sea.

You just had to get on with life, I thought.

Outside Mr. Suzuki's office, the gleaming black Daimler was streaked with rain. The door to the hut was half open. Something was wrong.

I pushed open the door gingerly and walked inside. The room was lit by the single black metal lamp on the desk. A haze of blue smoke hovered by the ceiling and there was a smell in the air like matches. Mr. Suzuki sat on his chair, his close-cropped, bullet-shaped head tilted to one side. His mouth was stuffed with dirty, crumpled pages of newspaper.

The grey suit jacket was hanging on the chair behind him. His stubby fingers, bitten to the quick, were clutching at a dark, gaping crimson and black wound in the middle of his chest, blood seeping like ink into the white cotton of his shirt.

I sat down on the chair on the other side of the desk. The skin on his face was stiff and waxy and I felt awkward looking at him, as if I'd disturbed him whilst he was doing something private.

I remembered how, the week after my father's ship went down, the military affairs clerk brought a wisteria box to the house, painted with his name. "The Great Sea Battle of Leyte Gulf," the newspapers had called it. My teacher had given me the honour of sticking the little Japanese flag to the map on the wall that day. We'd spent the rest of the afternoon drawing lavish pictures of the battle, sketching the smoking funnels of aircraft carriers and whizzing Zero fighters.

My mother and Satsuko and I sat together in the house that evening. The box lay on the floor in front of us. I stared at the whorls and knots in the wood; they looked just like the shapes of the Philippine islands on the map.

The next day, I'd hammered the cedar sign to our front door. *A House of Honour.* "You're the man of the house, now," the military affairs clerk told me.

Blood was soaking slowly outward in Mr. Suzuki's shirt. *The man of the house.*

I closed my eyes.

Finally, I stood up and walked to the door. As I pulled it shut, I caught a final glimpse of Mr. Suzuki in the lamplight. His fedora lay upside down beside him on the floor.

I walked over to Mr. Isamushi's noodle stall and sat at the counter. He wiped it down and poured out a big bottle of beer in front of me. "Where's the boss tonight?" he asked.

I shrugged.

"Well, you're very welcome anyway, sir," he said. "You've got a new suit."

I nodded and swallowed. "What soup are you using today, then, granddad?"

He ladled steaming broth into a bowl. "Rat and snake today, sir. Delicious." He spooned a pile of noodles on the top.

As I sat there, I held up the noodles on my chopsticks and blew away the steam just like Mr. Suzuki had always done. When I'd finished, I carefully slurped away the soup and lit a cigarette, gazing at the smoke as it twisted in the air in front of me.

I put my hand in my jacket pocket, rubbing the banknotes between my fingers. I glanced around at the covered stalls, wondering if Yotchan was around tonight. I forced myself to picture her lying beneath me, her breasts heaving away.

I left three copper coins on the counter and slipped away into the market passageways. The food stalls were packed with ex-soldiers, their faces lit by orange lanterns. At the liquor stand on the corner, I drank a glass of "special" that made my eyes water. One of the ex-students slapped me on the back and poured me out another.

My head was swimming as I crossed the road to the station. The place was swarming with men and women coming back from the demonstrations, their signs all tattered as they crammed through the doors into the ticket hall, down the stairs beneath which the children and I had once slept.

Around the back of the station, in the wasteground beneath the railway arches, I saw whores at last. They stood around the big puddles, and they called out to me, my stomach coiling into knots. I glanced at them furtively as I stumbled on through the darkness.

The red brickwork of the railway tunnel was brightly lit. The struts of the ironwork began to tremble and squeak as a train rolled overhead. My heart started to pound. A solitary girl was sitting on a railing in a pool of light in the middle of the tunnel, wreathed in a white cloud of cigarette smoke. I fingered the notes in my pocket and swallowed, my flesh hopelessly tightening as I made my way toward her.

33
May Day
(*Hal Lynch*)

For a moment, as I awoke, I couldn't remember where I was. The room seemed naggingly familiar, and the light coming through the window had the distant, luminescent effect of sky seen from beneath water. There was a desk, the whitewashed wall, a flower-print dress draped over the schoolroom chair. A pale ivory body lay beside me, silken black hair splayed upon the pillow. A ridge of spine beneath the skin rose and fell minutely as Satsuko slept on.

As I dressed, she woke up and slid her arms around my chest. Her head rested on my shoulder as she buttoned my shirt with careful fingers. I kissed her hands, pressing her palms to my lips. In a low voice, she whispered that she would like me to meet her later on that evening by Asakusa Pond. The bench where we'd sat and watched the cherry blossoms on our first date.

I decided to tell her everything that night. Explain my plan, ask her to come away with me, to wait for me. To trust me. Our reflections gazed back at us from the mirror against the wall, and I felt suddenly romantic and chivalrous and sure of myself.

I'd promised to meet Ward at the press club before going over to watch the May Day protests. Judy was due to arrive at Yokohama on the USS *New Mexico* tomorrow. Perhaps we could all go out and celebrate together, I thought, somewhere expensive and exquisite, before I embarked upon its long return voyage two days later.

As I walked out into the road, men and women were emerging from the muddy side streets carrying placards and banners. Protesters packed like sardines into the tram as it curved on its rails toward the Imperial Plaza. I alighted at Yurakucho and walked over to Shimbun Alley. The lobby of the press club was deserted. Everyone was already gone, covering the action.

Upstairs, the ballroom was empty and a dusty haze floated over the tables as I waited for Ward to appear. There was a stink of old cigarettes and spilled liquor. I glanced at my watch. It was late already.

A dense crowd surged beneath the bridge by the Imperial Hotel. A great swathe of the population was represented on the street: students, young women in kimonos, men in suits, elderly folk in yukatas. When I reached the edge of the park, I was astounded. It was a forest of red flags and hand-painted banners. Some were written in Japanese, but most were in crude English for the benefit of the Occupiers. The bandstand was festooned with flags, and applause came from the crowd as a trio of men emerged onto the stage, holding up their hands. The bull-like man in the jersey whom I'd seen before bellowed into a microphone, his voice overwhelmed by shrieks of static. The crowd erupted, drowning him out with their applause. Wind gusted over the crowd, setting the banners fluttering. The park darkened perceptibly, as apocalyptic storm clouds began to swallow the sky.

As the man on the podium began his oration, rain began to fall. The gaunt faces of the people remained determined as the drops soaked the banners and dripped down their cheeks. They began to chant, their voices rising up in chorus, their forearms beating the air, and as the rain swept over their heads, the noise swelled and strengthened. Another man stepped onto the rostrum, and his shrill voice was welcomed with a huge surge of applause as he waved an accusing finger toward the high stone wall of the palace beyond.

"The emperor sits behind that moat," he cried, "gorging himself with delicate dishes while outside, the people starve!"

There was a sharp tremor in the air. A bright flash of lightning pierced the grey sky and the crowd jostled forward. Suddenly, a strange, warrior-like cry rose from their throats: "*Washo . . . washo!*" A low rumble of thunder rolled over the park, like some ethereal call to arms, and I was caught up in the crowd as they began to run, the figures on the rostrum waving them forward. We surged over the soggy grass, the horde clapping and howling as they swarmed over the bridge into the Imperial Plaza, fanning out along the stone banks of the moat. Just for a moment it seemed as though they were going to try to storm the palace, that the emperor would finally come face to face with the wrath of his people. But a solid line of white military jeeps and uniformed American troops stood beside the bridge house with its medieval gates and the turret of a tank swivelled casually to face us. The crowd jittered, the muscles tightening in their faces. From a bullhorn came the bark of an order to retreat as rifles were raised in unison.

Tiny clouds of smoke drifted from the barrels of the guns a split second before the thundering shots cracked open the sky. The crowd writhed backward like a shoal of fish, falling and stumbling onto the sodden yellow gravel. Rifles reported again and panic gripped the crowd, people slipping and screaming as they were trampled underfoot. The rain lashed down and the banners toppled to the ground, the letters smeared and the paper disintegrating. I was carried along by the mob toward the fortress of the Dai-ichi building—General Headquarters— where a phalanx of military police and soldiers surrounded the granite columns, their rifles directly levelled at us. A shot erupted above our heads. The crowd swerved away and pounded onward through the driving rain, in the direction of the prime minister's Lloyd Wright residence further on up the avenue.

It was at moments like this that revolutions could break, I thought, that great tragedies occurred. That the world could slip its bonds of gravity and calamity could come raining down. There were hands at my back. A man fell in front of me. I tripped over his body and flew through the air. My head collided with the road, hard, and I curled up into a stunned ball as boots thudded around me.

The asphalt was wet and cold against my cheek. The air was filled with shrieks and pumping rounds of gunshot. A hand grabbed my throat and pulled me up; I felt the scratch and stink of an overcoat against my face. A tall Japanese man was gripping my shoulders. He was dressed in a long camel hair overcoat, a black bowler pinned to his head. His round glasses were speckled with raindrops.

"Had enough, Lynch?"

The voice was purest Brooklyn. With unexpected strength, he took hold of my arm, and, striking out with his elbow, pulled me through the crowd. After a moment, we reached the line of troops. He flashed a badge and they parted to let us through. We paused for a moment on the steps of the building. My jacket was ripped all the way down one seam and my pants were smeared with mud. Fresh blood stained my hand, though whether it was my own or someone else's I did not know. The man popped a piece of gum into his mouth as he watched the mob surge past.

"So, Lynch," he said, scratching the side of his face. "How long have you been a commie?"

G2, Intelligence Division, was sequestered on the top floor of the GHQ building. The ceilings grew lower, the atmosphere more muffled, as we ascended the echoing stairwell. By the time we had reached the frosted glass door of the office, the tumult outside had softened almost to a rumbling melody, punctuated by the occasional whistle. The spook led me into a small windowless room, where a short trim man with a neat blond moustache stood up behind a desk and twisted his hand in salute.

"Afternoon, Lynch. Colonel Wanderly. The sumo wrestler is Captain Ohara."

I saluted back. "Harold Lynch."

"We know who you are."

The room was lined with metal drawers, and the entirety of one wall was taken up with a large map of China, Siberia and the Japanese islands. As the door closed, the office became silent. I was suddenly put in mind of my sealed cabin in our F-13, a moment before takeoff.

"Why don't you park yourself down there, Lynch?" Wanderly said, gesturing at a hard metal chair. "Sorry about the mess. They won't let me get a woman in."

He placed a pair of spectacles on the end of his nose as Ohara perched on the edge of the desk.

Wanderly licked his fingers as he flipped through a thick manila file, picking out photos and press clippings. I recognized my photo of the railway men in the hospital at Hiroshima, then my first piece in the *Stars and Stripes*. I almost smiled. Our rat man, from way back in September. I felt a wave of nostalgia at the sight of the old man's face, gazing forlornly up the river. Wanderly chuckled.

"Well, I've got to hand it to you, Hal. You've got a good eye. And a fine way with words."

"What's this about, Corporal?"

"How long have you known Mark Ward, Lynch?" Ohara interrupted. His face was pockmarked. I remembered him now, from the lobby of the Imperial Hotel, the night when Ward and I had gone there for drinks. General Willoughby's hawk eye behind the monocle, scrutinizing Mark, as the man pressed upon his tailored uniform arm.

"About six months. We met on a train."

"Never met him at Columbia—your alma mater?"

"Must have been before my time."

"Tell you much about his career during the war?"

"He spent time in China."

"Ever tell you where?"

"All over, I guess. I was stationed in Chengtu for a time myself."

"We know you were. Ward was based mainly in Shaanxi. That ring a bell?"

"Well. Sure."

Shaanxi had been the headquarters of Mao's forces, his "Golden Land" up in the hills, where the Red Army had ended their long march and the exiled Japanese communists had holed up during the war. I recalled Ward's distraught face the day after he'd been dragged in by G2, after his return from the Snow Country. *Don't you see, Hal? I'm next on their goddamned list!*

"Where he enjoyed the hospitality of Mao Zedong for several months. As did Wilf Burchett."

"Burchett?"

I frowned, recalling Burchett's gleaming eye, as he pulled tight the straps of his kit bag. *Good luck, mate. You're going to need it.*

"Well," I said, "they were both war correspondents, after all."

Wanderly's eyes softened and his voice took on the tone of a sympathetic teacher. "Look, Hal. I think you're tangled up in something you don't understand. I think people may have taken advantage of you. They sense you're vulnerable. You reek of self-pity. They've used your misplaced guilt to their own advantage."

"We've seen your medical, Lynch," Ohara butted in. "Reads like a horror movie. Still can't sleep?"

Wanderly glanced up at him in apparent distaste. I folded my arms. The room had darkened, but he didn't switch on the lamp. He spread his hands out on the desk, like a priest about to begin a sermon.

"You tell me, Hal. What are we to make of it? You ask for a transfer almost the day the war ends. You turn up in Tokyo and start knocking on the door of every red agent in town. You travel to a prescribed area with what looks like the express intention of embarrassing the Occupation. What are we to make of it, Hal? What are you doing here, anyway?"

I pictured Tokyo from the sky, looking down at the neighbourhoods and parks, the schools and the temples.

"I guess I just wanted to see what was left."

Furtively, I glanced at my watch. Satsuko would be on the tram by now, heading toward Asakusa Pond.

"This Hiroshima piece," Wanderly said, as if embarrassed to mention it. He flipped through the folder and I made out the original carbon of my story.

"'Aftermath of the Atom.' Very portentous, Hal," Wanderly said.

"Did Ward tell you what to write?" asked Ohara.

As Wanderly held up the ink-stained article, I pictured Frayne Baker in his office, flinging the pages into the air. *Radiation disease. Horse—shit!*

"I've already been fired for that, Colonel."

"And a decision regarding your tenure in Japan has been made, Hal."

There was a pulse in my stomach.

"You know I met a Jap last week, Lynch?" Ohara had come around and now stood behind me, resting his hands on the back of my chair. He bent over, and I could feel his hot breath on my neck. "Worked as a doctor at a medical institute up north during the war. A planeload of our boys crash-landed not far away one day. The Japs took them along for treatment. Hell, you might even have known them. Smiling boys, about your own age. Well, I asked the man what they'd done to them, how they'd died. He was as cool as you like. Do you know what he told me?"

Ohara's hands moved to my shoulder blades, his fingers squeezing.

"He said they'd performed live experiments on them, Lynch. Cut out their lungs. Injected them with chemicals. Just to see what would happen. As if they were rats. How do you like that?"

It was grotesque, macabre. I tried to resist the bait. "And what was Hiroshima, gentlemen? Wasn't that an experiment? The live vivisection of an entire city?"

"It was just a bomb, Hal," said Wanderly. "A bomb that saved the lives of thousands of young American men."

"But they're still dying in Hiroshima, Colonel."

"That can't be helped. Here's something that might interest you, Hal." Wanderly slid another sheet from the dossier. He held up a glossy photograph of Ward. He raised his eyebrows. "Your friend. Maxim Alexandrovich Warszawski. Born in Minsk, Russia, 1905. Studied at the Soviet Institute for Teachers, Librarians and Propagandists, 1920 to 23. Moved to New York to study at Columbia University, 1925. Quite a coincidence, wouldn't you say?"

My stomach knotted as his words sank in. I saw Ward coming aboard the train at Kyoto, wheezing as he slung his kit bag onto the luggage rack. At the press club, that first night, exchanging fluent jovialities with the Soviet correspondents. *Don't get them mixed up, Lynch—they'll break your arm!*

"Two summers ago, Hal, the FBI raided Ward's office in Chicago. They discovered documents recently stolen from the Office of Strategic Services, concerning the battle plans of Chiang Kai-shek. Six months later, Ward was in Shaanxi along with Mao, Burchett and all the other Reds. Six months later, he arrived in Tokyo. What's he doing here, Hal?"

A vein pulsed in my forehead. I remembered the glow of

Ward's cigar in the train carriage, his crinkling face as I unburdened myself to him. My fierce, wounded sense of self-pity.

"He help you write that piece, Hal? Or was it just spiritual encouragement?"

Are you still bothered by what you did up there, Lynch? There'd been such sympathy in his eyes, behind the wide spectacles, and I'd bowed my head, like a boy in a confessional box.

The big hand on my shoulder, as I told him about my trip to Hiroshima. *You know I'm proud of you, don't you, Hal?* My profound feeling of solace. As if he was a priest, granting me absolution from my sins.

"You've been a sap, Lynch, a first-class fucking sap," Ohara spat. "Ward sure sucked you in. Had you eating out of his hand. Radiation disease. They'll give you the Order of fucking Lenin. Thought you were a hotshot, Lynch? Or did you know you were taking pictures for Joe Stalin?"

Wanderly paused, looked at me, then continued.

"I'm going to be frank with you, Hal. You're an intelligent man. Mark Ward is a Stalinist agent. That's a simple statement of fact. Now. There's another war coming soon, Hal. Did you know that? Sad but true. In fact, it's already begun. There will soon be a time when we will need a strong Japan, Hal, when we will need this country on America's side. This kind of thing could tip the balance. The Russians know that. That's why Ward is here. He's no teacher, and he's certainly no librarian. You've been made a fool of, Hal. You can see that now. Bad people have taken advantage of your weaknesses to damage our position. We'd like to give you a chance to show us whose side you're really on."

Ohara moved from my chair and went to the other side of the table. The room was almost entirely dark now, the map on the wall obscured. Wanderly leaned forward.

"Tell us about Ward, Hal. He's your friend, isn't he? He trusts you. He confides in you."

"What are you asking me, gentlemen?"

"Hal, he's been using you. Don't you see that? You don't owe him a thing."

"Where are the fucking negatives, Hal?"

Ohara's words reverberated in the darkness. Wanderly smiled thinly, his fingers drumming the manila envelope. I felt a sudden flash of unexpected advantage as I pictured Dutch handing me the envelope. My trumps. Hidden in a cigar box, under the floorboard of an anonymous room in a downtown Tokyo saloon.

"I don't know what you mean."

"Fuck off, Hal!" bellowed Ohara. "You know what we're talking about!"

I leaned slowly back in the chair, holding his gaze.

"What are you asking me?" I repeated.

Wanderly tapped the envelope, the smile lingering on his face. "We're asking you to consider your position, Hal. Your future."

I slowly shook my head. "No."

After a long pause, Wanderly sighed and shrugged his shoulders. "Oh well."

He replaced the outlying documents in the dossier and closed it carefully.

"The *New Mexico* is leaving for San Francisco in two days, Lieutenant. You'll be on it."

I tried not to smile as I pictured the ticket in my jacket pocket. I imagined the moment, six months from now. Standing on the dock at Oakland. Watching the ship steam beneath the San Francisco Bay Bridge. The passengers coming down the gangplank. Satsuko pausing, her dark eyes searching the crowd.

"You can't take the girl, Lynch."

My heart jolted. Ohara's face was hidden in the shadows. "Sure," he said. "We heard all about her."

Another photograph appeared on the desk. Satsuko and I, squinting in the spring sunshine outside the Senso Temple.

Smile!

Eugene. Just the kind of bright, callow boy that Intelligence liked to employ. Ambitious. Venal. Naive. *They started it, didn't they, Hal?*

This, then, was the reason for his sudden desire to see the world; his unexpected passion for journalism. His nocturnal visit to the newsroom on the night of my return from Hiroshima. The look on his face as he saw me come into the office the next day, like that of a whipped dog.

"Pretty girl," Ohara said.

I swallowed. "The Exclusion Act won't last six months."

Wanderly placed a square sheet on the table. I glanced down. The paper was covered with Japanese writing, unintelligible stamps.

"Going to tell me what that is?"

Wanderly picked up the sheet, and drew his finger across the ideograms at the top.

"'Recreation and Amusement Association,'" he read. "How do you like that?"

"You know they register their whores here in Japan, Lynch?" Ohara said. "They're a bureaucratic bunch."

My senses were suddenly alert. Wanderly stared at me over his spectacles.

"Not the kind of girl we want in America, Hal. Sorry."

"Undesirable is what they call it, Lynch."

"Tend to be crawling with all manner of disease and such. The rules are very clear. She won't make it past immigration. Not now. Not ever."

A hollow pit opened up in my stomach. Just as I had felt every night, as our plane had lurched from the end of the airstrip, pitching just yards above churning indigo waves. The words and stamps wavered before me, the green ink blotting into the cheap fabric of the paper, as I pictured Satsuko, sitting on the bench by Asakusa Pond, pulling her shawl around her. *An undesirable.*

Ohara was gazing steadily at me. "They'll never let her into America, Lynch. I will personally make damned sure of that. And you will never come back to Japan, as long as we are here."

"Let's make this easy, Hal," sighed Wanderly. "Give us the negatives. Forget about Hiroshima. Forget about the war. Go back to your nice saloon. Make an honest woman of her. You can take that sheet away with you if you like. Start again from scratch."

I pictured her, helpless in my arms, as we'd stood in the ruins of her house. Clinging to me, burying her face in my chest. The intensity of that feeling—as if we were the only two people left on earth.

I picked up the sheet and rubbed the rough paper between my fingertips.

"Why don't you start again, Hal. Make a new life from all this ruin."

A soft explosion came from somewhere far away. The men's voices seemed to spiral around me in the darkness.

"What do you say, Lynch?"

"There's another war soon coming, Hal. Sad but true. Whose side are you on?"

"It's them or us, Lynch. You need to make a decision. What's it going to be?"

34
THE FLOWERS OF EDO
(*Satsuko Takara*)

A t Asakusa Pond, rain drummed against my umbrella and dripped into puddles by my feet. The water had soaked into my sandals now and my socks were quite saturated. Men walked past my bench, faces glowing behind cigarettes as they leered at me from the darkness.

The night was cindery and bleak and I remembered a neighbourhood fairy tale my mother had once told me, about the tap-dancing girls from the Casino Folies, whose ghosts, she said, had danced upon the roof of the building long after it had burned down. It was just the kind of story she had loved.

I glanced at the little wristwatch that Hal had bought me. It was very late. I wondered whether I had made our arrangement quite clear, whether Hal had understood me properly when I'd told him the time and place to meet. His cologne had been cedary and strong, the starched cotton smooth around the swell of his back as I'd buttoned his shirt that morning. In my mind's eye, I saw the pigskin suitcase, the locked typewriter case. A stab of panic suddenly went through me. Was he planning to leave? Had he already gone? Sailed away for America, without so much as a goodbye?

I struggled to recall the times we'd spoken those past weeks. There had been the joke about taking me to America, but nothing after that. Certainly nothing had been decided one way or another. Was I just his Japanese plaything? A temporary mistress? A pang of ridiculous jealousy went through me as I imagined his wife back home. She would be beautiful, charming, like Ingrid Bergman. My heart sank as I remembered the rash letter I had posted to Michiko. Blithely declaring that I'd soon be off to California, to take up my new life in the sun.

What an idiot I had been.

I prayed that the letter had never arrived, that it had been lost in the post before reaching her studio.

What a stupid, ignorant girl.

What had made me think that he was any different from the other Americans? What vanity was it that had let me flatter myself that I was somehow special? I was just one more girl amongst thousands. I clutched my swollen stomach, picturing myself from above, a pregnant, unmarried woman, sitting alone in the rain in a soaking kimono . . .

Footsteps thudded across the arched wooden bridge. Hal was stumbling toward me in the rain. As he came closer, I almost screamed. His trousers were dark and wet, ripped along the seam, buttons torn from his shirt. His eyes were wild as I reached up to embrace him, pushing my fingers through his soaking hair.

I cringed as I imagined some brutal gang of ex-soldiers assaulting him. "Are you hurt?" I asked, desperately.

He stood motionless as I buried my face in his chest. I held him for a long moment.

He wasn't responding. Something was wrong. I stepped back. His eyes were downcast, and his arms hung loosely from his sides. Finally, he lifted his head and gazed at me. He placed his hands upon my shoulders with a gentle, almost tender motion.

"Hal-san," I murmured. "What is it?"

His mouth twisted into a terrible smile. Rain dripped down from his hair onto his cheeks.

I somehow knew that something dreadful had happened, something final and irrevocable. A hard lump rose into my throat as I pictured the hours I'd spent in Mrs. Ishino's parlour room that afternoon, as she brushed my hair and softly spoke to me, as if soothing a jittery horse. I'd imagined Hal and me, sitting on this bench in the last of the evening sunlight, his deep blue eyes filling with wonder as I told him about our baby, the child that was growing inside me. This wasn't how I'd imagined it. No—this wasn't it at all.

He was shaking his head. Over and over, he was shaking his head.

He took my hand. Barely able to swallow, I let him lead me through the park to the battered arcade where we sheltered beneath the eaves of an overhanging stall.

He patted his pockets for his cigarettes, and finally lit one with his metal lighter. His fingers were trembling as he turned to me with a terrible smile.

"Well, Satsuko," he said. "I'm going home."

Rain tapped on the wooden roof as I looked up at him. With my heart in my mouth, I held a hand up to his cheek.

A sharp image came into my mind. The day of the surrender, as we'd all knelt down in the gravel of the factory yard, the cicadas whirring, the hot sun on our backs, listening to the emperor's speech. I remembered how, just for a second, my heart had leaped when I thought his Imperial Majesty had said that Japan had won the war.

"Take me," I whispered. "Please."

He took my hand, kneading and squeezing my palm. Suddenly, he dropped my hand and slammed his fist against the wooden shutter of the stall. I cried out as it rattled in its frame. He put his head in his hands.

Rain was falling all around us, making patterns in the wide puddles in the gravel path. His clothes were saturated, his face hidden. A wave of hatred and revulsion suddenly clawed its way through my heart.

I had been right, after all. Mrs. Ishino had been wrong. He was just another American, like all the others.

"I'm so sorry," he whispered.

So sorry. I felt a cold sense of calm. He would go. I would stay. "Okay."

A sudden urge to batter his face with my fists flashed through me. Instead, I leaned down and grasped him under the arm.

"Get up."

He tried to clutch my hand again, but I slapped him away. Slowly he faced me, dripping in the darkness.

"You," I said, pointing. "Come."

I stalked away beneath the scaffold of the Treasure House Gate and into the precincts of Senso Temple, the hem of my kimono wet and heavy. Stray dogs lurked by the ginkgo stumps, barking from behind the stacks of timber that lay soaking in the yard.

The rain blew in fine, blustery clouds. At the far side of the shrine, I paused until I heard the American trudging behind me. He was calling out my name. I waited until he was a dozen paces behind me, and then turned sharply down Umamichi Street.

The patch of earth was overgrown with tall, wild grasses and littered with saturated lumps of charred wood and broken brick. Ghostly walls seemed to hang around me as I stood there, imagining the eel tank, the rows of tables. Up above had been the overhanging wooden balcony where we used to sit in the summer as the smell of broiling food floated up in the air. The room where Hiroshi and I had fallen asleep to the sound of the shop sign creaking like a frog in the summer rain.

The American was standing behind me. I pointed at the black, abandoned earth.

"Here," I said, in Japanese. "My house."

He nodded, a muscle trembling in his forehead. He tried to put his hand on my shoulder, but I jerked away.

I sprinkled my fingers in the air.

"Your planes," I said. "Fire."

A strange look came over his face, and he slowly squatted down. He looked up into the sky, as if he could see them now, roaring in over Tokyo.

I remembered the first vibration on the horizon, the air quivering like the struck string of a shamisen. The American was trembling, like a child left alone in the dark, and I hated him then, and I was glad, because I had never wished to hate anything as much before in my life.

The high wind came from the west, batting at the paper lanterns along the alley and rattling the wooden shutters of the shops. The last thing my mother did that night was to feed a few pinches of crumbled rice cracker to the goldfish that she kept in a bowl in the family alcove, and which she insisted were a lucky charm against fire.

I woke around midnight to a dull thudding. The roar of the American planes in the sky grew louder and louder until it sounded like a continuous peal of thunder. Then the house was shaking and Hiroshi and I sat up in bed, the room flickering with shadows. Outside the window the sky was as bright as day, filled with whirling orange flame.

Just then, there was a flash and a trail of blue sparks shot across the room. I screamed and leaped out of bed, pulling Hiroshi up as he struggled to put on his padded air-defence helmet. Together we tumbled down the stairs to go to the underground shelter, but it was already too late. Outside the house, the world was like a glowing orange playground, the wind blowing fiercely hot as incendiary bombs pelted down from the sky. Our screaming neighbours filled the street, dashing wildly to and fro, some with coats over their heads, others trying to throw hopeless buckets of water at the incendiaries as they landed. Mrs. Oka stumbled out of her house carrying her cedar buckets of pickles, the bran bubbling with heat smeared along their sides.

My mother's voice called out my name: she was leaning over our balcony in her nightclothes, screaming at us to get away.

"Hurry, Mother!" I shouted back at her. "Please hurry!"

I clung onto Hiroshi's hand as great gusts of hot wind blew around us. A tongue of blue flame was crawling up the eaves to the roof. I screamed at my mother: "Jump, Mother, please jump down!"

She dashed inside, wasting precious seconds, before she finally emerged in a loose blue kimono. The roof of our house suddenly crumpled behind her in a shower of sparks.

Most of the street was on fire now, the flames crackling in great swirls, the heat terribly intense as the fire ate away at the buildings. My mother was in the street now, waving at us. Just then there was a blinding flash behind her. Heat blasted toward us. The store beyond ours that sold cooking oil had exploded. I felt my eyelashes crinkle away and I looked up with streaming eyes. My mother was running toward us, screaming. Her kimono was a sheet of flame and her beautiful hair was a dancing halo of fire. She tottered forward, still holding out her arms, then collapsed onto the ground a short distance in front of us, writhing as the flames devoured her.

People were running past us now, screaming, "We're going to die!"

Hiroshi started to shout, refusing to move as I tried to drag him along the street.

"Come on!" I shrieked.

"Father's pot!" he shouted. "I promised him! I need to go back for it!"

"It's too late!"

Flaming beams crashed around us in showers of blazing sparks. The sky exploded with shells that spurted flame and hissing blue tendrils like blazing morning glory. People were running helplessly toward the Kamiarai Bridge, and we were swept along with them, past the police station and Fuji

Elementary School. The shelters at the side of the public market were full of panicked people, pushing away the newcomers, shouting that there was no room left. As we approached the Yoshiwara canal, fireballs began to pelt down from the sky and a thick smoking wind gusted along so strongly that it almost swept me off my feet. We were in hell.

Through the cloud of whirling smoke, the buildings on the other side of the canal were on fire, red flame belching from inside the windows. The dark water was alive with dashing reflections, bobbing with people who had jumped in, steam rising from its surface. I held Hiroshi's hand, and together we leaped from the concrete bank, splashing down into the scalding water. When we came to the surface, he cried out. His face was yellow as we looked up at the burning buildings on the bank.

"Father!" he started to shriek. "I promised him!"

"Come back!"

I scrabbled for Hiroshi's fingers in the water, but he plunged away from me and seized hold of the iron ladder that led up to the bank. He clambered up, crouching down as he approached the flames. He turned back to face me, silhouetted by fire.

"Stay there, Satsuko!" he shouted. "I'll come back! I promise!"

It was madness. Overhead, the entire sky was filled with thundering silver planes, so low now that I could see the figures of the pilots behind the glass noses.

"Hiroshi!" I screamed, but he started sprinting along the bank, straight toward the firestorm.

A sharp whistle came from above, and there was a deafening explosion. The water swept up in a great boiling wave. The chemical works along the canal had exploded. The sky turned phosphorus white as I splashed forward and desperately tried to hoist myself up out of the boiling water onto the ladder. The iron rail was scorching now and the metal stuck to the skin of my hands. I wrenched them away in agony, the skin tearing away, sticking there like flapping cloth as I rolled onto the bank. People were crawling around me on all fours, their faces black, their clothes all burned away. Blazing timbers crashed into the water behind me and whirling figures screamed in pain as incendiaries pelted the water. I desperately searched for Hiroshi. There was nothing but fire. To the side of the street I saw an irrigation ditch and I crawled blindly toward it. A rushing cloud of black smoke blew toward me, and then the ground disappeared beneath me, and I was tumbling down the steep banks to the bottom.

The American was hunched over on the ground, rocking back and forth. I knelt down and wrenched his hand away from his face.

"Why?" I asked. "Why?"

His raised a shaking hand to my face, but again, I struck it away.

"I'm so sorry—" he whispered.

I stood up. "You go. I stay. Okay."

Leaving him in the wet earth, I strode away, past the ruined houses, along the incinerated alley. A strangled noise came from behind me, half sob, half shout, but I didn't look back.

Asakusa Market was bustling with people and I walked on until I reached a group of low stalls. There, ignoring the looks brought about by my sodden clothes and tangled hair, I ordered a glass of shochu from the ugly stallholder and drank it down in one. I ordered another. The rough liquor burned in my belly, and I drank another glass, and another, before stumbling along the alleys in the direction of Matsugaya, then Inaricho. Without knowing how, I found myself climbing the metal steps of the bridge overlooking the mass of shimmering train tracks that snaked out of Ueno Station.

Trains were shuttling in and out, their carriages lit, their wheels sparking. Speckles of rain flew against my face as I watched the white and red lamps of the carriages worming into the violet black night that covered the distant hills.

Almost without thinking, I took a pot of rouge from my satchel, and with my fingertip smeared it heavily across my lips and cheeks. I tugged the combs from my hair and hurled them over the railing so that my wet hair dangled loose around my face. I started to walk across the bridge, my sandals slipping on the metal as I crossed over the tracks and walked down toward Ueno Station.

On the other side, I took out my pocket mirror. I grimaced in satisfaction. The reflection was that of the cheapest kind of slut. *This is what I am,* I thought. *This is what I have become.* I laughed, my voice shrill and uncanny in my ears.

I stumbled toward the railway arches, where pan-pan girls were hunched around the wide puddles, bedraggled from the rain. I gazed at them as I walked unsteadily into the underpass that led beneath the tracks.

I stopped in the middle of the tunnel and perched upon the railing in a pool of streetlight. My fingers trembled as I lit a cigarette, sucking it hard and feeling myself enveloped by white smoke.

Footsteps were coming toward me. My stomach quivered. With my fingertips, I slowly drew aside the fabric of my kimono to show my white thighs.

The footsteps stopped and I felt a light hand on my shoulder. "Miss?"

I opened my eyes.

A boy was standing there, holding out a palm full of notes and coins. His face was horribly disfigured and scarred.

His eyes widened. The money fell to the ground.

The lights of the tunnel whirled around me as Hiroshi's clammy fingers reached out to touch my face.

PART FOUR
NIGHT TO NEXT DAY
July 1946

35

THE YOKOHAMA ROAD
(Hal Lynch)

There is a stretch of the Hudson Highlands where the cliffs shoot straight up from the river, deep and wide now as it curves around Mount Storm King. Heavy beech and oak line the ridge, an outpost of the green panoply that stretches over the whole northern half of the state. The Eastern Chief rides alongside here for a while, cutting through the forest as if through virgin land, before the track curves around, and on the distant horizon the spires of New York City appear, stabbing up into the sky.

I'd ridden trains all the way across America. Along the coast from San Francisco to Los Angeles, then inward over the arroyos and canyons and red earth of the southwestern states. I crossed the Mississippi and the endless, flat wheat plain of Kansas, curved up into the Midwest, finally arriving in Chicago on a grey, humid day in July. I ate a pizza pie in a red-stone Italian joint, and back at the station took a seat in the waiting room amongst a gang of long-bearded Amish men, dressed in white shirts and black pants, who spoke in singsong voices about the price of grain and chickens. Later, they sat contentedly in the observation carriage as I went to my cabin and sipped whisky and looked out over the vast, lonely expanse of the Great Lakes until I finally fell asleep for the last, long stretch to the Eastern seaboard.

The train paced itself like a steady racehorse as it rode the track high up above the tenements of Harlem, the first foundations of grand housing projects being laid down below. Then came the towering brick apartment buildings of Manhattan, the shining glass skyscrapers, and then the gargantuan mechanical workings of the city, grimy with oil and dirt, the screeching tunnels and dark galleries drifting away on each side as we pulled into Grand Central Station. I slung my kit bag over my shoulder and clambered out onto the platform. I stood there alone as the commuters pushed past me, not knowing where the hell I was going next.

I took a room in a boardinghouse on West 28th Street, not far from Penn Station, where I lay low, sweating in a box room, smoking cigarettes and taking no other diversion than the occasional slaughter of a cockroach beneath my shoe heel. The Sicilian operetta of the couple who ran the place drifted endlessly through the floorboards. New York was wilting hot. The sun poured right down from the sky. I prayed in the evenings for the summer storms, for the thunder that would crack open the night and drench the earth for a few sacred minutes, before the moisture evaporated and the restless heat rose up to smother the city once more.

The Yokohama road had been as bad as I remembered, pitted with holes and craters. Life along the highway had grown more vigorous now—shanties extending along each side, swarms of people, young and old, eking out an existence amongst the crinkled tin, chicken wire and tarpaulin. Garden plots lined the perimeter, tended by withered old men and women with babies on their backs. Stray dogs and naked children watched from the side of the road as my taxi passed, no longer curious enough to either wave or bark. At the dock, young GIs stood fresh off the boat, laughing and joking as they sold off their gear to grinning yakuza men in white summer hats and vests.

The press club had been all a clamour when I'd stumbled back there the night before, alive with the day's events. The prime minister's residence had been stormed; troops were still out on the streets; the government was about to fall. The faces of the newspapermen were alight as they traded rumours and swapped war stories, snapping their fingers for drinks. Chaos was their amphetamine, I thought, as I sifted the room for any trace of Mark Ward. Sally Harper from *TIME* was comforting a graceful blonde woman who sat on the piano stool, dabbing her eyes in a daze. Judy Ward—Mark's wife.

"Where is he?" I asked above the din. Sally stared at me in astonishment.

"I thought you were his friend!"

"What happened?"

"Haven't you heard? Where have you been?"

"Heard what?"

"Mark's been arrested. They're saying he's some kind of subversive!"

I wondered if he'd still been wearing his Japanese robe as the burly MPs stormed through the screen door. Seizing him by the arms, dragging him from his wicker chair. The ballroom was heavy with smoke and the furore of relentless gossip and confusion. I crept away, helpless, behind the curtain and lay down on the carpet.

I walked over to Mrs. Ishino's the next morning. The place was a wreck. The curtain was gone from the entranceway and chairs were tipped over on the floor. Big tin signs were nailed to the wall, warnings scrawled in red paint over the front of the building: "Off-Limits to Allied Personnel. VD."

Upstairs, my room had been trashed. Everything was gone. My notes, my cameras, even my typewriter. All that was left were a few ripped paperbacks and the zinc pail on the floor, overturned, water saturating the tatami. This, then, was the reason for the untimely visit from the public health inspectors. For my extended interview with Wanderly and Ohara. Just another thing to add to my conscience. With a prayer on my lips, I knelt down in the corner of the room, pulled up the mat and prised up the floorboard.

The cigar box was still there. I picked it up and held it in my hands, my eyes closed, breathing in the smell of cedar and tobacco. Then I stuffed it deep into my jacket. Downstairs, I paused in the wreckage and took one last look around. I scribbled a hopeless note for Satsuko: the name of my ship and the time of its sailing. I took out most of the remaining yen notes from my wallet and left them in a useless stack on the splintered bar.

Over the rail of the USS *New Mexico*, I gazed down as Japanese girls hugged their American boyfriends, as kisses, tears, and fervent promises were exchanged. The ship gave a great mournful bellow as the massed turbines cranked up. The last of the lovers hugged each other and the men hastened up the gangway as it was pulled home. On the dock, the girls waved white handkerchiefs, calling out in plaintive, high-pitched chorus to the GIs who jostled around me on deck, shouting out wild endearments, pledges of eternal love and return.

The horn gave a deep bellow, and a quickening vibration pulsed through the deck as the chains drew up the anchor. With a great shudder, the ship began to pull unmistakably away from the quay. Another high-pitched wail came from the assembly below; the men around me whistled and shouted. A sea of handkerchiefs fluttered up and down, and my eyes searched the crowd restlessly for Satsuko. Up and down, up and down the handkerchiefs went, every one a love story, every one a heartbreak.

No part of me wanted to leave. And yet, here I was, suddenly on the deck of a vast, oceangoing ship, Japan drifting irrevocably away from me. A yawning gulf opening up, a chasm that grew wider, deeper, and more achingly lonely with every inch that we pulled out to sea.

The island was finally lost beyond the carved sapphire horizon as the lonely screams of seabirds gusted around me in the sky. I went below deck and climbed onto my bunk. A young, ratlike man in uniform lay on the bed beneath mine, his leg in a plaster cast. He was reading the funny pages of the *Stars and Stripes*, chuckling to himself.

"Going home, huh?" he said, without looking up. I grunted forbearingly, but he carried on talking. "Old Nippon sure is a swell place. No place like home though. Say, where's home for you, fella?"

I willed him to shut up. I desperately wanted to be left alone in my despair, as if the banality of his conversation might somehow impinge upon the purity of my bitterness.

"New York," I muttered.

"New *York*, huh? You don't say . . . "

He appeared to contemplate the feasibility of human beings inhabiting New York City for a while, and then, apparently satisfied, he began to speak again, his voice brimming with knowing locker-room insinuation.

"Say. How about those Jap girls, huh? Sure are cute, ain't they?"

Satsuko's face arose before me—her dark, harrowing eyes.

"Foxy little geisha girls . . . You ever have one of them? Huh? You ever have one of them little geisha girls?"

Her look of distress. Of fury.

Take me. Please—

I buried my face in my blanket with an uncertain noise, my hands over my ears.

Throughout those dog days of summer, I walked the New York streets like a hunted animal. It seemed almost overwhelming in its banality. Cabs went up and down Lexington Avenue. Steam rose from the manhole covers. Old women walked their poodles in Central Park and messenger boys sprinted between the office buildings. At five-thirty sharp, men in suits poured out from the skyscrapers into the bars by Grand Central Station, before hurrying off to their air-conditioned lives of domestic bliss.

The city was like an impenetrable fortress. The world might lie in ruins, but it was business as usual in New York, heir to the postwar world, its citizens engrossed in their buying and selling, eating and drinking, their greatest victory this vast, blithe antipathy—this insurmountable wall against which I pounded my head. I stopped in the middle of the streets as the crowds rushed past, clutched onto walls for support. The cars and the people went by like an endless zoetrope, and it was all moving so fast that I was terrified of stepping into the current, of being swept away entirely.

I was standing outside the 42nd Street subway station one evening when a chubby man asked me for a match for his cigarette. As I held out my lighter, he made an amiable remark on that evening's performance by the Brooklyn Dodgers. A sudden, liquid fury passed through me. Before I knew it, I was clinging onto his shirt, shaking him furiously.

I saw myself suddenly from above—a madman, gripping onto another like some desperate succubus. I slowly forced myself to release him. He sprinted off up Broadway, clinging onto his hat as he glanced back at me in terror.

I walked all across Manhattan that night. The next morning at the boardinghouse, I settled up with Mrs. D'Annunzio and told her I'd be leaving later on that week. Something had to change. Something had to give.

At a photography studio in Murray Hill, I methodically worked up my Hiroshima prints. As I stood in the dim red light, leaning over the enlarger and counting off the seconds, the trip came back to me in vivid bursts. The lonely train guard in the ruined station. Snowflakes, hovering in the air outside the police station. As the images swelled in darkening hues from the developing fluid, I stared once again into the eyes of the aged dance teacher; studied the faint, fragile smile of the railway man, who thought that the wind would come and carry him away like a feather. It occurred to me that they would all now, most likely, be dead. As the prints hung dripping on the line, I felt a profound affinity, as if I, like them, were now just a ghost, a restless shadow on the fabric of the world.

I packed sets of the prints into envelopes and over the course of the next few days delivered them personally, with a short typed note and full release, to the offices of *TIME*, *Atlantic Monthly*, *LIFE* and *Harper's*. Then I knew that I needed to rest. I went up to Vermont and rented a cabin in the White Mountains. I fished and swam in the nearby lake, chopped wood, took long walks in the forest. I retired early and lay in bed, listening to the wind in the pines and thinking of Satsuko.

Gradually, I felt my strength start to return. The great perpetual roar that had been in my ears for so long was slowly beginning to fade.

Every other day, I hiked the five miles to the village to pick up groceries at the mom-and-pop store. They had the occasional magazine there, and one morning, I arrived to find that month's edition of the *New Yorker* on the rack. The cover showed a typical Manhattan summer scene: a cartoon of cheerful citizens playing games in the park. As I leaned down to pick it up from the stand, I noticed a strip of paper binding the magazine, printed with an editorial message.

"Hiroshima," it read, in underlined type. "This entire issue is devoted to the story of how an atomic bomb destroyed a city."

A strange, distant sensation coursed through me. I paid the old lady and walked away up the street, reading. The whole magazine had been given over to a piece by a correspondent whose name I didn't recognize: John Hersey. A writer who'd just returned from Japan. It followed the stories of five survivors of the A-Bomb, from the moment of the blast until now, more than a year later, when the city had finally been opened up again. I sat outside my cabin that morning and read the magazine from cover to cover, over and over again.

It painted a picture of fractured lives, of souls caught outside of time. It depicted citizens shocked and confused, still struggling to comprehend the thing they had witnessed in those bright, searing seconds that fine August morning. I recognized much of the description: the points of reference, the landmarks and cardinal points. Then, toward the end of the article, I gave a great cry of vindication. To my fierce delight, the story began to talk of radiation disease, of "Disease X." The story documented its victims, its symptoms and its causes. And it presented it all as medical fact. Not as propaganda. Not as a bargaining tool. Not as "horseshit."

The story went on until the very last page. There were no pictures. But after the words, they would come, I thought. My pictures.

A tranquillity descended upon me as I reread the article in the silence of my cabin. It was done now, I thought. It was over.

That evening, I sat on the bank of the lake and looked up at the moon as it slowly rose above the treetops. The water lapped against the shore and a million stars stretched out against the sky. I thought about Satsuko with a terrible ache in my heart. Where would she be tonight? What cramped back room, what urgent back alley? I broke down and shook with tears for a long time; one man, alone in a forest, beneath the starry sky.

Finally, my sobs subsided, and all that was left was the freshness of the night around me. A cool breeze sprang up and the tops of the trees sighed as they waved back and forth in the moonlight. I stood up and brushed myself off, then walked back through the wood to my cabin. I took off my shirt and climbed into my narrow bunk. Within moments, thank God, I had fallen into a profound and utterly dreamless sleep.

36
ONE WONDERFUL DAY
(*Osamu Maruki*)

W rap!" Kano cried, as if pronouncing a wonderful blessing over the assembled cast and crew, crowded now below the edge of the soundstage. Michiko Nozaki stood for a second, her hand frozen in tableau. Slowly, her face dissolved into that wonderful, trademark smile of hers, and she flung out her arms and rushed down the steps toward Kano, kissing him on both cheeks in the French manner. Kinosuke, her leading man, strode over and spun her about in his arms. Hoots and catcalls came from the crew as she emerged from his embrace, blushing and breathless. Only then did she notice me and hurry over.

"Sensei!" she said. "You've come to see us at last."

She pecked me chastely upon the forehead. Kinosuke slid a brawny arm around her waist and held up his other hand in the air.

"Well, then," he called, "I propose now that we all offer a heartfelt *banzai*—"

Disconcerted noises came from the crew and he stopped himself with a chuckle.

"Excuse me—perhaps I should propose instead that we offer 'three cheers'—to our director, Kano. That we might express our respect and gratitude to him from the bottom of our hearts."

He turned solemnly and touched his hands to his forehead. An appreciative purr came from the rest of the crew and Kinosuke raised his fist in the air: "Hip, hip, hooray!"

Kano smiled, his face half-hidden behind a pair of thick American sunglasses.

"Thank you," he said. "Though it is I who should really be expressing my thanks. To our stars—" He gestured at Kinosuke and Michiko, and everyone applauded enthusiastically. "—the artists—" He turned to the smocked designers, who held up their paint brushes and grinned. "—and to the crew." He waved up at the lighting box, from which bright bulbs flashed.

"You must all be very tired!" he said. "But there is just one more 'thank you' I would like to add, one that has perhaps so far gone unexpressed in the production of this picture. I would like to dedicate this film to its true creator."

Michiko Nozaki's bright eyes fell upon me. I tingled with pride, and bashfully bowed my head as Kano raised his hands.

"To Tokyo. To the city, and to the spirit of its people."

My head jerked back up.

"To a city that will one day emerge from the ashes again, as it has so many times in the past."

Heavy applause came from all around as I cleared my throat.

"I have expressed before the idea that a city cannot simply rebuild itself like some robotic automaton. Its true spirit lies in the hearts and the habits of its people."

The crew nodded earnestly.

"This is to what we pay tribute today. And as long as the spirit of Tokyoites lives on—gruff and arrogant as it may be— so will their city survive. Thank you for your hard work!"

Everyone began to applaud. We moved forward, and then, abandoning all dignity, we flung our arms around each other and began to laugh out loud.

At that moment a deep and quickening sense of dignity passed over me, a feeling such as I had never had before in my entire life. I embraced them all, trying not to weep. My colleagues; my comrades; my friends.

I sat at my usual spot at the counter of the Montmartre, drinking Scotch, tapping the stiff toe of my russet Oxford brogue against the stool. I wondered about the reviews that would appear in the cinema magazines the next week. *Dreamy and melodramatic*, they would say. *Inaccurate—naive.*

I shook my head. The critics, for once, did not concern me. I only hoped that I had perhaps managed to capture something of the peculiar spirit of the times—the spirit of the burned-out ruins. Of the curious resilience of human hearts in the face of chaos and destruction; of our potential to rise again from tragedy, to cast off the burden of time as a butterfly shrugs off its chrysalis.

The gala premiere performance was held, at Kano's insistence, in the ruins of an old theatre in Shinjuku that he had regularly visited as a child. The roof was still mostly open to the sky and battered chairs were lined up in the amphitheatre to face an improvised canvas screen. Michiko Nozaki sat down in the front row, chattering to the friends she had brought along. A matronly lady sat on one side of her, and on the other was a teenage boy, smartly dressed in long shorts and a white shirt. Beyond him was another woman, and as I gazed down, in the last light of dusk, she turned, so that for a moment, I could clearly see her face.

Such a strange and curious thing.

Satsuko Takara wore a flowing cotton summer dress, her hair pinned and fastened with a simple comb. How odd, how fateful, for her to appear right now, just moments before the drama that was so inspired by her was to be enacted. Would she recognize something of herself up there on the screen?

A profound sense of humility and providence coursed through me. Here, for surely the last time, was my heaven-sent chance. I swore that I would go down to her after the film had ended. That I would offer her the hand of companionship again. That I would ask, if I was not too ashamed, for her forgiveness.

The lights went out and the projector began to whir. A thick beam of smouldering light hit the screen, and the symbol of a torch flickered onto the canvas. The name of the film appeared in stuttering ideograms, followed by the name of Kano, then of myself. With an excited murmur, the audience settled back in their seats.

It was like nothing I had ever dreamed of. A new world came into being for me as Michiko Nozaki appeared on the swaying screen and her birdlike voice emerged from the speakers. Everyone in the crowd seemed to sense it too, and a sound rose from the auditorium like a soft, collective sigh.

Up above, the beautiful face turned this way and that, smiling and nodding, her skin translucent, her eyes glistening. With the blurry backdrop of the ruined city behind her, she began to run down a narrow alley of low tenement houses . . .

The audience gazed at the screen as, above them, stars glimmered in the sky. With spectacular longing in my heart, I closed my eyes, willing myself to cling tightly to that beautiful image forever.

Wonderful faces, shining over and over with light.

Michiko skipped along a street of low wooden houses, dodging puddles in her path and throwing her hands this way and that like a dancer. Blurry ruins were painted behind her, distant buildings and a smudgy sky. She stopped at the edge of the stage and put her hands on her hips, and flashed her beautiful smile. With a flouncing curtsy, she skittered off to one side, where handsome Mr. Kinosuke stood holding a lacquer box of powdered mochi cakes. She pinched his nose, giggling, and promptly popped one into her mouth.

Hiroshi stood on a crate, squinting through the view finder of the camera, supported by Mr. Mogami the cinematographer, who was spinning him smoothly around to film the action. The film made a sound like a flittering clock as it whirred through the contraption. The director, Mr. Kano, stepped forward and raised his hand.

"Cut! Cut!" he called.

The rest of the assembled actors and stagehands laughed and clapped as Hiroshi opened his eyes. He blinked in the bright stage lights, a bashful smile slowly growing on his face.

I came to, lying in the tunnel beneath the railway arch that night, overwhelmed by an almost unbearable sense of excruciating shame. My kimono was soaked, my crimson nails chipped. Hiroshi's eyes were still wide as he stared at me.

Slowly, I got to my feet. I could hardly believe how grown-up he looked. He wore a collared shirt and smart woollen trousers. But his face was covered with thick, swirling welts, and I felt a stab in my heart as we stood there in the tunnel, in silence.

Finally, he spoke.

"Big sister," he said, his voice deep. "You're alive."

A sob rose in my throat. "And you," I whispered.

He bowed his head, and placed his palms formally together.

"Please forgive me," he murmured.

Tears filled my eyes. "Forgive you?"

He knelt on the ground and touched his forehead solemnly to the concrete. "Please forgive me. For leaving you alone that night."

I saw him, silhouetted by fire. I desperately shook my head, unable to speak. He finally sat down cross-legged on the ground.

"I needed to fetch the pot, you understand," he said, frowning. "Father was counting on me."

"Of course."

He drew his arms around his legs. I wondered what could possibly be passing through his mind.

"Did you find it, Hiroshi-kun?" I finally asked.

He shook his head.

"Well. Perhaps we might go to look for it together one day."

He glanced up at me.

"Are you still in pain?" I said, gesturing to his face. His cheeks looked angry and shiny in the streetlight. He shook his head again.

"Hiroshi-kun—" I started. He glanced at me. "Please, Hiroshi-kun," I said. "There's no need for us to talk about anything that has happened."

He stared at the ground, and nodded.

I walked over to him, and held out my hand.

"Please, brother," I said. "Will you come with me, now?"

As we approached Mrs. Ishino's shop, something was very wrong. On the wall outside there were scrawled letters and tin signs, just like the Americans had put up outside the Oasis.

Inside, it was as if a typhoon had swept through the place. Chairs had been thrown aside, streamers pulled down, and broken glass littered the floor. I shivered as a memory came to me—of how the Americans had torn away the little curtains outside the girls' rooms at the International Palace.

Mrs. Ishino was slumped over at the back of the bar, her thick arm hugging a bottle of shochu. On the table was the photograph of her husband in his flying jacket, the glass shattered in the frame. The gramophone was playing a mournful fragment of "The Apple Song" over and over again.

Hiroshi's eyes were so wide that I was frightened he would bolt. I wouldn't have blamed him. But instead, he sat on a stool as I shook Mrs. Ishino and tried to pour water down her throat. There was the sound of a motorcar in the alley outside.

The whole scene had the feel of a dream, as the rain blustered in through the window. I heard a soft knock. A voice called my name.

Standing there by the doorway, dressed in a pleated white skirt and wool sweater, was Michiko.

The workmen tottered on a ladder in the alley and I called out in direction as they hoisted up the sign with the name of our new shop painted upon it in large crimson letters: Twilight Bar. Inside, two carpenters were sanding down the new counter and there was a strong smell of paint and sawdust. Hanako and Masuko were sitting with Mrs. Ishino, poring over the shopping list for our opening week. Hiroshi stood with them. He had all kinds of connections at the market now, he said, and could get food especially cheap, though I didn't care to know how.

Several of his photographs were framed on the newly

painted walls. Shoeshine boys buffed the boots of American soldiers in Ueno Plaza; a packed four-car train travelled slowly through the countryside. Opposite the bar was a photograph he'd hung in pride of place: a portrait of a tough-looking gang-ster, dressed in a three-piece suit, scowling away beneath the big illuminated sign at the Ueno Sunshine Market.

Michiko had barely asked a single question that night. She had calmly stepped over the threshold, taking in the wreckage of the bar.

"Why, Satsuko. Aren't you going to introduce me?" She gestured at Hiroshi.

"This—this is Hiroshi-kun."

"Your brother?" she asked, staring at me in amazement. I nodded. She walked over to him and pushed the hair out of his eyes. *She really is a good actress*, I thought.

"Satsuko," she said, taking one last look around. "I think perhaps you should fetch everybody's things and come along with me."

We stayed all summer at her luxurious apartment. It was all her own now, Michiko having bought it after her admiral had been sent back to American following some scandal.

Every afternoon, on her return home from filming, she brought us gifts: slabs of chocolate; summer clothes for Hiroshi; fish, rice and vegetables. I cooked our meals in the evenings and we all ate together at her Western dining table. Mrs. Ishino had fallen quite in love with Michiko by then, and told stories of Tokyo theatres of the past, of the glory days when she had danced in the cabarets and operettas. Michiko regaled us with the antics of the actors and stagehands, gave us the gossip about her famous leading man Kinosuke.

One evening, the conversation turned to the subject of Hollywood. The film *My Darling Clementine* had just opened, and Hiroshi had come back from the cinema earlier that day, breathless with excitement.

"Hollywood—well!" Michiko said, a familiar look coming into her eyes. "Wouldn't that just be the dream."

My chopsticks hesitated over my dish. "Really, Michiko?" I said. "I should think it would be a very lonely place, despite all its glamour."

Michiko raised a quizzical eyebrow.

"Really, Satsuko?" she said. "I'm surprised at you. Didn't you once write to tell me you were intending to go away to America yourself? San Francisco, wasn't it?"

Silence fell and Hiroshi glanced at me curiously. Mrs. Ishino cleared her throat and helped herself to some more rice.

"What on earth made you think that, Miss Nozaki?" Mrs. Ishino asked pleasantly. "Why would a girl like Satsuko-chan possibly want to go to America?"

I laughed politely. Michiko's eyes narrowed, holding my own for a second.

"Please excuse me," she said. "I was thinking of someone else entirely."

As I say, she really was a very good actress.

But there was one matter which I couldn't brush over, of course, one that became harder for me to conceal as the summer went on, however much I might try to do so behind loose-fitting cotton dresses. Finally, Mrs. Ishino took me to one side and said that we would have to make preparations for any eventuality.

Certain officials, she said, could be persuaded to draw up certain documents, if the right gifts were slipped up their sleeves. She assured me it was for the best, that it would avoid all sorts of complications later on. She returned later that week with a stamped marriage certificate, with my name upon it. The other name was that of a twenty-five-year-old man, who had apparently been born in Gunma Prefecture. Mrs. Ishino told me that he had died soon after his return to Japan from Manchukuo.

"Your husband, Satsuko. A lightning affair. Poor soul."

My child would have a father, then, on paper at least. But I agonized over what the child would look like. Would the eyes be charcoal black, like mine? Or would they be sky blue?

In the meantime, Michiko had insisted that we were all to be the guests of honour at the gala premiere of her new film. That morning, Mrs. Ishino helped dress me in my green and gold summer kimono, and Hiroshi and I took the tram up to Asakusa. We had promised to light some incense for our parents in the ruins of our old shop, as well as have one last look for our father's pot. The neighbourhood was as busy as it had ever been, men in shirtsleeves going to and fro on bicycles in the warm afternoon sunshine. The Nakamise Arcade leading up to the Senso Temple was bustling with stalls, and the sound of sawing and hammering came from the temple precincts. Cedar prayer plaques were hanging in bundles from the gates in honour of the Star Festival, and we bought our own little plaques, writing our secret requests on the back in the hope that they would be answered by the Goddess of Mercy.

We bought the incense and then walked rather solemnly toward Umamichi Street. Flags fluttered, advertising new restaurants, theatres and vaudeville shows.

"Look!" Hiroshi said suddenly. Up above the shell of a building was a billboard advertising Michiko's new film, her painted face beaming out.

"The old neighbourhood's really coming back to life, isn't it, Hiroshi?"

He made a noise of assent. I studied him. He was so much taller now, his eyes so alert. I wondered what he could have possibly gone through during those long months when we'd been apart. I wondered if we would ever talk of it. Probably not, I thought. Not at least until we were very old.

We found the square cistern, and stepped into the rubble of our old shop, overgrown now with feverfew and stalks of wild sugar beet. Hiroshi poked about for a while, but found nothing but a few blackened fragments of ceramic. I looked at him in question. He gave a rueful smile and shook his head.

I placed the incense in the centre of the patch and he bent down to light it. We both clasped our hands and bowed our heads as the fragrant smoke twisted up around us.

I felt the child inside me, then, for the first time, kicking gently inside my belly. I gasped, imagining the little feet and toes, the tiny mouth and ears, as it lay curled inside my womb. It would be an autumn child, I thought, just as I had been myself. At that moment, the image of my mother came into my mind. I felt, quite intensely, that she was standing beside me, stroking my hair with her hand. I raised my head. The sunlight fell in my eyes, and I felt my father there too—they were both standing quietly behind me, one hand on each of my shoulders.

Cicadas were whirring loudly as we walked back to the street. I noticed a sign advertising a summer *matsuri* and I wondered out loud how lavish the processions might be this year, whether the men would still heave portable shrines up to the temple.

"It's strange," Hiroshi murmured. "I was just thinking the same thing."

It would be firework season soon, I thought. Bright flowers would burst in the sky above Tokyo through those hot summer nights and we would light candles, offer prayers and food to the spirits of the dead, set lanterns adrift upon the water. There would be so many offerings this year that the river would be like a galaxy of floating stars.

Autumn would draw in, and before long we would prepare to go up to Asakusa together to listen to the ringing of the New Year's bell. The child would be with us by then, I thought—my baby.

Winter would deepen then slowly dissolve. The days would lengthen once more.

Before long, there would be plum blossom.

ACKNOWLEDGEMENTS

This novel was inspired and informed by numerous works of nonfiction and fiction, of which I am particularly indebted to the following:

Embracing Defeat: Japan in the Wake of World War II by John W. Dower

Japan at War: An Oral History by Haruko Taya Cook and Theodore F. Cook

Japan Diary by Mark Gayn

Hiroshima by John Hersey

The Japan Journals: 1947–2004 by Donald Richie

Democracy with a Tommygun by Wilfred G. Burchett

Further reading:

Modern Japanese Literature: From 1868 to the Present Day by Donald Keene

The Scarlet Gang of Asakusa by Yasunari Kawabata

The Setting Sun by Osamu Dazai

Confessions of a Mask and *Runaway Horses* by Yukio Mishima

Confessions of a Yakuza by Junichi Saga

The Sea and Poison by Shusaku Endo

The Children and *The Makioka Sisters* by Junichiro Tanizaki

A Drifting Life by Yoshihiro Tatsumi

The Essential Haiku: Versions of Basho, Buson, & Issa by Robert Hass

Onward Towards our Noble Deaths by Shigeru Mizuki

The author would like to thank the following people for their help, advice, and support during the writing of this book:

Will Eglington

Pete Harris

Kieran Holland

David, Gordon and Sally Mitchell

James Parsons

Carrie Plitt and all at Conville & Walsh

Averil & Conor Sinnott

Jo Unwin

Susan Watt

Janie Yoon, Sarah MacLachlan and all at House of Anansi

ABOUT THE AUTHOR

Ben Byrne was born in 1977. He studied drama at the University of Manchester and later lived in San Francisco, New York and Tokyo, working as a consultant, ethnographic filmmaker and musician. He returned to England to dedicate his time more fully to writing, and his short fiction has appeared in *Litro* magazine. *Fire Flowers* is his first novel.